CRIME CLASSICS

Lonely Magdalen

Also in the Crime Classics series:

Lonely Magdalen

AN INSPECTOR POOLE MYSTERY

HENRY WADE

ABOUT THE AUTHOR

Henry Wade was the pseudonym of Henry Lancelot Aubrey-Fletcher (1887–1969). He was educated at Eton and then at Oxford and went on to have a distinguished military career, serving in World War I.

One of the founding members of The Dection Club in 1930, Wade was a major figure in the development of the Golden Age period, writing twenty novels and two short story collections, the most famous of which were his Inspector Poole novels.

This edition published in the UK by Arcturus Publishing Limited
26/27 Bickels Yard, 151–153 Bermondsey Street, London SE1 3HA

Design and layout copyright © 2013 Arcturus Publishing Limited
Text copyright © Henry Wade, 1940

Cover artwork by Steve Beaumont
Typesetting by Couper Street Type Co.

AD003693EN

Printed in the UK

CONTENTS

PART III: WORKING FORWARD

This story, of which the first and third parts are laid in the year 1939, having been largely written during the spring and summer of that year, takes no account of the war which broke out in the autumn. Certain details will consequently be found to be incorrect; summer-time, for instance, did not end on October 9th, and certain posts have been removed from a corner of Hampstead Heath. Otherwise the topography may be described as fact, as may the war of 1914-18, whilst the other circumstances and the characters of the story are fiction.

H. W.

A map of the area of London with which the story is concerned will be found at the end of the book.

PART I

WORKING BACK

CHAPTER I

'THE RED KNIGHT'

'This is the National Programme. You have been listening to Jay Fillister's orchestra playing at the Municipal Pavilion, Bournechester. Before going on to the next item here is an urgent police message that has just come in. At 7.40 p.m. this evening the dead body of a woman was found near the boundary hedge at the north-east corner of Hampstead Heath close to the point where Millfield Lane passes by the most northerly of the Highgate Ponds. The woman appears to have been strangled and probably died some time between 7 and 7.30 p.m. Her description is as follows: age between forty and fifty, height five feet seven inches, slight build, small hands and feet, hair brown parted in the middle and dressed low over the ears, eyes blue or grey, face heavily made up, right cheek disfigured by a scar probably caused by a burn. The woman was wearing a blue serge skirt, white artificial silk blouse, knitted jumper, blue stuff overcoat trimmed with grey fur, small black hat, artificial silk stockings and high-heeled black shoes, all in rather worn condition. A worn black handbag containing an unmarked handkerchief, a lipstick and some coppers, was found in a ditch about ten yards from the body. The police are anxious to get in touch with anyone who can identify this woman, or who saw her near Millfield Lane or Ken Wood this evening, or who saw anyone else in this neighbourhood between 7 and 7.30 p.m. whose behaviour might suggest connection with the crime. Will anyone who can give information on these points please communicate with New Scotland Yard, Telephone number Whitehall 1212, or with the nearest police station. It is emphasised that the speed with which information reaches the police is of vital importance. And now here is Professor Harold

Dickerson, who will give the second of his weekly series of talks on "Woman and her sphere to-day"...'

'Not 'ere 'e won't. Switch it off, Ted.'

The large and rubicund landlord of The Red Knight reached for the radio switch and the husky voice of Professor Dickerson was lost to the occupants of the public bar.

Ted Boscombe glanced at the clock above him.

'Pretty quick work, gettin' that on the air before 8.30 an' the body only found at 7.40,' he said with the conscious pride of the ex-policeman.

'Bit of an 'urry, ain't they?' asked the small man in a tilted billycock hat who had turned down his thumb for Professor Dickerson. 'Why couldn't they wait till the nine o'clock news? Interferin' with the programme, these effin' police . . . no offence, Ted.'

'You 'eard what was said, didn't you?' demanded Boscombe sternly. 'Speed. That's the essence o' the contract in detection. Get a quick identification or a quick word about someone seen near the body an' we can maybe get on to the feller before 'e's made up 'is story. Speed; that's what 'angs 'em, nine times out o' ten. This wireless, it's a great 'elp to the police, properly used. I call to mind . . . Why, Bert, what's the trouble? Not feelin' well?'

The little group at the bar counter turned to stare at a big man in a dirty macintosh and cap who was sitting alone at a small table in the corner. His fleshy face was white, his mouth wide open, and when the landlord's eye was attracted to him he had been staring glassily at his half-empty pint tankard. Now he looked up quickly, his small eyes flickering over the inquisitive group.

'Nothin' wrong with yer beer, is there?' enquired Boscombe anxiously.

'Swallowed a frog, I expect,' said a tall thin man whose frayed coat-sleeve betokened clerk.

The landlord shot him an indignant glance.

'It's my belief 'e's 'ad a shock,' said a collarless labourer. 'Somethin's upset 'im.'

'Ah, all this talk about corpses; what did I say?' cut in billycock. 'Why can't they keep their nasty stories till the proper time? Spoilin' a man's beer.'

There was a laugh from the little company, but the landlord was gazing thoughtfully at the object of all this sympathy.

'Don't know anythin' about it, do yer, Bert?' he asked.

The big man scowled.

'Anything about what?' he asked. 'What's all the fuss about?'

Boscombe shrugged his shoulders.

'Only you was lookin' mighty queer after that police message came over the wireless. I thought maybe . . . well, you lives over the far side of the 'Eath from 'ere, don't you? I thought maybe you'd walked across and might 'ave seen something.'

Again the big man scowled, shifting in his chair. The men at the bar were staring at him curiously now.

''Oo is 'e?' he heard one of them ask.

'Bert Varden,' came the reply. 'Tic-tac or somethin'.'

'I don't see how Mr. Varden could have seen anything,' said the tall clerk in a slow drawl. 'He was here before me and I got here before eight. Body was found at 7.40, they said, and what's Ken Wood from here? Three miles if it's one, and three miles into twenty minutes won't go – not unless he's got a Rolls-Royce.'

Pleased with his analysis the clerk took a long pull at his Guinness.

'Body was found at 7.40, ah,' said the landlord pontifically, 'but death might 'ave occurred any time between 7 and 7.30, it said; you want to get your facts right, Mr. Hawkins, in detective work.'

Varden pushed the small table away from him.

'What the hell are you all talking about?' he asked angrily. 'What d'you think you are? A bloody jury?'

'Now, mate; now, mate, no offence,' said the navvy. 'You've spilt yer beer and there's no call to do that. Ted Boscombe 'ere's only lettin' off a bit o' gas, ain't yer, Ted?'

The laugh evidently soothed Varden's feelings and he sank back into his chair. But Boscombe saw that the man's usually florid face was still white, and he was curious.

The subject of the police message soon slid away into the more congenial one of the young football season. After a time Boscombe went through into the saloon bar, leaving his barmaid in charge. Five minutes later he returned and, walking across to the corner where Varden sat, sank into a chair beside him.

'You wanted to see Mr. Lewis, didn't you?' he asked quietly.

'Yes,' said Varden quickly. 'Has he come in?'

'In the saloon,' replied Boscombe, nodding towards the door through which he had come.

Varden started to rise but the landlord put a hand on his arm.

'Talkin' to Sam Cockburn,' he said. 'Business, I guess; better leave 'em be a bit.'

He leaned closer to Varden.

'Did yer know that skirt?' he asked.

Varden stared at him and the Adam's apple worked twice up and down in his throat before he answered – and that was answer enough for ex-Police Constable Ted Boscombe.

'Skirt . . . ?' Varden cleared his throat. 'What are you talking about?'

'That skirt that's been done in,' said Boscombe, looking steadily at his companion.

Again Varden hesitated . . . and no doubt realised that he had hesitated too long.

'As a matter of fact I believe I do know her,' he muttered. 'At least, I know a woman with a scar like that on her cheek. Might be another one. What of it, anyway?'

Ted Boscombe glanced round the bar. Except for the ever-changing group at the bar counter there were not many customers in. The corner where they sat was otherwise empty. He leaned back and, taking a cigarette from a packet in his waistcoat pocket, lit it with careful deliberation.

'What of it?' he asked slowly. 'You 'eard the police message. They want information. "Information received"; that's detection, ninety per cent. An' they want it quick.'

'Well, let them get it,' growled Varden. 'I'm not shoving my nose into any police-station.'

He gave a quick glance at his companion.

'And look here, Boscombe, none of your g
your old pals. If you do . . .'

Varden did not finish his sentence, but ther
small eyes.

Ted Boscombe drew slowly at his cigarette, i
smoke to trickle out through his nostrils.

'I'm not in the Force now, Bert,' he said, quietly; 'I've got my business
to attend to, an' gettin' the wrong side of a customer isn't part of it. I'm
just givin' you a word o' friendly advice: if you've got anythin' to tell, tell
it quick; the police look funny at a man that keeps things to 'imself . . .
especially when it's a case o' murder.'

He gave Varden a nod and, rising ponderously to his feet, strolled
behind the bar counter.

After he had gone Herbert Varden sat for some time motionless in
his chair, staring at his now empty tankard. His heavy shoulders drooped
forward and his heavy jowl drooped with them; the pouches under his
eyes followed the general line. It would have been difficult for an outsider
to guess his age; under the cap his hair could not be seen but the lines
on his face were those of a man who would not see fifty again – or of a
dissolute liver; but his hands were strong and firm and the sinews of his
neck had not begun to drag. Probably a good judge would have put him
at a dissolute forty.

Presently he pulled himself together with a start and, after a quick
glance round the room to make sure that he was no longer the object of
general attention, rose to his feet and walked across to the door of the
saloon bar. Opening it, he looked inside.

It was a snug room; too much red plush and painted glass for the
higher taste, but with its heavy curtains, sporting prints and coal fire,
undoubtedly cosy. There were not many occupants; to be accurate there
were seven, arranged in two pairs and a threesome, each group engaged
in earnest and apparently intimate conversation.

As the door opened all the occupants of the saloon glanced towards
the newcomer and their conversation stopped, as if they were conscious

ce of an alien spirit. Varden hesitated, then slouched across
the pairs.

nything for me this week, Mr. Lewis?' he muttered.

The man addressed, a small tubby fellow with dark hair and a rosy
clean-shaven face, had frowned when he saw who the newcomer was.
His expression did not clear when Varden spoke to him.

'No,' he said curtly. 'And when I do want you I'll send for you.'

He turned to his companion.

'Mrs. Cockburn well, I hope, Sam?' he asked casually. 'Mrs. Lewis was
telling me she'd seen her and the girls at the Troc one night last week.'

Sam Cockburn took up the lead and Varden was left standing beside
the two seated men, awkward and embarrassed. He scowled down at
them, hating their sleekness, their round bellies, their double-whiskies,
their large cigars, their general air of prosperity. He knew that his education
had been better, his start in life more propitious than theirs, and now he
had to stand a suppliant, insulted, ignored . . . Bitter anger shook him
and a surge of the violent temper that had been his curse through life.
With a supreme effort of self-control he crushed the impulse to send
flying the table with its drinks, to knock the sleek heads together. He
turned on his heel and slouched out of the room.

The other two groups had watched the little incident with amusement
and Lewis was aware of it. He was angry and uncomfortable.

'Tiresome, those fellows,' said Cockburn, with a sympathy tinged
with malice. He himself had no dealings with men of Varden's type. He
despised Montie Lewis for making use of a bully.

'Useful at times,' said Lewis shortly. 'Some of the rougher meetings
. . . you don't bother with them, Sam, I know. I hope to cut them out
before long. Have another.'

He walked across to the hatch, tapped on it, and presently returned
with two fresh double-whiskies. The three little groups in the saloon
settled down to their routine of gossip and private business, forgetting
the man who had intruded and disturbed them.

Varden's anger was still simmering in him when he got back into the
public bar. But he had more than anger to think about tonight. He sank

back into his old seat, looked into his tankard, half rose with the intention of getting it refilled but changed his mind. For ten minutes he sat staring glumly at a spittoon, then looked up suddenly at the clock. It stood at five minutes past ten.

Varden shifted uneasily in his chair, indecision pictured on his sullen face. His right hand fingered his chin, scratched his ear; again and again he looked at the clock. He was conscious that the landlord eyed him from time to time but nobody else was interested in him now. Why should they be? Why the hell couldn't people mind their own business? Varden forgot that that was exactly what he had resented in the sleek bookmakers next door.

'Last orders, gentlemen, please,' proclaimed the mellow voice of Ted Boscombe.

Varden glanced quickly again at the clock, pushed back his chair and walked across to the bar counter. He did not go to the end where Boscombe was serving but gave his order to the barmaid.

'Double-whisky,' he growled.

The woman measured out the double tot, slid the small glass towards him and picked up the money. With a quick turn of the wrist Varden tilted the neat spirit down his throat, turned on his heel and strode towards the door. With a thrust of his foot he flung it open, then walked out into the night.

Out of the corner of his eye Ted Boscombe watched him go, then glanced up at the clock.

'Time, gentlemen, please,' he said.

WHO WAS SHE?

A group of square-shouldered men in thick overcoats and bowler hats stood on the damp grass at the north-east corner of Hampstead Heath. There was no lamp near them, but the glow of London reflected from the low clouds just gave light enough for them to see each other's faces. They were standing at the edge of a slight slope which fell away towards the foot of the boundary hedge; it could hardly be called a ditch and yet that was probably what it had originally been. On the slope, a few feet away from the group of men, lay a dark object covered by a rug.

'Seen all you want to, doctor?' asked Chief-Inspector Beldam, a stocky man with the squarest shoulders of the lot.

'All I want to by the light of a torch,' said Dr. Blathermore shortly. 'And I gather that the local man . . . what's his name again?'

'Dr. Faber, sir,' said another voice.

'Faber; I gather he'd already seen all there was to see here.'

'Yes, sir, but you had to see it *in situ*' said Chief-Inspector Beldam soothingly. 'I don't suppose we've learned much from it but you never know.'

'Except the point about the grass under the body, sir,' suggested Divisional-Detective-Inspector Hartridge.

'Ah, about it's being wet; yes, that was a good point of yours,' said the senior man generously. 'That ought to give us a limit one side or the other. What time *did* that rain begin?'

Nobody answered.

'Couldn't say at the moment, sir,' said the Divisional Inspector at last. 'I was in the Station from 6.15 on; it hadn't begun then. It was raining all right at 7.45 when I came out after the gentleman – Mr. Gooden – rang me up.'

'Ah, yes; the man that found the body. He may have noticed. Anyhow we must get that point fixed. You'll do that best locally, Inspector Hartridge; it might have begun at a different time down at the Yard.'

'Yes, sir, I'll see to that.'

'And what about Gooden, anyway? You kept tapes on him, I suppose?'

'Have I got to listen to all this?' asked the sour voice of the Police Surgeon.

'Sorry, doctor; no, of course not,' replied Beldam blandly. 'We'll get the body along for you at once.'

He hesitated a moment, then went on:

'It might be better, till we've got identification, to keep it up here. Where's the nearest mortuary, Hartridge?'

'One at the North Eastern Hospital, sir; quite close to us.'

'Good. I wonder if you'd mind if we sent her there, doctor . . . I mean, for you to do your examination there? Bore for you, I know, but . . .'

'Oh, don't mind me. My evening out's wrecked anyway. I'd rather like to get some dinner first, but no doubt you're in a hurry.'

'Plenty of time for that, sir. Look here, my car'll run you wherever you want to go, if you wouldn't mind telling it to come back here . . . or better come to Hampstead Police Station.'

'Thanks, Chief-Inspector. I'll do that and then arrange for Dr . . . what's his name? Faber? . . . to come and give me a hand. Good of you to let me have some dinner. I'll let you have a report. Good-night. Good-night.'

Chief-Inspector Beldam's love of a witticism nearly got the better of his sense of discipline, but not quite. He waited until the Police Surgeon was out of earshot, and by that time discipline had won the day.

'You'll keep this place clear, Inspector Hartridge? I want to have a look at it in daylight.'

'Of course, sir.'

'Oh, and by the way, I followed up your suggestion of a broadcast;

got straight on to the B.B.C. after you spoke to me and worded an urgent message. They promised to get it on the air almost at once – 8.25 at the latest, they said. So there may be some result in at the Yard already, or possibly at your Station. Taking a bit of a risk putting that through to them without knowing anything about the case myself, but I know you and I know you're reliable.'

In the darkness Inspector Hartridge flushed hotly. It was grand to work with a man like Chief-Inspector Beldam; he could be unpleasant enough when he wasn't pleased but at least he wasn't afraid of giving praise when he thought it due. It would put him in good with the other Yard men who were still standing silently by, waiting for orders.

'I don't know the Heath well,' went on Beldam. 'Seems a lonely sort of place after dark, this corner of it. Is it the usual place for this sort of thing?'

'This sort of thing, sir? Murder?' asked Inspector Hartridge, momentarily dense.

'No, no; soliciting. This poor woman's a prostitute or I'm a Dutchman. Seems an unusual place for her to find customers, especially on a wet October evening. What's the character of the place?'

'I see what you mean, sir. I hadn't thought of that – about her being a prostitute. I expect you're right, sir. But the place is respectable enough, what I know of it. I'm not really intimate with it though; some of the older constables'll know it better.'

'Check up on that, will you? Well, I don't know that we can do any more good here. You got all the flashlights on the spot you want, Sergeant Cook?'

'All we can do here, sir,' replied one of the dim figures.

'Right. Then you and Smith had better go along in the ambulance to the mortuary and get your close-ups there. I want good ones for identification before the doctors start taking sections. Right, we'll be off. Information's what we want and we're more likely to get that at your Station or the Yard. Give me that torch, Gower.'

Detective-Sergeant Gower handed over a large electric torch with a bulbous head. Beldam pushed forward the switch and instantly the scene was flooded with an astonishingly bright light. The boundary hedge, the bushes and scattered trees, even the distant masses of Ken Wood were revealed as the detective swung the beam round in a last survey. On the path fifty yards to the north stood two uniformed constables; further south, at the point where Millfield Lane slipped through the barrier and ceased to be a lane, stood two more while beyond them were visible a number of curious onlookers.

'The ambulance can get up to the barrier all right, eh?'

'Get up, sir, but it could only turn in one of these narrow drive gates – a job in the dark. Better to put her on a stretcher and carry her up to the end of Merton Lane.'

'Right; you know best. Was that your car standing there when I came up? You can give us a lift to your Station, Hartridge?'

'Easy, sir,' said the Divisional-Inspector, making a mental note that the Chief-Inspector had not lost his powers of observation. 'I'll leave Sergeant Berringer here to see about getting the body away, if you agree, sir; I want to get back to the Station.'

After a few more words of instruction the group broke up, four men walking towards Millfield Lane where the two constables stood. As they approached the barrier a tall man in a soft hat detached himself from the little crowd of onlookers and came forward.

'Evening, Chief-Inspector,' he said. 'You'll give us a story, I hope?'

Beldam peered into the newcomer's face.

'Whitfield, eh? Got the whole crowd with you? You fellows don't lose much time; I'll hand you that. But I can't hand you any more at the moment – no more than you got over the wireless, that is. If you come along to Hampstead Police Station in one hour from now – say 10.30 – we can probably give you something. That'll be time enough for the London editions, eh? Provincials too, probably, but they don't matter, so far as we're concerned. Look here, you fellows, I'll give you all I can and in return I want your help. Publicity's what we need in a case like this and I want you to splash it. Here's a woman strangled in a quiet corner of the Heath after dark. I think she's a prostitute but I don't know yet so don't say anything about that; she may be a Duke's aunt and I don't want to be run in for slander. But the point is that it's a quiet corner and dark; nobody's likely to have seen it happen. But somebody may have heard something, or seen her beforehand, or seen someone hanging about. And of course we must identify the woman. That shouldn't be difficult but we want everyone who knew her to come and tell us tell us all about her – who her clients were, if she's what I think she is . . . but don't put that in yet. You see my point, eh?'

'That's all right, Chief,' said the spokesman of the Press reporters. 'We'll splash it all right and we count on you to give us the dope. 10.30 at Hampstead Police Station it is. Come on, boys, they aren't shut yet.'

The little crowd faded away up Millfield Lane. Chief-Inspector Beldam waited till they had gone, said a word or two to the constables who had to keep vigil through the night, then led on.

'You've got a man trying these houses that overlook the Heath, I think you said, Hartridge? There's quite a chance that someone heard something, even if they didn't see anything. It isn't easy to strangle a woman without her letting out a scream or two . . . or at least a pretty noisy sort of gurgle.'

'I've got a good man on that, sir – Winterbourne,' said the Divisional-Inspector. 'He won't miss anything there is.'

'Good; by the way, Hartridge, you never answered my question about Gooden, the man who found the body; you haven't lost sight of him?'

'No, sir. The doctor interrupted before I could answer. We know all about Mr. Gooden, sir. He's a barrister; lived up here since the war – one of these houses leading off the Lane; churchwarden at St. Simon's, too. He was taking his dog for a run.'

Chief-Inspector Beldam sniffed.

'H'm. Churchwardens may have their weaknesses like the rest of us . . . and I've seen a barrister in the dock before now. Still, I don't say. . . . I'll have a word with him before I go back.'

They had reached Inspector Hartridge's car by now, and five minutes later they were at Hampstead Police Station. Chief-Inspector Beldam at once went in to pay his respects to Superintendent Hollis, who was working in his office. He had not met him before.

'Glad to have your help, Chief-Inspector,' said Hollis politely. 'There have been one or two reports in but I haven't acted on them because I felt sure you'd be in before long. Two messages from the Yard, too; I took 'em down and I'll give you the gist of them; then you can ring up if you want to.'

'Thank you, sir,' said Beldam, who thought the Superintendent ponderous but probably sound.

Hollis pulled a message pad towards him.

'In the first place, the two Yard messages: both identifications. A Mr. Tom Porritt of 125 Spital Crescent, West Ham, reports that he hasn't seen his wife for a week. He thinks she's about the build of this woman, brown hair, never noticed the colour of her eyes; when she left him she had a gash on her cheek that was healing nicely. She's got a wooden leg. I gather the Yard told him that as nothing had been said about a wooden leg probably in this case there wasn't one and that for the moment it wasn't worth while his coming up to identify. I take it that's right, Chief-Inspector . . . I mean about there being no wooden leg? Of course, one wouldn't be looking for it and in the dark . . . but it'd be a bit awkward if we had overlooked it.'

Beldam laughed.

'That's all right, sir,' he said. 'This isn't Mrs. Tom Porritt. This lady wouldn't have had any use for a wooden leg, unless I'm much mistaken.'

The Superintendent looked at him doubtfully but did not press for an explanation.

'Then there was a call from a Miss Wicherton of Leeds – 21 South Bascombe Street. She said the description sounded exactly like her sister, Fanny, whom she hadn't seen since the war, when she married a Canadian soldier. Fanny was just like the description said, brown hair, grey eyes, such pretty hands and feet – I'm quoting your chap at the Yard who seemed to think it funny. She hadn't any scar on her cheek when Miss Wicherton saw her, but then of course that might have come since; fifty-three would be the age now. Miss Wicherton will be glad to come down and identify but will her expenses be paid as she's not well off?'

Chief-Inspector Beldam did not look impressed.

'Pretty vague, sir, isn't it? I mean, no scar and just a general similarity. I don't think this woman's as much as fifty-three either.'

'I fancy Miss Wicherton wouldn't mind a free trip to London,' said the Superintendent calmly.' 'We can do better than that locally, though there's no name yet. A Mr. Scott of 27 Greenhill Road – that's on the edge of the Heath, or rather of Parliament Hill – came in ten minutes after the broadcast and told me that about a fortnight ago he was accosted near Highgate Ponds by a woman answering to the description given.'

'Ah,' said Chief-Inspector Beldam.

'He says there was a lamp nearby and he noticed the scar on the cheek, though he couldn't remember which. He thought she must have been a good-looking woman once, but I gather there was nothing doing. He hasn't seen her since, doesn't know her name or anything else about her. I told him I'd give him a ring when the body was available for identification.'

'That confirms one thing, anyhow, sir,' said Beldam. 'We're bound to get an identification soon, though the men who know her may not be too keen to come forward. None of your constables have noticed her, I suppose?'

'None that I've asked so far; there are others out on duty or off duty. Darby, one of my elder constables, thinks she can't have worked that beat long or he'd have seen her. He knows the Heath well.'

'Ah, I'd like to have a talk with him before I go if he's about, sir; he can tell me a lot of things I want to know.'

'I'll get hold of him. Now there's one more bit of local information. A Mrs. Joliffe, living in Viking's Court, Bishop's Wood – that's just north of Ken Wood – rang up to say she'd seen a motor car standing in Millfield Lane at about seven o'clock. There were two people in it, one of them certainly a woman; she couldn't be sure about the other. She hadn't noticed them particularly nor, of course, the number of the car, but it was an old dark saloon; she thought it *might* be a Morris or a Standard.'

'Very helpful,' said Beldam bitterly. 'Still, I'll put someone on to that straight away.'

He went out into the charge-room, where the two officers whom he had brought up with him from the Yard were still patiently waiting for orders.

'Here's a job after your own heart, Poole,' he said to the younger of the two. 'An old saloon car, dark, possibly a Morris or a Standard but possibly not, was seen in Millfield Lane about 7 p.m. Two people in it, one at any rate a woman. Information from a Mrs. Joliffe, Viking's Court, Bishop's Wood. If I remember rightly you specialise in finding the un-traceable – especially motor-cars. I want this one, alive or dead . . . or rather, I want the people in it.'

The young detective smiled.

'Sounds pretty hopeless, sir, doesn't it. Still, you never know.'

He put on the overcoat that he had discarded and went out. Beldam returned to the Superintendent's room, to find him telephoning.

'. . . yes, that sounds all right. Have you got a car there? You might send her along here at once, will you; we'll get her home. Thank you; good-night, Lampson.'

He hung up and turned to the Scotland Yard man.

'That sounds more like it,' he said. 'That's Kentish Town. Woman's just come in to say that she thinks this was her lodger. They're sending her right along.'

'Good, sir. May I ring up the Hospital? I want to make sure the body's got there all right. Your Sergeant Berringer doesn't seem to have got here yet.'

'It's all right, sir,' said Inspector Hartridge, who had just come in after attending to some local routine work; 'Berringer's been in and I sent him back to have another look round. The body's at the mortuary all right and your camera man's at work. Doctor's not got there yet.'

'So much the better. I don't think the medical report will help us much, unless they can give us the size of the hands that strangled her. And they do make such a mess of a body; it doesn't help identification.'

There was the sound of a car pulling up in the street outside. Inspector Hartridge went out and presently returned with a small, shabby woman who was obviously torn between the conflicting emotions of excitement and nervousness.

'This is Mrs. Twist, sir,' said Hartridge.

Superintendent Hollis motioned to a chair.

'Sit down, Mrs. Twist,' he said in a friendly voice. 'Tell us what you know. Nothing to be nervous about. You think this poor woman was your lodger, eh?'

Mrs. Twist swallowed violently but after a short delay managed to find her tongue.

'Well, sir, it did sound like it, what it said on the wireless. Twist an' me, we'd just 'ad our supper when it come through an' we both said the same thing at once: "That's 'er." Struck us all of an 'eap it did. There was the scar, you see, an' the clothes and the black bag and the bit about them all being shabby-like. She didn't make much, poor thing, 'count o' the scar p'raps an' she couldn't afford new clothes though they might've brought in more money. Shall I 'ave to see 'er, sir?'

'Presently, if you don't mind. But tell us a bit more about her first. What was her name?'

'Knox, sir. Miss Bella Knox she called 'erself. Never 'ad no letters, though, so I never see it in writing.'

'How long had she been lodging with you?'

Mrs. Twist pondered.

'April,' she said. 'Six months that'd be, wouldn't it? I call to mind it was April because Miss Castani what was with us before that – Italian she was or Polish or something outlandish, though a nice-mannered young lady – she got took bad the day of the National, that's towards the end of March, and she was in 'ospital two days later an' 'opin' to come back she was, and the next day they come round and said she was dead. Give Twist an' me quite a turn it did and it was two or three weeks before I could let the room, people bein' that superstitious and then I 'ad to drop the rent a couple o' bob to make it draw. That was 'ow Miss Knox come to me because the two bob made a difference to 'er, she said. April that was.'

Superintendent Hollis turned to the Scotland Yard man.

'Carry on, Chief-Inspector,' he said.

Beldam hesitated. It might be a waste of time asking a lot of questions now. Better get a proper identification first. Still, there was one point . . .

'What about this lady's friends,' he asked; 'can you tell us about them?'

'Friends? She 'adn't got no friends. Leastways, I never saw none.'

'But surely . . . I mean . . . well, her clients, you know. Didn't they come to the house?'

'Ow, them. I shouldn't call them friends. Yes, she'd bring one now and again. I'm a respectable woman meself but I'm not one to stand in the way if all's quiet and decent. 'Course, it's not much of a room to bring a gentleman to; matter of fact it's top floor back with a skylight. It's a small 'ouse and that's the only spare we got, what with Gertie and Madge gettin' big girls now; they can't sleep with the boys any longer. We don't ask much rent for it, but it 'elps.'

The police-officers listened patiently to these domestic details.

'But what about these men, Mrs. Twist; can you tell us any of their names?' asked Superintendent Hollis.

'Well there now, I wouldn't know that, would I? I mean, it 'adn't nothin' to do with me 'oo they were. Mind your own business and there'll be no bones broken, that's my motto.'

'But would you recognise any of these men if you saw them again? You must have seen some of them, mustn't you?'

'Well, I might . . . an' then again I might not,' said Mrs. Twist helpfully.

Beldam glanced across at the Superintendent.

'Perhaps we'd better get on to the identification first, sir.' he said. 'We can follow up the rest afterwards if it's all right.'

Hollis nodded and within a minute Mrs. Twist was seated in the police car in company with Chief-Inspector Beldam and Inspector Hartridge. Three minutes' drive took them to the Hospital, and after some brief formalities they were ushered by the night porter into the mortuary, where Detective-Sergeant Cook and his assistant were just packing up their traps.

Mrs. Twist was silent now, swallowing a good deal, and nervously picking at the lapel of her coat.

Beldam walked up to the marble slab and quietly turned down the sheet that covered the small, still body of the murdered woman.

'If you'd just step up and have a look, madam,' he said gently.

Mrs. Twist took two or three nervous steps forward, gave a loud hiccough and burst into tears.

'Yes,' she sobbed. 'That's . . . that's 'er.'

CHAPTER III

'WE KNOW WHO SHE WAS'

Superintendent Hollis had gone home, leaving Chief-Inspector Beldam the run of his office and the help of Divisional-Detective-Inspector Hartridge. The latter was now engaged in tabulating the various messages and reports that had come in as a result of the broadcast. From 9.30 p.m. onwards they had been arriving in increasing numbers; it seemed as if people with information to give had taken something like an hour to make up their minds to take the plunge and had then all plunged at once. Some had been lured by the familiar telephone number to communicate direct with Scotland Yard; others preferred their own local police-stations. Some of the information given appeared to be completely irrelevant or hopelessly vague, but all had been taken down and passed on to the man in charge of the case, whose duty it would be to decide what should be followed up and what ignored.

Two women in the Kentish Town area reported having noticed someone answering the description shopping in that district, but neither knew who she was. A Kentish Town grocer said that during the past few weeks he had frequently served a woman with a scarred cheek, but always over the counter for cash; he did not know her name and had not noticed that she was much made up. An errand boy had gone all the way down to Scotland Yard to describe how he had seen a woman sitting on a bench near Highgate Ponds only two evenings ago; on interrogation there seemed no particular point of resemblance except 'a lot of scent' – it had been too dark to make much of her face; in any case he did not know anything more about her and it seemed probable that the visit to Scotland Yard was largely one of adventure.

More exact identification came from Mrs. Twist's next-door-neighbour, who not only recognised the victim by description but had observed various comings and goings and was prepared to give some description of visitors though she knew no names, not being inquisitive though herself surprised that anyone should be willing to take a lodger of this type. There was evidently some neighbourly feeling behind this and Beldam made a note that information from this source might not be unbiassed, but he decided that the possibility of hearing something about Bella Knox's visitors called for a personal visit to Mrs. Babworth from himself.

Two identifications came from other parts of London, one south of the river and one from Ealing. In each case a different name was given and the Ealing lady appeared to belong to a higher social status than did the dead woman, but the descriptions did correspond fairly closely and local enquiries were set on foot. Another report came from Liverpool but as the woman concerned had only left her house that morning Beldam thought he could safely ignore it.

A ticket-collector at Highgate Underground Station said that he had twice recently seen a woman hanging about in the Station. He had noticed the grey fur – which he described as 'rabbit' – on the coat and he had noticed the scar. He had not seen anyone speak to the woman and he had not done so himself, though he had contemplated a word to superior authority if the 'hanging about' became a nuisance.

All very vague and indefinite; probably only the information given by Mrs. Twist and Mrs. Babworth would prove to be of any real help. Still, more might be expected when a photograph could be published.

While Inspector Hartridge was tabulating the various messages and reports Beldam himself was having a talk with Police-Constable Darby, who had twenty-seven years' service, most of it spent in the neighbourhood of Hampstead Heath. Darby was of the old-fashioned type of police-officer, massive, slow and imperturbable. With some reluctance he obeyed the Chief-Inspector's invitation to take a seat, and thereafter talked with steadily increasing freedom.

'The 'Eath, sir? Known it fer nigh on fifty years I 'ave, ever since I come to 'Ampstead as a kiddie when my Dad got a job with the Borough Council. 'Course, I was away part o' the time; did me three years with the Colours in the Coldstream and that meant Aldershot, Windsor, and Chelsea. Then in 1912 I joined the Force, was posted to this Division, and, 'cept for the War, 'ave been 'ere ever since. Oh, yes, I know the 'Eath.'

Darby slowly stroked his luxurious dark moustache.

'Then you're the man I want,' said Chief-Inspector Beldam, with a mental reservation as regards long-windedness. 'Now, this Millfield Lane, is that a place much used by women for this purpose?'

'Soliciting, sir? Well, no; I wouldn't say it was. Quiet, respectable, not much doin' there at this time o' year I'd have said. Of course, you'll understand, sir, that the 'Eath's a different place in winter to what it is in summer. Lots of people comin' and goin' all day and 'alf the night in summer, but winter time it's often nigh on deserted.'

'And October's neither one thing nor the other, of course. Still, go ahead. You were saying you wouldn't expect to find a prostitute in Millfield Lane.'

'Ah, I wasn't exactly sayin' that, sir. I'd never be surprised at wherever I found one; some fancies a crowd and lights and some prefers a quiet corner. Not that I'd like to be thought to say a word against Millfield Lane. I've never seen nothin' wrong there meself, nor never 'eard of it. What I do say is that if a pol lets 'er friends know where she's likely to be, well, they knows where to find 'er. And there's the 'Eath all 'andy like.'

Chief-Inspector Beldam looked doubtful.

'Surely, at this time of year, it's a bit cold and damp, eh?'

Darby sniffed.

''Appened to be damp tonight, sir, but it's been fine and dry enough till then. Lots of chaps prefer that to the sort of room what's all that some of these ladies 'as to take 'em to.'

Beldam made a wry face.

'And this corner of the Heath, where the body was found, is pretty quiet at this time of year?'

'That's about it, sir. There's that bit of a dip; you'd be 'idden from the path even if it was light enough to see.'

The Scotland Yard man rubbed his chin.

'Well, it doesn't impress me as a likely pitch,' he said. 'Still, you know best, I expect. Funny that you should never have seen her on it though, if you know the place so well.'

Again the slow smile spread over Darby's face.

'The mouse don't show up much when the cat's around, sir. Mighty quick they are to spot a police officer. All they've got to do is to walk on; it ain't too easy to spot them if they ain't paradin'.'

Beldam tapped the blotting-pad in front of him with a pencil.

'Were you on the Heath yourself this evening?' he asked

'Not on the 'Eath itself, sir. I was down Spaniards Road, what crosses it.'

'What time was that?'

'Between six and six-thirty, sir.'

'Were there many people about then?'

'Oh yes, plenty, sir. That's a busy road and a busy time o' day; people comin' 'ome from work. But that's best part of a mile from Millfield Lane, sir, and I understand the murder was committed after seven. That makes a lot o' difference; by seven most people are back in their 'ouses gettin' their supper.'

'Ah, that reminds me,' said Beldam. 'Mr. Hartridge, have you checked up on that point about the time the rain began?'

'Not yet, sir. I've made a lot of enquiries but people are mighty vague about a thing like that. You'd think,' said the detective bitterly, 'that a police officer would notice it but I haven't come across one yet that can tell me anything exact. "About 7 p.m." one says; "about 7.15" says another. What's the good of that? As I said, I was indoors myself at the time.'

Police-Constable Darby had listened imperturbably to this tirade.

'Beggin' your pardon, sir,' he said when it was over. 'I don't call to mind your askin' me about it. As it 'appens, I did notice what time the rain started.'

Never was smug self-satisfaction more clearly marked upon a human countenance.

'Well,' said Chief-Inspector Beldam sharply. 'What time was it?'

'7.15 p.m., sir.'

'How do you know?' snapped Hartridge, who thought that old constables, like old soldiers, were not always as respectful as they might be to their superior officers.

Darby, who was enjoying the attention of the upper ranks, settled down calmly to tell his story in his own time.

'There's a friend of mine what's cook to a lady in Weedon Grove – that's off East 'Eath Road; 'er family 'as their supper at 7.30 sharp and if I 'appen to be along any time before that there's generally a cup of 'ot soup goin'. She's a good cook is my friend. 'Er Tomater, or 'er Cream Vollay, as she calls . . .'

'Yes, yes; never mind that,' said the irritated Inspector. 'How can you fix the time?'

'I was comin' to that, sir. I 'appened to be along the Grove this evenin' and I thought that maybe I was 'a bit too early. I looked at me watch and it was 7.10 p.m., so I thought it'd be all right. I give a whistle when I got to No. 27, and me friend comes up the area steps with a nice cup o' green pea; bottled she said they was but I wouldn't 'ave known it. It was 'ot and I takes me time and 'as a friendly word or two and as I 'ands 'er back the cup the rain begins. I noticed it all right because it come on sharp and sudden an' I tells 'er to slip down and not get wet. I put me cape on and sets off for the Station. Five minutes I was talkin' to 'er and drinkin' the soup; I make no doubt it was 7.15 as near as no matter when the rain begins.'

'You were on duty at the time, I suppose?' asked the Inspector sharply.

'I was on duty, sir,' replied Darby, blandly confident of his established position. 'And many a useful bit of information I've picked up talkin' friendly to the in'abitants. Superintendent Bentcastle, what was 'ere before Superintendent 'Ollis, 'e said to me, I call to mind: 'Darby, 'e says . . .'

'That'll do,' snapped Hartridge. 'I expect I shall be able to check up on that, sir.'

The Scotland Yard man, who did not care a hoot about the derelictions of duty of a Divisional police-constable, was delighted to get so exact a time check. He knew now that the murder had been committed after 7.15 p.m. As the body had been found at 7.40 p.m. there was a gratifyingly small difference between the outside limits.

He dismissed Darby with a word of thanks and turned to Inspector Hartridge.

'We must concentrate on that time tomorrow,' he said. 'Between 7.15 and 7.40. Rake the whole neighbourhood to find people who were in Millfield Lane or anywhere near the Highgate Ponds between those times. Somebody *must* have seen this woman and very likely they saw someone with her. Only people are so confoundedly unobservant; they won't *think*. The Press ought to be able to help us there; they'll know how to stir up imagination. The trouble is that they may stir it up too much and then we have to weed out a lot of rubbish before we get to the real stuff. However, that's better than having nothing at all. By the way, what about those Pressmen; what time did I tell them to come?'

'They're here now, sir,' replied Hartridge. 'I heard them come in while you were talking to Darby.'

'Oh, right. Let's have them in.'

'You don't want them all, do you, sir? There's a whole crowd of them. If you had one in – that chap you spoke to; Whitfield, wasn't it? – you could give him your statement and he'd pass it on to the others.'

Chief-Inspector Beldam laughed.

'You don't know the Press,' he said. 'He might pass it on but the others would never believe he hadn't kept something up his sleeve as a scoop for his own paper. We must have three at least; they'd probably trust three to give each other away.'

Hartridge went out into the charge-room but immediately put his head back round the door.

'Inspector Poole's just come in, sir,' he said.

'Send him in.' Then, as his subordinate entered: 'Any good, Poole?'

'Not much, sir, I'm afraid. Not a very good witness.'

'Well, just hang on while I deal with these Press fellows. All right, Hartridge.'

The small deputation came in, headed by the red-haired Whitfield of the *Morning Despatch.*

'Sit down, boys,' said Beldam. 'I've not got a great deal of fresh stuff for you but we do at least know who the dead woman was.'

'That's the stuff,' said Whitfield. 'Make it a heartthrob.'

'Not much of that, I'm afraid. She's what I suspected but you'd better not say so in so many words. Name of Bella Knox, lodged in Bunt Street, Kentish Town. Description's the same as we've already given – can't improve on that – but there's one new point; her landlady says she "spoke like a lady." Not that I should say Mrs. Twist was much of a judge, and anyway with modern education I suppose most girls do. Anyhow she had no foreign accent and no marked twang or dialect.'

'Doesn't much matter, does it, Chief, if you know who she is?' asked Whitfield.

'Matters to this extent; we want to trace her friends – that's what you'd better call them though no doubt you can word it so that people can read between the lines. The men themselves may be shy of coming forward, but the better description of her we give, including her voice, the more chance there is of people having noticed not only her but anyone she was with. That's where I want your help, gentlemen. I *want to trace her friends.* Work on that; work that up all you can.'

Whitfield grinned.

'You want us to do your work for you, eh, Chief?' he said.

'That's what the police always want,' replied Beldam calmly. 'We like to sit still and wait for people to bring us information. Seriously, this is what I mean; you can do this job in a way we can't. We can call for people with information to come forward and one or two will, but for each one that does there'll be five that don't even know they've got information to give, or are doubtful about it and afraid of making fools of themselves. I want you gentlemen of the Press to make people think, stimulate their imagination – even if it brings us some false news. You can do it in a chatty sort of way that we can't use. You can . . . oh, well . . . don't you see what I mean?'

The detective's inspiration was petering out when it came to putting it into words.

'I know,' said Whitfield. 'You leave it to us. "The police want the best information; you've got it." "Friends, Londoners, Citizens, lend us your eyes." "Where were *you* on Monday night at seven?" On the whole I suppose the police can't use that style.'

'That's it. I want people to realise they've got a part to play in this. A man may say to himself: "I was round that way but I don't think I noticed anything," and that's all that comes of it. Then I want you or his conscience or something to say: "Yes, but are you *sure* you didn't? Didn't you *notice* any woman of that size round about there?" "Yes," says the man, "I think I did, now you put it that way; there was a woman near the Ponds, I think, but I can't say I noticed her particularly." "Are you sure?" says Conscience, "not the shape of her hat? or whether she smelt of scent? what sort of scent? was she alone? There might have been a man, eh; what sort of man – big? small? shabby? looked like a gentleman? bowler hat? Trilby? cap? moustache? Did you hear her voice or his voice?" . . . That's the sort of thing I mean, gentlemen. You'll each have your own way of doing it, but drag it out of them.'

'Can do,' said Whitfield. 'And you've no more facts for us?'

'Nothing at the moment, but I hope to let you have a photograph any time now. That ought to bring people forward. We know who she was, of course, but we want to know who her friends were.'

CHAPTER IV

A RESPECTABLE LOCALITY

'And now, Poole, what about that car?'

'Wash out, I'm afraid, sir.'

'Better tell me about it. Then I must . . .' Beldam glanced at his watch. 'Good Lord, how time flies; it's past eleven o'clock and I wanted to see that man Gooden tonight. In bed by now, probably.'

He reached for the telephone directory and began to flick over the pages.

'Where's Hartridge?'

'Gone across to the Hospital, I think, sir. I heard him telephoning to a Mr. Scott asking him to come and identify the body.'

'Scott? Ah, yes; that's the man that was accosted; I want to see him. Here we are – Jasper Gooden; that was the name.'

He put through a call and presently a man's voice replied. Beldam spoke.

'That Mr. Jasper Gooden? Mr. Gooden's butler, eh? Well, this is Chief-Inspector Beldam of New Scotland Yard. I want a word with Mr. Gooden. Has he gone to bed? Then perhaps you'll kindly enquire whether I can come round and see him any time within the next half hour. Yes, of course I'll hold on; look alive, man.'

An expression of mingled impatience and amusement crossed Beldam's face.

'These gentlemen's gentlemen,' he muttered.

He heard the sound of steps returning to the telephone and then the affected voice of the butler.

'Mister Gooden will not be retiring before midnight.'

'Right; I'll be round before then.'

He slammed down the receiver.

'Go ahead, Poole.'

'Mrs. Joliffe was not at her house, sir, when I went round. She had gone to a Bridge Club at Golders Green. I followed her there and she wasn't very pleased.'

'I'll bet she wasn't.'

Poole smiled.

'She came out into the hall to see me while she was dummy and she thought that would be enough. I managed to persuade her to give me ten minutes in the secretary's office. Not a very good witness, sir; impatient, not really trying to help.'

'Lady, eh?'

Again Poole smiled.

'Perhaps, sir. Smartly dressed, made up, cigarette, red nails, loud voice; not the old-fashioned kind, anyway. She had seen a car standing in Millfield Lane as she was walking back from a Registry Office in Highgate Road where she had been to see about a servant. The car was standing on the near side of the Lane, next the grass, facing north and about opposite where Merton Lane joins it. Mrs. Joliffe was walking up the path on that side. She said she just wondered why it was waiting there but didn't pay much attention to it. She noticed a woman in the front seat on the near side and thought there was someone in the driving seat, but did not notice whether it was a man or a woman; it was a low car and Mrs. Joliffe is a tall woman so she might easily not be able to see the driver as she walked past. About the car itself she could give me no help at all. When she reported she had said she thought it might be a Morris or a Standard, but when I pressed her she could give no reason for quoting either. She said that all she meant was that it was "one of those popular cars" and shabby at that. Didn't notice the number, of course. I couldn't get another tiling out of her and I had to let her go back to her Bridge.'

Chief-Inspector Beldam frowned.

'No good at all, then,' he said.

'I wouldn't quite say that, sir. By itself it's not enough to give us much chance of tracing the car. But it may work in with other reports. I thought, sir, that if you agreed we might call for information from anyone who had seen a car in the Lane at about that time.'

'Ah, yes; what time?'

'I'm sorry, sir, I forgot that. She was vague about that too; thought it might have been about seven o'clock, as she was back at her house in Bishop's Wood in time to dress for dinner, which she usually did at about half-past seven. I asked her where she was when the rain began and she seems to have noticed that anyhow; she said she had passed Ken Wood and got out into Hampstead Lane and the rain made her look about for a taxi but there wasn't one. I don't know what time the rain did begin, sir, but I calculate that between the point where she saw the car and the point where she was when the rain began would be about ten minutes' walk for an active woman.'

'Good work,' said Beldam. 'The rain began at 7.15; we've checked that. So she must have passed the car at about 7.05. Now look here, Poole, get out an information on that for all Stations and get it through to the Press, too; look sharp about it because we must have it in the morning editions – a call for information about a car . . . damn it, what is it now?'

Inspector Hartridge had come into the office.

'I've got Mr. Scott here, sir; the one that was accosted a fortnight ago. He's pretty sure that this was the woman though he can't absolutely swear to it. Do you want to see him, sir?'

Beldam looked at his watch.

'Can give him five minutes,' he said. 'Then I must get along and see your churchwarden friend before he "retires".'

Mr. Scott was a tubby, rosy-cheeked man of about forty; Beldam judged that normally he would be a hearty, genial fellow but at the moment he seemed slightly subdued.

'Sit down, sir,' said the Chief-Inspector. 'I don't want to keep you long because you'll have told your story to Inspector Hartridge. I just want to ask you two things. I understand you've only seen this woman once; is that so?'

Mr. Scott nodded.

'So far as I know, that is so,' he said.

'Did you at that time notice her talking to any other man?'

'No. I think I was the only man about at the time.'

'Thank you, sir. And can you tell me how she spoke? I mean, was there anything noticeable about it – a foreign accent, or Cockney, or did she speak like a lady?'

Mr. Scott's face slowly broke into a cheerful grin.

'Bit difficult to say: "Hullo dear, do you want a little friend?" like a lady, isn't it, Chief-Inspector? But I certainly didn't notice any special accent, Cockney or foreign.'

'I see, sir; probably it doesn't matter. And you've nothing else to tell that might help us?'

'Only what I've already told your Inspector. At least . . .'

Mr. Scott hesitated.

'Go on, sir.'

'Well, this isn't a fact. It's just . . . well, I'm a novelist and I'm given to imagining. After the woman spoke to me I began to think . . . I was walking alone, you see, with nothing special to think about. I began to wonder what her story was, how she came to take to that life, especially as her face was marked by that scar. It seemed pretty sad, you know, and I wondered . . .'

'Yes, sir, quite,' broke in Beldam, 'but I'm afraid I haven't time now. Quite natural, of course, for a novelist to imagine things, but not much use to the police. If you'll excuse me, sir, I've got another witness to see.'

Beldam pulled on his overcoat and swung out of the door, leaving Mr. Scott looking rather crestfallen.

'Bit crushing that, wasn't it?' he asked when the winds of the Chief-Inspector's departure had ceased to blow.

Inspector Poole laughed.

'He didn't mean to be unkind, sir,' he said, 'but he's in a hurry. He's got to see an important witness before twelve o'clock. I wonder if you'd tell me, sir, what was in your mind?'

Inspector Hartridge had gone out into the charge-room and Scott instinctively felt that with the younger man who was now talking to him he was in a more sympathetic atmosphere. He looked thoughtfully at Poole.

'You a detective, too?' he asked.

'Yes, sir. I'm a Detective-Inspector from the Yard. Chief-Inspector Beldam is from the Yard too. Inspector Hartridge, who you came in with, is attached to this Division; this is his Station.'

'I see,' said Scott; 'he's on his own dunghill and you aren't.'

Poole smiled.

'That's about it, sir.'

'Then perhaps we'd better get off it – if you want me to spout any more of my imaginings. I'm afraid I should wilt under another snub. I've got my car outside; can I give you a lift anywhere?'

Poole hesitated.

'That's very kind of you, sir,' he said. 'I've got to get back to the Yard to draft something for the Press. It's miles out of your way . . .'

'Not at this time of night. Come along . . . and for God's sake stop calling me' "Sir"; it's too damned official for my informal spirit.'

Poole had a final word or two with Inspector Hartridge and then joined the novelist in his small two-seater, which was soon buzzing merrily down Haverstock Hill.

'What I'd got in my mind,' said Scott, 'was that there must often be a story behind these poor women's lives. I know that's not a very original idea, of course.

> *She was poor but she was honest,*
> *Victim of a rich man's crime.*

We've all laughed at that little ditty but it's a jest that may sometimes hide a true word. After all, there can't be many of them that set out with the intention of adopting that line as a career.'

'Very few, I should imagine,' said Poole, 'but, after all, it must be a perilously easy step to take when your adopted career falls down on you, especially if you've got looks and not much else.'

'Yes, and that's what this woman had, I feel sure. Not now, poor thing, not when I saw her; but not many years ago. Your Chief asked me about her voice and I confess I hadn't particularly noticed it, but it was a shrewd question. It might well give you a line on her past . . . if you really need one.'

'Probably we shan't,' said Poole. 'The odds are that this is just a case of some vicious brute, a more or less casual bit of violence that went too far. But, as you say, it might be worth remembering. Pity you didn't notice it yourself.'

'Our conversation was confined to formula,' said Scott, spinning the small car round the red bulk of a belated bus. 'Otherwise I might have noticed. Have you discovered who she is? Perhaps I oughtn't to ask.'

'There's no secret about that,' replied Poole. 'The Press have got it already. At least, we know the name she was using.'

'Exactly. And it's damned unlikely to be her own. You know her name and her profession, but that doesn't really mean that you know who she is. That's the point I was making for when your Chief-Inspector crushed me.'

Poole was silent for a minute, wondering how much he ought to say. Casual conversation was not encouraged for police officers, especially detectives, but this man seemed intelligent and might yet be useful.

'That's very true,' he said. 'She may well have an identity very different to what we imagine. At the moment, so far as the police are concerned, she is just an unfortunate woman with a rather artificial name. She called herself Bella Knox.'

Scott looked quizzically at his companion but decided against the jibe he would have made among his own cronies.

'A woman of imagination,' he said. 'She's beginning to take shape in my mind. Look here, Inspector . . . you didn't tell me your name.'

'Poole.'

'Well, if it isn't asking too much and if you get stuck over this case, I wish you'd come and have a word with me about it. You know my address – it's a bachelor flat with a barrel of strong ale. I feel quite intrigued about this story and if the normal theory of the brute beast breaks down I might be able to suggest an alternative. Come along and smoke a pipe with me one evening when you're free; you owe me that for the lift and I promise not to try and pump you unduly.'

Poole thought it extremely unlikely that the novelist could provide any useful suggestions, but he could hardly refuse the offer of hospitality.

'That's very kind of you,' he said. 'I'd like to come in one night.'

In the meantime, while Poole was being human with the novelist, Chief-Inspector Beldam was finding himself compelled to extreme formality with the barrister. Mr. Jasper Gooden was a small, thin man of about fifty-five. He wore rimless *pince-nez* glasses and his voice was dry, with a slightly querulous note. He was wearing evening clothes, with a black velvet smoking jacket, but there was no sign of smoke in the small study where he received Beldam.

Having indicated a chair Mr. Gooden consulted a gold watch.

'It is my custom not to work into the small hours, Chief-Inspector,' he said. 'I am still engaged upon a brief but I can give you a quarter of an hour.'

Beldam repressed an inclination to tell the lawyer that it was his duty to give the police as much of his time as they required.

'Very good of you, sir,' he said. 'I have had the bare fact that you found this poor woman's body – or rather that your little dog did.'

To his surprise Beldam saw a twinkle appear in the lawyer's eye.

'Ivan,' he said quietly.

From the shadow behind the desk at which Mr. Gooden was sitting there rose a gigantic, shaggy dog, which, yawning, displayed a set of extremely formidable teeth.

'Siberian wolf-hound,' said Mr. Gooden in his precise voice.

The dog walked slowly round the desk and approached Beldam, sniffing him carefully. Seated as he was, the detective found the dog's head almost on a level with his throat, and for a moment he was conscious of a sensation of extreme discomposure.

'Quite harmless,' said the barrister. 'But perhaps *not* a little dog.'

'I'm sorry, sir, I'm sure,' said the detective. 'A stupid mistake on my part. Lucky you had him with you, or the body might not have been found till tomorrow and our job would have been more difficult.'

'It was quite a chance, really,' said Mr. Gooden. 'These dogs hunt by sight, not by scent. He happened to be ranging rather wide and came right on to the woman. I was in a hurry to get back here because of the rain and when he did not come to my whistle I had to stop and wait for him. Of course, it was dark and I could not see where he had got to till I moved off the path.'

'You saw nobody near the body, sir?'

'Not a soul. That part of the Heath is often very quiet after dark at this time of year and of course the rain would tend to keep people away.'

'But not the murderer, sir,' said Beldam quietly.

Mr. Gooden seemed rather taken aback.

'No, no, I suppose not. Have you any evidence as to the time the murder was committed?'

'Some evidence, sir. It was committed after 7.15 . . . and you found the body, I understand, at 7.40.'

'Precisely. I at once consulted my watch. Fortunately I was carrying a torch, which I do when I go out on the Heath after dark. 7.15 you say? Dear me, that was not very long before I was on the spot.'

'7.15 was the earliest time, sir, but it is likely to have been later than that – at least five minutes later and probably more.'

'How do you . . . ? But I must not ask you questions. I am afraid I cannot help you in the way you would like; I saw nobody anywhere near the spot. Millfield Lane itself was quite deserted.'

'That's a pity, sir, but of course I expected it. You would have told us if you had seen anybody. But there is one way in which you might be able to help us. I take it that you often exercise your dog on the Heath?'

'Yes, practically every evening, but not often as late as that. I was delayed by a conference.'

'Quite so, sir. What I wanted to ask was whether you had on any previous occasion noticed this woman in that neighbourhood.'

The barrister shook his head.

'Not to my knowledge,' he said.

'Have you noticed any soliciting?'

'No, not in that neighbourhood. If I had I should of course have reported it. This is a respectable locality, I hope and believe.'

Beldam wondered whether the barrister would regard murder as respectable, though soliciting was not.

'I have, of course,' continued Mr. Gooden, 'seen a certain amount of the public love-making which people allow themselves in these days, but there is nothing illegal in that, so long as there is no act of indecency. And of course I have from time to time noticed people waiting about, as if they had an assignation; again, nothing illegal there.'

'Have you noticed any particular men hanging about?'

'Any particular men? What does the word "particular" imply?'

Beldam felt a twinge of irritation.

'I'll put it differently, sir,' he said. 'Have you noticed any man hanging about whom you might recognise or describe?'

The barrister nodded, as though acknowledging a point. He pondered for a moment or two.

'I am afraid I am not in the habit of noticing people,' he said, 'not, at any rate, unless I know them personally or there is something unusual about them. My mind is usually concentrated upon my thoughts. But now you press me I did one evening notice a man waiting near the Bathing Pond, on the grass between the Pond and the Lane. He struck me as an undesirable character to have hanging about in this locality.'

'Can you describe him, sir?'

Mr. Gooden carefully polished his glasses before replying.

'I can give you no exact description,' he said. 'The impression I received – the unfavourable impression which caused me to notice him – was probably more to do with the expression on his face than to any particular feature. He was a large man, certainly; tall and with heavy shoulders. He wore, I think, some kind of macintosh and a cap. He had one of those fleshy faces with an unhealthy colour that means drink, and his eyes were shifty. I am so well accustomed, Chief Inspector, to forming a quick judgment of character when I have to deal with witnesses, that I would not hesitate to say that this was an undesirable character. But I can say no more.'

'And of course there was nothing to connect him with this woman, sir, or with any other woman?'

'Nothing; he was alone and appeared to be waiting for somebody, but that is little more than a guess. There were a fair number of people on the move then, if I remember rightly. It was earlier in the evening and, of course, before the change to winter time, so that it was quite light.'

Beldam had made a note of this description, though it seemed long odds against its being required. Still . . .

'Would you recognise this man again, sir?' he asked.

'I think so. Yes, I think so.'

'If you do see him, sir, perhaps you would communicate at once with Hampstead Police Station. There is just a chance . . .'

'Quite so. And now, Chief-Inspector, I must ask you to bring interview to a close. You will observe that I have given you considerably more than the quarter of an hour that I promised.'

'Very good of you, sir,' said Beldam, feeling that he had learned very little that he had not known before.

He agreed with Mr. Jasper Gooden, however, that it was time for bed.

CHAPTER V

CHARGE-ROOM INTERLUDE

Sergeant Jameson sat at his high desk in the charge-room of Hampstead Police Station. It was still early, barely eight o'clock, and the Station-Sergeant had the place to himself, for which he was profoundly thankful. He could read at his leisure the reports, 'informations,' orders, and other literature which it was his duty to absorb. His brain had never been quick and now that he was over fifty he found concentration increasingly difficult. Last night it had been impossible; the Station had been infested by Scotland Yard detectives, witnesses, and, worst of all, journalists – reporters of the most persistent type, men who worried him for information which he could not give and who refused to take 'no' for an answer. How Superintendent Hollis had come to allow such people in the Station passed Sergeant Jameson's comprehension; no doubt it was the demoralising influence of the Scotland Yard detectives, men who had no respect for dignity and who treated the Divisional police as if they were an inferior class.

In his judgment of the Scotland Yard officers Sergeant Jameson was not being just, but that happened to be his personal prejudice, an idiosyncrasy which no amount of courtesy from Chief-Inspector Beldam or Inspector Poole or Sergeant Gower or any other C.I.D. officer would ever alter. In early life Jameson had had ambitions which had never been realised and, quite unconsciously, he had allowed his disappointment to warp his judgment. In other respects he was a fair-minded man, especially where the unfortunates who passed through his hands were concerned. He could sympathise with people in trouble, and beneath a rather crusty exterior he had a surprisingly tender heart. He hated murder cases; it was not so much that he was sorry for the victim as that he could realise the agonies of mind which the murderer must suffer – the man or woman who was being hunted by the implacable detectives who were his own pet aversion. Jameson had played no direct part in cases of this kind but he had twice entered charges against men who had been arrested for murder and he would never forget the look of fear in their eyes; one had been a navvy who had killed his wife in a drunken fury and one a young clerk who had cut the throat of a girl of whom he was jealous – both brutes in their way but to Jameson human beings who felt the icy fingers of death closing upon their hearts.

So this morning the Station-Sergeant was glad of the routine work that kept his mind from uncomfortable thoughts. His pen was busy now, entering his own report in a round and beautifully legible script, moving slowly but with all the relentless dignity of the law across the yellow paper. A gleam of autumn sunshine threw a patch of brightness on the wood-block floor, and a large blue-bottle banged itself eagerly against the dusty window-pane as if it realised that a police-station was no place for a free spirit.

A smart young constable came in through the swing door and, after hanging up his helmet, bent down to smooth the creases which a pair of bicycle clips had made in his stiff blue trousers.

'Cat came back with the milk this morning,' he said with a grin. 'Been out on the tiles like any other cat but the maid says the old lady's no end fussed about it; never done such a thing before and it's a pedigree something or other and a lady at that and goodness knows what company it may not have been keeping.'

Sergeant Jameson grunted, sensing impropriety.

'Put it in writing, and no sauce,' he said gruffly.

'Yes, sir; no, sir,' said Police-Constable Bliss cheerfully. He knew his sergeant well and was not afraid of the gruffness, which was only skin-deep.

Very soon two pens were scratching and only the clumsy blue-bottle competed with them. The constable's worked the more smoothly and swiftly of the two but its course was frequently checked, perhaps by the throes of composition which attempted to combine veiled humour with absence of 'sauce.'

After a time there was a gentle tap at the outer door.

'Come in,' said Sergeant Jameson without looking up from his work.

Nobody did come in but after a time the tap was repeated, even more timidly than before. Bliss walked across to the door and admitted a small, shabby woman who corresponded exactly to her tap.

'Yes, ma'am; what can I do for you?' asked Sergeant Jameson, putting down his pen.

The woman stood not very far from the door, nervously twitching a corner of her threadbare coat with work-worn hands.

'I . . . you 'aven't . . . it's me 'usband,' she said at last.

Jameson sighed and pulled a sheet of paper towards him. Another wife-beater, no doubt.

'Will you come up to the desk,' he said, 'and give me your name?'

'Dench, sir; Emily Dench.'

'Give Mrs. Dench a chair, Bliss. Now, will you tell me all about it?'

Mrs. Dench hesitated, evidently not knowing how to begin.

'I wondered whether you'd got 'im 'ere,' she said at last. ''E's not been 'ome all night. 'E's been in trouble before but not 'ere; we only come to 'Ampstead in July.'

Sergeant Jameson had exchanged glances with his subordinate.

'Can you describe him?' he asked.

''E's a big man, sir; not fat-like but 'eavy shoulders and strong. Got a big moustache an' . . . an' a bit of a temper,' said Mrs. Dench nervously. 'When 'e's 'ad a drop 'e sometimes forgets 'imself.'

'Better not tell me about that, Mrs. Dench,' said Sergeant Jameson quietly. 'We've got him here, I think, but he either couldn't or wouldn't give his name. Police-Constable Bliss here found him on a seat by the Spaniards at eleven o'clock last night; he was drunk and disorderly. He'll appear before the magistrate at eleven o'clock this morning. Do you want to see him?'

'Oh, no, sir,' said Mrs. Dench with an involuntary shiver which told the kind-hearted Station-Sergeant a great deal. 'Not now I know where 'e is. I didn't know but what somethin' might 'ave 'appened to him.'

Being run in as drunk and disorderly was probably not a 'happening' in the life of Mrs. Dench.

'Well, his night in a cell hasn't done him any harm,' said Jameson, glancing across at a young man who had just come in and who now stood nervously uncertain, just where Mrs. Dench had stood.

'Take a seat, please,' said the Sergeant, pointing to a bench which ran along the wall opposite him.

'Now, Mrs. Dench, if you care to give me your address you can, though you need not. I'll keep an eye on your husband and if you want any help at any time just come and have a word with me.'

Mrs. Dench, looking rather bewildered by this generous offer, allowed herself to be escorted to the door by Police-Constable Bliss. Sergeant Jameson beckoned to the young man on the bench.

'And what's your trouble?' he asked, his experienced eye sizing up the shiny right sleeve of the coat, the ill-cleaned shoes and the unassured manner as not calling for a 'sir.'

'I . . . I've lost a bicycle, Sergeant.'

'Oh, have you? And do you expect me to go and look for it?'

This was rather disconcerting.

'Oh . . . oh, no. But I thought . . . I hoped . . . I didn't quite know what I ought to do. It isn't . . . I mean, it might have been stolen, mightn't it?'

Sergeant Jameson grunted. People who could not talk straight always irritated him.

'Better tell me where you lost it,' he said. 'What's your name?'

'Cadby; Frank Cadby.'

'Address?'

'27 Morton Buildings, Webster Street.'

'Go on.'

'Hampstead, N.W.'

'Damn it, I know where Webster Street is. How did you come to lose it?'

'Oh. Well, you see, I was on the Heath last night with a friend and I put it down and when I looked for it again I couldn't find it.'

Jameson controlled his irritation with difficulty.

'Where did you put it down? What time?'

'Well, it was near Ken Wood; near the trees, I mean, not the house.'

'What were you doing there with a bicycle?' asked the Sergeant sternly. 'There's no bicycle track there.'

'I . . . I wasn't bicycling, Sergeant. I rode across from East Heath Road by the path that you're allowed to bicycle on to the Bathing Pond, where I was to meet my friend. She wanted to walk and I didn't like to leave my bicycle there so I wheeled it. We went across towards Ken Wood and she . . . well she said the bicycle was a nuisance and that I was to put it down, so I did and we walked up the hill a bit over the grass towards Spaniards Road and then we sat on a bench a bit.'

Cadby's tongue was working more freely now, if not very coherently.

'Better tell me the time.'

'I was to meet her at seven o'clock. She was a bit late but not very. We sat on the bench for a good time, talking. We're thinking of getting married, when I get a rise, and I didn't notice that it was getting dark. I'd forgotten about its getting dark an hour earlier . . . I mean, summer time only ended on Sunday. And . . . well, we sat there longer than I'd realised and when I looked at my watch it was after eight. I'd got to be down in Bedford Square at nine to take some notes – shorthand – for my boss, so we went down the hill quick and then I couldn't find my bicycle. I don't know that part of the Heath and I wasn't sure, in the dark, where I'd put it, and I was afraid of being late so I thought I'd better leave it and come back and look for it in the morning and . . . well, it's not there.'

'Nor likely to be. Why didn't you report your loss at once?'

Frank Cadby fidgetted. Sergeant Jameson began to wonder whether he was lying.

'I only just had time to get down to Bedford Square. You see, we had to walk as far as the tram stop in Highgate Road and then I had to get the Tube at Kentish Town. There'd have been a row if I'd been late.'

'What time did you leave your boss?'

'About a quarter past ten.'

'Why didn't you report it then?'

Cadby hesitated.

'I thought I'd find it this morning,' he said lamely.

'You must be a fool. Serve you right if you don't see it again. What make of bicycle?'

The young man's jaw dropped.

'I . . . I don't know,' he stammered.

Sergeant Jameson put down his pen and looked searchingly at his visitor.

'Was this your own bicycle?' he asked curtly.

Cadby was silent, his eyes falling before the Sergeant's penetrating stare.

'Better answer my question, Cadby. Was this your own bicycle?'

'N . . . No, sir.'

'Whose was it?'

'Jack Pickford's. He keeps it at the end of our landing. He's away in hospital. He's let me use it before now.'

'I see. So you borrowed it without leave. And I suppose that's why you didn't report the loss at once?'

'Yes.'

'It looks as if you'd landed yourself in trouble. Can you describe the bicycle?'

'I . . . I think so. It's a sporting kind; low handlebars. It's got an electric lamp in front and an oil lamp behind, as well as the reflector. The grip has come off one of the handles.'

'Which one?'

'The left, I think. Yes, the left.'

Sergeant Jameson looked across at Police-Constable Bliss, who had been listening to the conversation. Bliss nodded.

'Well, Cadby,' said Jameson, 'I think we've got your bicycle here. One of the park keepers found it last night and brought it in here. It was lucky for you that he did or you might have found yourself charged with larceny. This constable will show you the bicycle and if you identify it as Pickford's you can take it away, when you've signed for it. He will go with you and get confirmation of your story. We shall report the matter to the owner and he may or may not charge you. In any case let this be a lesson to you not to make use of things that don't belong to you without leave.'

He turned to the constable.

'You can go on your bicycle, Bliss, and get back as quick as you can. We've wasted enough time already this morning.'

CHAPTER VI

BUNT STREET

Sergeant Jameson had not had five minutes' peace for the contemplation of his own work when the door of the Charge-room opened again and in strolled Inspector Hartridge.

'Morning, Jameson,' said the detective cheerfully.

'Good morning, sir.'

'Anything come in during the night?'

'A drunk, sir; enquiry about a cat; enquiry about a bi . . .'

'I mean about this murder case,' cut in the Inspector impatiently.

Jameson's manner remained impeccably respectful . . . and frigid.

'I understand that there was a further report about a car seen in Millfield Lane, sir. Detective-Constable Winterbourne has the particulars for you.'

'Right. Super come in yet?'

'Not yet, sir.'

Jameson's air was one of illimitable patience. Inspector Hartridge shrugged his shoulders. He was aware of the uniformed Sergeant's prejudice against the plain-clothes branch and regretted it; Jameson was a good old chap in his way but it was a bore always being met with the correct answer and nothing more.

He walked down the passage to the small room which was all that could be spared to the detective branch of the Division. Winterbourne was sitting at a minute table in a corner, busily scribbling away at his report.

With some difficulty the young detective extracted his long legs from under the table.

'Morning, Winterbourne. Let's hear about this car.'

Winterbourne picked up his report.

'At 9.45 p.m. I visited Westerham Lodge, Millfield Lane. In the course of . . .'

'In your own words, man; not that stuff.'

'Yes, sir. You told me to visit all the houses round there to see if anyone had heard or seen anything. A manservant named Hoskin at Westerham Lodge told me he was coming back up the Lane from the direction of Highgate Road and saw a car standing nearly opposite the entrance to the Lodge. It drove off before he got up to it; he thinks he must have been a hundred yards away at the time and he didn't notice what the driver was like or even whether it was a man or a woman. Didn't notice anything about the car either, except that it was a dark saloon and seemed shabby. He didn't notice the number.'

'He wouldn't. What about time? Could he fix it?'

'Roughly, sir. When he got into his pantry he looked at his clock to see if he'd got plenty of time to get dinner laid. He says it was 7.25 then, and allowing for one thing and another he put the time of the car moving off at between 7.15 and 7.20.'

Hartridge nodded.

'Not too bad,' he said. 'But what a hope for tracing it. Still, the Yard'll want to know about it; I expect . . .'

A buzzer sounded twice.

'There's the Super. I'll send for you if he wants to hear the story.'

Hartridge walked back into the Charge-room where he found that one of the Scotland Yard men, Inspector Poole, had just arrived and was trying his hand on Sergeant Jameson.

'I'm afraid we're being rather a nuisance to you, Sergeant, cluttering up your Station.'

'We've all got our duty to do, sir,' replied Jameson stiffly.

Inspector Hartridge laughed.

'You won't do any good there, Poole,' he said. 'Sergeant Jameson doesn't love us. I'm just going in to the Super. I expect he'll want to see you too.'

Poole nodded.

'I ought to have a word with him before I go on,' he said.

'I'll let him know you're here.'

Hartridge knocked at the Superintendent's door and disappeared. In a moment he was back again and beckoned to Poole to come in.

Superintendent Hollis, who never allowed his night's rest to be curtailed if he could help it, was looking fresh and cheerful.

'Good morning, Inspector,' he said. 'Mr. Beldam coming along?'

'Not just yet, sir. He's detained at the Yard; some hitch about a case he's been on. He told me to come up and see if anything fresh had come in and then to go down to Mrs. Twist's.'

Superintendent Hollis nodded.

'Hartridge has got some report about a car in Millfield Lane. I thought you'd better hear it. Go ahead, Hartridge.'

Inspector Hartridge repeated the story which Winterbourne had told him. The Scotland Yard man jotted down a few notes and said that he would go to Westerham Lodge after his visit to the Kentish Town lodging. He told of two fresh reports of possible identification which had come in to Whitehall 1212 during the night, reports which were being investigated but, in the light of what was now known about the dead woman, were not likely to have any bearing on the case.

'I expect it'll turn out to be a local job, sir,' he said. 'If you could spare Inspector Hartridge to come with me he'd probably pick up the local threads much quicker than I should.'

'Kentish Town's N Division,' said Superintendent Hollis. 'Of course, this is our case but now the Yard's on it we'd better leave anything outside our area to you. Get in touch with Superintendent Buxton if you want local help in Kentish Town.'

'Very well, sir.'

Inwardly Poole cursed the water-tight compartments in which the older police officers so often liked to confine themselves; in the Metropolitan Police there should be no such hindrance to quick work, whatever might be necessary with the County Constabularies.

'I'll keep Hartridge on hunting round the Millfield Lane area,' went on Superintendent Hollis. 'There's quite likely something to be found in daylight but we shall want all our men on the spot. Let me know if you pick up anything useful in Kentish Town.'

Poole did not know what his Chief-Inspector had arranged over-night, but he thought that if the Divisional detectives were going to be kept hunting round the scene of the murder they might just as well have been at it since daybreak. However, it was not his job to say so and he set off without further delay for Kentish Town.

As a matter of courtesy he called in at the local police-station, hoping that he might be rewarded by some useful information about Mrs. Twist, if not about her lodger. Very little, however, was known about the former and nothing about the latter. Twist was a railway porter employed at St. Pancras; he was believed to be a steady man and his wife was known to take a lodger or lodgers. The police had no illusions as to the type of lodger admitted by Mrs. Twist but there had been no complaint about the conduct of the house and there was a limit to the extent to which they concerned themselves with morals; of the lodgers themselves nothing was known.

Poole decided not immediately to ask for local help in his investi-gations, which might need delicate handling. If he could get a line on Bella Knox's 'friends' then he thought that the local men could be of great help, but he wanted to visit Mrs. Twist alone.

Bunt Street, Kentish Town, is not one of the most attractive residential areas. It is narrow, dirty, and at night time ill-lit; though the roar of traffic in the busy Camden Road reaches it, it does not cheer it; Bunt Street remains a desolate spot and its small, mean houses have a desolate appearance not wholly accounted for by their lack of paint.

Poole felt his spirits sink as he walked up it in the drizzling rain. His talk with the novelist, Gordon Scott, on the previous evening had aroused his own interest in the victim of the murder and he found his imagination busy picturing poor Bella Knox in her almost hopeless quest for a liveli-hood, sometimes bringing a client back with her to this unattractive home but more often, probably, returning alone, worn out, hungry, lonely and miserable. He had only caught a glimpse of the limp body lying on the grass and had not seen it after its removal to the mortuary, but somehow he did not feel that Bella Knox had been one of the cheerful, careless type which is unaffected by its surroundings. Perhaps the novelist's imagination was responsible for this opinion, but it was supported by the very nature of the locality which the woman had chosen for her pitch and by the fact that so little seemed to be known of her.

Number 53 differed very little from its neighbours. Three steep and unwashed steps led up to a door which had not known a coat of paint in twenty years. The single ground floor window was screened by a pair of ragged lace curtains that might once have been white, while a large aspidistra did its best to block out the light which might otherwise have filtered through the dirty window panes. From the basement window, a crack of which was open, the smell of boiling cabbage rose into the damp air.

Poole's knock was answered by an untidy girl, thin and pasty-faced. She declared that mother was in the kitchen, and showed the detective into a back room which, from its furniture and its smell of stale food, had the appearance of being the communal dining-room.

While he waited for the landlady Poole studied his surroundings. The table, too big for the room, had six chairs round it; presumably when Bella Knox was alive there must have been seven and that meant a tight squeeze. The chairs themselves were an odd lot and the remaining furniture, sideboard and dresser, was of poor quality. On the dark red walls hung the usual enlarged portraits of whiskered Father and bomba-zined Mother, supported by a patriotic oleograph and a cracked mirror. In search of cheerfulness Poole looked out of the window and saw a tiny yard, entirely devoid of green, which yet provided a home for half a dozen draggled hens in a wire pen.

The door opened and Mrs. Twist, of whom Poole had only caught a glimpse on the previous evening, came in. She wore an overall and her hair was hidden by a twisted duster but, as mistress in her own house, she now carried an air of confidence that had been lacking at the police-station. She looked at Poole with an interest which was tinged with disappointment.

'You ain't the one I saw last night,' she said sharply. 'Where's the 'ead one?'

'Chief-Inspector Beldam was detained at the Yard, Mrs. Twist,' replied Poole politely. 'He's sure to want to see you himself but he sent me on to have a first look round. I am Detective-Inspector Poole and I am working under Chief-Inspector Beldam.'

The resounding titles seemed to appease Mrs. Twist, who pulled a chair out from the table.

'Sit down,' she said. 'I'm not sorry to get off me legs for a minute. 'ave they found 'oo done it?'

'Not yet, I'm afraid. We have not received as much information as we hoped for. I understand that you don't yourself know much about Miss Knox's friends; is that so?'

'She 'adn't got any friends. I told your boss that. Not except us, that is; we was friends in a manner of speakin'. She wasn't one to mix much but she was polite. We rather liked 'er.'

'She had her meals with the family?'

'Yes, she did; and why not?' said Mrs. Twist, quickly on the defensive. 'We're a large family; two boys livin' in and two girls, besides Twist. The kitchen's too small for us all to eat in and besides there ain't nowhere for a lodger to cook 'er own food. I wouldn't 'ave no one else messin' round in my kitchen.'

'No, of course not; naturally,' said Poole hurriedly. He did not want to upset this important witness. 'A very happy arrangement for your lodger, Mrs. Twist. But about Miss Knox's friends; I really meant her acquaintances – professionally.'

It was always so difficult to know how far the veneer of respectability must be observed. Some women in Mrs. Twist's position liked plain speaking; others did not.

'Oh, them; I didn't take no notice of them; not unless they made a row, which wasn't often. Now and then one would 'ave 'ad a drop more than was respectable but Miss Knox 'ad a proper feelin' about 'oo she brought to the 'ouse; she didn't give us no trouble and we asked no questions.'

Poole listened patiently. He wondered whether Mrs. Twist was really as ignorant as she made herself out to be or whether she was trying to blanket his enquiries with a smokescreen of words.

'You didn't know any of them by name?'

'No. 'Ow should I? They didn't often come twice. She'd only been 'ere six months.'

'Can you describe any of them?'

Mrs. Twist hesitated.

'One was a black man,' she said. 'A young feller; one o' them students, like as not. Then there was an old fellow with a beard; respectable 'e looked; 'e did come two or three times, now I come to think of it. Mostly I didn't see 'em at all. She 'ad 'er own key and she always come in quiet. There was one big chap, what 'ad 'ad too much; she took 'im away 'erself; I saw 'em goin' down the street from the kitchen window but I didn't see 'is face. That's all I can tell you. She'd only been 'ere six months,' reiterated Mrs. Twist.

Poole wondered whether any other member of the family could give him more exact information.

'Do your daughters both help you at home, Mrs. Twist?' he asked.

But the landlady quickly put her foot on that gambit.

'I won't 'ave my girls brought into this,' she said sharply. 'It ain't nice. They're respectable girls.'

For the moment it might be wiser not to pursue that line; it was a matter of tactics which his Chief had better decide.

'I don't want to be troublesome, Mrs. Twist,' said the detective quietly. 'As a matter of form we shall just have to know what the family consists of and where they work. You've got two boys, I think you said?'

Rather grudgingly Mrs. Twist gave the required information. Fred, the eldest, was a railwayman like his father; Gertie, nineteen, worked at Ford and Wilson's in the Holloway Road; Madge, seventeen, helped her mother in the house; Billy was still at school. Poole jotted down the particulars and closed his notebook.

'Perhaps I might see Miss Knox's room?' he said.

'It ain't much of a room, you know,' explained Mrs. Twist, leading the way up the narrow stairs with some reluctance. 'It's the only spare we've got now. Used to 'ave two but the girls got too big to sleep in the same room as Fred; it wasn't nice. Billy used to sleep with Twist an' me then, but now 'e shares with Fred and the girls 'ave one to themselves.'

By this time they had reached the second floor, which was also the top.

'That's the girls',' said the landlady, indicating the front room. 'I wanted to keep it for lodgers, but Gertie wouldn't sleep in the back one 'cos it's only got a skylight. Got swelled 'ead since she's been working at Ford & Wilson's. We didn't think the boys ought to be up 'ere with the lodger, she being a lady.'

Poole pretended a polite interest in this domestic detail but he was glad when the back room was opened and he could get to work. He begged Mrs. Twist not to let him detain her from her cooking and, after some hesitation, she left him.

The room was certainly no Venusberg. It was small, with a sharply sloping ceiling in which was the skylight that had not attracted Miss Twist. Nearly half of it was taken up with a large brass bedstead that had no doubt been picked up cheap and whose springs had long since lost all resilience; its size was its only virtue. The sheets were coarse, the blankets threadbare; whatever the contents of the pillow might be they had not come from the breast of an eiderduck. It was, however, carefully made and the whole room was as neat and clean as it could possibly be made.

There were only four other pieces of furniture; a hanging cupboard with drawers at one side, a washstand, a bedside cupboard, and a chair, all of painted deal and very much the worse for wear. Poole opened the hanging cupboard and was surprised to find in it two dress-hangers on which were suspended two dresses; one of these was of some dark woollen material and the other a thin flowered muslin. Poole knew nothing about women's dresses, nor how to describe them, but these two seemed to represent summer and winter and were probably all that poor Bella Knox possessed, except the serge skirt and overcoat in which she had been found. Cheap and worn as they undoubtedly were, however, the detective was again struck by the care with which they had been tended and mended. There was no doubt that this woman, poor and degraded as she might be, took trouble about her appearance and was making a gallant fight to retain her self-respect.

There was no name-tab nor other mark on the dresses, nor was there on any of the lesser garments which lay neatly folded in the drawers. Everything was clean and carefully mended, everything was sadly worn . . . and there was not much of anything. Doubtless Bella Knox had washed and ironed her own clothes, just as a brush and a tin of blacking showed that she cleaned her own shoes.

But all this neatness, interesting as a guide to character, provided no clue to the identity which must lie hidden behind the pseudonym; still less did it help in the discovery of her acquaintances. There was no letter, no paper, no scrap of writing nor even of print. There were no trinkets, no photographs, no 'personal effects' of any kind apart from the clothes, and it was only after an exhaustive search that Poole found seven £1 notes in an envelope tucked into the back of the wardrobe. When he left the room the detective felt that he knew even less of Bella Knox than when he entered it; she remained a disembodied spirit with a palpably false name.

CHAPTER VII

MEN FRIENDS

After transferring the key of Bella Knox's bedroom to the outside, Poole locked the door and put the key in his pocket. He made his way down to the basement and told the landlady what he had done. To his surprise Mrs. Twist made no protest. She prophesied gloomily that she would get no fresh lodger for many a long day; the death of the previous one in hospital had forced the price of the room down two shillings and now this murder would make it unletable. The detective sympathised, promised to reduce police interference to a minimum, and took his leave.

But police interference there had got to be, and not only in Number 53; the whole of Bunt Street must be subjected to their busybodying enquiries. Poole did not intend to do this himself; it was a job eminently suited to the unimaginative but indefatigable talents of his assistant, Detective-Sergeant Gower. Gower was always ready for any tiresome job; he was a pessimist by nature but he produced surprisingly successful results. He had worked on several cases with Poole and was a devoted admirer of his young superior officer.

There was one more person in Bunt Street that Poole intended to see himself and that was Mrs. Twist's neighbour, Mrs. Babworth, who had volunteered information over the telephone on the previous evening. But the detective was not anxious to go straight from one house to the other; to do so might well arouse hostility in the breast of Mrs. Twist and that was a state of affairs that wise detectives always tried to avoid. So he walked off down Bunt Street as if he had no more interest in the place and went straight to Kentish Town Station, where he had arranged to meet Gower.

The Sergeant had spent the last two hours visiting garages in the

Highgate area in an attempt to get news of the 'dark and dirty' saloon seen by Mrs. Joliffe. It was a pretty hopeless task and Poole had expected nothing of it, so that he was not disappointed to receive a blank report. The area of enquiry would now have to be extended and could probably be left to the Divisional Police.

In the meantime, in order to give Bunt Street time to settle down before he disturbed it again, Poole decided to try the local shops and public-houses. There was, in particular, a grocer who had telephoned information on the previous evening and no doubt enquiries would unearth further information. This again would be tedious work but then most detective work in real life *was* tedious. It could, of course, be done by the local police but Poole always liked to take the cream off himself if possible. By using his imagination, which by implication should be superior to that of the local men, it should be possible to pick out the most likely sources of information without wasting time on the unlikely. For instance, now that he knew that Bella Knox had taken her meals with the family it was hardly worth while tackling butcher, greengrocer and other food shops. The fact that information had already come from a grocer rather upset this theory, but it was quite possible that she had only bought from him some luxuries – biscuits, chocolate, and so on – to eke out the fare provided by Mrs. Twist. Anyhow, that point could soon be cleared up.

So Poole allotted to himself Mr. Chadwell the grocer, the post office, the public library, chemists and drapers, while to Gower he gave the special objective of the public-houses, a field of enquiry in which the Sergeant might be regarded as a specialist. It was now eleven o'clock and the two detectives arranged to meet in the saloon bar of the 'Cup and Candle' at one.

Photographs of the dead woman taken in the mortuary on the previous evening were now in the detectives' possession and Poole was struck by the skill with which Detective-Sergeant Cook had removed the appearance of horror from his subject. Bella Knox appeared to be asleep and the likeness seemed to be excellent. One photograph had been taken with the eyes actually open (how the photographer had done it

Poole did not know) and in this the appearance of horror had been less successfully avoided – the expression in the dead eyes gave even the hardened detective an uncomfortable sensation.

Armed with these photographs Poole worked slowly and methodically over his allotted field. Mr. Chadwell was the best witness; he remembered well the woman with the scarred face though he had never heard her name. As Poole had guessed, she had only made small purchases, a cake of soap, a tin of cocoa, an ounce or two of starch, but Chadwell had noticed her because, though her general appearance suggested her profession she had not been either 'bold' or shamefaced; Chadwell – evidently a man of some imagination – described her as 'her own mistress,' from which Poole gathered that she had assurance without assertiveness. It gave a useful indication to character, but once again there was nothing more; no man had been seen with her and no conversation had taken place.

By the same patient method Poole established small purchases at draper and chemist, but at both post office and public library he drew blank. By the time he reached the *rendezvous* he felt that once more he was in the uncomfortable position of being none the wiser for some good and technically successful work. He had obtained contact with Bella Knox but none with any possible murderer.

The Cup and Candle was a modest inn and, as Poole had hoped, the saloon bar was empty. Here he was presently joined by Sergeant Gower and over their plates of bread and cheese and their tankards of bitter the two detectives exchanged notes. In one way Gower had been even less successful than Poole, because it was fairly evident that Bella Knox herself never entered a public-house. On the other hand, he had obtained information which was much more promising than anything Poole had got. The landlord of the Gay George which stood at the corner of the street by which the inhabitants of Bunt Street were most likely to enter Camden Road, had at once recognised the dead woman by her photograph. He had a habit, just before the house 'opened,' of standing at the window of his public bar and looking out upon the busy world which was Camden Road. He had, he said, more than once noticed this woman come to the corner of the street outside his house and wait about – not for long, not long enough to be a nuisance or to call undue attention to herself, but he had twice seen her pick up a man who was probably waiting for the Gay George to open; one of these had been a regular customer, and the landlord had been annoyed to see good money deflected to another channel, but he was a kind-hearted man, he was, with no wish to get a poor woman into trouble, and he had said nothing to the police.

With some reluctance he gave the name of the customer in question, begging that if possible his own name would not be mentioned by the police. To this request Sergeant Gower had made a non-committal reply; so long as he got the information he wanted the feelings of his informants did not interest him. He now passed on his report to his superior officer and waited for orders.

Poole thought that before doing any more he ought to report to his Chief-Inspector, so he went to a telephone kiosk and was lucky enough to catch Beldam just as he was setting out himself for Bunt Street. After a moment's thought Beldam decided that he would himself get in touch with the Gay George customer, one George Fenley, a bricklayer, as this was the first direct contact with a man that had been established. Poole was told to get on with his intended task of questioning Mrs. Babworth, while Sergeant Gower was to work slowly through the rest of the street.

Mrs. Babworth had to be extracted from a post-prandial slumber but, once aroused, she proved a willing and voluminous talker. She took in no lodgers herself, being a capitalist in her own right as well as the recipient of a full scale war widow's pension. She lived in Bunt Street because she had done so all her life and was not one who cared to chop and change, but she evidently was not fond of her next door neighbour. Mrs. Twist, it appeared, not only took in a disreputable lodger but was a back-biter and mischief-maker, and while it was a judgment on her that ill-fame had descended upon her dishonoured house it was a cruel shame that her neighbours should be forced to share in her notoriety and to suffer the attentions of the police.

Poole refrained from pointing out that Mrs. Babworth had herself invited this attention on the previous evening. He listened patiently to a good deal of neighbourly gossip and then began to steer it in the direction he required. Mrs. Babworth had not, it appeared, kept any sort of watch upon Mrs. Twist's lodger or her friends, but it had not been possible to avoid noticing things occasionally. There was a big man with a nasty face, clean shaven she thought, who had been there twice in the last month to her certain knowledge; she thought she would recognise him if she saw him again. There was an old man who should have known better; he had a white beard and as like as not he spent his Sundays preaching to better people than himself. There was a young lad with spectacles and two nondescripts of whom no particulars could be recalled. Mrs. Babworth made no mention of the black man and had presumably been so unfortunate as to miss that particular piece of scandal.

On the whole it was not an impressive list and did not suggest a flourishing business, but Poole remembered that the summer was only just over and that the dead woman had apparently favoured the wide open spaces for her craft. Neither was it a very helpful list at the moment because Mrs. Babworth did not know the identity of any of the men she described; she had not seen them about anywhere else in the neighbour-hood, though possibly other people might know them.

Poole expressed regret on this point.

'I'm much obliged to you, madam, for your help,' he said, rising from his chair; 'I'm only sorry that you don't know the name of any of Miss Knox's friends.'

'Well, I do know one, anyway,' said Mrs. Babworth sharply.

'Oh? Which is that?'

The widow hesitated.

'Not one of them I've been telling you about, I don't mean.'

Poole sat down again.

'Perhaps you will tell me about him,' he said quietly.

For a moment it seemed as if Mrs. Babworth regretted her last impulse. She fidgetted in her chair and did not at once continue.

'Well, I mean to say, I can't help knowing *his* name, can I now?' she said at last.

'Who do you mean?'

'Well . . . Twist, of course.'

'Twist? Oh yes, of course; Mrs. Twist told me that the family were all friendly with Miss Knox. They had meals together.'

'Friendly!'

Mrs. Babworth's sniff was eloquent.

'He could be friendly without taking the creature to the pictures, couldn't he?'

'Did he do that? I daresay they all went sometimes.'

'I daresay they did but that wouldn't be much use to Twist, would it? I saw him at the Pandeon with her not a fortnight ago and that when Mrs. Twist was laid up with a bad leg. Oh, yes; Twist was friendly enough. Not that I suppose for a minute that there was anything *in* it; oh, no.'

Mrs. Babworth was trembling. Whether this phenomenon was due to suppressed emotion, righteous indignation, or mere excitement Poole did not know. Her feelings in any case were strongly aroused and he thought it best to soothe them.

'I'm sure you're right, madam,' he said. 'Just a bit of kindness on the part of Mr. Twist. I've been told that he is a very steady man.'

But this was too much for Mrs. Babworth. Her voice rose almost to a scream.

'Oh, yes, Twist's steady enough when a respectable woman wants to pass a friendly word with him, but when a dirty little tart makes up to him – ugly, too, that scar and no chicken – where's his steadiness then? Can you tell me that?'

Before the detective could answer the slighted widow burst into tears and Poole tactfully withdrew. As he walked away he turned over the interview in his mind. He had at first had some hopes of getting valuable information from so observant a witness, but as Mrs. Babworth could put no name to anyone she had seen her talents had been largely wasted. At first the insinuation against Twist himself had been suggestive but it had soon become apparent that this was a mere outburst of spiteful jealousy. No doubt the widow had set her cap at her neighbour's husband and, receiving no response, had allowed her resentment to carry her over the bounds of truth. She had hesitated before launching out upon her tale; hesitated to commit herself to a slander.

But, thought Poole, as he walked down Bunt Street, slander may be true, or at least contain a germ of truth. It might be worth while having a word with Twist. The local police had given him a good character but they were hardly likely to know anything about his morals, and a married man who gets into trouble with his wife's lodger . . . yes, it would be worth while having a word with Twist.

On the other side of the street Sergeant Gower emerged from a house, strolled along to the next one and rang the bell. He had a small case in his hand and Poole was prepared to bet that it contained samples of cheap stockings. Sergeant Gower was an artist and like all artists had his special tricks. He took no notice of his superior officer, though he had undoubtedly seen him; he would not spoil his 'character' by any such elementary blunder as that. So Poole strolled on to the end of the street and waited round the corner. Five minutes later Gower appeared.

'Nothing much doing so far, sir,' he said. 'They're mostly hard-worked folks and don't do a lot of snooping. I thought I wouldn't be a police-officer, at any rate for a start, so I didn't use the photograph but I'd heard about the murder and was naturally curious. Three of the four that I've seen so far knew about Mrs. Twist's lodger but only one had seen a man with her – an old fellow with a white beard.'

'Yes, I've heard about him,' said Poole. 'Your friend didn't know who he was, I suppose?'

'No, sir.'

'Nor did mine. Well, go ahead. I'll be back at the Yard about six, I expect. This is going to be a dull job, I'm afraid, but we're bound to get a line soon.'

During the course of his career in the C.I.D. Poole had been lucky enough to be mixed up in several cases of exceptional interest. He was rather a protegé of the Assistant Commissioner, Sir Leward Marradine, and on two occasions had been put in charge of cases which would normally have been entrusted to a Chief-Inspector. Both of these had concerned men of considerable distinction and had brought Poole into contact with a very different world to that in which he was now working, so that the present case did appear to him by comparison rather drab and uninteresting. However, he was not a man who suffered from swelled head and as he was a conscientious officer he set about his present task with all the thoroughness and skill that he could command.

Robert Twist, he had been told, was a railway porter at St. Pancras, so he now made his way to the big terminus in the Euston Road, a matter of ten minutes' walk. He had to get leave from the Station Master to detach the porter from his work but it was not a particularly busy time of day and the Station Master was considerate enough to allow him the use of a small office for the interview.

Twist proved to be a short, sturdy man of about fifty-five. He was clean-shaven and when he removed his cap on entering the office he disclosed a head of close-cropped black hair, slightly tinged with grey at the temples.

'Good afternoon, Mr. Twist,' said the detective, motioning the porter to a chair. 'I am a police officer and I am making some enquiries about the woman, Bella Knox, who has been lodging at your house.'

The porter made no comment, but a wary look had come into his eyes. That might, of course, be natural enough even with the clearest conscience; nobody likes to be mixed up with the police.

'I have seen your wife,' went on the detective, 'but I want to ask you one or two questions. Mrs. Twist told me that Miss Knox sometimes brought friends to the house – men friends – but she was not able to tell me who any of them were. I wonder whether you can help me.'

Twist shook his head.

'I don't know nothing about them,' he said curtly.

'Nothing at all? You've seen them, I suppose?'

'I might 'a' done.'

'Can't, you be more definite than that?'

'All right,' said the man grudgingly. 'I did see one or two occasional-like. She didn't often bring 'em 'ome. It ain't much of a room to bring 'em to.'

The detective nodded.

'Can you describe the men you have seen?'

Slowly and painfully Poole extracted from the porter a list which in the end corresponded pretty closely with that already given him by Mrs. Twist and Mrs. Babworth; the old man, the black man, the big man who had had a glass too much, the young fellow with glasses; the nondescripts referred to by Mrs. Babworth received a slightly more exact description as 'a fellow in a blue suit with sticking-out teeth' and 'a chap with one leg shorter than the other.' But Twist knew, he declared, nothing about any of them, not their names, their address, nor their professions. Poole had hardly expected that he would.

'You never heard or saw any of them use or threaten violence to Miss Knox?' he asked.

'No, I didn't. And they wouldn't 'a' done it twice in my 'ouse,' said Twist sturdily.

'I'm sure they wouldn't. But violence has been done and you will understand that we have to ask about it. Now there's one question I've got to put to you, Twist, that I am afraid you may think rather impertinent, but it's a matter of routine and you aren't obliged to answer it. On what terms were you with Miss Knox yourself?'

Instantly the wary look deepened in the porter's eyes.

'What d'jer mean . . . terms?' he asked.

'Were you friendly with her?'

'We was all friendly with our lodgers,' said Twist. 'Why shouldn't we be?'

'No reason at all; very natural. But you yourself; were you on good t. . . were you specially friendly with her?'

'No, I wasn't,' said the man gruffly. 'What are yer gettin' at?'

'You didn't, for instance, go about with her after your work was done?'

'No.'

'Did you ever take her to a restaurant . . . or to a cinema?'

'No, I tell yer.'

Poole looked steadily at the porter.

'What would you say,' he asked quietly, 'if I told you that you had been seen at a cinema with this woman only a week or two ago?'

Slowly the colour drained from the man's face. His eyes shifted from the detective's face and be remained silent.

'Better tell me the truth, Twist.'

The porter passed his tongue over his dry lips. He squared his shoulders.

'All right,' he said. 'What of it? I took 'er once, that's all. My missus was laid up and I 'adn't no one to go with. I likes to go to the pictures once a week. She was standin' at the corner of 'Art Street in the rain and she looked pretty miserable. I asked her to come with me and she did. I give 'er a glass o' port, too,' he added defiantly. 'Is that a 'angin' matter?'

'That was the only time?'

'Didn't I tell yer? What's the 'arm, anyway?'

'No harm, probably. But you told me a moment before that you had never taken her to a cinema. Have you told me anything else that's not true?'

Twist was silent.

'Well?' said the detective sharply. 'What about those men? Do you know who any of them are?'

Twist shrugged his shoulders.

'No, I don't,' he said. 'But I've seen one of them somewhere else.'

'Which one?'

'The big chap.'

'Where have you seen him?'

''Ere; in the station. 'E's in one of these race gangs. I seen 'im goin' down in the race specials to 'Orton Park, 'im and a lot of others. Seen 'im come back, too; 'e 'ad drink on 'im then.'

CHAPTER VIII

MAGDALEN

Chief-Inspector Beldam was annoyed. He had wasted a whole morning, entirely owing, in his opinion, to the stupidity of the Director of Public Prosecutions – or more probably one of his staff. And now he had wasted a whole afternoon and the greater part of an evening entirely owing to the stupidity of a builder's clerk. How any builder could employ as his clerk a man so inefficient as to say that a certain bricklayer was engaged on a job in Brentford when in fact he was working at the exactly opposite side of London in Brentwood passed Beldam's comprehension. The fact remained that one of the busiest police-officers in England had spent an hour or more in the western suburb searching for a street and a building which did not exist there, and had then had to go right through London and out into Essex to find that the men had just knocked off work and gone home – an hour early because of winter-time.

When Mr. George Fenley was at last run to earth in the bosom of his family Beldam had had to waste further time in tact; after all, it was hardly fair to question a man about his relations with a prostitute in front of his wife. And when at last George Fenley had allowed himself to be taken for a walk he had, after reluctantly admitting a casual acquaintance with the dead woman, produced a cast-iron alibi for the previous evening, the confirming of which was the only quick job that Beldam had done all day. No, George Fenley, captain of the Gay George darts team in the annual All-Camden Championship last night, could not at the same time have been throttling a wretched woman on Hampstead Heath three miles away.

So that was the end of the single male contact so far obtained. It was true that Sergeant Gower had obtained another, but he had also effectually smashed it. The result of his painstaking canvassing of Bunt Street had not added to the list of Bella Knox's clients but it had enabled him to trace one of them, the 'young lad with spectacles.' He had proved to be of local extraction, not, it was true, of Bunt Street itself but of Brighton Crescent, the other side of Camden Road. Gower's informant had recognised him as an assistant in the Imperial Stores and Gower had no difficulty in running him to earth. Frederick Percy White had been a very frightened young man when the detective questioned him, but he was not guilty of murder. From 7 to 8.30 p.m. on the previous evening he had been attending an Evening Class in Mathematics, since it was his ambition to graduate to the accountancy branch of the great business; his master had not only confirmed his presence by personal recollection but had shown Gower the book in which attendances were entered. So Frederick Percy played his brief part upon the tragic stage and left it, the better for a nerve-shaking lesson.

And here was Inspector Poole, with another story of frustrated contact. Robert Twist's alibi, it was true, had not yet been tested; he had told Poole that his previous evening had been spent in the bosom of his family, and Poole had decided not to set that household immediately by the ears by interrogating them; that was a matter for the Chief-Inspector to decide. But it seemed extremely unlikely that such an alibi would have been given if it was false; Twist could hardly have hoped to persuade wife, daughter of seventeen and son of thirteen to lie successfully – the two elder children had been out upon their own affairs.

'What did you make of him yourself?' asked Beldam.

Poole hesitated.

'On the whole I'm inclined to think he was telling the truth, sir, when he said he had only taken the woman out once. After all, now that she's been murdered and the police poking their noses into her affairs, he wouldn't want to let out that he had been in any way friendly with her. If he had been about constantly with her he would hardly have dared to lie, but he might reasonably hope that a single occasion would not have been noticed.'

Beldam nodded.

'We'll get the local men on to following up that point,' he said. 'If he's been about with her much they're bound to find out about it. But what about in his own home? He might have been friendly with her there without any outsiders noticing.'

'If by "friendly" you mean "intimate," sir,' said Poole, 'I don't think that would be possible. It's a tiny house, full of people. Twist sleeps with his wife in one room, the boys are next door to them, the girls are upstairs next to Bella Knox's room, the walls are thin, the stairs rickety. I don't think such a thing would be possible without the whole family knowing.'

'Perhaps not, and I suppose he wouldn't often be alone in the house with her. If Mrs. Twist was out shopping or visiting one of the family would probably be in.'

'I should imagine so, sir.'

'Right. Then, for the moment, that washes out Twist. I'll think over the question of whether we check his alibi for last night with the family. That leaves only the unknown race tout or whatever he is. There must be ten thousand of them in London, but what's that to the C.I.D.? You'd better work on that, Poole; find out when the next race-meeting on that line is held and we'll see if we can get Twist to spot him. In the meantime . . . oh, by the way, no more news of that car?'

'Nothing, sir; we've tried the local garages but the description's so vague that it's almost hopeless. The Divisional men are working all the houses in the neighbourhood.'

Beldam snorted.

'Divisional men?' he said. 'That old . . . well, I'd better not get insubordinate. Hartridge seems to have spent his day looking under blades of grass for footprints and not finding them. They've collected an odd assortment of stuff from the hedge near where the body was found but none of it seems to have any relevance. You'd better have a look through it. Now I'm going to get something to eat.'

But the Chief-Inspector's supper had to wait. There was a knock at the door and a uniformed constable appeared.

'Gentleman asking for you, sir,' he said, handing over a printed slip.

Beldam glanced at it.

'Reverend Wilbraham Battisley,' he read. 'Business: Hampstead Heath Case.'

He looked up at the constable.

'What's he like?' he asked, evidently seeking an excuse not to postpone his meal.

'Gentleman, sir. Distinguished appearance. C. of E., I should say.'

Beldam sighed.

'Show him up. Better wait, Poole, though I don't suppose he's got anything worth hearing.'

The constable was right. Mr. Battisley was a man of considerable distinction, so far, at any rate, as appearance was concerned. He was tall, upright; he had a fine aquiline nose and a smooth clean-shaven face of which the chin was the only doubtful feature; his hair was white and rather long; he had very beautiful hands, which he used freely to point his conversation.

'Chief-Inspector Beldam?' he asked in a pleasant voice.

Beldam rose from his seat and indicated a chair in front of his desk.

'I understand that you are in charge of the distressing case which was reported in this morning's paper – the woman found dead by Highgate Ponds, I mean.'

'That is so, sir. Have you any information you can give us?'

Mr. Battisley's hand indicated doubt.

'I hardly know,' he said, 'whether what I have to say will be what you regard as information. Indeed I have been doubtful whether I am justified in bringing it to your notice; it verges close upon the confidence which a priest may not betray. However, having spent the day in meditation I have decided that it will be no breach of trust and I have come, leaving it to you to decide whether what I have to say has any significance from your point of view.'

Beldam hoped it had. He was not fond of verbiage but he realised that others were and he was prepared to be patient if the end justified it.

'Perhaps you will tell me, sir,' he said politely.

'I hold the benefice of St. Egbert's, Bethnal Green. I have some private means and I have always maintained that it is the duty of a man in my comparatively fortunate position to take a poor living. St. Egbert's is a very poor living, but it is an important one. It is a large parish and the people are the poorest of the poor but they are none the less fine for that, courageous, cheerful and, for the most part, honest. There is always a strong vein of the living faith to be found in such a community but it needs to be found and worked with as great care and determination as a vein of gold in the solid rock. To have such a task is a noble charge; it is a man's work and it brings its own reward.'

Beldam sighed inwardly; it seemed that information might be as hard to come by as gold – and perhaps as elusive.

Mr. Battisley may have sensed the detective's doubt.

'You may be wondering,' he said with a smile, 'what all this has to do with a dead woman on Hampstead Heath. I will tell you. There may be living faith in a community such as ours without any noticeable outward sign. Attendance at the Sunday services may be thin and largely confined to elderly women without household duties. Working people need rest on the day of rest and the habit of church attendance has largely disappeared in recent years. One may – one does – regret it, but one must not shut one's eyes to hard fact. The fact here is that though Sunday services are poorly attended that must not be taken as a sign that there is no living faith; the acid test is observance of the Sacrament and in this, I say with deep thankfulness, my people show that their faith is indeed alive. I do not refer, of course, to the regular weekly Eucharist but on the great festivals of the Church – Easter, Whitsun, Christmas – the attendances are truly encouraging.'

The vicar of St. Egbert's paused. His eyes were glistening with enthusiasm and he had probably forgotten where he was. He brought himself back to earth with an obvious effort.

'Now, what I have to tell you is this,' he continued, tapping the table in front of him with a long finger. 'Last Christmas day, at the conclusion of the eight o'clock Celebration, the second service of the day, I was leaving the vestry intending to have a word with the Clerk before going home to breakfast. The church was empty by then – or so I thought – and I did not at first see the Clerk. I walked down towards the west door and then saw that there was a woman still kneeling in one of the rear pews. She evidently heard my footsteps because she looked up, then rose to her feet and began to walk out of the church. I had not recognised her as one of my regular flock, so I hastened my steps to see who she was. I caught her up in the porch and saw that she was a stranger. I noticed that there was a scar on the right cheek, a sad disfigurement to what I judged must once have been a beautiful face. Having seen the photograph in this morning's paper I have no doubt that this poor victim was the woman I saw that Christmas morning.'

Beldam was listening with more interest now. There might, after all, be some useful contact to be obtained here.

'I was struck,' went on Mr. Battisley, 'by the sadness of the woman's expression. Her face was pale and her lips thin and colourless, but it was in the eyes that the sadness lay. I felt that I wanted to know more about her; she interested me apart from the fact that she appeared to be devout. I said "Good morning" and asked her her name. She was silent for a moment and then her face broke into a smile that has remained firmly in my memory. It was a smile that I have often tried to describe to myself but never to my complete satisfaction. The word "whimsical" is as near as I can get to it but that does not go deep enough. I should have said "mischievous" had it not been for the extreme underlying sadness of the eyes, which no movement of the lips seemed able to blot out. For a moment I thought that she had not heard my question and I repeated it. "Magdalen," she replied and turned her back on me and walked quickly away. I was so taken aback that I did not follow her.'

The vicar stopped speaking. His expression suggested that he was still sensible of the hurt to his feelings. Beldam wondered whether that was all that he had come to say.

'Did you see her again, sir?' he asked.

'Yes,' replied Mr. Battisley. 'Yes, I did. About a month later I saw her late one afternoon in Victoria Park, which lies just outside my parish. She looked very different then; her face was painted, her lips a bright red, there was an automatic and quite meaningless smile on her face as she talked to a man who had been walking just in front of me. I realised then what the poor woman's profession must be and the realisation was a shock to me. I felt quite unhappy for the rest of the day. Later I wondered whether I had neglected my duty in not speaking to her again but I am sure that I should only have received a rebuff. However, I had another opportunity, for a few weeks later – I think it must have been at the beginning of March – I saw her turn into a street in my own parish – Darley Street. She was only a hundred yards ahead of me and, determined to learn more about her, I set out to catch her up; but before I could do so she stopped at a house, opened the door, and walked in. I don't know now whether she had seen me.

'I knocked at the door and after an appreciable time it was opened by another woman whom I did not know; I had never visited at that house. I said that I would like to speak to the lady who had just come in. She looked me up and down in a most unpleasant way and then slammed the door in my face.'

Beldam had difficulty in restraining a guffaw. He quickly passed a hand over his own face. But he did not deceive the Reverend Wilbraham Battisley.

'Yes,' said the clergyman with a rueful smile. 'I can see that that has its funny side, but at the time it gave me a very unpleasant shock. There was nothing that I could do. I turned away, hoping that nobody had seen my humiliation.'

Beldam felt a twinge of remorse.

'It must have been very unpleasant, sir,' he said. 'Did you see her again?'

'No. I ought, perhaps, to have made another attempt at some later date to visit her, but my courage failed me. This morning, when I read of her death, I felt ashamed.'

This was getting too near sentiment for Beldam's liking.

'Can you tell me the number of the house in Darley Street, sir?' he asked curtly.

'Yes; it was number twenty-five.'

'Thank you, sir; we'll look that up. I'm much obliged to you for your information.'

He rose to his feet and walking to the door, opened it. Slightly taken aback by this abrupt dismissal Mr. Battisley murmured 'good-night' and went out into the passage. Inspector Poole started to follow, intending the small courtesy of seeing the clergyman off the premises, but his superior checked him and closed the door.

'Much ado about precious little,' said Beldam.

He looked at his watch.

'Thirty-five minutes. Five would have done it. "I saw this woman at my church one day. She looked ill and sad. She wasn't made up. When I asked her her name she pulled my leg. A month later I saw her accost a man in Victoria Park; she was made up then. At the beginning of March I followed her to No. 25 Darley Street and had the door slammed in my face." That's all there was in all that rigmarole and precious little use it is, too.'

Poole felt jarred by this reception of a story that he had found strangely moving. Of the clergyman himself he had at first felt uncertain; there was a touch of unctuousness about him that was not attractive, but there seemed little doubt of his sincerity.

'The address is useful, sir,' he suggested.

'Well, is it?' replied Beldam. 'She left there more than six months ago. You're not going to tell me that this murder has anything to do with such ancient history as that?'

CHAPTER IX

A MAN DETAINED

The last race of the day was over and Montie Lewis was paying out. It had been a good day for him – up to the last race, when a short-priced favourite had just got home and spoiled the book. A great many backers had been on this horse, in a desperate attempt to recover from a disastrous day, but fortunately the ring had been sufficiently united to force down the price and no great harm had been done. Still, it meant that a large number of people had to be paid and that delayed the return journey to the railway station.

Montie Lewis did not like delays. He was a nervous man and he had seen funny things happen between the course and the railway station when the greater part of the crowd had cleared off. Once, some years ago now, he himself had had a very unpleasant experience and had had to part with a lot of money under threat of something worse, so now he liked to get away sharp when there were still plenty of people – and policemen – about. Still, it could not be helped; he had got to pay out, just as others were doing.

He glanced down the line of rails and saw that the majority of his fellow bookmakers were packing up; some were already making off, while in front of his stand there was still a little group of impatient punters. He had been delayed – was still being delayed – by a tiresome fellow, a stranger to him, who disputed the odds that he had accepted. Lewis's clerk had shown the man the entry in his book against the number of his ticket; the fellow still argued . . . and the other backers were becoming angry. Lewis was a weak man and disliked taking a strong line; he should have paid the man what was due to him and called the next; instead of that he had continued to argue . . . and now he realised that the group in front of him was larger than it had been and that among it were men whose faces he knew and feared.

With a quick glance over their heads he reassured himself with the sight of a big man with heavy shoulders and a clean-shaven, sullen face who was lounging about in the background. He was glad that he had brought Varden with him; however much Sam Cockburn might sneer it was a comfort to have an escort. By the entrance to the ring, too, a policeman was standing; no mischief could happen here – but it might happen on the way to the station if he did not get this gang cleared off.

'Here, take your money and clear out,' he said roughly, thrusting greasy notes into the arguer's hand. 'Come on, you. 27534,' he read out from the next man's ticket.

'27534. Two ten,' chimed his clerk.

The policeman strolled over to the group.

'Come along,' he said. 'We don't want to be here all night.'

'No more we don't,' agreed Lewis, cheered by the support of the law. 'One of these blighters has been arguing.'

The policeman, who was not without race-course experience, remained close at hand and the group began to dissolve; several of the men were evidently not holders of winning tickets after all, and in a very short time the pay-out was complete. Lewis and his clerk packed up and five minutes later were on their way out through the deserted enclosures, the big man in close attendance. A group of policemen were standing outside the entrance but the last of the crowd had gone.

'We must shove along,' said Lewis. 'We don't want to miss the last special.'

'I didn't much like the look of that lot,' said his clerk. 'I thought one or two of them belonged to Mason's gang.'

'They did. I don't know what they were up to in the ring; couldn't play any tricks there.'

'Delaying things,' said the clerk. 'There's that narrow passage by the black shed we've got to go through; might be trouble there.'

Lewis blenched. He beckoned Varden up beside him.

'Keep your eyes open till we get to the station,' he said.

Varden nodded. His hands were in his coat pockets.

They reached the narrow passage and Lewis, clasping his leather bag tightly under his buttoned overcoat, allowed his clerk to go first. Varden brought up the rear.

They had nearly reached the end of the passage and were passing the open doorway of one of the sheds when the clerk stopped with a gasp and Lewis nearly bumped into him. Varden's hands, with a flash of brass on the knuckles, sprang from his pockets . . . and were immediately thrust back again. Two policemen were standing just inside the door of the shed.

'My God, you made me jump,' exclaimed Lewis, wiping the cold sweat from his forehead.

'Better jump if you want to catch the train,' said one of the policemen, eyeing Varden suspiciously.

'He's all right. Friend of mine,' said Lewis, noticing the look.

'I think you had some other friends looking out for you not long ago,' said the policeman quietly. 'Better get on now.'

The three men hurried on towards the station, followed at a more leisurely pace by the policemen. A train was standing at the platform, the last of the crowd piling into it. Lewis, gasping for breath, was pushed into a crowded carriage, the door slammed behind him. For some seconds he lay back on the seat panting, trembling a little, too, from reaction after fear. Then he realised that neither his clerk nor Varden had followed him into the carriage – they must have been pushed into another – and he looked nervously round the carriage and was relieved to find that none of the men he dreaded were in it. Slowly his nerves quieted down and presently he was discussing the day's sport with his neighbours.

In the next carriage Varden and the clerk also panted for some time from the exertion of catching the train, neither being in very good condition. The clerk soon recovered his equanimity and entered into the general conversation of the carriage, but his big companion remained aloof. His sullen face, even through the disfigurement caused by excessive drinking, bore signs of having once been handsome and even distinguished, but his expression was wholly unpleasant. Apart from sullenness it was furtive; the eyes, which were in any case too small, were made to look even more so by the fleshiness of the cheeks, a fact which added meanness to the other unattractive ingredients.

After one or two attempts to draw him into the conversation had failed, his companions left him alone and he sat staring in front of him for the whole of the journey back to London. It might have been thought that he was in a day-dream but for the play of expression which a close observer would have seen in his eyes – expression which bore witness to a troubled and anxious mind.

It was not a long journey but the succession of specials caused delay; the nearer they got to the terminus the more frequent were the stoppages, and it was quite dark by the time the train pulled up at the platform. The men tumbled out and stretched their cramped limbs. Montie Lewis joined his companions.

'There you are,' he said. 'You oughtn't to have got separated from me, Varden. There might have been trouble on the way up.'

'How could I help it?' growled Varden. 'The porters shoved us in anywhere.'

Lewis was so relieved to have got safely back to London after his fright on the race-course that he did not pursue the point.

'Well, we'll do with a drink,' he said, and led the way up the platform. Varden would have liked to be paid and to get away from his companions, who were not congenial to him, but he wanted that drink. He followed the others towards the barrier where tickets were being collected, his eyes all the time shifting restlessly from side to side as if he were searching for something which he did not wish to find.

As they reached the barrier Varden saw just beyond it a porter standing with two men in dark overcoats and bowler hats. He checked, but the pressure of people behind drove him forward. He noticed that the porter was scanning the faces of the passengers as they gave up their tickets, whereas the two men with him seemed less interested. The fact seemed to give Varden some reassurance, but only for a moment; as he gave up his own ticket he saw the porter's face change; he turned and said something to his companions.

Through the barrier, Varden hesitated. Lewis and his clerk were ahead of him and, quite apart from the drink, he wanted his money, but . . . the younger of the bowler-hatted men came up to him.

'I'd like to have a word with you a minute, please,' he said quietly.

Instinctively Varden glanced over his other shoulder and saw that the elder man was standing just behind him now.

'What's the matter?' he asked roughly.

'If you'll come with us I'll explain. Better not attract attention here. We are police-officers and we want to ask you some questions. There's a car just outside.'

For a moment Varden hesitated, but it was obviously useless either to run or argue; with a shrug of the shoulders he walked on, the elder man beside him. The other had stopped to say a word to the porter but he soon followed. The little scene, so startling to Varden, did not appear to have attracted the attention of his fellow-passengers.

Near the entrance Lewis and the clerk were waiting for him. They looked with surprise at his companions and Lewis took a step towards them.

'Lead on, Gower,' said a quiet voice just behind, and Varden felt his sleeve gently pulled. He walked past the bookmaker without a word.

The younger detective came up to Lewis.

'Is that man a friend of yours?' he asked.

The bookmaker stared at him.

'I employ him,' he said. 'What about it?'

'I'm a police-officer. I have to make some enquiries about him. Can you tell me his name, please?'

'Well, if you don't know that you don't know much. His name's Varden – Bert Varden, he's called. What's he done?'

Poole took no notice of the question.

'If you'll kindly give me your own names and addresses I won't detain you any longer now, gentlemen,' he said.

With some reluctance the required information was given and Poole walked to a telephone box, where he put through a call to Scotland Yard. A minute or two later he rejoined Sergeant Gower and Varden in the police-car.

'What's all this about?' demanded Varden angrily as the car moved off. 'You've no right to take me up like this.'

'We just want to ask you some questions,' said Poole. 'You wouldn't like us to do that in a public place like a railway station. I'm taking you to Hampstead Police Station where you will be questioned by Chief-Inspector Beldam, who is in charge of the case.'

'What case?'

'The case of Bella Knox, the woman who was found dead by Highgate Ponds a fortnight ago.'

Poole felt the body of the man beside him stiffen. He was silent for a minute or more.

'What's that got to do with me?'

The words seemed to be forced out of Varden, as if by some impulse which he would have liked to restrain.

'Better wait, Mr. Varden,' said Poole quietly.

This time the big man controlled himself and the journey was finished in silence.

Arrived at Hampstead Police Station they walked into the charge-room and Sergeant Gower, leading Varden to the seat which ran along one wall, sat down beside him. Poole went across to the high desk and talked in a low voice to the uniformed sergeant who was sitting behind it. Then he tapped at an inner door and disappeared.

Varden sat, staring at the floor in front of him, a muscle in his jaw working spasmodically as he struggled to control his nerves. Gower sat stolidly beside him, paring his nails with a pen-knife. The uniformed sergeant, after one look at the man who had been brought in, turned his attention to his papers.

For nearly ten minutes there was silence, except for the rattle of traffic in the street. Then there came the sound of vigorous feet, the door was flung open, and a stocky, square-shouldered man with a dark moustache strode into the charge-room. He gave one searching glance at the man on the wall-seat, nodded to the station-sergeant, and walked across to the inner door, which he opened after a perfunctory knock.

Two minutes later the younger detective appeared in the doorway and beckoned. Sergeant Gower touched his companion's arm and they walked into the inner room. A big man in sombre blue uniform with a crown on his shoulder straps was seated at a desk; beside him sat the stocky man who had just arrived, while Inspector Poole stood near the door. At a small table in the window sat a young constable with writing material in front of him.

Superintendent Hollis nodded to the man at his side.

'Go ahead, Beldam,' he said.

'Your name's Herbert Varden, eh?' asked Chief-Inspector Beldam.

Varden was silent.

'Well, is it?' snapped the detective.

'Look here, what's all this about?' asked Varden angrily. 'You take me in charge in a public place, damaging my character. I'm marched into a roomful of policemen to be questioned . . . and you aren't even sure who I am. What's the meaning of it, I want to know?'

Poole, standing unobtrusively in the background, had leisure to study the man now. He noticed, which he had been too much occupied to do at the station, that in spite of his sodden face and shabby appearance, Varden spoke like an educated man. Well, there were many of them about in the lower strata of life nowadays.

Chief-Inspector Beldam was not accustomed to counterattack from a man in such circumstances.

'Where were you between seven and eight on the evening of the ninth? Monday, it was,' he asked aggressively.

But Varden was not so easily cowed.

'You've no right to ask me questions and have my answers written down without cautioning me,' he countered.

But that was a mistake and it restored Beldam's equilibrium.

'You're wrong there, my man,' he said. 'We only have to caution people whom we intend or expect to charge. We haven't got as far as that . . . yet. Now answer my questions civilly. If you've nothing to hide there's no harm coming to you. Let's have your full name.'

After a moment's hesitation Varden shrugged his shoulders and answered.

'Herbert Varden.'

'Address?'

'16 Taylor Street, Crouch End.'

'Age?'

'Forty-two.'

'Profession?'

Varden hesitated.

'None,' he said.

Beldam sniffed.

'Private means?' he asked.

'That's my affair.'

'It's mine too at the moment. Come on, you don't live on air. No regular profession, I suppose you mean. You were with a bookmaker to-day; were you working for him?'

'Yes,' replied Varden sullenly.

'What as? Clerk? Tic-tac?'

Varden shook his head.

'What, then?'

'Call it "escort" if you like.'

'Oh, that's it, is it?'

Beldam made a sign to Sergeant Gower, who stepped in front of Varden and put out his hands. But Varden stepped back quickly out of reach.

'Here, you can't frisk me!' be snarled. 'I'm not under arrest.'

'Oh, can't I?' said Beldam with a grim smile. He rose from his chair and walked up to Varden, whose arms were now held by Gower on one side and Poole on the other. Unbuttoning the man's macintosh Beldam ran his hands quickly over his body; then he put them in the pockets of the macintosh and drew from each a set of brass knuckle-dusters.

'That's your game, is it?'

He dropped the ugly weapons on to Superintendent Hollis's table.

Varden glowered at him but said no more. Beldam nodded to the detectives, who let go the man's arms but remained at his side.

'"Escort's" a good word,' said Beldam. 'I've heard it called "bully".'

A sudden smile crossed Varden's face.

'You've got me wrong,' he said. 'I'm for protection, not aggression . . . like the bloody British Empire.'

'We'll see about that. Now then, about this woman, Knox; you knew her, eh?'

'If you say so.'

'Well, did you?'

'Yes, I did,' replied Varden doggedly. His face had grown paler and the muscle worked in his jaw.

'Intimate with her?'

'Technically, yes.'

'Known her long?'

'A few months.'

'You knew her pretty well, didn't you?'

'No, I did not. I told you. I'd been with her two or three times. Half a dozen, perhaps.'

'We'll leave it at that for the moment. Now I'll ask you again: where were you between seven and eight on the evening of Monday the ninth of October?'

Poole felt the man beside him stir uneasily. Glancing at him he saw beads of sweat break out on the forehead.

'How should I know where I was a fortnight or more ago?' asked Varden roughly. 'I don't keep a diary. One day's like another to me. I might have been anywhere.'

'That won't do for me, Varden,' said Beldam quietly. 'A friend of yours . . . an acquaintance, say . . . was murdered that day. You must have read about it in the papers next day, if you didn't hear about it on the wireless the same night. That would pin the day on any man's memory. Tell the truth, now; where were you?'

There was a moment's silence.

'As a matter of fact, I did hear about it on the wireless, now I come to think of it,' said Varden. 'I was at the Red Knight; the police message came through while I was there. I'd been there a long time.'

Beldam looked thoughtfully at the man in front of him.

'We'd better get this exactly, Varden,' he said. 'Where is the Red Knight?'

'Battery Street, near Kilburn Station.'

'End of Maida Vale, eh? That's a long way from where you live, Varden; don't they keep the beer you fancy in Crouch End?'

'I went there to see the bookmaker I generally work for. He always goes to the Red Knight – lives near there. Lots of bookies go there.'

'I see. How did you get there?'

'I walked,' said Varden sullenly. 'I don't keep a car. I hadn't had a job for some time and buses cost money.'

Beldam walked across to a map of North London that hung on the wall. When he spoke again there was a note of quickened interest in his voice.

'Kilburn's pretty nearly exactly the other side of the Heath from Crouch End,' he said. 'Did you cross the Health that evening?'

Poole felt the arm beside him stiffen.

'Yes,' said Varden. 'That's the way I always go if I walk. Not across the Heath itself but over the bottom end of Parliament Hill, past the Fever Hospital and Swiss Cottage.'

The man, Poole thought, was trying to speak casually but there was a tense note in his voice.

'You went by Millfield Lane, eh?'

Something of the same note appeared in Beldam's voice now. To Poole's imagination there came the rasping sound of crossed rapiers.

'No, I didn't,' said Varden quickly. 'Not within hundreds of yards of it. Not within half a mile of where the body was found. You needn't try to fasten that on me. I wasn't there.'

'Weren't you?' said Beldam quietly. 'You seem to know just where you ought not to have been.'

'It was all in the papers, wasn't it?' said Varden hotly. 'I know you're trying to fasten this on me because you haven't found anyone who did do it. You're not giving me a square deal.'

'Oh, yes; you'll get a square deal all right,' said Beldam, and his milder tone seemed to ease the tension. 'Now, let's just go into the question of time. Did you start from your home? What is it – a lodging house?'

'I've got a room in a house. Yes, I started from there.'

'What time?'

'Haven't the faintest.'

'You must have some idea.'

Varden appeared to ponder.

'Well, I wanted to get to the Red Knight before eight because that's about when Montie Lewis always gets there. I didn't want to miss him; sometimes he only stops for a few minutes. It takes me best part of an hour and a half to walk across, so I must have left home before half-past six. I was at the Red Knight before eight because I'd been there some time before he arrived; must have been there by a quarter to.'

'We'll put it at 7.45 . . . for the moment,' said Beldam.

He walked across to the map again.

'Is your house near the station?' he asked.

'Yes. Within a minute or two.'

'Show me which way you went.'

Varden with his escort walked across to the map. With a grimy finger the big man traced his route, down Hornsey Lane, past St. Pancras Infirmary, the south edge of Highgate Cemetery, the Duke of St. Albans, at the edge of Parliament Hill, some way below the most southerly of the Highgate Ponds . . .

'That'll do for the moment.'

With the top joint of his little finger Beldam measured off the distance on the map.

'Walking a good pace?'

'Just ordinary.'

'Say three miles an hour? Stop on the way?'

'No.'

'Then if your times are right you must have got to the edge of Parliament Hill in about half an hour. Say seven o'clock.'

Beldam looked significantly at Superintendent Hollis.

'That's about a quarter of an hour or twenty minutes' walk from the place, sir,' he said quietly.

The Superintendent pursed his mouth into a silent whistle. He remembered that Beldam had fixed the time of the murder at between 7.15 and 7.40 p.m.

'That's right, isn't it, Varden?' asked Beldam quietly.

'If it suits you,' said Varden bitterly. 'I'm admitting nothing. I never went near the place.'

'Well, we'll leave that for the moment. Now show me how you went from there.'

Again Varden pointed out his route, across the lower end of Parliament Hill, past the Fever Hospital, down Belsize Avenue, Swiss Cottage, Belsize Road, Kilburn Station, to Battery Street, just north of Paddington Recreation Ground.

Carefully Beldam measured off the distance, frowned, measured it again.

'Just over three miles I make it, sir,' he said, with rather less assurance in his voice.

'An hour.'

'Yes, and you said it was another quarter up to where the body was,' said Varden triumphantly. 'Fit that in if you can.'

'How do you know what time she was killed?' Beldam shot at him.

Varden gave a little gasp.

'I don't, but the papers said between 7.15 and 7.40. Even if she was killed at 7.15, how could I have got to Kilburn before 8?'

'We don't know that you did.'

'You'll find I did.'

'Perhaps.'

Beldam walked across to the Superintendent and held a muttered conference with him.

'Very well, Varden,' he said, straightening up. 'We'll check your statement. You'll be detained here in the meantime.'

Again the colour ebbed from the big man's face.

'Does that mean I'm under arrest? You told me . . .'

'It doesn't. We're entitled to hold you for twenty-four hours without arrest while we make enquiries. At the end of that time you'll either be charged or discharged.'

CHAPTER X

THE TORN NOTE

'Well, sir? What do you think of that?' asked Chief-Inspector Beldam as soon as Varden had been led off to his cell.

But Superintendent Hollis believed in the principle of the Military Court Martial in which the senior officer speaks last and so has the less chance of saying something silly.

'What do you?' he countered. 'You're the expert.'

'Sticks out a mile, doesn't it?' replied Beldam, who had not really wanted to know the old buffer's opinion. 'He knew the woman; he's a tough; he was near the spot at the time of the murder – admits it.'

'That's the point that struck me in his favour,' said Hollis slowly. 'Taking into account his general character and the position he found himself in, I thought he answered you very frankly.'

Beldam stared.

'There is that way of looking at it, I suppose,' he said. 'But he pretended at first that he didn't know what day we were talking about and then admitted that he'd heard all about it on the wireless.'

'Only human, that first reaction of his – about the day, I mean,' said the Superintendent. 'I think most of us would have said that . . . "How should I know where I was a fortnight ago" . . . however innocent we were.'

Beldam felt a dawning respect for his senior's intelligence.

'He told you quite frankly that he'd been near where the body was found,' went on Hollis. 'He needn't have. He could quite well have said he'd gone by another route or by bus or something. I was impressed by that frankness,' he repeated.

'Might be cunning, sir. It's risky to tell a lie about where you've been

. . . or where you haven't been. Someone might have seen him near Millfield Lane and then, if he'd denied being near there, he'd have been in the soup. He's an intelligent man, I fancy.'

'Yes; I think he is that. It would be as well to trace his early history. In the meantime perhaps we're theorising too much; there's a good deal of fact to be checked, isn't there?'

Beldam realised with something of a shock that he was not as completely in control of the situation as he was accustomed to be.

'I'll see about that at once, sir,' he said stiffly, and walked out of the room, followed by the inwardly chuckling Inspector Poole.

In the charge room Sergeant Gower was once more patiently waiting for any job, dull or dangerous, that might be allotted to him. Beldam addressed him.

'Get on up to Crouch End. You heard what Varden said. Check it. Find out what time he left the house. Find out if anyone saw him about. You know what's wanted.'

'Yes, sir.'

Sergeant Gower walked out into the street, followed almost at once by the two senior officers. The police-car in which Poole had brought Varden from St. Pancras was still waiting and they got into it.

'Red Knight, Battery Street, Kilburn,' snapped Beldam to the driver. 'We shall have to check these times and distances carefully, Poole – that is, if we find he was telling the truth about the Red Knight.'

'You think he's the man we want, sir?' asked Poole, who knew that Beldam would like to let off steam.

'Of course he is! Didn't I say it stood out a mile? People are too damn fond of being clever. These cases always turn out to be plain simple, once you've got your hand on the man.'

That, Poole knew, was very true. Subtlety played a very small part in the detection of crime – or rather, it played a part in a very small proportion of cases. Everything pointed to this being a straightforward case now that they had got the contact that had at first eluded them.

'We must find out who the fellow is, of course,' went on Beldam. 'Probably he's on the records already, with a long history of violence;

that'll simplify matters for us, even though the jury aren't allowed to know about it. "British justice"! Everything to give the criminal a chance to get away with it.'

Poole smiled.

'The judge'll know, sir; that's always a help.'

'Sometimes . . . but we haven't got him in the dock yet. Here we are.'

Poole glanced at his watch. It was just on eight o'clock.

'May kill two birds at once, sir,' he said. 'If Varden's right, Lewis may be here.'

'So much the better. Wait round the corner, Smith.'

He pushed open the door of the public bar.

Ted Boscombe, handing change to a customer, saw the two detectives come in and at once knew what they were; he had half expected a visit for some time. Raising the flap of the bar-counter he walked up to them.

'This way, gentlemen,' he said quietly, and led the way through the saloon bar to his own snug parlour.

Beldam had followed with some surprise.

'You know who I am?' he asked.

'Not your name, sir,' said the landlord with a smile. 'I'm out of touch now but I was in the Force before I took this on.'

'So much the better. I'm Chief-Inspector Beldam; this is Inspector Poole. What's your name?'

'Boscombe, sir.'

'Well, Boscombe, we want to check some facts given us by a man named Varden – Herbert Varden. You know him?'

'Yes, sir.'

Boscombe answered quietly but he was inwardly excited enough.

'Is he a frequent customer here?'

'Not very frequent, sir. He comes sometimes to see Mr. Lewis or one of the other bookmakers who come 'ere regular.'

'Oh, yes; he told us about Lewis. Has he been in this evening?'

'Not yet, sir; might be in any minute now. He's pretty regular at eight o'clock.'

'Tell one of your people to let us know if he comes in. I want a word with him.'

Boscombe went out and a minute later returned.

'Just come in, sir. I told him you wanted a word; he'll wait.'

'Right. Now this man, Varden. Have you any means of remembering what days he has been here in the last month, say?'

Boscombe smiled.

'You're not wanting to lead me, of course, sir, but it may save time if I tell you he was 'ere on Monday evening, the 9th of this month.'

Beldam nodded approvingly.

'You've got your wits about you still, Boscombe, I see. Tell me about that evening.'

'Yes, sir. Varden came in that evening some time before eight. I remember the evening well because of the police broadcast; we 'ad a bit of a discussion about it like. And I remember Varden being 'ere because some of the fellows was chippin' 'im about it.'

'Oh?' put in Beldam quickly. 'Why was that?'

Boscombe pondered his answer, as if he were anxious not to do anyone an injustice and yet willing to do his duty as a citizen.

''E looked a bit queer,' he said. 'When that message come through, I mean. Someone asked 'im if 'e'd 'ad a shock, but I don't call to mind that there was any answer because they all got laughin' and jokin' – talking about 'is beer bein' wrong . . . you know the sort of thing. Varden was angry but then e's not a friendly sort of chap, I'd say.'

'That's interesting,' said Beldam. 'I may want to ask you more about that later but I want to fix the time first the time, of his getting here. Can you help me?'

The landlord slowly nodded his large head. He was anxious to tell as much of the truth as possible, because he was conscious of being guilty of *suppressio veri* – though he might not have known it by that name. He had not told, and did not intend to tell, the Chief-Inspector anything about that private conversation of his with Varden, in which the latter had admitted acquaintance with the dead woman. If he had been going to tell about that conversation he should have told it at once; keeping it to himself he, as an ex-police officer, knew perfectly well had been a reprehensible if not actually a criminal act, and if he revealed it now he would get into serious trouble. He had refrained from volunteering that information to the police because it would have done him no good with his customers, and his customers must now be considered before his old colleagues. He had little fear that his concealment would ever come to the knowledge of the police; if he himself did not mention the matter of that private conversation it was extremely unlikely that Varden would do so; nobody else knew about it.

But he would tell as much of the truth as possible, now that he was being questioned.

'I think I can tell you that, sir,' he said. 'When Varden come 'e asked me if Mr Lewis was in. Lewis uses the saloon bar and so Varden wouldn't know whether 'e was in unless 'e asked. Mr. Lewis is very regular, as I told you; comes in eight o'clock most nights, sharp as a whistle, for 'is double whisky or sometimes a glass o' port; 'is 'ouse ain't more a few 'undred yards from 'ere. So when Varden asked me that I glanced up at the clock and saw that it still wanted five minutes to eight. So I says: "Not likely to be in for another five or ten minutes" and went on servin' my customers. Later on I went through into the saloon bar and as it 'appened Montie Lewis wasn't there. 'E come in some time between a quarter an' 'alf past, the potboy told me. I didn't see 'im meself till past 'alf past and then I told Varden and 'e went in and 'ad a word with 'im, but that was after the police message come through on the wireless.'

Beldam thought for a moment, then asked the landlord why he was so certain that all this had happened on the particular night he was interested in. The question disconcerted Boscombe; he was certain of it because he had wondered whether Varden might really know something about the murder, but he was not going to say that to the C.I.D. men.

'Well, sir, perhaps I can't say I'm dead certain – not to swear to,' he hedged. 'But I make no doubt about it. 'E was 'ere right enough, because of all that chaff when the message come through, and I don't think I could be mistook about that bein' the night 'e asked if Lewis was in.'

Beldam pondered for a minute. He did not want to fix the fact too definitely in this witness's mind; he might want to have him shaken in the witness box if that hour – 7.55 – proved a snag to his case.

'Tell me a little more about that chaff,' he said. 'You said that he seemed as if he'd had a shock; how did he show that?'

"E looked a bit white and stare-y, but then that might not 'ave 'ad anything to do with the broadcast.'

He did not want to prejudice the police against Varden, though he had certainly thought at the time that it was the news that had upset him.

'Tell me who else was here at the time.'

Boscombe gave the names, so far as he could remember them. Of addresses he knew nothing.

'Any of them in now?'

'Not when you come in; might 'a' come in since.'

'Have a look.'

Boscombe was back in a minute. None of the men he had named happened to be in at present, though they might come in later.

'That'll be your job, Poole,' said the Chief-Inspector. 'Now there's one thing more, Boscombe. When Varden arrived – assuming that you're right about its being on that night that he got here at 7.55 – did he seem normal in every way? He wasn't out of breath – as if he'd been running – or anything like that?'

Again Boscombe took his time to reply. He realised that a man's life might depend on his answer.

'No, sir,' he said slowly. 'I don't call to mind anything like that.'

'Right. Then tell Mr. Lewis I'd like a word with him. Poole, you'd better settle yourself in the public bar; I daresay the Receiver'll stand for a pint.'

'That'll be all right, sir,' said Boscombe with a grin. 'That'll be on the 'ouse; it ain't every day I 'ave the honour of a visit from the C.I.D.'

The landlord and Poole went out and were shortly replaced by Montie Lewis. The bookmaker seemed uneasy but Beldam motioned him to a chair with a friendly gesture.

'I won't keep you many minutes, Mr. Lewis,' he said. 'I just want to ask you a question or two about the man, Varden, who I understand does a job for you now and then. Have you known him long?'

Lewis scratched his rubicund cheek.

'On and off I must have known him for a couple of years,' he said.

'Steady sort of chap?'

'Steady enough so far as I'm concerned. He likes his glass but he does his work all right.'

'H'm. Well, I won't bother you at the moment about what that work is. You wouldn't say he was inclined to be violent, eh?'

Lewis did not relish the trend of these questions. He did not want the police to get wrong ideas about his own activities. They had prejudices about race gangs and might not understand that he only employed Varden for protective purposes.

'Nothing of that sort, I should say,' he replied.

'That's all right then. Now, do you happen to remember the night of Monday the 9th of this month?'

Lewis stared at him.

'I can't say I do,' he answered. 'What about it?'

'It happens to be the night that that woman was found dead by Highgate Ponds. You may have heard the police message on the wireless – 8.25 p.m. it was given.'

The bookmaker's jaw dropped.

'I didn't hear the message,' he said slowly. 'I remember reading about it in the paper next day.'

'Does that refresh your memory about where you were on that night? The Monday night?'

'I . . . where *I* was?'

'Yes.'

Montie Lewis showed every sign of acute discomfort. It was the first time that he had ever been called upon to account for his movements to the police.

'Why, I . . . I wasn't anywhere particular,' he stammered. 'I remember the night now, because of course we were all interested about that murder when we saw it in the papers next morning. I had my supper at home with Mrs. Lewis, same as I generally do, and then I came on here and had a glass or two with Sam Cockburn – that's a colleague of mine. Then I went home to bed. Sam'll be able to tell you that's right.'

'I'm not doubting you, Mr. Lewis,' said Beldam, who believed in keeping his witnesses happy – unless he had reasons for doing otherwise. 'Now, can you tell me what time you got here that night?'

'I generally get here round about eight o'clock,' said the bookmaker. 'We keep regular hours, Mrs. Lewis and I. Supper at 7.30 and then I come straight over here for my glass; it's only a step.'

'Yes, but that particular night,' persisted the detective. 'Were you punctual at eight that night?'

Lewis pondered, then smacked his hand on his knee.

'No, I was not,' he said. 'Someone came to my house to see me just when supper was being put on; kept me best part of a quarter of an hour. Mrs. Lewis was quite put out about it, I recollect, because she'd done up an omelette and waiting spoiled it. I can't have got here till a quarter or twenty past.'

That seemed pretty definite confirmation of the landlord's story. For reasons already mentioned Beldam did not want to stress the point too much.

'Did you see Varden that evening?' he asked.

'Yes, I did,' replied Lewis crossly. 'The fellow came barging into the saloon bar when I was talking to Cockburn. Wanted to know whether I'd got a job for him. Made a perfect nuisance of himself and I told him to clear out.'

'Any particular reason for his worrying you that night?'

'Not that I know of, but he sometimes did if he was short of money.'

'Oh, he was short of money, was he?'

That seemed to confirm what Varden had said about walking and the price of bus fares.

'And did you give him a job?'

'Not then. He's worked for me once or twice since.'

'Still short of money?'

The bookmaker, his confidence now restored, grinned cheerfully.

'Pretty chronic with him, I fancy,' he said, lifting his elbow significantly.

That seemed to be all there was to be got out of Mr. Montie Lewis at the moment, so Beldam thanked him and let him go. After thinking things over he walked into the public bar, nodded to the landlord, took no notice of Poole, and went out into the street. He had only gone a few yards when a thought struck him; he returned, put his head, inside the bar and beckoned to Boscombe. Rather unwillingly, because he did not want his customers to start asking questions, the landlord went outside.

'I'm told that Varden was short of money that night,' said Beldam. 'Did he have a drink when he got here?'

Boscombe started.

'Holy Jake!' he exclaimed. 'I'd forgotten all about that. Yes, 'e did 'ave a drink – a pint of bitter. And 'e 'ad a double whisky when he left, just before closing time, after 'e'd 'ad his talk with Mr. Lewis. Mabel served him but I happened to notice. But what I'd forgotten was that 'e paid for his pint with a note – a ten-bob note.'

'Eh?'

Beldam stared at the landlord, a stare that hardened as he concentrated on this piece of information.

'Funny thing your not telling me about that before, Boscombe,' he said sternly. 'You seem to have remembered everything else that happened that evening clearly enough.'

'I . . . well, I don't know how I come to forget about it, sir, and that's a fact,' stammered the discomfited landlord. 'Takin' in money comes so automatic when you're servin' at the bar that I never really notices. You'd be surprised the number of notes that's paid across the counter for a pint o' beer, especially on pay days; there's nothing out of the ordinary about it. But I did notice this one, I remember now, because it was torn.'

'Torn, was it?'

The detective's tone was soft, but Boscombe liked it none the better for that.

'And what did you do with it?'

'Paid it into the bank, same as usual, sir.'

Beldam eyed the man malevolently.

'You blasted fool,' he said, still in that quiet voice. 'You may have thrown away the one clue we want. I don't understand you and your memory . . . but I mean to.'

CHAPTER XI

DISCHARGED

It was too late to do anything about tracing the torn banknote that night. The remorseful landlord had given Beldam the name of his bank and there was still a faint hope that it might be found. In the meantime the detective wanted his supper . . . and time to think.

It seemed fairly certain that they had got their hands on the right man. Varden was a friend of the dead woman's; by his own admission he had been within a very short distance of the place where she was murdered, at the approximate time of the murder: he was a man of doubtful character, with a reputation for violence; the medical evidence as to the position of the bruises on the dead woman's throat suggested that the killer had large hands – which Varden certainly had; finally, within half an hour Varden had paid for a drink with a ten-shilling note, whereas he had stated that he walked nearly five miles because 'buses cost money' . . . and, according to Lewis, he came to the Red Knight to ask for work 'when he was short of money.'

But Beldam knew that a case that was clear to the police might not be good enough for a jury, might not even be strong enough to justify an arrest. A good deal of supporting evidence, with substantial proof, must be collected before he could be satisfied. And the time problem must be cleared up; that might prove to be of vital importance, one way or the other.

In the meantime, supper.

By the time he got back to the Yard neither Inspector Poole nor Sergeant Gower had returned, so the Chief-Inspector settled down to write his own notes and followed this by drafting an 'information' for circulation throughout the Metropolitan Police area, giving a description of Varden and asking that particular steps should be taken to find anyone who had seen him on the night in question, particularly between the hours of 6 and 8 p.m. A photograph would have been a great help for this purpose and Beldam decided that an attempt must be made to get one.

Shortly before 10 p.m. Sergeant Gower appeared, with a report that confirmed what Varden had told about his lodging and the time of leaving it on 9th October. Mrs. Gooche, his landlady, after some prompting as to the date, succeeded in remembering that her lodger had been in his room – sleeping, she thought – all that afternoon, that he had had his supper at half-past five as usual and had left the house immediately afterwards, probably between six and a quarter past. Actually Varden had said 'before half-past six' but the slight discrepancy did not matter; he could, even by his own statement, have got to Millfield Lane in plenty of time to commit the murder.

Gower had spent a good deal of time in hunting up Varden's acquaintances in the Crouch End neighbourhood but he had not been very successful. It was evident that Varden was not liked. Although he frequented public-houses he did not make friends; he apparently thought himself a cut above his fellows, even though his circumstances now were not such as to support that idea; he was quarrelsome and, on occasions, even violent. People left him alone and consequently knew very little about him ... and cared less. Nobody remembered having seen him on the evening of 9th October, but then very few of them remembered that night as being different from any other night, even when reminded that it was the night on which Bella Knox's body had been found by the Ponds; that, of course, had been something of a 'nine days' wonder,' but it was now sixteen days old and the police having apparently failed to spot the murderer, it had been largely forgotten.

None of this was much help to Beldam but he had not hoped for more. Poole had not come in yet and he decided not to wait for him; he was a man who believed in regular hours of sleep whenever they were obtainable and he liked to be in bed by eleven. So he said good-night to Sergeant Gower and caught a bus home to Pimlico.

*

On the following morning Beldam went straight to the Kilburn branch of the London and Continental Bank into which the landlord of the Red Knight paid his daily takings. It was a small branch and the manager, having had little experience of police enquiries, was at first suspicious and on his dignity. Knowing the strong position of bank managers *vis à vis* the police, the Chief-Inspector was gentle.

'I don't want to ask for any breach of confidence, sir,' he said. 'It's a matter of trying to trace a bank-note – a ten-shilling note. We don't know the number and in any case I know you don't usually keep a record of the numbers of small denomination notes, but this note was torn and I thought it just possible that we might be able to trace it in that way.'

The manager thought it unlikely but asked for further particulars. Beldam gave such as he had and waited anxiously, realising that the whole case might turn on this issue.

'Provided that the note is complete,' said Mr. Wittingham, 'it is legal tender and we accept it as such. If it is badly torn it is returned, through our head office, to the Bank of England for cancellation. In that case we should keep a note of its number.'

'But this particular note,' asked Beldam eagerly; 'can we trace it? How often do you send them for cancellation? Might it still be here?'

Mr. Wittingham was not too certain about this point himself.

'I will send for the Chief Cashier,' he said.

The Chief Cashier explained that torn notes were kept until a sufficient number of them had been collected to make it worth while sending them for cancellation. He knew nothing about the note paid in by the landlord of the Red Knight but he would make enquiries.

Two minutes later he was back, carrying a slim bundle of notes in his hand.

'The last lot were cancelled on 1st of October, sir,' he told the manager. 'Since then only eight have been collected, five pound notes and three ten-shilling notes. I don't know which the particular note paid in by Mr. Boscombe was, but if it was torn it was one of these three.'

He held out the three brown notes. The manager took them and handed them to Beldam, who examined them eagerly. One was almost torn in two, the halves being joined only by a tiny corner. One was torn across one corner and repaired with stamp paper. The third was also torn across the middle but had been more neatly mended with the semi-transparent adhesive paper used by stamp collectors and others.

Beldam held each to his nose in turn; the third one had a faint smell of beer! The fingers of the landlord would be enough to account for that ... and it was a pretty little piece of evidence.

'Would you two gentlemen kindly smell these three notes?' he asked.

The manager and chief cashier rather unwillingly did as they were asked and each, after slight prompting, discovered that one of them had an alcoholic odour. Beldam wrote the number of the note on a sheet of paper and got the two bank officials to sign a statement to the effect that on 25th October that note had smelt of beer.

'Smell may wear off,' explained the detective. 'Might prove to be an important point. Now, may I take these three notes away? For identification purposes I ought to have all three.'

After the first shock of this startling suggestion had worn off the manager, not without some reluctance, agreed that if the detective gave a signed receipt and if in due course the notes, or their cash equivalent, were duly refunded, he would allow them to be impounded.

Concealing his impatience Beldam completed the necessary formalities, took a verbally grateful leave, and hurried off to the Red Knight. He found Ted Boscombe supervising his staff's preparations for the mid-day rush. Boscombe was not too pleased to see him but he did his best to conceal the fact.

In the landlord's parlour Beldam produced the three torn notes.

'Seen any of these before?' he asked.

Boscombe examined them carefully.

'That looks like the one Varden gave me,' he said, pointing to the note which smelt of beer.

'What makes you say that?'

The landlord, suspicious of a trap, scratched his head.

'Well, the note was torn,' he said slowly. 'And that's what it looked like. That sticky paper's the same.'

'You definitely identify it?'

Boscombe hesitated.

'Well, it seems like it,' he admitted. 'There might be others mended like that.'

'There might,' said Beldam irritably. 'But that's the note you paid into your bank.'

'Oh, well, if it is, that's the one Bert Varden gave me,' agreed the unhappy landlord.

'Well, don't let your memory slip you again, Boscombe,' said the detective, and took his leave.

Well pleased with his morning's work, Beldam returned to Scotland Yard and found Inspector Poole waiting for him. Here, too, there was support for Varden's own story, as well as for that of Ted Boscombe. Poole had got in touch with three men who had been present at the Red Knight when the police message about Bella Knox came through. In the case of two of them nothing much was remembered about Varden except that there had been a bit of chaff which seemed to annoy the man – a surly fellow at the best of times, they thought. But one witness had been more precise.

Mr. William Hawkins, clerk to a Paddington solicitor, had himself noticed that Varden, whom he knew by sight as an occasional customer at the Red Knight, was looking white and startled after the police message about the woman found dead on the Heath. The landlord had asked Varden whether he knew anything about it but the latter had not given a direct answer; he had seemed annoyed by the questioning.

Poole had questioned Mr. Hawkins carefully about the time of Varden's arrival at the Red Knight and had got a very clear answer. The clerk himself had reached the public-house at a minute or two before eight and Varden was already there. He particularly remembered the point because when Boscombe asked Varden whether he had 'seen anything' he (Hawkins) had pointed out that it would have been impossible for anyone to be near Ken Wood at 7.40 and at Kilburn before 8; not – he remembered saying – unless he had come in a Rolls Royce. To this Mr. Boscombe had replied that though the body had been found at 7.40

the message said that death might have occurred any time between 7 and 7.30 p.m.

Beldam was impressed by this evidence. It was clear that any attempt to throw doubt upon Varden's statement that he had reached the Red Knight before 8 p.m. would be extremely difficult. It was evident that the time schedule would have to be carefully examined.

'He'll have a job to explain why our message upset him like that,' said Beldam.

Poole looked doubtful.

'I don't know, sir,' he said. 'Even if he knew nothing about it he might well recognise her by the description. It would be a bit of a shock. He may even have realised that he might himself be suspected of the murder, especially as he'd been quite close to the place where her body was found.'

Beldam looked at his subordinate with some displeasure.

'It's our job to prove that he did do it,' he said sharply, 'not that he didn't.'

That was a sentiment that Poole could not agree with, but he was not so unwise as to argue about it. He held his tongue.

'Come on, we'll have a go at the time table,' said Beldam.

On a table near the window was spread a copy of the same large-scale map of North London that decorated the wall of Superintendent Hollis's room at Hampstead. The two detectives settled down to a careful study of it, helped by a protractor, a pair of compasses, and a magnifying glass. With minute care they measured out first the route which Varden had said that he followed from Crouch End, over the south end of Parliament Hill, to Kilburn, and then the shortest route which he might have followed if he had gone from the scene of the murder to the Red Knight.

The latter route also meant crossing Parliament Hill, though a different part of it to that described by Varden. He would probably have left the Heath by Parliament Hill Road, passed Hampstead Heath Station, and so on past the Fever Hospital and down Belsize Avenue and Belsize Road as described by himself. The distance at its very shortest was more than three and a quarter miles.

'Take him best part of an hour to walk it,' said Beldam glumly. 'How long would it take to run?'

Poole smiled.

'He doesn't look in much condition to run, sir,' he said. 'Might do a sort of Scout run and walk – say five miles an hour.'

He worked out a quick sum in Rule of Three.

'Forty minutes, sir. If he got to the Red Knight at 7.55 that means starting at 7.15 – the moment the rain started.'

Beldam frowned.

'The murder must have been done at least five minutes after that,' he said. 'The ground under the body was definitely wet, not just damp. Personally I put it at nearer 7.30 than 7.15. If he went on foot at all he must have run damned hard.'

'He'd have shown it when he got to the pub, sir. You can't run three miles in half an hour without getting pretty badly blown, not if you're in the sort of trim Varden is. They must have noticed it.'

'Boscombe might have and said nothing about it. I don't trust that fellow.'

'There were others there, sir. Hawkins came in after but other customers must have noticed. Besides, a man running through London streets attracts attention quicker than anything.'

Beldam nodded.

'You're right,' he said. 'Then he didn't run and he didn't walk. What about a bus or the Underground?'

'I'll get the London Transport people to look that up, sir, but from the look of the map it seems unlikely. All the railways seem to run south-east, not south-west; they cut across the line he'd have had to follow.'

'And all the buses go miles round. I don't like the look of it, Poole.'

'It must have been taxi or car, sir, if it was anything.'

The suggestion did not appeal to the Chief-Inspector.

'How'd a tough like Varden get hold of a car?' he growled. 'Not unless he stole one, and we'd have heard of that.'

'And he wouldn't easily pick up a taxi that side of the Heath, sir,' said Poole thoughtfully. 'They don't cruise down Millfield Lane; I doubt if they even do in Highgate Road or Hampstead Lane, and there can't be a stand anywhere near where the body was found.'

'Well, if he took a taxi we're bound to trace it in no time,' said Beldam. 'I'll get on to that at once while you see the London Transport people. We shan't be able to hold him over the twenty-four hours, Poole; nothing like enough evidence to take him before a magistrate.'

'I'm afraid not, sir,' said Poole tactfully.

It did not take Chief-Inspector Beldam long to set in motion the machinery for tracing any taxi-cab that might have picked up a passenger – such an easily remembered passenger as the large, uncouth Varden – in the neighbourhood of Highgate Ponds on the evening of 9th October. When he had done so he asked for an interview with the Assistant Commissioner.

Sir Leward Marradine, when he left the Army and accepted this appointment in the Metropolitan Police just after the War, had believed that his clever brain and active imagination would enable him to achieve brilliant results where the plodding methods of the professional detectives failed. Twenty years of experience had radically modified that belief. He knew now that these steady, methodical officers of the C.I.D. got their results with almost unfailing regularity; he respected them and he seldom interfered with them or criticised their methods. If they asked for advice he was glad to give it and he thought that sometimes he was useful to them, but beyond that he confined himself to his own duties, which were strategical rather than tactical.

To him very often fell the task of taking a difficult decision, particularly in cases which involved men and women of position. In the case which Chief-Inspector Beldam laid before him this morning there was no such complication to affect his judgment, and no need for him to do more than give the opinion that Beldam asked for.

'I expect you've got the man all right,' he said, 'but I agree that there's hardly enough to charge him on at the moment. Why does the ten-shilling note excite you so much?'

'The man said he'd got no money, sir – and then we find him pulling out bank notes to pay for a drink.'

'"Notes" is rather an over-statement, isn't it? It might be his only one, his last in the world. But in any case, what of it? Are you suggesting robbery as motive for the murder? What we know of Bella Knox doesn't suggest that she was worth robbing. She wouldn't carry money about in her handbag, would she, even if she had any to carry?'

Beldam realised that he had allowed that rather obvious point to escape him. The word used by the Assistant Commissioner hit the nail on the head; the unexpected information about the note had 'excited' him and warped his judgment.

'He'll have to explain it, anyway, sir,' he said.

'Oh, yes, by all means get an explanation. Have we any previous record of him, by the way?'

'Not by that name, sir. I'm going to get his prints this morning if I can. I'd like a photograph, too.'

'Yes, you ought to get that. And then very likely he'll be better out of your hands than in them; if you keep a close eye on him he may do something stupid.'

Beldam was glad that the A.C. took that view; it made it easier to discharge the man without loss of prestige. So, after a few more words about another case, he took himself off to Hampstead Police Station.

Superintendent Hollis was out, which was a relief to Beldam. On the previous day the older man had rather cramped his style and had even administered something not far removed from a snub. He had thought-fully left word that the Chief-Inspector was to have the use of his room if he wanted it. Beldam had Varden brought in, Divisional Detective-Inspector Hartridge being also present.

'Have you been through our hands before, Varden?' Beldam asked abruptly. He had decided on a sharp attack . . . but Varden had had time to prepare his own plans.

'You've got your records,' he said. 'Have a look at them.'

'Are you willing to have your finger-prints taken?'

Varden frowned.

'No. I'm not,' he said.

'You realise that if we charge you they will be taken automatically, whether you're willing or not?'

Varden did not answer but the muscle in his jaw twitched.

'Is Varden your real name?'

'It's the name I gave you and it's all you'll get.'

'You'll not do yourself any good by being truculent, Varden. Where were you born?'

'I don't remember. I was very young at the time.'

Beldam saw a spasm of amusement cross the face of the young constable who was acting as escort. He did not like being scored off, but he was not going to be deflected from his course.

'Where were you at school?'

'Eton and Oxford.'

'I've warned you, Varden. What were you after you left school? What employment were you in? You weren't always a bookmaker's bully, I suppose?'

For some reason this question appeared to infuriate Varden. His face flushed angrily, then the colour ebbed away, leaving it white and set. He made a visible effort to control himself.

'I'm not going to answer all these damn-fool questions,' he said harshly. 'If you want to know you can find out for yourself.'

'Very well, Varden,' said Beldam quietly. 'You've chosen to take this line and you mustn't complain if it counts against you. We shall find out. Now I'm going to ask you a question that you will be well advised to answer. . . . Where did you get the ten-shilling note that you paid for your drink at the Red Knight with?'

He shot the question at Varden, but if he expected to startle the man into a disclosure he was disappointed. Varden stared at him.

'Where did I get it? Probably Lewis gave it me or I may have got it from one of the other bookies. I have a bet myself sometimes. Why?'

'You told me you walked to Kilburn because you'd got no money.'

'That's a lie,' said Varden hotly. 'You're putting things into my mouth.'

Beldam turned over the transcript of notes taken on the previous day.

'Here are your own words,' he said. '"I walked. I don't keep a car. I hadn't had a job for some time and buses cost money".'

'Well, so they do. I was short of money, it's true, but that doesn't mean I hadn't got any. As a matter of fact that note was all I'd got left; that's why I wanted to get a job from Lewis. I'd got my rent to pay.'

'So you stood yourself a pint of beer . . . and a double whisky.'

That shot did go home.

'That bloody swine Boscombe's been shooting his tongue at you,' Varden said angrily. 'Acting the spy on his customers to keep in with the police.'

'Why did you want it hidden?'

'I didn't want it hidden. You're trying to trap me.'

Beldam shrugged his shoulders. Truth to tell, he did not feel that he was getting anywhere with this interrogation; scoring points was not going to help him unless they produced evidence. He came to a sudden decision.

'Very well, Varden; you can go,' he said.

The big man's jaw dropped. His small eyes flickered from side to side at the police-officers in the room.

'D'you mean . . . d'you mean . . . ?' he stammered.

'I mean that I'm not holding you.'

'You're . . . you're not going to charge me?'

'No,' said Chief-Inspector Beldam shortly. 'You can clear out.'

CHAPTER XII

FADING OUT

Beldam returned to Scotland Yard in no very amiable frame of mind. He realised that he had not succeeded in shaking Varden's story and he had the uncomfortable feeling that the case, which only yesterday had promised so well, was slipping away from him. The only two minor successes of the morning had been scored, not by himself but by subordinates. As soon as Varden had gone, Divisional-Detective Inspector Hartridge had calmly announced that he had succeeded in getting an admirable set of finger-prints on a drinking mug specially prepared for the purpose, whilst a minute or two afterwards Detective-Sergeant Cook had come in to say that he had secured an excellent snapshot of Varden as the discharged man left the police station. With these crumbs of comfort Beldam returned to Scotland Yard.

He found Inspector Poole awaiting him with his report on his visit to the London Transport offices. Any question of Varden having used a train to get from Ken Wood to Kilburn in quick time was at once ruled out; there was no line that would have been the smallest use to him. Neither was there any tram or trolley bus service that would have helped. There were, on the other hand, two possible bus routes. If, from the scene of the murder, Varden had gone north to Hampstead Lane he could have taken a 210 bus, going either east or west, by which he might have got to Kilburn by the following routes.

Route A, going east, was as follows: 210 eastwards to Highgate Station, change, 134, 135 or 137 southwards to Camden Town Station, 31 westwards to Swiss Cottage and Kilburn Station. The London Transport officials estimated that the quickest possible time for this journey, allowing no time lost over changes, was forty-five minutes.

'No good,' said Beldam. 'What's the other?'

Route B was: 210 westwards to Golders Green, change, 28 southwards down Fortune Green Road and West End Lane to Kilburn. They put this at thirty to thirty-five minutes, allowing the quickest possible conditions.

'That's just possible,' said Beldam. 'Putting the earliest time of the murder at 7.20, thirty-five minutes just gets him to Kilburn at 7.55.'

'Yes, sir, but not to the Red Knight,' said Poole. 'That's another four minutes. I walked it last night.'

'Well, the Transport people may be a few minutes out; they said thirty to thirty-five.'

'There's the other end, sir,' persisted Poole. 'He had to get from the spot to Hampstead Lane; that must take five minutes even if he ran.'

Beldam frowned.

'Seems to me you're out to prove he didn't do it,' he said irritably.

Then he laughed.

'Sorry. I shouldn't have said that; you're quite right. You must test those bus times yourself, Poole; we can't depend on the officials. Talk to the conductors and drivers and see whether they ever go quicker than schedule; they might do, to make up time if they've been delayed.'

'Yes, sir. I asked the Transport people to make enquiries from their conductors. I gave them a description of Varden. He's fairly noticeable and if he'd been hurrying or was rattled he'd have been even more so.'

'Yes. That's a line. And we ought to have a photograph ready any minute now. Cook got one this morning. All the same, I don't like the look of things, Poole. These closefitting times don't make a good case before a jury.'

'Any chance of our being mistaken about the time of the rain beginning, sir? We're fixing our time of the murder almost entirely by that, aren't we?' asked Poole.

'Yes, we are. It may be wrong but that old constable was very cocksure. We're bound to put him in the box now as our witness, but it looks as if he'd be more use to the defence.'

At this point Sergeant Cook appeared with a print of his snapshot, a really excellent likeness of Varden. Beldam made arrangement for copies to be issued to the officers working on the case, as well as for wider distribution through the *Gazette*.

Soon afterwards the finger-print department reported that Varden's prints had been examined and a search made in the records; there was no previous record of them.

Inspector Poole having been despatched to work the bus routes, and Sergeant Gower to distribute photographs to the Highgate and Kentish Town police, Beldam wondered what he should do himself. The Divisional detectives were keeping an eye on Varden, a task which was in any case beneath the dignity of a Chief-Inspector, as was all the detailed drudgery of investigation on which he, as the brains of the case, had to work. Probably the best thing would be to put the whole thing out of his mind for a time. Resolutely he turned to the file of a case that had been dragging on for many months, bursting into a fitful flame of life from time to time and then dying down again for lack of fuel to feed on. In a short time the troublesome problem of Bella Knox and Herbert Varden was forgotten.

Late in the evening Poole returned to the Yard. He had tested the time of both bus routes and found that the official times had not erred on the side of over-estimation. Route A – via Camden Town – was clearly out of the hunt; even though he had been lucky in his connections at Highgate Station and Camden Town Station, the journey had taken Poole only a few minutes under the hour. Route B was much quicker; the bus had made fast time along Hampstead Lane and Spaniards Road and had reached Golders Green Station in sixteen minutes. Then there had been a considerable wait before a 28 came along, but, even leaving that out of account, the rest of the journey had been much slower, the Finchley Road being congested, while Fortune Green Road and West End Lane were narrow and winding. From Golders Green to Kilburn Station had taken twenty-three minutes, making thirty-nine in all, to which had to be added an optimistic five minutes from body to bus and three from bus to Red Knight. Poole was convinced that Varden could not have made the trip in less than three-quarters of an hour and he thought an hour would be more likely.

A 210 bus conductor had told him that the service ran at ten-minute intervals, so that Varden would have had to be lucky if he had caught one directly he got into Hampstead Lane. The conductor was certain that the journey to Golders Green could not have been done more quickly than it was done that day. The 28 bus conductor thought that two or three minutes might on occasions be knocked off the trip from Golders Green to Kilburn, but it was equally likely that two or three minutes would sometimes be added to it. The service ran at six-minute intervals.

Poole had got from London Transport Headquarters the names of conductors on the 210 and 28 routes between 7 and 8 p.m. on 9th October. Of these he had managed to interview five, none of whom remembered seeing Varden on that night; that left eleven still to be questioned on the morrow.

On his return to Scotland Yard on the following morning Chief-Inspector Beldam set himself once more to review the Bella Knox case. He realised that he had allowed himself to minimise his task. He was so sure that Varden was the murderer that he had got it into his head that if only he could break down the Red Knight alibi his difficulties were over. Actually this was far from being the case. Even if he were able to prove that Varden *could* have got to Kilburn by 7.55 p.m. after committing a murder at Ken Wood at about 7.20 p.m. that was no proof that the man *had* committed the murder. The only real facts against him were that he was a friend of the dead woman's, that he was near the place where she was murdered at about the time when she was murdered, that he had shown signs of agitation when the police announcement of the murder came over the wireless, and that he was a violent type.

None of these facts were in themselves sufficient proof of guilt, though collectively they were highly significant. Before he could charge the man he must not only break down that alibi but he must either get some witness to Varden's presence near the spot where the body was found, or at least some witness to prove that his own story of his movements was untrue. If Poole could find a bus conductor who could identify Varden as travelling on the 210 or 28 route, that would be of first-class importance, as would be a taxi-driver who took him from the scene of the crime to Kilburn. That line was being worked; was there any other that could be followed?

'Presence near the spot where the body was found.' Failing a witness to the actual murder that would be the best evidence of all. But no such witness had been found. It occurred to Beldam that the Press had been singularly unhelpful. He had counted on their stimulating imagination or re-awakening memory, but not one witness of this kind had come forward. No one appeared to have seen Varden near Highgate Ponds or Ken Wood on the night of the murder; indeed, if it had not been for his own story it would not have been known that he had been anywhere near the place that day. Beldam realised that the defence would make strong play with that point.

Methodically the detective read through his notes of the case and it was only in the evidence of Mr. Jasper Gooden, who with his dog Ivan had found the body, that he found the slightest help. Towards the end of that interview Mr. Gooden had said that he had 'one evening' noticed near the Bathing Pond a man who had struck him as being an 'undesirable character.' The description he gave of this man did tally closely with that of Varden – 'tall, with heavy shoulders; one of those fleshy faces with an unhealthy colour that means drink, shifty eyes.' Yes, that might well be Varden. And he had 'appeared to be waiting for somebody.'

That was a suggestive piece of evidence. The Bathing Pond was within about six hundred yards of the place where Bella Knox had died. It was, too, in that locality that she had accosted Scott, the novelist. It was a fair guess that on the 'one evening' of which Mr. Gooden spoke Varden had been waiting for Bella Knox, and it was only one step farther to guess that on the 9th October he had met her there, gone with her to the quiet corner near Ken Wood, and there, for some reason so far unexplained, had murdered her. But it *was* only a guess.

And what about that 'unexplained reason'? What possible motive could there be for such a deed? Well, there must be a motive, because it had been done. At first Beldam had pounced on that ten-shilling note as indicative of the motive – robbery. But was it enough? Was it likely that a poor woman, so ill-dressed, ill-housed, whose total worldly wealth was probably represented by the seven £1 notes found by Poole behind the wardrobe, would have carried in her handbag sufficient money to tempt even a tough like Varden to robbery . . . let alone murder? It seemed unlikely. Violent temper seemed a more likely explanation, and that did at least fit in with Varden's known character,

Beldam sighed. There was altogether too much guesswork about this case. One could not expect to get a witness to the actual fact of murder, but there must be *some* facts before a case could be presented. There was, of course, one other fact; the car that had been seen standing in Millfield Lane. It had been standing at the junction of Merton Lane and Millfield Lane; that was within two hundred yards of the Bathing Pond which might be Bella Knox's *rendezvous* with Varden; it was also within four hundred yards of the spot where Bella had been killed. It had been seen there by Mrs. Joliffe and Poole had fixed the time of her seeing it at 7.05 p.m. It had also been seen – presumably it was the same car – by the butler at Westerham Lodge, which was close to Merton Lane, and this man had seen it move off at a time which he put with some certainty as between 7.15 and 7.20 p.m.

That time seemed a shade too early to fit in with the murder, but it would not do to be too precise about that. Could it be taken to fit in with the case against Varden? How could Varden have a car waiting for him? Could he have driven there in it himself and then driven away, after the murder, to the Red Knight? That would dispose of the alibi, but of course it did not fit in with his own account of walking from Crouch End to Kilburn. But that account was so far unsupported by any independent witness. It seemed extraordinarily unlikely that Varden would have a car of his own. It seemed little less unlikely that someone else had driven him there and driven him away again. That meant complicity in the murder, and complicity in murder was very rare, except in one of great elaboration. There had been the Browne and Kennedy case, of course; they had been of the same type as Varden; it might be a similar case.

But how was that car to be traced? Poole, an expert in such work, had tried and failed; Sergeant Gower had tried and failed. The description of the car was hopelessly vague. It was a million to one chance against its being traced now, nearly three weeks after it was seen. Still, in the absence of anything better, that clue must again be examined.

It was at this point that Beldam realised to the full how thin his case had worn and it was at this point that a telephone message came through from Kentish Town Police Station to say that a man had been found who had seen Varden near the Duke of St. Albans public-house at the edge of Parliament Hill at 7 p.m. on the 9th October. The man, whose name was Vesper, was a London Transport official on duty at the Tram terminus at the end of Highgate Road, which was where the Duke of St. Albans was situated. Vesper was a good witness, apparently reliable and definite in his statement. He had recognised Varden by the photograph shown to him by a divisional detective. He had had no particular reason for noticing him, apart from the fact that he did not like the look of him. He knew the time was 7 p.m. because he was to go off duty at that hour, and he knew it was 9th October because it was the first week-day of winter-time.

That, Beldam realised, was good, clear evidence. It supported Varden's own story . . . up to that point. It did not mean that he could not have committed the murder because the Duke of St. Albans was only a quarter of an hour or twenty minutes' walk from the scene. Quick work, but possible.

Vesper's story would have to be carefully checked, and checked by himself, Beldam, but if it was true it did at least crystallise the situation. It also reduced the likelihood of the car having had anything to do with Varden.

By the end of the day some more clearing up had been done. Beldam had seen the tram official, Vesper, who repeated with quiet assurance the story he had already told to the divisional detective. He had also learned from headquarters that the man was steady and reliable. Poole had completed his task of interviewing bus-conductors on the 210 and 28 routes and had learned that none of them remembered Varden, whose photograph was shown to them, travelling on their buses on 9th October. The conductors on the 210 route had felt pretty sure that they would have noticed him because people did not come aboard in large numbers in Hampstead Lane in the vicinity of Ken Wood. The 28 men were less certain; Golders Green Station was a busy stop.

Finally, though this was negative information, no taxi-driver had come forward to report having taken a fare from the Highgate area to Kilburn on the night in question.

Beldam decided that unless something turned up during the weekend he would have to ask for another conference with the Assistant Commissioner and obtain a decision as to whether there was sufficient justification for continuing the present concentration of man and brainpower upon a case which showed such ominous signs of fading out.

CHAPTER XIII

THE AMETHYST BROOCH

On Monday morning Chief-Inspector Beldam found one interesting piece of news awaiting him. The Brodshire Constabulary reported that Herbert Varden was a Brodshire man, born at Little Cattington in February 1896; his father had been a schoolmaster and at the time of his death was headmaster of Brodbury Grammar School, a man highly respected in the county town. Herbert Varden had received a good education and had served during the latter part of the Great War in the Brodshire Light Infantry, but owing to an attack of dysentery acquired in Salonika had not seen much active service. After the War he had completed his training as a school teacher and had been employed as an assistant master at Hollington, one of the smaller county secondary schools. He was a good teacher but owing to his violent temper had not made a favourable impression on the education authorities.

In 1926 an incident had occurred which had ended his connection with Brodshire. He had been suspected of an offence against a young girl, but owing to the reluctance of the parents to incur publicity the police had not been able to proceed against him.

Local feeling against him, however, had been so high that the School Managers had asked him to resign and Varden, in a violent outburst of temper, had given them an excuse to dismiss him. Varden had left the county and had not been heard of since.

As far as it went, this information was useful as an indication of character; it established the man's identity and accounted for his educated speech and for his general air of grievance and unwillingness to associate on terms of friendship with the people among whom his life was now cast. It was not difficult to imagine the stages in his downfall. He would have found great difficulty in obtaining further employment in his profession and probably had not tried. Drink and ill-temper would account for the rest of his unhappy story.

All this, however, was no help in establishing a case against Varden in connection with the murder of Bella Knox, and Chief-Inspector Beldam duly asked for an interview with the Assistant Commissioner. Sir Leward, having heard Beldam's report, asked if there were no other suspects on the active list. Beldam was obliged to admit that there were not; of the men known to have associated with Bella Knox, Fenley, the customer of the Gay George, had proved an unshakable alibi, as had also Frederick Percy White, the 'young lad with spectacles'; Robert Twist, Bella Knox's landlord, had only a family alibi, but there was no proof that his association with her had been in any way a guilty one nor any other evidence to connect him with the murder.

'What do you think yourself, Chief-Inspector?' asked Sir Leward.

'I think Varden did it all right, sir,' said Beldam doggedly, 'but unless we can get some evidence of a car or taxi taking him from the spot to the Red Knight in half an hour I don't see how we can charge him.'

'Nor do I,' said the Assistant Commissioner. 'You must just work on that line. Or rather, you must put somebody on to it.'

He turned to Chief-Constable Thurston, who was present at the interview.

'You want a Chief-Inspector for that Boddington case, don't you, Mr. Thurston?'

'Yes, sir, I do,' said the Chief-Constable. 'We're shorthanded now, with Chief-Inspector Fairbridge sick. If you think Chief-Inspector Beldam can be spared from this case now I shall be thankful.'

That was exactly what the Assistant Commissioner wanted and Chief-Constable Thurston knew it. Sir Leward never liked to keep a man on a job once he had lost heart, but he was careful not to hurt the feelings of his senior officers. Furthermore, he had particular faith in the ability of the comparatively young Detective-Inspector, Poole, who was at present employed on the case under Chief-Inspector Beldam. The

A.C., Thurston realised, would welcome the opportunity to give Poole his head.

So it was arranged that, for the time being at any rate, Chief-Inspector Beldam should be transferred to another case while Inspector Poole was instructed to take charge of the Knox problem, with special directions to work on the tracing of a car which might account for Varden's apparent alibi. The arrangement suited Poole admirably; he had been fortunate enough in the past to have charge of two or three cases which would normally have been entrusted to a senior officer and he had faith in his own ability; he was an ambitious man, in his quiet way, and he knew that to succeed where a Chief-Inspector had – to put it bluntly – failed, would greatly improve his chances of promotion.

At the same time, Poole was under no illusion as to the difficulty of his task. He himself must take a share in Beldam's failure up to date; he had done, he knew, useful work in providing grist for Beldam's mill but that mill had not delivered the goods. Would he, Poole, be able to produce any better result?

Although Poole had been working on the case from the beginning it was only in a subordinate capacity and he had not seen all the detailed reports. His first task, therefore, was to get himself fully acquainted with the case, so he spent a couple of hours in reading through the file and re-checking times and distances on the map. At the end of that time he felt very much as Beldam had done: that Varden *ought* to be the man they were after but that there was very little proof that he was.

Was it possible that they were on the wrong track altogether? Chief-Inspector Beldam had been certain that Bella Knox must have been murdered by one of the men with whom her profession brought her in contact, some vicious brute who killed for a little money or in a fit of temper; Varden had filled that role very well. But was the whole idea wrong? Poole remembered the 'imaginings' of the novelist, Gordon Scott, who had bored Chief-Inspector Beldam by wondering what the woman's 'story' had been. Beldam had snubbed him but, later, Scott had enlarged on his ideas to Poole, quoting the rude little song that had made so many generations laugh, the ditty about the 'victim of a noble squire,' who 'had fled to London City for to hide her awful shaime.' The idea that there was a 'story' behind the sordid murder on Hampstead Heath had naturally appealed to the novelist; he, Poole, had been more polite than Beldam in his reception of it but he had put it firmly on one side, assuring Scott that these cases almost always had a simple explanation . . . and a squalid one.

Had he been wrong and Scott right? Reading through the file had reminded Poole of another witness who had made a very similar suggestion – the Reverend Wilbraham Battisley, with his story of 'Magdalen' at the Christmas Day Celebration. At the time Poole had been moved by that story but he had allowed the Chief-Inspector's contemptuous dismissal of it to put it out of his mind.

Then another point struck Poole. He had suggested to his chief that one useful piece of information had come out of Mr. Battisley's story – the address of the house to which he had followed 'Magdalen' and at which he had been so rudely treated by the landlady. There again the Chief-Inspector had applied the wet blanket; the woman had left the house six months before the murder, he said; such 'ancient history' could have nothing to do with the case. And that little tag – the house in Bethnal Green where Bella Knox had once lived – had remained loose.

It should remain loose no longer. In the present state of suspended animation in which this case found itself no clue was too slight or too ancient to be tested. Poole decided to go straight down to Mr. Battisley's parish.

Darley Street, Bethnal Green, differs from Bunt Street, Kentish Town, only in its relation to its neighbours. Darley Street is one of the better streets of a poor quarter; Bunt Street one of the poorer streets of a better quarter. Each owes much of its air of depression to its uniformity, but in Darley Street some of the houses did show signs of a successful struggle against the surrounding conditions. No. 25 actually had some paint on the door and clean curtains in the windows. Poole rang the bell with a feeling of encouragement.

The door was opened by a tall, gaunt woman with hard grey eyes.

Poole decided at once that it was no use to try and wheedle information here; he must be official and depend upon a sense of duty.

'I am a police officer, madam,' he said, showing his warrant card. 'I have come to ask you for some information.'

After a moment's hesitation the woman led the way into a back room where a small fire was burning. Shutting the door behind Poole she stood silently waiting.

'I'm afraid I don't even know your name,' said Poole.

'Norris. What do you want?'

'We have been given to understand that Miss Bella Knox once lodged with you,' said Poole.

It seemed to him that a little flicker of perturbation appeared in Mrs. Norris's eyes but her expression did not change.

'Well, what if she did?'

'You know, perhaps, that she was found dead on Hampstead Heath three weeks ago?'

'I read about it.'

'But you did not give us the information we were asking for.' Poole's voice was quiet but there was a stern note in it.

It had little apparent effect upon Mrs. Norris.

'I had no information to give. When the news of a woman being murdered first appeared I did not connect her with my lodger. It was only after the name was published that I realised who the woman was and then I had nothing to tell; that was all I knew about her.'

'That would be for us to judge,' said Poole. 'It was your duty to tell the police what you know. It is your duty to tell me now.'

The woman's face hardened but Poole soon found that he had struck the right note.

'Very well,' she said. 'I don't want to get drawn into this. I am a respectable woman. But I will do my duty.'

Bella Knox, it appeared, had come to Darley Street in November of the previous year. Mrs. Norris had not at that time realised, she declared, what 'sort of woman' her new lodger was; she had said that she was an actress, which had accounted for her being out till late and also, in Mrs.

Norris's view, for her appearance. She did not bring men to the house, but neighbours started talk. Mrs. Norris would have liked to turn her out but she was hard up then – she had since come in for a little money – and satisfactory lodgers were not plentiful in that neighbourhood. Miss Knox paid regularly for a time and then began to get behind with her rent.

One day she did bring a man there and Mrs. Norris had turned him out at once. Bella Knox had promised that it should not happen again but she got more and more behind with her payments and at last, when she owed nearly five pounds, Mrs. Norris had given her notice.

'She hadn't got anything I could seize,' said the landlady grimly, 'or I should have done it. I needed the money. But she gave me a pawn ticket and said it was for a valuable brooch and that if I could redeem it perhaps I would keep it and give her a chance to buy it back if she was ever in a position to. I thought that was nice of her; she needn't have given it me.'

'Did you redeem the brooch?' asked Poole.

'No. I went round to the pawnshop but they wanted fifteen pounds and I couldn't afford it. I kept the ticket.'

At Poole's request Mrs. Norris hunted through a drawer in her small writing-table and produced the ticket. Poole gave her a receipt for it and promised that it should be returned in due course. The landlady could tell him no more. She knew nothing of where Miss Knox had come from and had seen or heard nothing of her since her departure.

Poole was interested in the little he had learned. The 'valuable brooch' did give some slight support to the theory of a 'story.' He formed the opinion that Mrs. Norris was not quite so hard as she liked to appear, in spite of her cavalier treatment of the vicar. Poole had not mentioned that incident, not wishing to give Mr. Battisley away.

The name of the pawnbroker on the ticket was J. Colenstein and his shop was in the East End, so Poole went straight to it from Darley Street. Mr. Colenstein was an elderly man and his shop was dark and not very clean. With extreme willingness he produced the brooch, which was of amethysts set in gold, the centre stone being large.

The pawnbroker explained that, though the stones were good and the gold, of course, of some value, the setting was old-fashioned. There was not likely to be a ready sale for it now. It would probably have to be broken up if it were not redeemed.

The lady, he thought, attached a sentimental value to it. She had pawned it with him three times, though each time he had only been able to offer a smaller amount. She had begged him not to break it up, saying that she was sure she could redeem it again some day. That was why he had kept it as long as he had, though it had been last pawned as long ago as September 1937. He had hardly hoped to see his money back.

September 1937 was, of course, a year or more previous to Bella Knox's arrival at Darley Street. Poole asked whether the pawnbroker had got a note of the address at that time. He had. With jewellery he always took particular care to satisfy himself of the *bona fides* of his customers. The lady had explained when she first pawned the brooch that it had been a present from an old friend and he, Mr. Colenstein, had had no reason to doubt her; but he had taken her address then and also the address, different from the first, when she had pledged it in 1937. The first transaction had taken place as long ago as 1929; the address then had been 2 Titchcombe Street, Finsbury. The brooch had been redeemed three months later. It had been pledged again in 1935, from the same address, and had remained in his hands for nearly a year. When pledged in September 1937 the address had been 184 Banbury Street, Hackney.

All this information Mr. Colenstein produced from a large and well-thumbed ledger. Poole realised that the pawnbroker was a methodical man who would, if necessary, be a useful witness. The brooch itself might be an even more important piece of evidence.

'I'd like to take this brooch, Mr. Colenstein,' said the detective. 'I'll give you a receipt and you shall have it back in due course.'

Mr. Colenstein raised not the slightest objection. His principle through a long life had been to keep on good terms with the police, which he interpreted as meaning honesty unless dishonesty could profitably be pursued without serious risk of discovery.

Blissfully ignorant of Mr. Colenstein's principles but well satisfied with his practice, Poole made his way to the more recent of Bella Knox's addresses, Banbury Street, Hackney. Here he met with no success at all, the present occupier of No. 184 having only come in two months previously, whilst two further tenants were known to have been in and out since September 1937. Poole took a note of the landlord's name and address but postponed a visit to him until he had tried the earlier address.

He had some hopes from this address because the brooch had been pledged from it both in 1929 and in 1935, which suggested that Bella Knox might have been better known there than at any of the subsequent houses, at which her stay had been in each case rather brief.

Finsbury is a district of different character to Bethnal Green or Hackney or Kentish Town, and Poole was curious to see the type of house at which Bella Knox had lodged in earlier days. Titchcombe Street, when he found it, proved to be one of its more remote quarters, but it was a decided improvement on Bunt Street, Darley Street, or Banbury Street, and No. 2 a house of fair size and in good repair. It seemed likely that the years between 1929 and 1935 had been less pinched for poor Bella Knox than had the four subsequent ones.

As Poole approached the house the door opened and a woman came out. She was generously decorated and fairly young. Even at a distance of some feet an aroma of violets reached the detective and so did a glance of calculating gladness. Poole hesitated, then stopped and raised his Trilby hat.

'I beg your pardon,' he said, 'but are you the occupier of this house?'

The girl stared at him.

'I live there, if that's what you mean,' she said in a thin metallic voice.

The stare had made Poole realise that he was talking in the stilted manner that official enquiry so easily made a habit.

He smiled.

'I meant, is it your house? I'm trying to find somebody who once lived here.'

'Oh, are you? Well, if it's not me you want to find you'd better ask Ma Pearson.'

The girl turned back to the house, opening the door with a latchkey. Inside the hall she raised her voice to a strident scream.

'Ma-a!'

After a pause a door at the back of the hall opened and a large woman with flaming red hair appeared.

'What is it, dear? Such a row you do make.'

'Boy friend of yours. Well, ta-ta.'

'Thank you so much,' said Poole.

The girl eyed him thoughtfully; then her face slowly broke into a smile even more overpowering than the scent of violets.

'Well, you know where I live, dear, don't you?' she said.

She slipped a card into his hand and walked out of the house.

'Well, what's it all about?'

Poole turned his eyes back to the landlady. She must have been very handsome at one time but age and over-indulgence had spoilt both figure and complexion. The red hair was unmistakably dyed. Her clothes were brightly coloured but untidy, and her feet were thrust into a pair of felt slippers.

'Might I have a word with you, Mrs. Pearson?' asked the detective, feeling rather out of his element.

'I daresay you might. What is it; business or pleasure?'

'Business, I'm afraid.'

'Well, some business is pleasure, isn't it?' said Ma Pearson with a vivid smile. 'You'd better come into my little snuggery.'

Standing in the hall, Poole had been conscious that violets formed only one ingredient of the bouquet of scents that impregnated the atmosphere. As he walked into the small sitting-room he almost gasped as the hot and heavy air reached him. He decided to remove all possibility of misapprehension at once.

'I'm sorry to trouble you, Mrs. Pearson,' he said, as soon as the door was shut. 'I'm a police-officer and I have to make some enquiries about a woman who I believe once lodged here.'

At the word 'police' Mrs. Pearson's face froze into a mask of suspicion and hostility. Even behind the colour on her cheeks Poole could see that her face had paled.

'You've nothing against me.'

Poole took a quick decision, judging that here he would learn more by friendliness than intimidation.

'Nothing at all, Mrs. Pearson,' he said quietly. 'In fact I've only just learned your name. I am making enquiries about a woman who, I believe, lived here some years ago – some time between 1929 and 1935. I don't know even whether you lived here yourself then.'

The suspicion remained in Mrs. Pearson's face but her colour had returned.

'Well, it's the first time I've ever had the police in this house,' she declared. 'Still, you'd better sit down, I suppose.'

That was better. Poole sat down and leaned confidentially towards the landlady.

'Did you know Miss Bella Knox?' he asked.

'Bella! Oh, Bella!'

To his intense surprise Poole saw the hard face in front of him slowly pucker and wrinkle into an expression of heartbroken grief. Ma Pearson's fat lips quivered and two large tears slowly trickled down her raddled cheeks.

CHAPTER XIV

AN OLD PHOTOGRAPH

Mrs. Pearson's tears ceased almost as abruptly as they had appeared. She dabbed her eyes, blew her nose, and heaved a voluminous sigh.

'I don't know what's come over me to do that,' she said. 'But there, I was fond of Bella and I won't deny it. When I read about her being done in on Hampstead Heath it made me feel real bad.'

'You knew all about that?' asked Poole, astonished at this calm admission. 'Didn't you see that the police were asking for information about her?'

'Oh, yes, I saw that,' said Ma Pearson. 'But I didn't know who'd done it.'

'But we asked for information about Miss Knox. You could have given us that.'

'Well, gracious me, you don't expect me to walk into a police station and make myself conspicuous, do you? What an idea!'

This was the second lady, though of different type to the first, who had said the same thing. Poole wondered whether the police were unreasonable in their expectations. He decided not to waste time on pressing the point.

'Perhaps you'll tell me about her now, Mrs. Pearson,' he said.

Probably Ma Pearson realised that the detective was being very forbearing. She looked at him with a more friendly eye. 'You're not going to get us into trouble?' she asked. Poole shook his head.

'I'm only interested in the murder of Bella Knox,' he said. 'If you can help me to find the man who did it I shall be grateful – and I expect you want that found out, don't you?'

'That I do. Bella was a dear, though always in trouble.'

'Trouble? What sort of trouble?'

'Ma' lifted her elbow significantly.

'Couldn't keep away from it when she had money,' she said. 'And of course that didn't help her to get money. Spoilt her looks, quite apart from that scar. I couldn't keep her. Twice I had to give her notice; she came back and I gave her another chance twice but it was no use; she had to go and I only saw her once after that.'

Poole asked questions and gradually extracted what Mrs. Pearson knew about her lodger. It was disappointingly little. Bella Knox had come to Titchcombe Street first in about 1928. She had then a little money and had been able to pay the small deposit that Ma Pearson required from her lodgers. Everyone liked her but she became intimate with nobody; she told her landlady and her fellow-lodgers nothing about herself and Mrs. Pearson had no idea what her earlier history had been nor where she had previously lived. She thought that she 'worked' round Liverpool Street Station but nobody was inquisitive at No. 2 Titchcombe Street and no prying questions were asked.

To Poole's eager enquiries about Bella's men friends Mrs. Pearson gave a completely negative reply; she never noticed who came into the house, she asked no questions as long as people behaved themselves, and in any case it was donkeys' years ago; how could she remember? The detective realised that Ma Pearson was not going to remember, whether she could or not; he felt that he could hardly blame her, but it was a bitter disappointment to him. He had built a good deal of hope upon this contact, because it covered so long a period – not so long as he had thought, because Bella had been away for two periods between 1928 and 1936, but still long enough to encourage a hope that her landlady would be able to tell a good deal about her.

It seemed, however, that Bella Knox, without being unfriendly, had managed to hide any personality she might have possessed, and certainly had disclosed nothing that might suggest that this final tragedy had its roots in her early history.

The detective made one final effort.

'Did you ever see this brooch, Mrs. Pearson?' he asked, pulling the amethyst brooch out of his pocket. Ma Pearson looked at it with interest.

'Why, yes; I did see it once,' she said. 'She wore it one evening when we had a party to celebrate my coming in for a bit of money; went to the Troc. we did, and then on to a show at the Palace; quite like old times it was for some of the girls who'd been on the stage when they were younger or luckier. Bella wore that brooch and we teased her about it. I remember; she said it was a present from her grandmother to a good girl, but of course we didn't believe that. That must have been about '30 or '31 – I never saw her wear the brooch again and to tell the truth I always thought she must have popped it. Where? . . . but there I suppose I mustn't ask questions, must I?'

Poole laughed.

'Well, I've asked a good many,' he said, 'so I don't mind telling you that you guessed right. She hadn't any other possessions of this kind, I suppose, that might help me? No photographs? Nothing to show who her parents were or anything like that?'

Mrs. Pearson slapped her ample knee.

'Well, there,' she said. 'I nearly forgot all about it. She did have one photograph, but not of a person. It was of a house and she left it behind when she went away the last time; must have forgotten about it or mislaid it because I found it on the floor behind her dressing-table after she'd gone; it wasn't in a frame. I kept it in case she came back for it but she never did. I expect it's somewhere now if I could find it.'

'I wish you'd have a try, Mrs. Pearson,' said Poole. 'It might be a guide.'

'Well, of course, it might and yet again it mightn't,' said Mrs. Pearson. 'I recollect now that it had a name on the back that wasn't Bella's. Something like Margaret, it was, or Catherine.'

Poole's interest quickened. 'Do see if you can find it,' he urged.

Reluctantly Mrs. Pearson turned to an untidy cupboard and rummaged through shelves and drawers. Then she tried drawers in a table and a cardboard box on top of the cupboard.

'Well, there, I don't really know where it might be now,' she said, evidently bored with her task.

But Poole was not going to give up so easily. He decided to apply a spur.

'Mrs. Pearson,' he said firmly, 'I want that photograph. I feel sure that you can find it if you try and I'm going to remind you that you put yourself in the wrong with the police when you did not respond to their appeal for information in the first place ... quite apart from anything else. I don't like using threats, especially as you've told me so much, but if I don't get that photograph I shan't feel quite so sure that you are helping us as much as you can.'

Ma Pearson shot a shrewd glance at the detective. He had been gentlemanly enough up to date, she thought, but there might be a hard hand behind those pleasant manners.

'Oh, all right,' she said. 'A nod's as good as a wink. I'll have a real good turn out this evening. I've got drawers and boxes full of junk all over the house. I daresay I can find the thing but I can't do it till after supper. You run along now, like a good chap, and if I find it I'll let you know. Where do I write to?'

Poole gave the necessary information and decided that he must be satisfied with that promise. He knew that he could make out no case for a search warrant.

As he walked away from Titchcombe Street, breathing deeply to get the scent out of his lungs, the detective thought over his day's work. Taken in detail he realised that he had learned very little, but on the other hand the background of his case had filled out a good deal. He had begun to get a much clearer picture of the unfortunate woman whose death was causing him so much trouble.

How Bella Knox had come to take up her unhappy profession he did not yet know, but he could now follow some of the later stages of her downward path. The character of Mrs. Pearson's house in Titchcombe Street was obvious enough and morally reprehensible, but the house itself and the general standard of living there were clearly of better quality than at any of Bella's subsequent homes. She was evidently in more comfortable circumstances during those years between 1928 and 1936 than she had been in the subsequent years. She would certainly have had to pay Ma Pearson a higher rent than she gave Mrs. Norris or Mrs. Twist. Her miserable room in Mrs. Twist's house in Bunt Street undoubtedly marked the lowest ebb of her career.

The reason for the decline in her fortunes seemed obvious enough. Apart from advancing years – the medical evidence put her age at death at about forty-four – the fact that she was a drinker would inevitably tell against her. It was fairly clear that she was not the convivial type of drinker, who might in merry company carry on a successful business. If she had been that she would have been far better known locally than she was. One of the most striking facts about her, considering her profession, was just the fact that she was so little known. Poole could not help fancying that this poor woman was far from being a shameless creature; he felt that she shrank from her task and only faced it when compelled to by sheer necessity.

But in spite of her shyness, her secretiveness, her solitary drinking, there had emerged the fact that people liked her. Three landladies of more different type than Mrs. Twist, Mrs. Norris and Mrs. Pearson it would have been hard to find, and yet each had declared or admitted that she had liked Bella Knox, and Mrs. Pearson had evidently felt a real affection for her; in spite of her failing and in spite of difficulty over rent she had twice taken her back into her house after telling her that she must go. There must have been some very genuine charm to account for this.

However, this picture painting was no immediate help in the task of finding a murderer, and Poole, as he wrote up his notes at the Yard, felt that he had got an almost hopeless task in front of him. No taxi-driver had yet come forward to say that he had driven Varden from the neighbourhood of Highgate Ponds to Kilburn, and it was extremely unlikely now that such a one would be found. Sergeant Gower had made no progress in his attempt to trace the car that might have been used for the same purpose. To all intents and purposes Poole felt that, even if he were guilty, which seemed very doubtful, Herbert Varden had now very little to fear from the police.

*

On the following morning, however, he had a pleasant surprise. On arriving at Scotland Yard he was told that a Mrs. Pearson had rung up to say that she had found the photograph and would he come and see it or should she send it to him? Poole went straight down to the Underground and within half an hour was in Titchcombe Street.

Rather to his relief he encountered none of Mrs. Pearson's lodgers; no doubt they were not early risers. The landlady herself was tidier than on the previous day and wasted no time on idle tears.

'Here it is,' she said, thrusting a piece of cardboard into the detective's hand. 'It gave me a pretty hunt but I always was ready to oblige a friend.'

The photograph was faded and scratched but it certainly interested Poole. The house which it portrayed was a large one, so far as he could judge in Elizabethan style if not of that period. In the foreground was a stretch of grass on which two ponies were grazing, while at one side appeared a small group of people whose dress suggested a pre-war style; they were too far away for any faces to be distinguishable. The mount had been trimmed, possibly to fit a frame, so that no photographer's name appeared, a fact which represented, Poole thought, the usual cussedness of detective work.

He turned the photograph over and saw that the back, though equally free of printed matter, bore the one name 'Kathleen,' written in ink in a bold hand. If only there had been a surname as well. But that would be too much to expect.

However, here was something definite to work on. Poole thanked Mrs. Pearson for her help, gave his usual receipt, pocketed the photograph and hurried back to the West End. His objective was the establishment of Messrs. Cawston, Sproule and Pennyburn, the estate agents in Berkeley Square. If anyone could identify the house in the photograph at a glance, then it would be Mr. Cawston, Mr. Sproule, or Mr. Pennyburn, because their firm had been established for something like two centuries and had probably handled in that time three-quarters of all the large properties in England that ever came upon the market. And the house in Bella Knox's photograph appeared to qualify for that description.

Poole realised, of course, that he was unlikely to find bearers of all those illustrious names still representing the firm, but that would hardly affect the encyclopædic knowledge that must have descended through the ages. In the outer office he was surprised to find only an elderly ledger clerk half hidden behind a tall desk, and two younger clerks less deeply engaged. He addressed himself to one of the latter.

'Can I see one of the partners, please?' he asked.

The clerk eyed him carefully and probably decided that here was not a potential client of any importance.

'I am afraid that none of the partners are disengaged at the moment, sir,' he said politely. 'Can I give you any information?'

'You can take my card to one of the partners and ask if he will kindly see me as soon as he is disengaged,' said the detective, handing over one of his official cards.

The clerk glanced at it, started visibly, and disappeared up a flight of stairs. Within a minute he was back.

'Mr. Pennyburn will see you now,' he said, dropping the 'sir' but eyeing the detective with much greater interest than before.

Poole half expected to find a white-whiskered old gentleman in a swallow-tailed coat and stock, but instead, when he got into the partner's room, he saw a young man in a pinpoint grey suit with a red carnation in his button-hole. Mr. Pennyburn did not rise but waved the detective to a chair.

'What can I do for you, Inspector?' he asked pleasantly. Poole produced the photograph and handed it across the massive mahogany desk.

'I'm trying to identify this house, sir,' he said. 'I thought your firm was more likely to help me than anyone else.'

'Has somebody stolen it?'

Hardly expecting an answer to his mild jest, Mr. Pennyburn examined the photograph. His brow puckered.

'I know this house,' he said.

He tapped his desk with the end of a pencil, as if summoning help from some pigeon-hole in his memory. For a moment no help came and his finger hovered over a button in the house-telephone.

'I've got it,' he said suddenly. 'This is Chatterleys. It has been on our books for some four or five years.'

He looked up at the detective.

'What about it?' he asked.

'The photograph belongs to someone who has been murdered,' answered Poole quietly. 'I am trying to identify her, or rather to discover her early history.'

The estate agent nodded.

'In that case I must give you all the help I can. What exactly do you want to know?'

'Where it is; who it belongs to, sir, in the first place.'

'It is in Warwickshire, not far from Coventry. It belongs to a Mr. Fenley Morris. He asked us about four years ago to sell it for him but so far we have not been successful. It is a very interesting property but it has certain drawbacks; it has never been thoroughly modernised and would require a fairly large amount of money spent on it. Do you want details?'

'I should like first to hear something about Mr. Morris. Is he a married man? Has he a family?'

Mr. Pennyburn shook his head.

'I can't tell you very much about him,' he said. 'I believe he is a rich man – or was. I remember hearing something about a yacht.'

Again his hand went to the house-telephone; pressing a button, he picked up the receiver.

'Mr. Burton, would you come a minute, please?' he murmured.

A few minutes later the elderly man whom Poole had seen in the outer office came into the room.

'Mr. Burton, our chief ledger-clerk, knows everything,' said Mr. Pennyburn with a smile. 'Burton, Inspector ... er ... Poole wants to know something about Chatterleys, or rather about its owner. What do we know about Mr. Fenley Morris? Is he married? Has he a family? What age is he? You can speak freely.'

The old clerk coughed, as if deprecating the idea of parting with confidential information.

'Mr. Morris was unmarried at the time he put the property in our hands, sir,' he said. 'You will remember that he gave as one reason for wishing to part with the house that it was too large for a bachelor. There has been no announcement in the papers since then, but of course he might have been married quietly. I fancy that his age would be about sixty now.'

'And the point about children does not arise. What else, Inspector?'

'Is Mr. Morris living there now, sir?'

Mr. Pennyburn looked at the clerk, who shook his head.

'I believe the house has been unoccupied ever since it was put into our hands, sir. Mr. Morris lives largely abroad. He had a yacht but I saw that he sold it at the beginning of the summer. He is, I believe, at present in South America, where he has business interests.'

The young partner laughed.

'I told you Mr. Burton knew everything,' he said. 'Has he helped you at all?'

Poole hesitated, as if uncertain how to proceed. He realised that he had been in too much of a hurry in his visit to the estate agents; he ought to have made his plans beforehand, decided exactly what he did want to find out.

'Would there be anyone at Chatterleys now whose memory might go back some way, sir,' he asked; 'a caretaker, or a gardener, perhaps?'

Again Mr. Pennyburn glanced at the clerk.

'There is a caretaker, sir, who I believe has been a housemaid in times past. She married a gardener.'

While he answered, Mr. Burton's eye was upon the photograph on his employer's desk. He opened his mouth as if to speak again, but having answered the question that he had been asked he evidently decided to say no more.

'Then I think perhaps I had better go down there, sir,' said Poole. 'I may have to trouble you again but I shall have a clearer idea then of exactly what I want to know.'

'Of course. We shall be glad to do anything we can,' said Mr. Pennyburn heartily. 'By the way, will you go in your official capacity or would it help you if I gave you an order to view?'

A flicker of disapproval crossed the face of the faithful retainer but

Poole eagerly accepted the offer.

'That's very good indeed of you, sir,' he said. 'I may have to act officially but an order might enable me to find out enough without arousing curiosity.'

'Then, Mr. Burton, will you see about it?'

Mr. Pennyburn rose to his feet and walked with Poole to the door, smiling benignly on the detective as he took his leave.

CHAPTER XV

CHATTERLEYS

Mr. Pennyburn had acted with some shrewdness when he offered Inspector Poole an order to view Chatterleys. His clerk had naturally been shocked at the idea of a mere policeman posing as a prospective purchaser of a gentleman's property. But Mr. Pennyburn had realised that the young Detective-Inspector was no 'mere policeman' and that he could very well play the part without exciting unfavourable comment. John Poole had, in fact, been educated at a good public-school and at Oxford, and had been called to the Bar and practised for a year in Sir Edward Floodgate's chambers before taking up his chosen career as a police-officer. He was no 'Trenchard Inspector,' going straight to the Police College and gaining that high rank without going through the mill; Poole had joined the Metropolitan Police as a constable and had worked his way up through all the ranks. True, he had been given accelerated promotion, largely because he had been lucky enough to catch the eye of the Assistant Commissioner, but that promotion was due to merit and not to extraneous influence.

Mr. Pennyburn had not taken long to size up the detective. He had, moreover, realised the advantage of not having an official police visit paid to Chatterleys if it could possibly be avoided; such a visit might cause disquieting rumours to get about, which in their turn might put further obstacles in the way of finding a purchaser. So he had offered the order and had been pleased when the detective accepted it.

Poole travelled down to Coventry on the following morning, which was the 1st of November. A day in the country was always a pleasure to him and he did not get many of them, except on the rare occasions when a County Constabulary called for the help of the C.I.D. The autumn tints still lingered on the trees, and about ten minutes before reaching the town he had the rare pleasure of seeing hounds jogging along the road to a meet. The day was bright with wisps of mist still hanging about the low ground, and the detective wished that he was one of the lucky men who were going to spend it on a horse.

At Coventry he found that a bus would take him within reasonable walking distance of Chatterleys, and he welcomed the excuse to stretch his legs. Both the drive and the walk were all too short, and Poole guessed that the near proximity of the prosperous and spreading manufacturing town might partly account for the difficulty of finding a purchaser for a big country house. In these days there were not many people who could afford such a luxury and they could take their pick of the many which were on the market.

Poole had decided not to pose as a purchaser himself. Old family servants were very shrewd judges of 'gentlemen' and he thought that the caretaker might not be deceived even by his best blue serge suit, especially as he was arriving neither by car nor taxicab. Instead, he thought, he would present himself as the agent of the gentleman for whom he was making preliminary enquiries. In any case he realised that he might soon have to divulge his true identity.

His first view of Chatterleys was decidedly impressive. The house was undoubtedly Elizabethan in origin and was surrounded by a park with magnificent trees; a long range of stables stood at one side, while on the other a high brick wall suggested a large kitchen garden. Closer inspection showed that the house had been added to and altered at some very bad period of architecture, probably late Victorian, while the grounds were clearly suffering from neglect. There were broken windows and weeds growing even in the gravel sweep before the front door. Poole thought that if Mr. Fenley Morris was a rich man he must be a very foolish one – or else employ a very bad bailiff to look after the property which he wanted to sell.

Mr. Burton had promised to telephone to the caretaker to expect a visit, so the shutters of the house were open and the blinds drawn. Poole's ring was answered promptly by a middle-aged woman in a black stuff dress. She had black hair parted in the middle and dressed closely to her head; her mouth was thin and compressed and her grey eyes scanned Poole with none too welcoming a gaze. A quick thought flashed through the detective's mind; here might be another reason why the house did not find a ready purchaser – an old servant in a comfortable caretaking situation would not be too willing to quit it; she might easily influence the views of people who were not strongly attracted by the house.

However, a first impression might be a false one and Poole opened the engagement with a cheerful smile.

'Good-morning, Mrs. Batty,' he said – the omniscient ledger-clerk had supplied him with the name – 'I have an order to view from Messrs. Cawston, Sproule and Pennyburn. My name is Poole, but I am acting for Colonel Bunbury, who is looking out for a property in the midlands.'

The detective thought that Mrs. Batty's gaze became less searching when he announced that he was not a principal. However, she made no comment beyond asking him to come in.

The house was furnished but all the furniture was stacked in the centre of the rooms and covered with dust-sheets, so that it was not possible to judge of its quality. There were no pictures on the walls and the old-fashioned paper looked patchy and none too clean. The whole house needed painting and the heavy brass fittings were in many cases tarnished. As the pilgrimage from room to room and floor to floor proceeded the detective realised that many thousands of pounds would have to be spent on this house to bring it up to modern standards of comfort and efficient working, though no doubt it had been the last word in luxury a couple of generations ago.

Poole did not attempt to talk much to his guide, beyond asking general questions which he thought would not give away his ignorance as an agent. The caretaker answered politely but without enthusiasm; she volunteered no information at all and Poole doubted whether he would learn from her anything that might help him unless he brought his official card into play. However, he thought he would at least try.

The tour was nearly complete when they reached the housekeeper's room, which was evidently the present living-room of Mr. and Mrs. Batty. It was comfortably furnished and a cheerful fire burned in the grate.

'What a charming room,' exclaimed Poole, instinctively warmed by the contrast to the gloomy emptiness of the rest.

Instantly he saw that he had touched a responsive chord. Mrs. Batty smiled like a human being.

'It is a nice room, sir,' she said. 'I always used to envy Mrs. Curling this room and now I'm very comfortable in it myself.'

'Mrs. Curling?' queried Poole.

'Yes, sir; the housekeeper. She left when Sir Richard sold the house.'

The detective looked puzzled.

'What Sir Richard is that?' he asked. 'I only know of Mr. Fenley Morris.'

'Oh, it was him Sir Richard sold the house to,' said the caretaker. 'Mrs. Curling didn't stay after that. She had been with the Wayke family all her life and she wasn't going to change. Of course it was different for me; I only came here in 1917. When Mr. Morris asked me to stay on I didn't see why not. But Mrs. Curling wouldn't stay. She left the moment Sir Richard's things were out of the house. He sold all the furniture to Mr. Morris and only took just his own clothes and a few special family things.'

All this was rather confusing but Poole thought he could soon get the essential facts.

'Won't you have a glass of sherry and a biscuit, sir?' asked Mrs. Batty. 'Mr. Morris likes gentlemen who come to look at the house to have something. He says it's so tiring.'

'That certainly would be very nice, Mrs. Batty,' said Poole gratefully. 'I hope you will join me.'

The caretaker did not need much persuasion and soon they were seated comfortably in front of the fire with a decanter and some biscuits on a table between them. Poole was thankful that he had represented himself as a subordinate; Mrs. Batty's training would not have allowed her to do this with a 'gentleman.' He hoped that some useful information might now be forthcoming.

'When did Mr. Morris buy the house, then?' he asked.

Mrs. Batty pondered.

'1924 it would be,' she said. 'No, 1925, because that was the year the big storm blew so many trees down and Mr. Morris made a fuss; they were blown down in February and when he came in May he wanted to know what had happened to the garden. He'd seen the house in the summer of 1924 but there was a lot of haggle about price, I heard, and it wasn't sold till well into next year, 1925.'

1925, thought Poole, was considerably later than the date of the photograph in his pocket. He must start working back towards that now.

'Was Sir Richard an old man?' he said.

'Oh, no, sir. Sir Richard's not more than fifty, I'd say, but he was all broken up in the War – one of those air crashes – and he's quite a cripple now, poor man. He lost all his money, too, soon after the War and that's why he had to sell Chatterleys – that and being all alone. It was terrible lonely for him being here all by himself.'

'When did Sir Richard come into the property himself?' asked Poole.

'Oh, that was quite soon after I came; the last year of the War, I think. Old Sir Brandon had been very ill for some time and I never saw much of him myself. There'd been trouble in the family, I think, but that was before I came. 1918 it must have been he died.'

Even that, thought Poole, was later than the photograph. He decided that the time had come to produce this exhibit.

'By the way,' he said. 'I've got an old photograph of Chatterleys with some people in it. I wonder whether you can recognise any of them.'

He pulled it out of his pocket and handed it to Mrs. Batty, who seemed rather surprised. Poole thought he had better produce some sort of explanation.

'It was that photograph that first attracted Colonel Bunbury to the house,' he said. 'I don't know where he got it from and he didn't at first know what house it was but I traced it through the estate agents.'

Mrs. Batty looked at it with interest.

'That looks like Sir Brandon on the right,' she said. 'I always heard he was a tall gentleman, though I never saw him up. I couldn't tell who the others are; they're too small to see faces, aren't they? The two ladies might be his daughters.'

'He had two daughters?'

'Yes, Miss Helen and Miss Christine. Sir Richard ... Mr. Richard he was then ... was the eldest.'

'Oh,' said Poole.

He idly turned over the photograph, which Mrs. Batty had returned to him.

'I wonder who this would be,' he said, pointing to the name.

'Kathleen?'

The caretaker wrinkled her forehead.

'I call to mind the name, but ... oh, I know; one of the girls in the house was called Kathleen, I heard. One of the under-housemaids, but she used to maid Miss Christine.'

Poole's pulse had quickened. Was he on the trail at last? The excitement caused a momentary lapse of discretion.

'Did you know her yourself?' he asked quickly.

Mrs. Batty looked at him with surprise. A sudden suspicion came into her mind. What was all this questioning about?

Poole saw the look in her eyes and realised that he had blundered, that he could no longer expect to get any information unless he disclosed his identity. Now that there was promise of something definite to be gained by it he did not hesitate.

'I must apologise to you, Mrs. Batty,' he said. 'I have been misleading you but only because I did not want to cause talk unless it was necessary. I am a police-officer – a Scotland Yard detective – and I am investigating the murder of a poor woman in London. This photograph was found among her possessions and though we know the name she was using at the time we believe it was not her real name. If you had not known anyone of the name of Kathleen connected with Chatterleys it would not have been necessary to ask any more questions and no one need have known that a detective had been down here; I think the London agents were anxious that that should not be known unless it was necessary. But now I must ask you more, and it is right that you should know who I am and why I am being so inquisitive.'

Poole handed his warrant-card to the caretaker. She looked at it vaguely and gave it back without a word. The detective hoped that his quick confession had prevented her from becoming antagonistic.

'Will you help me, Mrs. Batty?' he asked.

'I . . . I suppose I must,' she said rather grudgingly. 'I hardly know . . . I've never had to do with the police . . . except the constable here.'

Poole smiled. He could imagine that he must appear rather different from the village bobby.

'Would you like to ask your husband?' he said.

'I don't think there's any need for that,' said the woman. 'He wouldn't know anything. He came here after I did.'

So much the better, probably. It would save time and there could surely be no difficulty in finding out all about 'Kathleen' now.

'All right, then; I'll go ahead. Can you tell me Kathleen's surname?'

Mrs. Batty shook her head.

'I don't know that I ever heard it,' she said. 'She left before I came. I just heard her spoken of as Kathleen. I saw her once. She came down on a visit to Mrs. Curling.'

'Do you know where she went to from here?'

'Oh, she went with Miss Christine when she married, but I don't think she stayed long.'

'Is there anyone else here who knew her?'

'Not in the house. I'm the only one here now. There might be some in the village would remember her. But the best to ask about her would be Mrs. Curling.'

That certainly would be best. Gossip in the village was the last thing that Poole wanted until he knew a good deal more.

'Do you know where Mrs. Curling lives now?' he asked. 'She is still alive, I suppose?'

'Oh, yes; she lives in Birmingham with a married daughter. She's a very old lady now but she's got all her wits about her still.'

This was a great piece of luck. But there was one other test to be made first.

'You say you saw this girl Kathleen,' said Poole. 'I am going to ask you if you can identify a photograph of her. I am afraid it may upset you rather as it was taken after she was dead, but I am sure you will want to help us in finding out who killed her.'

Poole drew from his pocket the envelope containing several photographs of Bella Knox taken by Sergeant Cook. He chose the least distressing and handed it to Mrs. Batty.

'Of course she was twenty years or more older than when you saw her,' he said, 'but you may be able to recognise her.'

Mrs. Batty examined the photograph calmly enough. Poole realised that people who read some of the modern Sunday illustrated papers were accustomed to horrors.

'I'm sure I couldn't say,' said Mrs. Batty after a pause. 'I don't recollect her having a mark on her face.'

'That might have happened later, of course,' said Poole. 'It seems to be a burn.'

Again Mrs Batty stared at the photograph.

'It might be her,' she said, 'and yet again it might not.'

Obviously this was no good as an identification. Poole realised that for the moment he must rely upon the old housekeeper, Mrs. Curling.

CHAPTER XVI

A VERY OLD LADY

Poole thought that he would get a more sympathetic reception from the old housekeeper if he had a personal introduction, so he invited Mrs. Batty to come into Birmingham with him at her country's expense. The caretaker jumped at the opportunity. She must give her husband his dinner – it was now nearly one o'clock – and she must arrange for a friend to hold the fort till her return; after that she would soon be ready and there was a good bus service into Birmingham every hour. Moreover, she invited the detective to share the meal; there was only a bit of cold mutton, as she had not had time this morning to do anything hot, but he would be very welcome. It was a bit of a walk, she said, to the nearest public-house and even there he was not likely to get much more than bread and cheese.

Poole accepted gratefully, thinking that it would be as well to have a talk with Mrs. Batty's husband himself. He was very anxious that there should not be any gossip about his enquiries and he knew that the caretaker would in any case tell her husband, however much he might swear her to secrecy.

Batty, when he came in to his dinner, proved to be a younger man than his wife, strong and good-looking in his way, but probably rather slow-witted. He seemed, however, a very decent fellow and accepted the detective's explanation of his visit without comment and probably without much interest. In response to Poole's request for secrecy he said that he was not one to talk.

Mrs. Batty managed to find time to put on her best clothes for her visit to the great midland city and she showed every sign of enjoying the expedition, telling Poole all about the neighbourhood, the dullness of the life at Chatterleys and the enviable position of people like Mrs. Curling who were able to settle down in a town where there was a bit of life going on. She hoped to do the same herself some day, though it would be a job to get Batty away from his garden.

The run into Birmingham was a remarkably quick one and fortunately Mrs. Curling's home was on the near side of the city, in a very pleasant suburb. It was arranged that Mrs. Batty should go in first and prepare Mrs. Curling for the visit; after a quarter of an hour Poole was to call, and while he was having his talk with the old lady Mrs. Batty would go and do some shopping and perhaps visit a friend. After his visit the detective was to feel free to do what he liked; Mrs. Batty was quite accustomed to returning home alone; she might even stay late and go to a picture with a friend. There were plenty of late buses and she had warned Batty not to expect her till he saw her.

Poole walked about with some impatience until the fifteen minutes were up and then rang the bell of 'Rosemary'; the door was opened by Mrs. Batty herself.

'She's a bit upset, though she won't show it,' whispered the caretaker.

Poole followed her into a parlour that was completely true to Mrs. Curling's 'period'; the red and blue turkey carpet, the plush curtains, the family photographs, the ornaments on brackets, even the broad-leafed fern in a pot – all were there, looking like a set in a well produced late-Victorian play. And in a high-backed chair by the fire sat the leading lady, slim, erect, dressed in black bombazine with a cameo brooch at the neck, her small blue-veined hands folded on her lap, a lace cap on her neat white hair. Mrs. Curling's face was thin and the skin wrinkled, but her dark eyes were full of life and she looked at her visitor with dignified interest.

'This is Inspector Poole, Mrs. Curling,' said Mrs. Batty in a slightly raised voice.

Poole was uncertain how the old lady would like to be treated. If she regarded a Detective-Inspector as just one kind of policeman she would probably expect a 'Mum.' He took a step or two into the room and made a polite bow.

'Sit down, Mr. Poole,' said Mrs. Curling, thereby showing that she knew all about the higher ranks of the force.

She pointed to a chair close beside her.

'Is this your first visit to Birmingham?'

The manners of her period would not, of course, allow a direct plunge into business.

'I'm ashamed to say it is, Mrs. Curling,' answered Poole. 'I know very little of the midlands.'

For five minutes they discussed city and county. Poole mentioned his pleasure at seeing hounds from the train.

'That would be the North Warwickshire,' said Mrs. Curling. 'If I remember aright Wednesday was one of their days. And now you want to ask me some questions, don't you? Emily, you can go and do your shopping now and you can please yourself about coming back to tea or not. Mr. Poole, I am sure, will join me in a cup when we have finished business.'

Emily Batty said good-bye, 'in case she found Mrs. Simpkins in,' and a minute later Poole and the old housekeeper were alone.

'It is about Kathleen Knox you want to ask me, isn't it?' asked Mrs. Curling.

Poole started. So that had been her real name after all; only the 'Bella' had been camouflage – or humour.

'It may be about her,' Poole replied cautiously; 'that's one of the points about which I want your help.'

Not wishing to start his interview with too severe a shock, Poole produced first the photograph of Chatterleys.

'This photograph was found in the dead woman's room,' he said, handing it to the old lady.

Mrs. Curling looked rather vaguely at it but made no comment.

'Is that Sir Brandon Wayke?' he asked.

'Chatterleys belonged to Sir Brandon, yes,' said Mrs. Curling.

'I meant: is that figure in the photograph Sir Brandon?'

'I don't . . . it may be,' said the old lady rather haughtily.

Poole noticed that she was not examining the photograph at all closely.

A sudden suspicion flashed into his mind. She was not wearing spectacles; there was no sign of any; there was no book near her, no work. But she was not blind; her eyes had followed his every movement and she had taken the photograph from him without any fumbling.

He produced the photograph of the dead woman, the least repellent of the clutch.

'This is where I most want your help, Mrs. Curling,' he said. 'I am afraid the photograph may distress you because it was taken after the poor woman was dead, but it is the only one we have got. It is absolutely necessary to get an identification and there is no one who is more likely to be able to help us than you.'

Mrs. Curling listened gravely but she displayed no great eagerness to look at the photograph. However, she took it when he held it out to her.

Again Poole noticed that she looked at it vaguely; there was no screwing up of the eyes, no effort of concentration or focussing.

'I have not seen Kathleen for many years,' said Mrs. Curling. 'I am afraid I cannot say if this is her or not.'

'Had she that scar on her face?'

'Scar? What scar?'

So that was it. The scar was clear enough in the photograph. The old lady must be so short-sighted as to be nearly blind, and so proud as to refuse to acknowledge it. The discovery was a severe blow to Poole. He had counted on getting just the identification he wanted from the old housekeeper without any serious risk of 'talk' being started. Now he would have to go seeking it elsewhere and 'talk' was bound to begin.

He had, of course, the identification of the name; that could not be a coincidence. At any rate it was enough to justify him in pursuing his enquiries from Mrs. Curling.

'I can quite understand that,' he said, putting the photograph away in his pocket. 'Would you mind telling me something about Kathleen Knox?'

Mrs. Curling collected her thoughts before replying.

'I cannot quite remember where Kathleen came from,' she said. 'She was not a local girl; that I do know. Most of the young girls who came

to Chatterleys came from the villages round, but Kathleen did not. She
must have come, I think, in about 1908 or 1909. She was a good girl
and more intelligent than most girls; she was ambitious, too, and wanted
to be a lady's maid. I thought she would do quite well so I obtained
permission for her to look after Miss Christine when she was at home,
though she still did housework as well. Then when Miss Christine came
home for good Kathleen gradually spent more and more time looking
after her. Miss Christine liked her very much.'

'And when did she leave, Mrs. Curling? Mrs. Batty told me that she
took Kathleen with her when she married, but I don't know when that
was.'

The old housekeeper was silent for a moment. Poole noticed that the
corners of her mouth had a downward droop.

'Miss Christine married in 1915,' she said shortly.

'Kathleen did not stay long with her after that, I understand. Do you
know where she went to?'

'No,' said Mrs. Curling, still with a note of displeasure in her voice.
'She never wrote to me after she left Miss Christine, nor came to see me,
as one of our local girls would have done.'

That probably accounted for the displeasure, thought Poole. It was
very unfortunate because it made the task of tracing Kathleen Knox's
subsequent movements still more difficult. Still, no doubt he would be
able to trace her through 'Miss Christine.'

'Can you tell me where I can find Miss Christine?' he asked. 'What
is her married name, please? She is still alive, I hope?'

But Mrs. Curling's mouth had set in a rigid line.

'I cannot tell you anything about Miss Christine,' she said. 'Sir
Brandon was displeased with her marriage and she never came back to
Chatterleys. I cannot tell you anything about her.'

The repetition was emphatic but Poole thought he detected sadness
rather than anger in Mrs. Curling's voice. Probably he would be able to
wheedle more out of her by roundabout means. He sincerely hoped so;
it did seem extraordinary how at every turn something seemed to crop
up to block his efforts to trace Kathleen Knox.

'There was no Lady Wayke at that time, I suppose?' Poole asked. 'You spoke only of Sir Brandon.'

Mrs. Curling shook her head.

'No, Lady Wayke died when Miss Christine was born. Such a tragedy it was; Sir Brandon never got over it. Such a sweet lady, she was; so full of life and spirits; none of us could ever forget her.'

The old housekeeper's eyes had softened when she spoke of her dead mistress. Poole felt as if he had caught a glimpse of that past tragedy, which must have affected so many lives. Evidently it would account for the later 'trouble in the family' of which Mrs. Batty had spoken and which no doubt had to do with the daughter's marriage, at which Sir Brandon had been displeased. Through her, too, it might be said to have affected the life of Kathleen Knox and even indirectly led up to her unhappy end.

'There was an elder sister, wasn't there?' asked Poole.

'Yes, Miss Helen. But she was only a half-sister of Miss Christine. Sir Brandon was married twice. His first wife only lived five years after her marriage; she gave him Mr. Richard – Sir Richard he is now – and Miss Helen. She died in 1893, and then Sir Brandon married again at the beginning of 1895 and lost his second wife before the year was out.'

An unlucky family, thought Poole; those two tragedies so close together, the trouble over the daughter's marriage, the crippling of the eldest son, and finally the sale of the old home.

Still, that was not his affair. He had got somehow to trace Kathleen Knox, maid to the younger daughter, whose married name he had not yet discovered. He was about to ask for it a second time when the door opened and a middle-aged woman came in. She was a stouter and younger edition of the old housekeeper and there was a cheerful smile on her face as she nodded to Poole.

'Sorry to disturb,' she said, 'but it's past half-past four; shall I bring tea, mother?'

But Mrs. Curling did not approve of such short-circuiting of manners.

'This is Inspector Poole, Margaret; my daughter, Mrs. Hackett.'

Mrs. Hackett shook hands.

'Pleased to meet you, Inspector,' she said. Her training had not been that of her mother.

'Now, what about tea? Have you finished your talk?'

Her eye fell on the photograph of Chatterleys which lay on the table. She picked it up.

'What a funny old picture,' she said. 'Why, mother, here's Sir Brandon. It's very old, isn't it? Wherever did you get it?'

'I brought it,' said Poole. 'I hoped Mrs. Curling might be able to recognise somebody, not in that photograph but in another. But she was not able to.'

Mrs. Hackett shot a quizzical look at her mother.

'I had not seen her for a very long time,' said Mrs. Curling defensively. 'I was not able to recognise her.'

'Why, mother, of course you weren't – not without your glasses.'

She turned to Poole.

'She won't use them,' she said with a smile. 'She's too proud.'

'I have very good eyes. I don't need them,' declared the old lady.

'Of course they're good eyes; they're wonderful – but not for anything near. I took her to the oculist, Inspector, and he gave her a nice pair of glasses for reading, but she won't wear them. Who is it you want her to recognise?'

Here again Poole realised that Mrs. Curling would be sure to tell her daughter all about it when he was gone.

'It's a photograph of a woman who was murdered in London not long ago,' he said. 'I have reason to believe that it is a Miss Kathleen Knox, who was once in service at Chatterleys. Did you know her, Mrs. Hackett?'

Mrs. Hackett shook her head.

'I remember the name Kathleen,' she said, 'but I don't think I ever saw her. I was away in Canada for a long time; my husband was a railway engineer. Can I look at the photo?'

Once more Poole produced the photograph of Bella Knox. Mrs. Hackett looked at it and gave a little shudder.

'What a dreadful picture,' she said. 'I'm glad you can't see it, mother, if it's anyone you know.'

The remark irritated Poole. It seemed hardly respectful to his important mission. Perhaps Mrs. Hackett realised that, because she changed her mind.

'Perhaps you ought to see it, Mother, if the Inspector wants you to. Shall I get your glasses?'

Mrs. Curling remained silent, an expression of mulish obstinacy on her face. Her thin hands were trembling slightly.

'I shall be really very grateful if you will use them, Mrs. Curling,' said Poole gently. 'This poor woman has been murdered and I am sure we all want to find who murdered her, don't we?'

For a moment the old lady bridled, but Poole's touch had been very light.

'Very well,' she said.

Mrs. Hackett left the room and returned in a minute with a pair of steel-rimmed spectacles which she carefully adjusted on her mother's nose.

Poole put the photograph into the old lady's hands. She looked at it, bent her head to look closer.

'Oh!' she said with a little gasp. 'Oh; that isn't Kathleen. It is Miss Christine!'

PART II

TWENTY-FIVE YEARS AGO

CHAPTER I

JULY 1914

In the big park at Chatterleys were two acres of closely mown grass surrounded by a fence of movable posts and wire. The fence was down now and its place was taken partly by a row of benches, whilst at one side there was a large marquee and a collection of deck and garden chairs. In the middle of the mown grass thirteen white figures, with two others white above and dark below, were disporting themselves for their own amusement and that of the occupants of the chairs and benches.

This was, in fact, the first match of the famous Chatterleys Cricket Week, the match between Sir Brandon Wayke's XI and a team of Free Foresters. Most of Sir Brandon's side and some of the Foresters were staying at Chatterleys itself – it was a two days' match – whilst others were at Festing Manor, Colonel Widdington's house at the other side of the park, or at other of the hospitable country houses in the neighbourhood.

It was a hot afternoon in late July, and there were many brightly coloured parasols in the neighbourhood of the marquee, whilst the one group of sycamores near the edge of the ground was heavily patronised for its grateful shade. Out in the middle the men who were running about in this sweltering heat seemed hardly conscious of it; at this late stage of the season devout cricketers were acclimatised to sun, and in any case it is always cooler to run about in it than to sit. The home team were batting, and the plum, green and white striped caps of the fielding Foresters gave a pleasant air of uniformity to the scene.

The score board showed 80: 2: 13. A young man in an I. Zingari cap was cracking the ball lustily to all parts of the field in the good old-fashioned style of country-house cricket, whilst an older man in a panama was keeping up his end and wishing that there was not so much running between the wickets. In the two hours before luncheon the Free Foresters had scored 180 for three wickets, but Sir Brandon's famous cider cup had been too much for them and the later batsmen had been shot out in the post-prandial hour by a local Kort-right for a mere 70 further runs. So now, faced with the unexpectedly low total of 250, the home team were reasonably well placed, and if the young hero in the I. Z. cap continued to play as at present, by tea-time they would be on terms.

On comfortable chairs in the shade of the sycamores sat two middle-aged ladies; they wore long dresses, one of silk, the other of taffeta, elaborately looped and draped, reaching to within an inch or two of the ground. A few inches of black silk stocking were visible and their feet were encased in tight, sharply pointed shoes. Large picture hats, perched precariously upon high and puffed-out coiffures, gave a rather skittish appearance to the ageing faces below.

The elder of the two was Mrs. Widdington, wife of the owner of Festing Manor; with her was her old friend Mrs. Morton Beale, who was staying at the Manor together with her daughter Miriam, for, while young men were the essentials of a cricket week, they expected young ladies to amuse them when the labours of the day were done.

From the shade of the sycamores the view of the cricket was not ideal because there was a constant promenade of spectators walking backwards and forwards between the trees and the boundary. This did not bother Mrs. Beale, who, having no man of her own engaged in the game, was able and willing to give her whole attention to her neighbours. Mrs. Widdington, on the other hand, had eyes for no one but the players; she would much have preferred a chair on the boundary itself, from which she could have got an uninterrupted view, but Gladys Beale had declared that her complexion would not stand the sun. To her companion's chatter Mrs. Widdington gave only half an ear, as her eyes followed every movement of the young man in the Zingari cap, whose white blade was flashing so brilliantly in the sunshine.

A sudden round of clapping drew everyone's attention to the game; someone was putting the figures 50 at the bottom of the score-board.

'What is it, dear?' asked Mrs. Beale. 'Is somebody out?'

'No. Jim has got his fifty.'

'Oh, has he? How clever of him. Who is that attractive child with Miriam?'

But Mrs. Widdington had given a little gasp and her eyes seemed to be following the flight of a bird into the sky. The young batsman, elated by the applause, had tried to lift the slow bowler over the boundary, his stroke had been played a fraction too soon and the ball was soaring high into the air; it reached its zenith, hovered a moment, and then fell steeply down into the safe hands of the Forester standing in front of the tea-tent. Jim Widdington retired amid a storm of applause, raising his cap an inch or two in acknowledgment before reaching the line of chairs.

Mrs. Widdington's eyes sparkled with pride and she clapped vigorously with the rest. Mrs. Beale, after a perfunctory gesture, returned to the subject which interested her.

'Who is the girl with Miriam?' she asked again.

Mrs. Widdington brought her thoughts back to her guest. She looked about her. A few yards to the right, talking to one of the batting side, stood two girls. The shorter of the two was talking vivaciously to the cricketer; her long flowered-muslin dress was beautifully made, though it could not hide the dumpiness of her figure. The other was an inch or two taller; she wore a simple white frock and a straw hat trimmed with pale blue, beneath which waves of thick chestnut-coloured hair were visible. She had the beautiful natural carriage of a healthy young animal, but her movements were correspondingly gawky. She was not joining in the conversation, but her grey eyes were alive with interest as she listened to her companions.

'Oh, that is Christine – Christine Wayke,' said Mrs. Widdington. 'She is just back from Paris.'

'Finishing? She hardly looks it.'

Mrs. Widdington laughed.

'Far from it; she hasn't begun. She has been in a convent. Her father has had her very strictly brought up and I doubt if the poor child will get a London season at all. You know about her mother, of course?'

'Her mother?' asked Mrs. Beale vaguely. 'Oh, yes, I do remember there was something funny about that second marriage; an actress or something, wasn't she?'

'She was Jennie Moon.'

'Oh, yes, of course she was. *Daly's* or *The Gaiety*, or something like that. I remember seeing her photograph, but Morton never cared much about musical shows.'

'She was the loveliest little thing,' said Mrs. Widdington. 'She was still very young when Brandon married her, but already half London was in love with her. She danced divinely and had a pretty voice too, though it was rather light. Brandon had been deeply in love with his first wife, and when she died he was completely knocked out. He was a serious young man and a keen soldier – the only one in the Blues, Jack always says, but I am sure that is a libel. Anyhow, when Blanche died he went all to pieces; he told his friends that he was going to send in his papers and go right away, though he had Dick and Helen, quite young children still, to look after. Then he met Jennie somewhere and she got hold of him and twisted herself round his heart. I don't mean that unkindly; she was not a designing little minx; she fell genuinely in love with him – he was very handsome then – even though he was a good deal older than her.'

'How old *is* he?' asked Mrs. Beale.

'He must be sixty now. That would make him nearly forty when he married. Perhaps I was wrong in speaking of him as a serious young man; he must have been a senior captain then, but he was serious all right. Anyhow, Jennie captured him and they were married in a few weeks. Of course; he had to leave the Regiment, but he had Chatterleys to look after then – his father died just before Blanche. They settled down here and it looked as if they would be ideally happy.'

'And why weren't they?'

Mrs. Widdington hesitated. She was very fond of Brandon Wayke and she did not want to rake up old troubles. But she had said a word too much and she knew that Gladys Beale would give her no peace till she had explained it. After all, Gladys was one of her oldest friends; she would not let it go any further.

'Jennie was a little wild,' she said. 'A real darling but she *was* wild. She loved being down here ... for about a month, and then she was mad to go back to London and dance and have a good time. Brandon humoured her at first but when he knew that there was going to be a child he tried to keep her down here. She wouldn't do it. Brandon could be hard – too stern for a little butterfly like Jennie – and she used her wings. She ran away to London. He followed her and brought her back. She ran away again and Brandon went to London to look after her there and try to keep her reasonably quiet. She ... I think she was a little too fond of champagne and things. She wouldn't take care of herself when Christine was coming but insisted on still going on having a good time, dancing and every mad thing. She kept herself going on champagne, and when Christine was born she died.'

'Poor thing,' said Mrs. Beale, looking with greater interest at Christine Wayke. 'Does she take after her mother? In looks, I mean.'

'She's not nearly so pretty – not at present, anyhow; she may become so.'

'If she does she will break a lot of hearts,' said Mrs. Beale, wishing that Miriam would not choose to walk with a girl whose unformed figure was even now so much more beautiful than her own.

'You'll have to keep an eye on your Jim.'

Mrs. Widdington laughed.

'Jim thinks of no one but Helen,' she said.

'The half-sister? Really? Are they engaged?'

'Not officially, but they've been devoted to each other all their lives. Helen and my Mary have been practically brought up together and Jim has always been their hero.'

So much the worse for their chance of a happy married life, thought Mrs. Beale, but she was too wise to say so.

'Here they come,' said Grace Widdington, looking with fond pride at the tall figure of her son walking towards them between two girls, each with an arm through his. The taller of the two was a splendid young creature, fair haired, her fresh complexion healthily tanned by an open-air life. The other, slighter and shorter, was also fair but she looked delicate by comparison with Helen Wayke. Jim Widdington looked thoroughly well pleased with himself, proud of his innings, happy in the companionship of the two girls of whom he was so fond. His own tanned face was still flushed with his exertions and his blond moustache, curled upwards and outwards, gave him the slightly stupid look of the traditional Guardsman.

But Jim Widdington was no fool; slow-witted perhaps, but with any amount of common sense. He was a keen and serious soldier and a born leader of men.

'Darling, that was splendid,' said his mother gently. She longed to jump up and hug him but two generations of Widdington men had taught her not to be demonstrative, especially in public.

'Glad you liked it, mum; Helen has been ticking me off for losing my head.'

'He wasn't thinking of his side,' said Helen calmly. She, too, was bursting with pride but she was not going to let Jim get swelled head.

'Of course he was,' said Mary Widdington, quick to defend her brother. 'That twiddly bowler is dangerous; if Jim had knocked him off his length the others would have made all the runs we want. Now they'll scratch at him and get out.'

She, too, wore the black, red and yellow of I. Zingari in a thin riband round her soft straw hat. She was an ardent follower of the game and had only handed over her duties as scorer in order to worship for half an hour at her brother's shrine.

Mrs. Beale looked enviously at the group. Jim Widdington was extremely handsome, she thought. He was wearing a double-breasted blue serge coat with brass buttons, the 'boating-jacket' of the Brigade of Guards. A white scarf was tucked round his neck and his straw hat had a dark red and blue riband. Yes, very handsome, and he had money. He would have done splendidly for Miriam but that dream must vanish; if Jim took after his father he would be very faithful to one woman. She herself knew that only too well.

'Look; he's got Peter stumped.'

'And they're coming in to tea. Come on, mum; come on, Mrs. Beale; I've bagged a table for us.'

Jim led the way into the hot and stuffy tent, answering the congratulations and chaff of his friends with a pleasant smile.

Mrs. Beale looked round to summon Miriam but she saw that the girl was still engaged with the rather over-blown major to whom she had been talking before. Christine Wayke had disappeared.

Dinner at Chatterleys that night was a gay event. The house-party was augmented by the party from Festing Manor. There was to be a litttle dancing afterwards, not a late affair, because there were still three days' strenuous cricket ahead, but enough to ensure that the ladies should have their share of the week's enjoyment. The home team were well pleased with themselves; in reply to the Free Foresters' 250 they had compiled a respectable 223, rather laboriously after the departure of their star, but enough for honour. If their fast bowler was in form tomorrow they might even yet give the Foresters a shock.

Jim Widdington did not find himself next to Helen; she, as hostess, was at the head of the table with two of the elder guests on each side of her. He was between the wife of one of the visiting team and Christine Wayke. He had not seen much of Christine since her return from Paris; she seemed a nice-looking kid but had not got much to say for herself. He decided that his duty lay with the married woman on his right, an entertaining lady who was very ready to devote herself to the attractive young Guardsman.

On Christine's other side was Peter Drake, a brother officer of Jim's. Helen, who wanted Christine to enjoy her first dinner party, had specially chosen these two young men to sit next to her half-sister; Jim would of course be sweet to her and Peter was amusing and easy to get on with.

For some time Christine did not benefit by this arrangement. Jim seemed entirely taken up with Mrs. Godfrey and the man on her left presented only a shoulder to her. She was too inexperienced to seize the little opportunities that presented themselves of attracting some attention to herself, so she concentrated on her food, which seemed to her a miracle of goodness. From time to time she glanced down the table and once, as she was trying the champagne – the first she had ever drunk – she caught the eye of her father, who frowned at her. Why should he do that, she wondered anxiously? She looked down at her dress; nothing wrong there – except that it was very high and maidenly compared with those of the other women. Perhaps she ought to be talking to one of her neighbours – but they both had their backs to her. Perhaps she wasn't sitting up straight – but the Mother Superior had attended to that.

Christine gave up the problem and tried a little more champagne. It wasn't very nice, but the effect was exciting. There had only been a little and she thought she would like some more, but to her annoyance Badger appeared with a jug of lemonade and poured that into one of the other glasses. Probably Father had . . .

'I say, I think you might talk to me. Why are you looking so cross?'

The man on her left was speaking to her. She saw a plain face with a snub nose and a moustache too big for its surroundings, but the eyes above were jolly.

'I'm not. . . I mean . . . it was you who wasn't talking.'

That sounded hopeless. The convent lessons in deportment had not prepared her for conversation with strange young men.

'I thought you'd have eyes for no one but Jim,' said the young man. 'He's the hero to-day. Didn't he play well?'

'I'm afraid I don't know much about cricket,' said Christine.

'Good. Nor do I, really, though I do enjoy this sort. It's awfully good of your father to have us all here. You've just come from Paris, haven't you? That must have been a lark.'

Christine looked steadily at him with her large grey eyes and Peter Drake suddenly wondered why he had been wasting the last twenty minutes on the over-decorated lady on his left.

'I didn't notice the lark. I was in a convent. Four years.'

'Oh, lord. That sounds rather grim. I thought you'd been doing the Opera and theatres and all the sights.'

Christine smiled.

'We hardly went outside the walls, except for music lessons and one or two rather dull concerts. That's why I'm so dull to talk to.'

Peter grinned.

'Don't you believe it,' he said. 'You've got a twinkle in your eye ... besides other advantages. I say, who is it that old Jim's so taken up with?'

Christine laughed.

'I don't know. It obviously isn't me, is it?'

'So much the better,' said Peter, slipping a little deeper into his eighteenth heart-break. 'Will you dance with me after dinner – all the time, I mean?'

'I can't dance ... at least ... we've got to go.' Helen, collecting eyes, had risen, and Christine followed demurely in the wake of her dazzling elders. Peter Drake watched her with a beating heart.

'I say, Jim,' he whispered to his friend, 'you didn't tell me what a stunner you'd got down here.'

Jim Widdington stared at him.

'Who are you talking about?' he said.

'Why, Miss Wayke, of course.' Then, seeing the surprise in his friend's eyes he blundered on. 'Not your girl ... I mean ... of course, she's grand too, but I meant her sister. Dash it, you've been sitting next her all the evening.'

Jim laughed.

'Oh, Christine,' he said. 'I hadn't noticed. Is she? You've got such a susceptible heart, Peter. Come on, one glass of port and no more because you've got to make a lot more runs tomorrow than you did today. I hope we shan't have our leave stopped before the week's finished.'

'You don't really think there'll be a war, do you?' asked Peter Drake, torn between the rival attractions of Mars and Venus.

'I think it's a certainty,' said Jim gravely. 'Russia won't let the Austrians swallow Serbia and if they mobilise the Germans'll do the same. That will bring in France and then us.'

At the other end of the table the older men were discussing the same subject. Colonel Widdington, an old Grenadier himself, who had lost an arm in South Africa, had taken his glass of port down to his host's end of the table.

'I wish to God we'd got a decent Government,' he was saying. 'These damned Liberals are just as likely as not to try and keep out of it.'

'Nonsense, Jack,' said Sir Brandon. 'Asquith's sound enough and so's Winston, though I don't trust that fellow Lloyd George. But it's always a Liberal Government that leads us into a war; the other countries think they won't fight at any price. Look at Aberdeen and the Crimea.'

But Colonel Widdington was not a student of political history; he was a practical soldier and he turned the subject to machine-guns; the Russo-Japanese war, he said, had taught the Germans their value and it had, as usual, taught us nothing.

The butler came into the room and murmured in Sir Brandon's ear, then came round to Jim Widdington.

'You're wanted on the telephone, sir?' he said.

Jim went out of the room and presently returned, his face grave. He went up to his host.

'I'm afraid Peter and I will have to get back to Aldershot, sir,' he said. 'All leave's been cancelled.'

Colonel Widdington looked at his son in silence, but his face had suddenly grown very old. All the men rose to their feet.

'That will affect some of the others, too,' said Sir Brandon quietly.

Two other soldiers in the room agreed that they were bound to receive their recall at any time and had better make their preparations.

'And young Ricketts from Foxley, and I believe two others of the Foresters are serving soldiers. It puts an end to this match,' said Sir Brandon,' but we may be able to arrange a pick-up. It would be a pity to upset everyone more than is necessary. After all, this is only precautionary; there may be no mobilisation.'

No one in the room now thought that this was more than a gallant attempt to avert gloom. Certainly no one felt inclined to sit down and drink more port, so a move was made to the drawing-room. Sir Brandon broke the news as calmly as possible, and Jim Widdington and Peter Drake began to say their farewells. Unfortunately, everybody thought it necessary to troop out into the big hall to see them off, so that Jim had no chance to say a private good-bye to Helen Wayke. Both of them wanted to, but each was afraid of doing anything in the slightest degree emotional or melodramatic. Deep feeling could only be relieved by apparently lighthearted chaff.

Mary Widdington clung to her brother's arm as they walked out to the little two-seater Straker-Squire that crouched in a corner of the drive. Peter Drake lagged behind, trying to find Christine Wayke. He caught sight of her in a corner of the hall, looking out of the window. He slipped back.

'Good-bye, Miss Wayke,' he said, trying to squeeze a romantic note out of his workaday voice.

'Good-bye,' said Christine quietly, holding out her hand. Peter took it and did not let it go.

'I say . . . if we go out . . . would you write to me?'

The girl looked at Peter with her big grey eyes but did not answer, though she quietly released her hand. Peter longed to fling his arms round her and kiss her, but even this promising young philanderer felt abashed in front of anyone so young and innocent.

'Well, I shall write to you,' he said with a laugh.

'Come on, Peter,' came a voice from the drive. Peter hurried out.

Jim Widdington was being very calm and reassuring. 'This'll blow over,' he was saying to Mary and Helen. 'We shall probably be back in ten days or a fortnight. Anyhow, if we do have to go out we shall get 'good-bye' leave before we go.'

There was no 'good-bye' leave. A fortnight later the Expeditionary Force slipped quietly across the Channel before anyone even knew that they were going.

WOUNDED

Jim Widdington sat on the hard seat of a French railway carriage and tried to make himself believe that he was no longer in hell. The carriage was for sitting cases and was attached to a hospital train that was slowly making its way westwards from Poperinghe to the coast. Jim's head was bandaged; a splinter of shell had struck him just below the right temple, embedding itself in the thick bone just above the jaw socket; an inch higher and Jim would not have been a sitting case . . . or, indeed, a case of any kind. As it was, the sliver of steel had cut the large artery and he had lost a great deal of blood, so that he looked white as well as haggard. There was nothing serious about the wound but the Casualty Clearing Stations were so full that the surgeons could only cope with urgent operations and minor cases were being sent down to the base hospital.

It was not the wound that made Widdington look and feel like a ghost; it was lack of sleep. After the prolonged strain of the retreat from Mons, the advance to the Aisne and the fighting on the slopes above that river had been almost exhilarating. Then had come the transfer of the B.E.F. to the left of the line and the fearful ordeal of the first battle of Ypres. For nights and days on end the thin lines of British troops had clung to their hastily dug trenches under a storm of shell fire that seemed never to cease; the German infantry, in the gallant folly of mass formation, had flung themselves again and again towards the shell-torn lines, sometimes to be driven back with terrible loss, sometimes to surge over the few survivors and stop for lack of leadership when there was nothing else to stop them.

For the exhausted British soldiers there was no rest. Days and nights on end they watched, shot, dug, shot and watched again, till their eyes could hardly focus and the very trees and bushes in front of them sometimes looked like attacking Germans, and a weary officer would call his men to arms and fling volleys of fire into emptiness. Sleep was seldom possible except in short snatches that seemed to intensify the need for sleep, and when relief came and the weary men had staggered back to 'reserve trenches' a few hundred yards back, there was still no sleep; reserve meant counter-attack ... or, at the best, counter-march in response to some false alarm, and return to the front line became almost welcome.

How mortal men endured those weeks of sleepless exhaustion was almost as great a mystery as how they survived, a few of them, the plunging shells, the whistling shrapnel, the streams of bullets and the bayonet's steel. But some survived and Ypres was held, and in four and a half years of concentrated effort to capture it no German set his foot in the old Cathedral town save as a prisoner of war.

Steadily the streams of wounded poured back, in train and ambulance and car and even on foot, towards the base, passing on their way the meagre reinforcements hurrying up to take their place. But the lightly wounded 'sitting cases' seemed to take little interest in these encouraging signs; they watched with eyes that held no light; they were tired, desperately tired. They knew that for the time their personal ordeal was over, but they were too numbed by exhaustion even to appreciate that wonderful release from the hell of war.

At the back of Jim Widdington's mind was a gnawing discomfort. He felt that he should not be in this train, running through peaceful country, running away from the blood and turmoil where his comrades were still struggling to hold back the swarming Germans. He could stand, though he was weak; he had his legs, his hands, his eyes ... almost useless though they were. He ought to be back in the line ... back in the line ...

He had been unconscious when he was carried to the field dressing-station, and could only dimly remember jolting through the night over the shell-pocked road – the Menin road – in some iron-tyred wagon. He had expected to have his wound dressed at the C.C.S. in Ypres and to be sent back at once. When he was told that he would be sent down to the base he had protested that he must get back to the line, and had been told curtly that he would go where he was sent. But he was conscious that his protests had been half-hearted, that he had not really tried to get back, that he was escaping from the horror in which his friends and his men – the few of them who still survived – were still playing their heroic part.

The journey would have been maddening to men whose nerves were not deadened by fatigue. At times the train ran swiftly enough but often it limped slowly from stop to stop, clearing the line for east-bound traffic, troop trains, ammunition trains, supply trains, hospital trains returning empty to collect another pitiful load of shattered men.

In Widdington's compartment there were eight soldiers, all officers like himself, but they hardly spoke to one another, sitting for the most part in wide-eyed apathy. Once, at a larger railway station, some good Samaritan brought cups of tea and cigarettes, and for a time they woke up and talked with some show of animation, but within a quarter of an hour they had relapsed into silence. It began to get dark and sleep became easier, the sleep which they so badly needed but were too exhausted easily to find. The man next to Widdington slumped against his shoulder; Jim shook him off with a burst of irritation, but before long he was back again and the young Grenadier let him stay.

At last the lights of a big town appeared, shrouded as far as possible but unmistakable from the train. The sight awoke real interest in the wounded men; there would be a bed to sleep in now, a bed for the first time for many weeks. The luxury seemed unbelievable, and one young fellow burst into hysterical tears as the thought brought memories of happy days to him.

Slowly the train came to a standstill. Kind hands helped them down on to the low platform. French railway officials, a British R.T.O., R.M.C. orderlies, women voluntary workers, bustled about and shepherded those who could walk to a waiting ambulance. A group of French civilians stared and murmured sympathetically. The ambulance bumped slowly over cobbles and in five minutes pulled up before an hotel. More orderlies and some V.A.D. nurses helped them out and led them through a hall, up stairs, and along a corridor where men lay on stretchers so closely packed that it was hard not to tread on them.

At that early stage of the war there was no segregation of ranks to different hospitals; the flow of wounded was too great for that. The wounded were taken wherever there seemed to be room, and only in the hospital itself could the officers be sorted out and put into rooms separate from their men. Jim Widdington found himself in a small room with three other officers, one of whom had travelled with him. There was a bed for each, and in that they were lucky; a large proportion of their men would lie on the stretchers on which they had travelled or on mattresses upon the floor, some in wards – the hotel bedrooms, sitting-rooms, billiard-room – some in the passages, some even on the stairs.

The smell of the place would have sickened anyone not hardened to it; chloroform, iodoform, the smell of blood and dirt and sweat, the more terrible stench of gangrene and putrefaction. Nobody seemed to notice it; the hospital workers had lived in it for weeks, the wounded had left worse smells behind. A few visitors came and were staggered by it, blenched and hardened themselves to face it, went out again and drew deep breaths of sea air to clear their lungs.

An orderly told the new-comers to undress and get into bed. Pyjamas made by loving but unskilled hands drew the first laugh that Jim had heard for many a day; the arms of his jacket emerged from half-way up the sides, so that a large part of the garment clung round his neck and his middle was bare; his companion had trousers which opened at the back! They got into bed and waited, hoping for some food, longing for a drink and a smoke. An R.M.C. captain came in with a nursing sister, had a look at the tags on their uniform jackets, said a cheerful word, promised to examine them in the morning and went out. Half an hour later came plates of tinned chicken and – miracle of miracles – a bottle of champagne, the gift of a rich man who really knew what was wanted. Ten minutes after the last drop was finished, Jim Widdington was asleep.

*

He woke twelve hours later, feeling immeasurably better. The one blessing of the over-crowding was that the nursing staff could not get everybody up at five in the morning. They had too much work to do and washing and bed-making had to wait. When at last Jim was awakened he was told by the orderly to stay in bed till 'the major' came to examine him; a plate of bacon, a chunk of bread, and a mug of scalding tea added to his sense of well-being, but ten minutes after it was finished he was asleep again. He was re-awakened an hour later to find the R.M.C. major standing beside his bed, smiling sympathetically down at him.

'Sorry to wake you,' the doctor said. 'I expect you need all you can get. I must just look at your wound.'

The bandages were removed by a nurse, the doctor's sensitive fingers felt round the wound, it was washed with warm water and iodoform, a fresh dressing applied and the bandages rewound.

'All right at the moment, but that'll have to come out. Might cause trouble.'

'Can it be done soon? I ought to get back.'

The doctor shook his head.

'Not a chance. Operating theatre's needed for urgent cases. Yours can wait. They'll do it in England.'

England! Was he going back to England? He had not for a moment expected it, hardly thought of it; it was too wonderful to be true. Then that horrible gnawing conscience re-awakened.

'I can't go to England,' Jim said. 'This isn't anything. I must get back.'

For a second the older man let his hand rest on Jim's shoulder.

'That's all right, my lad,' he said. 'You'll get back . . . only too soon.'

He turned on his heel. Jim Widdington felt the prick of tears in his eyes, tears of weakness, of relief, of shame; he slid down in the bed and pulled up the coarse sheets to his face as he struggled to control the sobs that shook him.

The boat was crowded with wounded men, most of them on stretchers or in the few bunks available; in the smoking saloon were the officer sitting cases. There was still very little talk; the same look of blank exhaustion was on almost every face. One officer tried to collect a bridge four; he did not succeed; nobody's brain could cope with bridge.

It was a still day and the port-holes on one side were open. Jim watched the harbour walls slip past, saw the squat battlements of the fort with its ancient guns, and then . . . the sea, the English Channel! Slowly he pulled himself to his feet and walked to the door, opened it and stepped on to the deck. The salt air invigorated him but when he tried to walk he realised how weak he still was and he had to cling to the rail that ran along the outer wall of the saloon. He looked at the grey sea slipping past; ahead was the low form of a destroyer; behind, the shores of France were fading into the low horizon. France, the war, behind him!

The white cliffs of Dover were a thrill that drew every man who could stand to the deck or to port-holes of the saloon. It was beginning to get dark but the glimmering bastions of England were not the less beautiful for that and everybody's heart beat the faster at the sight of them. As the boat warped alongside the jetty the sight of English civilians and especially of English women brought a new realisation of home that few of these men who had been through the hell of Ypres had hoped to see again. There was light in the tired eyes now and voices took on a ring of cheerfulness that had not been heard even on the way over the water.

The journey to London was a miracle of speed and comfort and very soon everyone was crowding to the windows to see the dimmed lights of the suburbs slipping by. It was quite dark now and the Thames was hardly visible, but a minute or two later the train was in Charing Cross and the bustle of detrainment had begun. It was still early enough in the war for crowds to collect to watch the arrival of wounded men from the front. As he drove out of the station Jim Widdington saw the white faces and waving hands of the watchers; he had dim memories of seeing wounded men come back from South Africa when he was a boy, and of thinking how wonderful it must be to return as a blood-stained hero; he realised with surprised amusement that he must himself be a 'hero' now. In the excitement of the moment the thought was a pleasant one and he forgot the plaguings of conscience which had so greatly depressed him in France.

Before getting into the ambulance he had been told that he was going to Mrs. George Bazeley's hospital. The name was familiar to him as that of an extremely rich woman who entertained lavishly, and he knew that she had a large house in Grosvenor Square; he even thought that he had once been to a dance there, but as during the season he seldom had less than three dance invitations a night his memory on the subject was rather hazy.

The drive was a short one and very soon the door of the big house opened to let out a blaze of light and a rush of smart-looking nurses. Mrs. Bazeley herself received the four officers who had been allotted to her. She was a tall and very decorative lady of about forty, and she greeted each arrival with a warmth and friendliness that was almost embarrassing. In spite – or because – of the excitement, Jim Widdington was beginning to feel extremely tired and he was glad to get to his ward and to be undressed and tucked into bed. He would have preferred to undress himself, especially as the nurse who fussed over him looked as if she might have been one of his earlier dance-partners, but she seemed to regard it as her duty to treat him as a child and he was too tired now to argue.

Soup, chicken – not tinned this time – and more champagne were his delicious and much needed dinner, but he was not allowed to drop asleep until a handsome young civilian doctor had examined his wound. Jim did not listen to the murmurings of doctor and sister, and as soon as they were gone he snuggled down into the white linen sheets that seemed such a luxury to him now, and fell asleep.

Mrs. Bazeley's hospital was only too rigorously efficient and correct in the matter of early waking and washing. Jim felt that he had only been asleep a few minutes when he was woken and thermometered and washed and his bed made, all by the 'dancing-partner' of the previous night. He suggested mildly that he was capable of doing most of these things for himself, but he was briskly told that until the doctor had pronounced upon him he must be regarded as a cot case. He had about two hours to wait for breakfast and resented the early calling, as hospital patients in their pitiful ignorance always do.

The doctor when he came was not the smart young man of the previous evening – a mere house-surgeon, as he later discovered – but a grave elderly gentleman in a tail coat and grey whiskers. He was accompanied by Matron, ward-sister, dressing-sister, and a young probationer pushing the dressing-trolley. Jim was too much taken up with the seniors to notice that the probationer, a young and attractive girl, smiled at him as she hovered in the unimportant background.

The grave doctor decided that the piece of steel should come out of Jim's jaw on the following morning, and that in the meantime he would stay in bed. The great man and his satellites passed on and Jim's wound was dressed and re-bandaged. This time, as the sister moved on to the next bed, Jim did catch the shy smile of the probationer as she followed; he returned it, wondering whether the vaguely familiar face was that of another dancing-partner.

For most of the morning Jim dozed, but in the afternoon came the thrill of a visit from his mother and father. Colonel Widdington was gruff and rather silent, his only way of expressing emotion, but Mrs. Widdington's love and tenderness quickly melted a great deal of the strained anxiety from which her son was still suffering. For half an hour they talked in whispers, not about the war but about home and friends, so that Jim felt the dark clouds of horror slowly lift from his mind. He had hardly realised how much the strain and agony of war had affected him, but Grace Widdington saw that her son who a few weeks ago had left her as a boy had come back a man who would never be really young again.

It was a blow to Jim to hear that Helen Wayke had gone to France to drive a Red Cross ambulance. He had not thought much about her during the weeks of marching and fighting, but it had been a comfort to have her at the back of his mind, to think about when he had time to think. He was very fond of Helen, had been all his life; he would not have described himself as madly in love, but then he did not regard himself as a passionate type of man, as some of his friends were. He and Helen would almost certainly marry some day, but neither of them was in a hurry.

His sister, Mary, he heard, was nursing in one of the big London hospitals; she was sure to come and see him as soon as she was off duty. Mrs. Widdington thought that Christine Wayke was also training as a V.A.D. somewhere in London, but she did not know where. Dick Wayke had joined the Flying Corps and was already in France. Sir Brandon was very busy running a recruiting campaign in Warwickshire; he did not often come to London.

When his parents had gone Jim Widdington lay back in bed and thought over the news that they had given him. He was ashamed to find how little interested he was in it all, how little he really cared what his friends were doing. He had lost many of his brother officers during the last two and a half months; the Grenadiers had not been heavily engaged at Mons or during the retreat, except at Villers Cotterêts, but there had been many casualties on the Aisne and during the Ypres fighting the officer losses had been terribly severe. Exhaustion had helped to soften the blow which the death of so many friends meant, because everyone was numbed by it and hardly able to realise the terrible truth. Even now, away from the fighting and back in a comfortable hospital, Jim was too tired really to care very deeply.

Mary did not appear till after nine o'clock that night – not a visiting hour, but as a nurse on day duty she was privileged. The warmth of her greeting really did bring Jim back to life for a time. She forced him to talk a little about himself – and it was good for him to get some of his troubles off his chest – but she was quick to note the look of strain creep back into his eyes after a time and then she switched over to her own doings, her adventures in a 'professional' hospital – with a note of amused patronage for the luxury affair in which Jim found himself.

'They only send light cases here,' she said with a smile, adding maliciously, in an undertone which would not reach the other ward-patients, 'and only the best-looking ones at that.'

Jim laughed and fondled the moustache that had lost some of its swagger in the last weeks.

'We have the best-looking nurses, too,' he said.

Mary raised her eyebrows.

'Oh, you've noticed that, have you?' she asked. 'I imagined you were too ill to have an eye for beauty. Christine said you wouldn't condescend to notice her.'

'Christine?' Jim stared. 'Oh . . . you mean the kid-sister; what about her?'

Mary laughed.

'I bet you won't call her that to her face . . . twice. And you really never noticed her? She was just going out as I came in; she told me that she stood by your bed for half an hour this morning and you didn't so much as bat an eye at her. She was pushing the dressing-trolley.'

CHAPTER III

CONVALESCENT

Jim Widdington's operation was a very modest affair, but it involved an anæsthetic and a lot of bandages, and these facts alone had a mollifying effect upon Jim's conscience. He no longer felt that he ought never to have left the line; obviously these things could not have been done in a field dressing-station and equally obviously there was plenty of time for him to get back there again as soon as he was fit. The fighting at Ypres had died down and his battalion was out, resting and reorganising: so much he had heard from a Coldstreamer in the same brigade who had been brought in to his ward on the previous evening.

For the rest of the day, after the operation, Jim felt sleepy and rather sick, but the following morning he felt wonderfully better and when the house-surgeon and dressing-sister came round he greeted the trolley-nurse with a cheerful grin, to which Christine Wayke responded with a friendly and very attractive smile. With an eye to hospital discipline he did not speak to her but he had a word later on with one of the junior nurses in his ward, as a result of which Christine snatched five minutes from her brief dinner-hour and came to talk to him.

Jim was struck by her attractiveness; he had hardly noticed her at Chatterleys but now he saw that she was an extremely pretty girl. Perhaps it was the uniform that became her, or possibly the simple fact that he had not looked at a woman at all with an appraising eye since he left England early in August. She was not a bit like Helen. She had chestnut-coloured hair, whereas Helen was fair: she was slim, whereas Helen, though in no way fat, was big-boned and strong. She had none of Helen's serene confidence and self-assurance but seemed shy and awkward. Jim found the shyness rather charming.

They talked mostly about Helen. The girl told him that her sister had gone straight up to London as soon as war was declared and, pulling every string to which she could lay her competent hands, had given the Red Cross authorities no peace until they sent her out to France to pester somebody else; Helen was now driving an ambulance and had mentioned a place called St. Omer.

The conversation did not last long, as Nurse Wayke had to get back to duty, but Jim had enjoyed it and he looked forward to the time when he was allowed out of hospital and might take his young friend out to dinner and a show. His mother had promised to send him up some civilian clothes; it would be a real treat to get into them.

Mrs. George Bazeley was enjoying herself. For the last two or three years, ever since she passed the accommodating age of thirty-nine, she had been conscious that life, the amusing part of life, was slipping away from her. She had made the fatal mistake of marrying young, and in the first flush of enthusiasm had given her husband a son and a daughter in quick succession. The son was all right, he was great fun and his friends even more so, but the daughter was now out and that fact, however much one joked about it and tried to enjoy it, did take the gilt off a London season's gingerbread.

Her husband was no use to her. He had been an extremely dashing and attractive young Guardsman with a lot of money when she married him, but recently he had taken up politics and gone all serious. He never took her out now, never went to dances or to Ciro's or to anywhere amusing. Fortunately he was very good about money, let her have all she wanted, and did not make a fuss about her entertaining and going about with other people without him; but even in these enlightened neo-Georgian days a married woman without her husband was at a certain disadvantage – especially now that she had a grown-up daughter to chaperone.

So Clarice Bazeley welcomed the war, with all its excitement and activities. The risk to George and Freddie, of course, was dreadful to think about; George had re-joined his regiment and Freddie, who was a

Territorial, had gone out to Egypt as A.D.C. to dear old Billy Walborough, who had always been so good to her. But in between the moments of anxiety there was a great deal of fun to be had . . . and the hospital had been an inspiration! The hospital kept her in touch with all that was going on; the authorities – Jack Pillow was a very big medical noise at the War Office – had been wonderfully good about sending her just the sort of wounded officers she wanted, mostly Guardsmen and Riflemen and Cavalrymen – the best cavalry regiments, of course.

And these poor wounded men were so very delightful, so friendly, so pathetically grateful for everything that was being done for them. Fortunately most of them were not very badly wounded and they were able to talk and chaff, and when they were allowed up she could have them to tea in the little sitting-room which was all, except her bedroom and bathroom and, of course, the dining-room, which she had kept for her own use. And when they were discharged from hospital, as some of them were now beginning to be, they were terribly sweet about taking her out to dinner and a show or a nightclub. Really she was having much more fun and excitement now than she had had in the season itself – especially since Gloria, as a V.A.D. probationer, was much too tired after her day's duty to do anything but go to bed and sleep. That was the one advantage one had over the young – one could do with much less sleep.

Of all the young men who had so far come into her hospital Mrs. Bazeley thought that there was none so handsome as Jim Widdington. He was extraordinarily like George as George had been when she fell in love with and married him. At the impressionable age of eighteen she had thought her young Guardsman a very god of manly beauty, with his broad shoulders and narrow hips, his fair hair and lazy blue eyes, his curled and brushed-up moustache; at the even more impressionable age of forty-two she did not think of Jim Widdington as a god but she did very much want him to make love to her. The thought of being kissed by that beautiful moustache gave Clarice Bazeley a very delicious thrill.

Within a week of his operation Jim Widdington was discharged from hospital and appeared before a medical board, which gave him a fortnight's leave. He went home to Festing Manor and was fussed over by his mother and idolised by her staff and the villagers. What pleased him more was that his father treated him seriously as a soldier and asked endless questions about the fighting in France, methods of supply, the effect of shell-fire from the German heavy guns and howitzers, and more particularly their use of machine-guns. At the age of fifty-five and with his empty sleeve, Colonel Widdington had little hope of getting to France himself, but he was doing active work on the Territorial Association, and the War Office held out hopes of employment in training Kitchener's Army.

On the day after his arrival Jim walked over to Chatterleys to pay his respects to Sir Brandon Wayke, and found himself being cross-examined upon questions of major strategy and imperial politics which were rather beyond his scope, but the old man was very kind to him and showed him the letters he had had from Helen and was evidently very proud of his elder daughter's courage and enterprise. Sir Brandon did not talk much about Christine, but he was glad to hear that Jim had been in the hospital where 'his little girl' was working, and asked him to say a kind word to her occasionally when he returned to duty.

The fortnight passed all too quickly and Jim went back to London and was given light duty at home; he would have another board in a month's time and had no doubt that he would then be passed for general service. The reserve battalion of his regiment was at Chelsea Barracks, and Jim soon found that, as one of the first returned officers from the front, he was called upon to play an important part in training the new officers and men who would soon have to take their place in the line.

As soon as he could get a free afternoon Jim went round to Grosvenor Square to call on Mrs. Bazeley and thank her for her generous hospitality. With the same stone he hoped to kill another dutiful bird, to 'say a kind word' to Sir Brandon Wayke's younger daughter.

Mrs. Bazeley had arranged for two of her less exciting patients to come and have tea with her, but on Jim's arrival she quickly sent word that she would have to put them off till another day and settled down to a comfortable little *tête-à-tête* in front of her sitting-room fire. Jim Widdington's fortnight in the country had done him so much good that he was much more alive and a much more entertaining companion even than Clarice Bazeley had expected. She knew just how to draw him out and make him laugh, without bothering him about the worries of life, so that Jim thoroughly enjoyed himself, stayed much longer than he had intended, and forgot all about Christine Wayke.

Mrs. Bazeley was delighted. The boy was adorable and could easily be made very fond of her – given sufficient opportunity.

'I suppose your family have got a house in London,' she said, knowing quite well that they had not. Jim laughed.

'Good gracious, no; they're country cousins dyed in the wool now. Nothing would induce them to live in London.'

'Then where do you live?'

'Barracks. Chelsea.'

'Oh, my dear boy, how terrible! You can't do that,' exclaimed Mrs. Bazeley, opening wide her beautiful brown eyes.

It had not previously occurred to Jim Widdington that it was terrible to live in barracks with his brother officers, but he pondered the idea.

'Well, it is a bit crowded,' he said. 'Of course there are a lot of officers now and we have to share a room. That is rather a bore.'

'Share a room! Oh, but how awful! When you're just back from the front and wounded. It's monstrous; you ought to be comfortable and happy and . . . and have a good time. Look here, Jim . . . you don't mind if I call you "Jim," do you?'

Jim flushed. He was still rather young and had not had much experience of married women.

'Of course, please . . . I hope you will.'

'Well, look here, Jim,' said Mrs. Bazeley, 'I've got an idea. Why shouldn't you have Freddie's flat?'

Jim stared at her.

'Freddie?' he asked. 'Who . . . ?'

'Freddie's my son. That makes me sound rather old, doesn't it, but I married out of the schoolroom. He's gone to Egypt and he won't want it. He'd far rather it was used by someone like you; he'd be delighted, I know.'

Jim was bewildered by the suggestion.

'Oh, but I couldn't,' he said. 'I don't even know him.'

'Oh, that doesn't matter. Anyway, I give it him – it comes out of my dress allowance, so it's really for me to say who uses it. There's a very nice woman who does it for him and cooks his breakfast, and her husband comes in to valet him. I'm sure you'd be very comfortable.'

'I should indeed!' said Jim warmly. 'It's too wonderful . . . I hardly know what to say.'

'It's settled; say no more,' said Mrs. Bazeley, clapping her hands. 'And as agent's commission you can take me out to dinner tomorrow night and we'll go to a show afterwards.'

The whole thing had gone with such a swing that Clarice Bazeley very nearly risked a kiss on the spot, but she had seen that blush and decided not to spoil a very promising prospect by being in too much of a hurry. For much the same reason she did not prolong the *tête-à-tête* but sent Jim away while he was still warm with gratitude.

It was not till he was back in barracks dressing for dinner at the Club that he remembered that he had not killed his second bird, but it was too late now to do anything about Christine Wayke. He couldn't very well look her up next day because he was to call for Mrs. Bazeley in the evening; it wouldn't do to live on the door-step. But he would try again a few days later.

The dinner and show were a great success and Jim thoroughly enjoyed himself. He liked being seen about with a beautiful woman and he was flattered by her evident liking for him. Mrs. Bazeley was extremely discreet. She quickly realised that Jim Widdington was a modest country flower, for all his Guardsmanship, and she knew that it would be fatal to rush him. When she said good-night and thanked him, she gave his hand an affectionate little squeeze – just enough to show that he was a special friend and nothing to shock him, poor lamb. She rather enjoyed the prospect of a slow siege.

Two days later Jim arranged another little party, this time with his sister Mary and Christine Wayke. He did not see how else he could do much with the girl. She was not really 'out' yet and was obviously shy;

she would much rather come out with Mary. It was a mildly successful evening. Mary was tired after her long day's work in hospital. She ought really to have been in bed but had not been able to resist the chance of an evening with her beloved brother. Christine was quiet. She did not look quite so young as Jim had expected, and she was cheerful enough, but she left most of the talking to the others.

Before dropping Christine at her hospital – having no relation in London, Mrs. Bazeley had very kindly found a small room on the top floor for her and another probationer – Jim suggested another evening the following week. Mary sighed and shook her head.

'Can't, alas,' she said. 'I switch to night duty. But do take Christine.'

Jim hesitated.

'I'd love to,' he said, 'but what about . . . I mean, ought there to be a chaperone?'

Christine was looking demure but there was a twitch at the corners of her mouth.

Mary laughed.

'My dear Albert,' she said, 'Victoria no longer reigns. And there's a war on. *And* Christine is Helen's sister – practically. Or are you really not to be trusted.'

Jim flushed hotly.

'Don't talk rot,' he said. 'I only thought . . .'

Mary thrust her hand under his arm and squeezed it.

'You're a darling,' she said, 'but it's quite all right. I take full responsibility.'

Jim took Christine Wayke to dine at a quiet and very respectable little restaurant in Jermyn Street. She did not get off duty till eight o'clock so that they were too late to go to a play, except possibly to a musical show or a revue, and Jim hardly liked to take her to one of those – some of the dresses were inclined to be daring and the jokes unsuited to a young girl. They went instead to a cinema where they saw a film of the new comedian, Charlie Chaplin, who made them both laugh immoderately. They also saw some war films, long columns of Russians who were believed to be pushing the Germans and Austrians before them by sheer weight of numbers, pictures of long wicked-looking French guns which seemed nearly to fall over backwards each time they were fired, and other pictures of 'Kitchener's Army' – men in civilian clothes training without rifles but looking very cheerful and determined. The audience sang a good deal and Jim felt a lump in his throat; he saw that Christine's eyes were brimming with tears and he felt a curious inclination to put his arm round her. He repressed the inclination.

Jim enjoyed that evening much more than he had expected to and he asked the girl to come out again the following week, which she eagerly agreed to do. When she said good-night to him there was a sparkle in her eyes that made him feel very happy; it was nice to be able to give a little pleasure to such a jolly girl, who was having a hard and rather lonely life.

He had another night out that week with Mrs. Bazeley, a much livelier affair. They dined at Ciro's and danced a good deal. Mrs. Bazeley danced beautifully and seemed to have lots of amusing friends. On the way back to Grosvenor Square in a taxi she slipped her arm through his and that was distinctly exciting.

The weeks passed pleasantly enough, especially as there was not much fighting on the western front now and no depressing news of friends killed and wounded. The medical board passed Jim fit for general service but he learned from the Regimental Orderly Room that there were plenty of officers to go out to the battalions in France when they were needed, and he was not likely to be sent back for some time. The hard work in barracks made him enjoy his evenings of amusement much more than he had in peace time. There were lots of good shows on and always friends to be met at the Alhambra and the Empire.

He had several more evenings with Mrs. Bazeley, sometimes in parties but more often just the two of them together. Jim could not help realising that she seemed fond of him and he was certainly more than a little in love with her. He had occasional qualms of conscience at the idea; after all, she was a married woman and her husband was at the front, probably having a pretty foul time. Still, everybody in London seemed to be doing the same thing and it was only for a short time; he was bound to have to go out again soon and then she would forget all about him. He decided to enjoy himself while he could; an occasional kiss in a taxi could do no one any harm; he had no intention of going any further than that.

He thought sometimes about Helen. She was still in France and they wrote to one another occasionally, but somehow she seemed to have faded slightly into the background. After the war – if he survived it – it would be grand to meet her again and probably by then he would want to get married, but for the present the idea seemed remote.

In the meantime he felt that he was keeping in touch with her through her sister. Christine was 'coming out' a great deal. She was not nearly so shy now and talked away happily when they went out together. She had even persuaded him to take her to some of the more amusing places to dinner and to dance. Christine was a natural dancer; she was as light as a feather and the look of happiness in her grey eyes as she looked up at him gave Jim a warm feeling of happiness too.

On one occasion when they were dancing together they met Mrs. Bazeley, who was with a General who had been in hospital at the same time as Jim. Mrs. Bazeley seemed rather annoyed and hardly spoke to Christine; probably she thought that one of her nurses ought not to be dancing, that she should be resting when she was not working. But after all, so long as the girl did her work properly there seemed no reason why she should not enjoy herself in between times.

Then came an evening that disturbed the even tenor of this pleasant existence. Jim had been lent a small Straker-Squire coupe by a friend and he went round in it to Grosvenor Square to collect Christine. The girl was delighted and when he asked her where she would like to dine she said:

'Oh, let's go for a long drive and have dinner right out in the country. It *would* be fun, Jim. Do let's.'

Jim laughed. She was absurdly young, he thought, but very attractive. It really would be rather fun to get out of London for a change, and the car was a beauty.

'All right,' he said. 'We'll go west and stop when we get too hungry to go on.'

He had no particular plan in his mind but instinct took him down the Bath road. He wished it was summer, so that they could go to the Household Brigade Boat Club at Maidenhead, but that would be closed now. Still, 'Rattles' might be open; one could get food there at almost any time of night. It was hardly the place to take a girl like Christine, but in war-time the old conventions seemed to have largely disappeared, and in any case there would be no one there who would know her.

'Rattles' was open. There were not many people about and no one in the dining-room at that hour, but there was no difficulty about food. There was a cheerful fire and the room, almost in darkness except for the shaded lights on one or two tables, was very romantic. They ordered a grill and Jim thought that a bottle of Berncastler Doctor would be cheering. It was a sweet wine, which women liked, and one glass could not do Christine any harm.

The Berncastler Doctor was a great success. Christine gave a little gasp of delight when she tasted it, and very soon Jim found himself pouring her out a second glass. His own second glass had somewhat relaxed his sense of discretion, and in any case he had not realised what a very potent wine it was.

Christine was wearing a dress that he had not seen before, a black velvet, very simple but most becoming. Jim thought it was cut rather low for so young a girl, but it was none the less attractive for that, and of course he did not pretend to know anything about women's fashions. Christine herself was looking very lovely and not really a bit like a girl who was not out. The drive – or the wine – had brought a flush to her cheeks and a sparkle to her eyes, so that she seemed quite a woman of the world; not, of course, like Mrs. Bazeley, but still less like the shy and awkward girl he dimly remembered at Chatterleys. Very lovely, thought Jim, wondering how he could have for a moment imagined himself in love with the older woman.

When dinner was over Jim said something about going back.

'Oh, no!' exclaimed Christine. 'Jim, let's go on the river!'

Jim laughed.

'All the punts and boats are put away in the winter,' he said.

The girl's face fell.

'What a shame. But let's go for a walk anyhow – along the bank. It's not a bit cold. It'll be lovely, Jim.'

The boy hesitated but her eagerness was too much for him.

'There's the garden,' he said. 'We could walk round that. It's lovely in the summer.'

'Come on,' said Christine, slipping her hand into his.

The touch thrilled him and discretion vanished.

It *was* cold, but Christine had a cloak and he a coat. There was a moon, too, though it was often hidden by drifting clouds. Hand in hand they walked round the big garden, with its fine lawns sloping down to the river, the old willow trees, bare now but very beautiful, and the great chestnut standing gaunt against the sky. In a sheltered corner they found a wooden bench and sat on it, close together because it *was* cold. They did not talk much but they were very happy.

Jim's troublesome conscience was at rest now, lulled by Berncastler Doctor, and Christine – though that he did not realise – had no conscience to lull.

She put her cheek against his shoulder and squeezed his arm.

'Jim,' she said, 'this is the loveliest evening I've ever had in my life. I shan't ever forget it.'

Jim felt an intense longing to take her in his arms, but generations of *noblesse oblige* restrained him.

'I've enjoyed it too,' he said huskily; 'frightfully.'

The lovely upturned face was very close to his. The generations turned their back just long enough to allow him a gentle half-brotherly but half not-brotherly kiss.

The car took them back to London all too quickly, but it was after twelve o'clock when they reached Hyde Park Corner. They had spoken very little on the way back but both were blissfully happy.

'Jim,' said Christine suddenly, 'I'm most frightfully thirsty. Could you get me a drink somewhere? There's nothing but beastly water at the hospital.'

Jim smiled.

'Everywhere's shut now. What sort of a drink do you want?'

Christine laughed; a rather high-pitched little laugh.

'I believe I should like a . . . a brandy and soda.'

It was Jim's turn to laugh.

'I'm quite sure you wouldn't,' he said. 'It's a foul drink. Whisky's much nicer.'

'Well, whisky, then. Jim, haven't you got some at your flat?'

'Good heavens; I couldn't take you there!'

'Why not? Oh, Jim, do,' urged the girl. 'Nobody will see. Don't be such an old prim and proper.'

Jim was genuinely shocked but he did not like – as no man would like – to be accused of primness by a pretty girl. Against all his instincts and good sense he drove to the block of flats in Half Moon Street, made sure that the coast was clear, and whisked Christine upstairs. He had no intention of letting her stay more than five minutes. The Berncastler Doctor was wearing off.

Christine sank into a large armchair and tucked her feet under her, looking as if she had no intention of being hurried. Jim took a decanter and a siphon out of a cupboard, poured a very small quantity of whisky into a glass and filled it with soda. He was carrying the glass to Christine when he stopped suddenly and listened. He had not closed the door of the sitting-room and his quick ear had caught the sound of a key being pushed into the latch of the flat door. There was a look of bewilderment on his face as he stood, hesitating, in front of Christine. Then, as he heard the front door open and close, he seized the girl's hand, pulled her out of the chair and hurried her across the room; opening the door of the bedroom he pushed her inside.

Christine looked more excited than alarmed.

'Who is it?' she whispered.

'I don't know. I'll get rid of him. Keep quiet.'

He shut the door quietly and had taken three steps back into the room, still with the glass of whisky in his hand, when the door of the sitting-room was pushed open and Mrs. Bazeley walked in. She was in evening dress and had evidently discarded her cloak in the hall.

'Jim; what luck!' she said, with a dazzling smile. 'I thought you might be asleep.'

Jim stood staring at her, his manners forgotten. She came up to him.

'Did you think I was a burglar? I've always had a key.'

She took the glass from his hand, sipped the whisky, and shuddered.

'How horribly weak,' she said. 'Do you like it like that?'. .

'It . . . I . . . I don't really but I'm trying to cut down.'

Mrs. Bazeley laughed.

'How like you, Jim. Are you glad to see me?'

She came closer still and put her hand on his arm.

'Of course . . . yes. I was just rather startled,' said Jim, utterly bewildered.

'Then you might give me a kiss.'

She put her hands up to his face, pulled it towards hers and kissed him on the mouth. Her arms slipped round his neck, she put her mouth to his ear and whispered.

Jim felt himself flushing hotly.

'I . . . I . . . I didn't know . . . I mean, I'd no idea . . .'

Clarice Bazeley laughed.

'You precious innocent,' she said. 'What do you think I lent you this flat for?'

With a quick turn she walked across towards the bedroom. Opening the door she took a step into the room, stopped suddenly and stared with widening eyes. On the bed was lying one of her probationer nurses.

CHAPTER IV

SPRINGTIME AND WAR

Mrs. Bazeley was too angry for discretion. If she had stopped to think she would have realised that she was herself in no position to risk a scandal; if either of those young people chose to talk, her 'friends' would be only too maliciously eager to believe them and there might be serious trouble. But she was too angry to think. The treachery of Jim Widdington in bringing a girl to the flat which she had provided for him maddened her – a flapper, one of her own nurses! She paid no attention to the young man's stammered explanations. In a cold fury she told Christine not to put foot in her hospital again; her luggage would be packed and she could send for it.

Christine, white but defiant, said nothing at all. Jim pulled himself together.

'You can't do that, Mrs. Bazeley,' he said. 'This is all my fault and I've told you that it's not what you think. Christine must go back to the hospital tonight; she's got nowhere else to go. If you really mean that she must leave she can leave tomorrow.'

His firm tone did succeed in penetrating to Mrs. Bazeley's conscience – or sense of caution. She checked the bitter answer that had sprung to her lips.

'Very well. Go tomorrow,' she said curtly, and strode out of the flat with more effect than dignity.

Jim Widdington was too much worried himself to realise how very little upset Christine was. She had not heard very much of what had been said before Mrs. Bazeley came into the bedroom, and she was intensely curious to know the explanation of the visit, but Jim's face did not encourage questions. He told her that he would take her back to the hospital now, fetch her the next day as soon as he could get off duty, and take her down to Chatterleys. Christine protested that she did not want to go home but Jim was adamant and the girl realised that without his help she had no idea where she could go.

It was a gloomy end to a happy evening and Jim was too miserable and ashamed of himself to say much. His mind was occupied with wondering how he could explain things to Sir Brandon Wayke and his 'good-night' to Christine suffered from his preoccupation. It was that fact, rather than the risk of scandal, that made Christine cry as she undressed and got into bed.

On the following morning Jim got leave for the day on 'urgent private affairs,' his Commanding Officer realising that he was not the kind of officer to ask for it without good reason. The cold light of day had done nothing to give a rosier aspect to the situation, and the journey down to Coventry was one of unutterable gloom. On Jim's advice Christine had telephoned to say that she was coming home and asked if she could be met; to their relief it was the car that awaited them, rather than the dog-cart in which Sir Brandon sometimes chose to meet people himself.

But after all, that relief was only a postponement of the uncomfortable moment. Sir Brandon greeted his daughter with pleasure but, at the unexpected sight of her companion, asked no questions while the servants were within earshot. He evidently sensed that Jim wanted an opportunity to talk to him, as he led the way to his study, after telling Christine to go and see Mrs. Curling.

The next ten minutes were the most difficult that Jim Widdington had ever experienced. He had to explain to the old baronet why his daughter had lost her post in the hospital and at the same time convince him that the previous night's episode had been entirely innocent. Christine had wanted to say nothing about it at all, to tell her father that she was leaving the hospital of her own accord because the work was too hard for her; but Jim knew that there would always be a risk of the truth reaching Sir Brandon's ears and then, if there had been *suppressio veri*, the worst would almost certainly be suspected.

So he told a modified version of the truth, slurring over the supper at 'Rattles' and saying nothing of the feelings that had – there was no blinking the fact – been wakened in his own breast and possibly in that of Christine too. He gave the true explanation of their visit to the flat but said that Mrs. Bazeley had happened to see them go in and had followed them up to his flat in a spirit of dutiful care for her charge; the whitewashing of Mrs. Bazeley went against the grain but it was obviously the story that she would tell herself if ever she had to tell it, and the real truth would only have blackened him more in the eyes of Sir Brandon.

The old man listened to his story without interruption, his eyes fixed upon Jim's with disconcerting steadiness. When it was over he was silent for more than a minute.

'I am glad you told me about this yourself,' he said at last. 'If it had been anyone else but you it would have been a disgraceful thing to do, but I asked you to amuse her and I know you are a great friend of Helen's. I must believe that you did not realise how unwisely you were acting. Christine will not return to London and it will be better if you do not see her again or write to her. She is young and impressionable; she must have every chance to forget about this.'

Sir Brandon spoke quietly but there was an icy tone in his voice that was far more disconcerting than anger.

'I'm terribly sorry about it, sir,' said Jim awkwardly. 'It was entirely my fault and not Christine's at all. She doesn't . . . I mean, it's not that . . .'

'We will not say any more about it,' said Sir Brandon. 'I think it will be best if you return to London by the 2.58; there is good time for you to catch it. You must forgive my being inhospitable.'

He rang the bell and ordered the car to come round at once. For five or six minutes he talked about the war and then, when the car was announced, accompanied Jim to the front door. Standing on the front steps, his face expressionless and unsmiling, he was a formidable figure and Jim had not the courage to plead for a word with Christine. As the car drove away Sir Brandon turned on his heel and walked back into his study. He sat down at his big writing-table and his eyes turned to the faded photograph of a very beautiful woman which stood in a silver frame on one side of the table. Slowly he put up a hand to cover his eyes and sat on in silence.

For weeks London drawing-rooms had been full of talk of a Big Push in France, and on March 10th it came; a few hundred yards of trenches were won at Neuve Chapelle, and a battalion of Grenadiers lost 16 officers and 325 men. The Reserve Battalion at Chelsea prepared to send out a large draft of reinforcements, and Jim Widdington was too fully employed to think about his own private affairs. He soon learned that he would not himself be one of the officers to go out, but he knew that his time must be drawing near.

He had respected Sir Brandon Wayke's wishes and had not written to Christine, nor had he heard from her, but she was often in his droughts and he realised that her sister had faded into a rather dim background. 'Before the war' seemed now almost like another life; he wondered whether he had really been in love with Helen. Certainly he had never thought of her with the thrill that he felt each time his memory returned to that dim garden at Maidenhead, with the lovely face of Christine looking up at him in the fitful moonlight. He no longer could persuade himself that there had been much of the 'brother' in the kiss that he had given her, and he realised that if he saw her again he might find it difficult not to fall seriously in love. To do that would be something like treachery to Helen, and among people brought up on rigid principles of honour as the Waykes and Widdingtons had been, that was an idea that could not lightly be faced. Probably, thought Jim, an early return to France was the best solution of his personal problem.

He had told Mary very much what he had told Sir Brandon. She had not said very much but he could see that she was seriously disturbed; Helen was her friend and her heart was set on his marrying her. She made a great effort to see as much of her brother as she could, but she was still on night duty at her hospital and it was not easy to arrange. During the weeks following the battle of Neuve Chapelle they were both hard at work and saw very little of one another, and as the tension eased Jim found himself giving more and more thought to Christine and wishing that he could go down to Chatterleys and see her.

He had, of course, vacated the flat in Half Moon Street and was living once more in barracks. One morning early in April he received a letter which shook all his good resolutions.

CHATTERLEYS,

COVENTRY.

> Jim (it ran), I am so unhappy here. It is worse than being back in the convent and Father treats me like a naughty child. Please come and see me, if it's only for half an hour. I know you can't get away in the morning but there's a 2.23 that gets to Coventry at 3.57. We could meet at Riddings Copse; I shall go for a walk there every day with Tiger till you come. You could go back by the 5.23 – 7.22, and that wouldn't make you very late for dinner, would it. Oh, Jim, do come! If you don't I shall run away from here.
>
> Your affec^{te}
>
> CHRISTINE.

Knowing how strictly the girl had been brought up Jim felt that things must be indeed bad to wring from her such an appeal. The last sentence offered an excuse to salve his conscience, and Jim was too little worldly-wise to realise that that was what it had been designed to do. The following day he caught the 2.23 and soon after four o'clock he found Christine in Riddings Copse.

Very punctiliously he shook hands and for half an hour behaved like a perfect brother, urging Christine to be patient; very soon, he said, her father would forget about the unfortunate episode and everything would be happy and normal again. Christine listened patiently and sadly. She spoke very little herself, until at a quarter to five she said she must go back to tea or her father would miss her. They rose from the tree trunk on which they had been sitting and walked down the primrose-bordered ride. They were nearly within sight of the road when Christine stopped and seized Jim's arm.

'Jim,' she said in a trembling voice. 'Take me with you.'

The young man stared at her.

'Christine, I can't! It wouldn't be right. Where could you go?'

The girl clung to his arm and he felt her body quivering.

'I don't care. I can't stay here. Jim, I can't. You don't know how awful it is, with Father sitting like an . . . an old Mandarin and never speaking to me and snubbing me if I say anything. Couldn't I go to Mary, Jim? Perhaps I could work in her hospital.'

'But, Christine, we couldn't do that; your father would never forgive us. You must be patient and perhaps later he will let you come.'

He felt that he was speaking like a prig, but what else could he do? He looked down into her tear-dimmed eyes and again felt the intense longing to take her in his arms and comfort her. But this time there was no moon and he mastered the temptation.

'I must go, Christine,' he said, 'and I mustn't come again. Perhaps Mary can get leave and come down and talk to your father. I'm sure he will be nicer soon; it's just . . . just that he's so fond of you, really, and he must be very lonely without Helen. Cheer up, Christine, and it will all come right.'

It was very lame, very unsympathetic, but he could not trust himself to say more. He squeezed her hand, patted Tiger, and walked away towards the road. At the gate he turned to wave his hand. Christine was standing disconsolately at the bend in the ride, the terrier looking up questioningly at his unhappy young mistress.

In those spring days of 1915 the shackles of convention were breaking down. To the normal restlessness of the season was added the still more urgent restlessness of war. Young men, knowing that the risk of death lay not very far before them, were eager to snatch a little happiness from life. They could no longer wait for formal periods of courting and engagement, and they found that the girls they loved were as little ready to wait as they. Marriages were rushed through, often on slight acquaintance – acquaintance enflamed into passion by the upheaval of all the normal restraints of life.

In his cold farewell to Christine Wayke, Jim Widdington had done what he believed to be his duty, but as he travelled back to London he knew that he was in love with her and that his affection for Helen meant nothing to him at all. He longed for Christine, longed to have her always with him and to find with her, in the short days that remained to him, the happiness which love could give.

For days after his return to London he struggled with the temptation to go back to Chatterleys and tell Sir Brandon that he wanted to marry Christine. He was restrained only by the knowledge that everyone – his father and mother, Mary, Sir Brandon himself – believed that he was in love with Helen and would be shocked at the idea of his throwing her over for her sister. The shackles still held him, but they were wearing thin.

There was talk of another 'push' in France, another attempt to help the French, who were suffering terrible casualties in their own offensives in Artois. At any time now, Jim knew, he might have to go, and he might never see Christine again, never even tell her of his love. Many of his friends were marrying, men and girls no older than himself; it was cruel that his own chance of happiness should be ruined by the mere fact of a boy and girl friendship that had really meant nothing to either himself or Helen but had been worked up by their families into an artificial romance.

His restraint was near breaking point when one afternoon he left the officers' gate at Chelsea Barracks on his way to the Club. He crossed the road, intending to walk down Ebury Street; as he reached the far pavement he found himself face to face with Christine Wayke.

'Christine!'

'Jim; I've run away.'

He stared at her with open mouth; then, realising that people were looking at them, he took her arm and pulled her along beside him.

'But Christine, where are you living? What are you going to do?'

'I've got a lodging near Euston. I'm going on the stage.'

Jim stopped dead in his tracks.

'The stage!'

Again he was staring, too startled to think of what he looked like. The idea horrified him. The stage! Christine!

Pulling himself together he signalled to a taxi and, pushing the girl into it, followed himself.

'What do you mean, Christine?'

The taxi-driver opened the door.

'Where to, sir?' he asked patiently.

'Oh, anywhere – just drive. Regent's Park.'

The man grinned and a moment later slammed his noisy gear into place.

Christine's eyes were sparkling. Jim saw now that she was no longer the wilting girl that he had left in Ridding's Copse. She was excited, and the excitement gave colour to her cheeks and character to her face. She was beautiful, even more beautiful than Jim had realised.

Hardly knowing it, he seized her hand.

'Christine, you can't do that! It's . . . it's impossible!'

'It isn't; I've done it. I came up yesterday afternoon and got a room near Euston Station. I've been round to some agents this morning and one of them seemed to think I might get a place in the new show at the *Frailty*. I'm to have an audition tomorrow.'

Jim knew – or thought he knew – what an audition at the *Frailty* meant; it was a leg show and the thought of Christine in such a thing horrified him.

'Christine, please . . . please don't go there!' he urged. 'You don't know . . . I can't let you . . .'

Christine smiled at him, delighted to see the effect of her news.

'You don't care what I do, do you, Jim?' she asked softly.

'Christine, I care most frightfully!'

Good resolutions, discretion, convention, family considerations, everything had flown away before the violence of Jim's emotions. The sight of Christine alone would probably have scattered them, but coupled with this was fear . . . fear of what might happen to his lovely darling. Jim's affections had crystallised very rapidly.

'Christine, I can't let you . . . I can't let you go!'

Again Christine smiled, a soft, loving smile that went straight to the young man's heart.

'I don't want to go, Jim,' she whispered.

The taxi chugged stolidly round the Outer Circle of Regent's Park while within it the two young lovers sat locked in each other's arms. The third circuit had been completed before Jim came back to earth, and then the driver was told to take them to Mary's hospital in South London; it was going to be a profitable afternoon for him.

It was decided that if Mary would undertake some degree of responsibility, Christine should write and tell her father that she was in her care and was hoping to get work in her hospital. That would allay his immediate anxiety. As soon as Jim could get a day's leave he would go home, break the news to his own family and ask for Sir Brandon's consent to the marriage. Jim was so happy now that he faced the prospect of that ordeal almost with a light heart.

They were fortunate enough to find Mary just up from her day's sleep, and preparing for 'breakfast.' They took her out to a restaurant and revealed their secret, but they need not have done so because the first sight of their faces had told her the truth. It was a shock to her but hardly a surprise; she managed to conceal her real feelings and behaved, Jim thought, like the perfect sister she was. Her brother, of course, could do no wrong, but it would have startled both Jim and Christine to know what Mary Widdington thought of Helen's sister.

Three days later Jim's visit to Festing Manor and Chatterleys took place, and there was very little of the light heart left at the end of it. Colonel Widdington was on Salisbury Plain, proudly training a brigade of Kitchener's Army, but one parent was enough to express the family feelings. Mrs. Widdington was deeply shocked that her son should throw over Helen in such a cavalier way; fond as she was of Jim she had never spoiled him and now she gave him the full benefit of a very capable tongue, though she was wise enough to say nothing about Christine; she still hoped that the thing could be stopped but she knew that to abuse the girl was the surest way to drive a high-spirited young man into precipitate action.

To hear his mother's unvarnished opinion of him was no doubt good for Jim Widdington, but it did not help him to face Christine's father; his tail was not very high when he was shown into Sir Brandon's study. When he left it half an hour later it was frankly between his legs. The old man had had more than an inkling of the truth after the flat incident, but he had hoped that the firm line he had taken would bring the young people to their senses. He was unaccustomed to such quick wooing, and to hear this young man, who was morally engaged to his elder daughter, now calmly asking for the hand of the younger, whom he had only known a few weeks, both startled and infuriated him.

Sir Brandon was not a man to burst into a fit of temper but his cold anger was far more intimidating than any violent fury. He told Jim exactly what he thought of him. He refused his consent to the marriage and said that if it took place without his consent neither Jim nor Christine should ever enter Chatterleys again. Christine had no money of her own and would receive no dowry if she married without consent. No father could have given a headstrong young couple clearer warning of what they might expect.

But Sir Brandon Wayke did not give his prospective son-in-law the one warning that might have saved all the people he loved most in the world from the tragedy that lay before them.

CHAPTER V

WAR AND MARRIAGE

The October night was already falling when Jim Widdington's company marched off from its billets in a shell-wrecked French village to relieve a Coldstream company in the line. The men were heavily laden, because there was a lot of 'consolidation' to be done in the old German trench which they would occupy and, in addition to their normal trench kit, they had to carry sandbags, wire, screw-pickets and other uncomfortable burdens. They were soon sweating, and the heavy air reeked with the odour of bodies and clothes that had been too long in company. The battle of Loos had only just died down; a week ago the great German counter-attack had been beaten off with terrible loss to the enemy, providing the British with their one solid success in an otherwise disastrous battle.

Along the shell-torn road the company marched in file, and while they were still well behind the line the platoons were kept closed up to one another, so that Jim and Peter Drake could walk together. There was very little shelling, but the occasional rattle of machine-guns and the popping bursts of hand grenades – the bombs which had recently come into unpleasant fashion as effective weapons of war – showed that men's nerves were still under the strain of many days' fighting.

The two friends talked in low voices of the eternal topic of leave. Now that the battle was officially recognised to be over, the normal routine of 'peace-time' warfare was beginning to function again and Peter Drake was due to go on leave as soon as the battalion's turn of duty in the line was ended. Jim, frantically envious as he was, was glad of his friend's good fortune and listened good-temperedly to the other's eager plans.

Whew–ew–ew–ew–ew–ew.

A heavy shell droned over them to crash in the village which they had just left.

'Late again,' said Jim.

'I believe they always know when there's a relief on,' replied Peter. 'They'll probably whizz-bang us on the way up.'

There was a faint tremor of nervousness in his voice which Jim detected. Peter Drake had been out for a very long time and his nerve was beginning to go.

'I'm as windy as hell now that my leave's so near,' he confessed, probably realising that Jim had noticed that tremor.

'I bet you are. So was I when I was wounded and going down the line. I felt as if the whistle had blown for 'time' and it wasn't fair that I should be shelled any more.'

Wh–wh–wh – wsh – SH – CRASH.

Not very far away that time. Peter Drake's face was white but his lips held in a firm line. The Commanding Officer knew all about him and was anxious to get him home before there was trouble. That was how he had managed to get special leave for him before that precious privilege was generally re-opened.

Jim Widdington's own nerve was still sound enough. He had played his part well in the battle that was just over and he knew that his company commander was pleased with him. But he was very far from being the Happy Warrior; he had been the Happy Lover for too short a time to allow him to feel anything but bitter resentment that his happiness should be interrupted and threatened by this madness of war; he longed with all his heart for it to stop, for himself to be out of it, for anything that would take him back to Christine and the love of which he had had so cruelly short a glimpse.

Jim had married Christine as quickly as it had been possible to complete the formalities of war-time marriage. Mrs. Widdington and Mary had come to the register office with them; Sir Brandon Wayke had not come, had made no acknowledgment of the letter in which Jim had told of their intentions and plans. On the other hand, he had not reiterated his refusal of consent, which would have made the legal position very difficult. As a minor, Christine could not marry without it – at least without incurring severe legal penalties. The law demands a declaration from each party that there is no 'lawful hindrance' and, for a minor, lack of parental consent is such an impediment. To make a false declaration on the subject is punishable by penal servitude – but it does not invalidate the marriage!

Christine and Jim decided, against the advice of their lawyer, to run the risk, feeling sure that Sir Brandon would not go to the length of having his daughter put in prison; at the worst they hoped that war-time indulgence would be shown by the Court and that nothing more than a fine would be imposed. No doubt it was a big risk to run – but they were madly in love and Jim might at any moment have to go out again. So Christine took Sir Brandon's silence for consent and made her declaration.

Jim had written to Helen too, a difficult letter, clumsily expressed; Helen had replied with characteristic straightforwardness, wishing him happiness but making no reference to Christine. It was an honest letter, but it hurt Jim cruelly – as he deserved to be hurt.

For a fortnight after that dry and formal ceremony before the registrar, Jim and Christine had lived a life of intense if rather feverish happiness and gaiety. Young as she was, Christine was a perfect lover and mistress, intoxicating Jim with the passion that enveloped him like a flame. But passion was not enough for Christine; she needed gaiety too. Tired as he might be, every evening she dragged Jim out to restaurant, theatre, night-club – the whirl of hectic enjoyment in which all the combatant capitals of Europe were trying to drown their fears and sorrows. Jim enjoyed it because he enjoyed being with Christine and seeing her happy, but he did have twinges of regret that she could not be happy alone with him in the little Knightsbridge flat that they had taken on a short lease. He was just a little worried, too, at her lack of discrimination in making friends with people whom she met in the restaurants and night-clubs which they visited, and – though this he hardly admitted even to himself – at the amount of champagne which she drank. He did once mildly remonstrate with her about this but she laughed at him and told him not to be an old Jeremiah.

Apart from these tiny doubts Jim was intensely happy and almost succeeded in shutting his eyes to the heavy shadow that clouded the happiness of half the world. Few as were those first days of their married life, Jim and Christine lived them to the full, so that they achieved a substance lacking in many longer periods of normal existence.

But few indeed they were; early in July came the order for two more battalions of Grenadiers to be sent to France to help in the formation of a Guards Division. Every fit officer of the Regiment who was on the list for active service, and everyone who could be released from staff employment was needed now. A few weeks of intensive training in England were allowed and then came the parting which the young lovers had so deeply dreaded. Christine's courage in those last days and hours were an inspiration to Jim. She shed no tears, she helped him cheerfully in his preparations, and she enriched him with all the passionate love which was her truly precious gift.

Over in France there was more training, the welding of several magnificent units into one superb whole. The rumour of a great battle – 'the greatest ever fought' – was in the air and everyone was keyed up to what they hoped might be the beginning of a triumphant end. Jim wrote long and cheerful letters to Christine and she wrote to him, but she was not a good letter-writer; none of her love flowed through her pen as it did through her body, and gradually Jim felt a little chilled at the insipidity of her replies.

But soon even the thought of wife and home was pushed into the background of Jim's mind. The Division moved up – too late, as it was to prove – to the battle area, ready to 'exploit success'; it was thrown in to block a dangerous break in the line; it fought hard in the final efforts to break through, fought to retain the foothold won in the great Hohenzollern Redoubt, fought to beat off the German counter-attack. There was very little time for thought, very little time for sleep – except in snatches at the bottom of a trench; men were exhausted, men were shattered and killed. And Jim Widdington came through it untouched, with added confidence and the respect of his men, with new lines at the corners of his mouth and a look in his eyes which Christine had never seen.

But that new-found confidence in himself did not make Jim Widdington any more in love with modern warfare or prevent him from longing to be out of it and back in his little home with Christine. As he marched with his company back into the line that night he felt bitterly envious of Peter Drake, who would so soon be on his way home. He did not grudge Peter his leave; no one deserved it better. Peter had been out since the beginning and had only been transferred to Jim's battalion when its heavy officer casualties made some readjustment necessary. It was time Peter had a good long rest and everyone hoped that he would be kept in England for a spell. In any case Jim knew that he could not expect leave himself for some time, so that envying someone else's luck was a dog-in-the-manger business. He pushed his envious thoughts into the background of his mind and turned attention to the work in front of him.

Very soon the company was plodding up the remains of a communication trench which had connected the old German support and reserve lines. There had been little chance to repair it after the British bombardment and the going was terribly bad, but it did provide some protection from the bursts of machine-gun fire that occasionally swept the front. Very soon the Coldstream guides were leading the Grenadiers to their places in the line and the relief was quietly and quickly effected. As soon as everything was taken over and the Coldstream were out, the night's work began; digging, sandbagging, wiring, revetting, patrols into No Man's Land, a body or a limb to be buried, the line to be made not only safe but sanitary.

There was little interference from the enemy, who were themselves busy on the same tasks. They had their stereotyped bursts of offensiveness, a few rounds of 4.2 or 5.9, at billets or road junctions, one or two trench-mortar bombs at likely spots in the trenches, an occasional sweep of machine-gun fire. For three and a half days the routine of trench warfare ran its normal course, rest by day and work by night, one or two more bodies to be buried, two or three stretchers taken down.

On the last evening before relief Jim Widdington walked down the front line trench, now greatly improved, to have a word with Drake. He saw at once that his friend was in a very nervous state. He was walking up and down his platoon front, smoking continuously; there was a twitch at the corner of his mouth and his eyes had a hunted look that Jim had never seen in them before. It was clear, too, that the men had noticed their commander's nervousness and that it was making them jumpy.

'These damn fellows are sure to be late; they always are,' he said irritably – and quite unjustly. 'If I can get back to Divisional Headquarters by two ack emma I can get a lift in a car that's going down to Boulogne to catch the morning boat; that'll mean the best part of an extra day's leave.'

'You'll do it easily,' said Jim. 'It's not like handing over to a strange battalion that has to be shown everything; the Coldstream know this line and we shall be able to get out at once.'

'Yes, if they're in time, but . . .'

So it went on, the unhappy Peter Drake looking at his watch every few minutes and making a most uncharacteristic exhibition of himself. Jim knew that his friend's irritable nervousness was natural enough but it made him feel very uncomfortable and he walked back to his own platoon. It was quite dark now and everything was ready for the relief. The night was unusually quiet; an occasional heavy shell droned overhead, to fall in some back area, but the line itself was left in peace. With any luck they would get out without any trouble at all, and four days out were something to look forward to.

Jim looked at his watch and saw that at any minute now the Coldstream might be expected. A heavy explosion a little way to the left gave him a moment of uneasiness; did the Bosch know of the relief? Were they hoping to catch it with a sudden bombardment? But there was no more 'strafing' and a moment later dark figures appeared up the communication trench. Jim glanced along his line to see that all was well; the men were whispering together. His platoon sergeant came up to him.

'That "Minnie," sir; got Mr. Drake, they say.'

Jim felt his heart stand still. He turned to the Coldstream subaltern who had just come up.

'D'you mind if I go along and see what's happened? There's a rumour that Peter Drake's been hit.'

'Of course. Your platoon sergeant'll show me round. You can hand over when you get back.'

Jim hurried down the trench which was now crowded with the double lot of men. In one bay they were looking at a group in the corner by the far traverse. The acrid smell of explosive still hung about and there was a litter of earth and torn sandbags.

Peter Drake lay on the floor of the trench, his head resting on a folded great-coat. Even in the darkness Jim could see that his face was ashy white but the nervous twitch had left his mouth; his expression was almost serene. He smiled faintly when he saw Jim.

'No need to catch that car now,' he whispered.

His head slowly rolled over and the expression faded from his eyes.

'Better look in his pockets, sir,' whispered a sergeant in Jim's ear. 'That blood'll soak through everything. His people may want something.'

Jim saw now that the lower part of his friend's jacket was dark; a touch told him that the sergeant was right. He felt in the pockets and took out the few letters and papers that were in them. In the breast-pocket was a note-book; carefully folded under its elastic band was a yellow form giving leave to Lieut. P. Drake, – Bn. Grenadier Guards, to proceed on leave to England.

Two days later the welcome news arrived that the Division was to be relieved in the line and would go to a back area to re-fit. After inspecting his billets that morning Jim Widdington came out into the street and met his Battalion Commander, who beckoned to him.

'Would you like to go on leave, Jim?' he asked.

The young officer gasped.

'Sir! Yes, sir, I . . . I should frightfully.'

Colonel Daubeny smiled.

'Pleasant surprise, isn't it? We're allowed to send two officers and none of us have been out long this time – none except poor Peter. I know you've only been married five minutes so you can have first cut if you like. Pooh-Bah is going too. Get off as soon as your Company Commander can spare you.'

He walked away, leaving Jim still bewildered by his good fortune. But he wasted no time in bewilderment. He squared things with his captain, got his pass from the adjutant, and by noon he and Pooh-Bah – Captain Wilbraham Paunceforte-Bouverie – were off. By great good fortune the Divisional Supply Officer, happy possessor of a car of his own, offered them a lift to Boulogne and they caught the evening leave-boat by the skin of their teeth. In his excitement Jim had forgotten to telegraph to Christine and there was no time at Boulogne, but he sent a wire from Folkestone. Even if it reached her very little before he did, the surprise would be all the more glorious.

The train reached Victoria soon after 9 p.m. and, saying a hurried farewell to Pooh-Bah, who was going on to Scotland, Jim jumped into a taxi and drove to Knightsbridge. He could hardly wait for the lift to take him to the third floor, and instead of ringing the flat bell he pounded eagerly on the door.

It was opened by the maid who had come with Christine from Chatterleys. She looked startled at the sight of him.

'Hullo, Kathleen!'

Jim dropped his kit-bag on the floor and pushed past the girl into the sitting-room. It was empty. An unopened telegram was lying on the table.

'Where's Mrs. Widdington? Doesn't she know I'm back?'

'She went out before the telegram came,' the girl said nervously. 'I didn't like to open it. I was afraid it . . . it . . .'

Jim laughed.

'Not His Majesty's regrets this time,' he said. 'But where is she?'

'She's dining out, sir.'

'Oh, hell. Do you know where?'

Kathleen hesitated.

'No, sir. I'm afraid I couldn't say.'

It was a bitter disappointment. Christine must have gone out very early to dinner. Perhaps she would be back all the sooner. He questioned Kathleen but could learn nothing of her plans. He felt no inclination to go out to a restaurant by himself, and as Kathleen 'thought there was an egg and some ham' he asked for that and while it was being prepared plunged into a glorious hot bath. There seemed no point in dressing properly, so he got into a pair of silk pyjamas and a dressing gown and revelled in the luxury of their sleek softness.

But his overstrung nerves would not let him settle down peacefully to wait for Christine's return. Every few minutes he looked at the clock, he paced round the room, he requestioned Kathleen – who seemed rather embarrassed thereby – and finally it occurred to him to ring up Mary.

After some difficulty with the hospital porter he got her to the telephone. She gasped with pleasure at the sound of his voice, and the warmth of her welcome soothed him. But when he asked for news of Christine she could give him none; she did not know where she was likely to be dining and had indeed seen and heard very little of her for some time. Her voice had lost, now, its warmth and Jim wondered whether she had not yet forgiven him for not marrying Helen. Women were very odd; they always thought a man ought to marry as *they* thought best, not as he did.

So Jim had to settle back in his armchair and presently the tiredness that was in his bones overcame him and he fell asleep. It was a troubled sleep, with a most disconcerting dream; he woke with a start, thinking that someone had spoken to him. But the room was empty and, looking at the clock, he saw to his astonishment that it was past midnight. He began to feel uneasy. She must be out with a party, and though there was nothing very startling about that, somehow he had thought that while he was at the front she would spend her evenings quietly at home – a positively Crimean conception of wartime womanhood.

He sat on in his armchair, brooding uneasily. The fire had gone out and he was cold, but he was not going to bed without Christine though he had paid several visits to the attractive bedroom and looked longingly at the big bed with its soft white sheets and pale salmon-coloured blankets. He sat on in the armchair and at last, well after one o'clock, he heard the rattle of the lift gate. He sprang to the door and flung it open just as Christine was putting her key into the latch. Her eyes opened wide in astonishment, and the next moment he had flung his arms round her and was crushing her to him.

'Jim! Oh, you're hurting me!'

There was a nervous catch in her laugh and then Jim's arms stiffened. He had realised that just behind Christine on the dimly lit landing was standing a tall man in uniform.

'What the hell . . . ?'

Jim's arms dropped and Christine slipped away from him. 'Oh, I forgot,' she said. 'This is Gerald . . . Major Weedon.'

Jim glared at the man, who in truth was looking very ill at ease.

'What are you doing here?' asked Jim grimly. But Christine had seized his hand and was pulling him into the flat.

'Don't be ridiculous, darling,' she said. 'Gerald's only come up for a night-cap. We've been to the Blue Moon and it was *terribly* stuffy. Come in, Gerald, do.'

Bewildered by the shock but instinctively disliking a melodramatic scene, Jim stood aside and the big man walked past him into the sitting-room. He was good-looking, with a black moustache, and he wore a military cross and a wound-stripe on his Gunner uniform. But the sight of them did nothing to appease Jim, who, with the typical intolerance of the Guardsman, had no use for a man who wore his uniform in the evening in England, whatever the war-time regulations might be.

'Are you just back on leave?' asked Major Weedon, with an attempt at heartiness in his voice.

'Yes,' said Jim shortly.

He was watching Christine bring a decanter and siphon from a cupboard. To his horror he saw that her walk was unsteady as she crossed the room. Her cheeks were flushed and her eyes sparkling. She looked very lovely.

Jim curtly declined a drink himself, watched in silence while Weedon swallowed his, winced automatically when the unhappy man said: 'Well, chin-chin,' and very shortly and with no waste of words ushered him out of the flat and into the lift. Then he walked back into the sitting-room. Christine was sitting on the arm of his chair, looking rather woebegone.

'What did you bring that man here for?'

His voice was hard, cold, and unfriendly.

'Darling, I told you; he only came in for a drink. Don't look so horrid. Jim, it's wonderful to have you back. I never knew . . .'

Her voice faded away into silence before her husband's angry stare.

'What have you been doing this evening?'

Jim hardly recognised his own voice. It was like listening to someone in a nightmare, someone speaking cruel words to his darling Christine. But an invisible force drove him on. He did not listen to her answer.

'You've been drinking, Christine.'

There were tears in the grey eyes that looked at him so reproachfully.

'But, darling Jim, of course I've been drinking. What else can one do when one goes out? It's all so terrible when you're away and I'm so unhappy. Oh, Jim, love me!'

She held out her arms and Jim's heart stirred inside him. But he could not stop.

'I thought I could trust you. Going to night clubs with a bounder like that and making an exhibition of yourself. Everyone must have seen you were tight.'

'Jim, I'm so tired.'

Christine walked across to him. The little trip in her walk was pathetic now. She put her arms round his neck.

'Unhook me, darling,' she whispered.

Automatically Jim's fingers felt for the hooks in the silver dress that he knew so well. The soft smell of her body intoxicated him. As the dress slipped to the ground he flung his arms round her and their two bodies melted into one.

CHAPTER VI

THE SHADOW DEEPENS

Jim Widdington never knew whether that short October leave gave him more of delight or pain. The blessed relief of being for a short time away from the noise and dirt and horror of war, the precious joy of being with and of loving his beautiful young wife, these were indeed matters of delight. But behind them a shadow. Christine had changed. She was still beautiful – perhaps more beautiful than ever before; she was still sweet and loving and gay. But from her gaiety was cast the shadow, in it lay the pain which counter-balanced his delight.

In the short first period of their married life, when they knew only too well how little time was left to them, it had seemed natural that Christine, after the strictness of her upbringing, should want to fling herself into the whirl of frivolous enjoyment that must have been so novel to her. Even then Jim had felt moments of disquiet but it had been easy to make excuses for her; how could a girl so inexperienced be expected to discriminate in the making of friends? If she was inclined to drink rather too much of the champagne that flowed so freely, was that not also natural in the excitement of their sudden happiness?

But now these two failings were more marked and less easy to ignore. Jim saw no more of the unhappy Major Weedon and did not worry himself seriously about that single incident, but – as Christine dragged him out each night to restaurant, theatre and night-club – he found that she had collected a wide circle of friends who were very far from being attractive. Men, some of them soldiers but others obviously *embusques* of the least attractive type, hailed her by her Christian name; women whom Jim knew to be expensive harlots were on terms of easy friendship with her. When he protested she laughed at him and told him once again not to be a Jeremiah, and he loved her too much to spend even one hour of his short leave in quarrelling with her.

And she was drinking. Not just the glass too much that made for gaiety and humour, and which had seemed so excusable before. She drank steadily now through dinner, at the night-club, and even at home. And not only champagne but brandy, the most insidious of all drinks. Jim tried to check it; in public she just laughed and paid no attention to what he said; at home she cried and he had no heart to be harsh with her. He did find one opportunity to talk to her about it quietly and seriously; she listened sadly and agreed with all he said.

'I know, Jim. I don't want to, but I can't help it. I get so excited and something seems to drive me to go on. I suppose I have no self-control, but perhaps if this beastly war would end and we could live together quietly, I might settle down to being placid and calm. I want to be a good wife to you, Jim. I love you so much.'

Poor Jim could only hug her and tell her how much he loved her too. But he felt helpless and desperately worried.

Their time was so short – only six clear days. They paid one flying visit to Jim's home. Colonel Widdington – with the temporary rank of Brigadier-General – was still training men on Salisbury Plain; he had, to his bitter indignation, not been allowed to take his Brigade to France; it had been given to a younger man as soon as it was ready for active service. He had come up to London to see his son but could only spare a few hours. Mrs. Widdington was at home and was overwhelmed with joy at Jim's visit, greeting Christine, too, affectionately, though she had taken little notice of her in the past months.

The question of Sir Brandon Wayke and his ban of excommunication was discussed. The old man had not written one word to Jim or Christine since their marriage, and now was living the life almost of a recluse. It was decided that Mrs. Widdington should go across to Chatterleys and ask him if he would see his daughter and her husband; she returned to say that she had completely failed to move him and that he seemed to have aged very greatly. She did not add her private thought – that he was getting very queer in his mind.

It was a visit both happy and unhappy, like the whole of Jim's leave. So, too, was the hour they spent with Mary, still almost fanatically bound to her hospital. She was sweet to her brother, kind enough to Christine, but Jim could see that the girls were not happy together and on the whole he was glad when their meeting was over – a fact in itself terribly distressing to him because, until his marriage to Christine, he had always regarded Mary as his inseparable friend.

So the six days of that first leave passed quickly by and in the gloom of a late October morning Jim Widdington and his wife once more faced the dreadful ordeal of a parting that might be final. He left her knowing that his love for her was deeper than it had ever been, deeper by reason of the dangers that hung over it, the known danger that awaited him over the water, the subtler peril that remained with her at home.

The winter of 1915 passed in the comparative peace of trench warfare. In February 1916 the Guards Division moved north to the Salient and dug and trained and gained its customary command of No Man's Land. A steady drain of casualties kept the personnel of each unit constantly changing, but Jim Widdington remained immune and before long was commanding a Company and really enjoying the added responsibility that it brought him.

It was as well that his mind should be fully employed by his work, because very little happiness came to him from home. Christine's letters, frequent and affectionate at first, gradually dwindled away and became little more than a few scrawled lines in response to his appeals. Mary never mentioned her and his mother, who seldom went to London, gave no real news of her. His brother officers, going on leave, told him – in reply to his enquiries – that they had seen Christine at a restaurant or a night-club, but they seemed strangely reluctant to speak of her, and their silence added to poor Jim's uneasiness.

Then one day, when winter was fading into a lovely Flanders spring, there came a letter from Mary that brought all his fears to a head.

JIM (she wrote), Do try and get leave and come home. I haven't said anything before because I have hardly seen Christine myself and I could not believe what I sometimes heard. But I did see her two nights ago at a restaurant and I feel terribly uneasy about her. I am sure it is the strain of the war and your being away, but she seems to have lost control and I can't bear that she should make you unhappy.

It's no good my talking to her; you are the only person who can do any good. Do come, darling Jim.

Your loving
MARY.

The letter, vague as it was, left poor Jim in little doubt as to its meaning. He knew that Mary would not write in such a strain without good reason, and yet he felt furious with her for even hinting a criticism of Christine. What could he do? He was not due for leave again in the normal course for some time; he could only get it now by pleading 'urgent private affairs' and that would mean revealing a trouble that he desperately wanted to hide.

For a week he nursed his anxiety, tormenting himself with doubt and anger. The thought of Christine being 'talked about' by Mary's friends maddened him; furiously he told himself that their tales were lies . . . and yet he knew that the very silence of his brother officers was corroborative. At last he could bear it no longer. He must find out for himself. He went to the Commanding Officer and, without giving any reason, begged for even a few days' leave. Colonel Daubeny, who knew that his young Company Commander was no swinger of the lead, at once gave up the turn which he had allotted to himself and sent him off without asking a single question.

This time Jim was careful to telegraph a warning of his return. He arrived at midday and found Christine at the flat. She greeted him with eager affection but Jim was staggered by the change in her. Her features had coarsened, her expression had become petulant, her mouth twitched nervously, even when her face was apparently in repose. Nor was it only in appearance that the change was evident. Affectionate though she was, there was a hint of artificiality about her that distressed Jim even more than her coarsened features. Her voice at times had a strident note that did not ring true, and her grey eyes no longer held the steady gaze that had been the hallmark of her sincerity. In the days of their hurried court-ship, on their brief honeymoon, even in her faults, in the wild moments of excitement that swept her into indiscretion, Christine had always seemed so utterly genuine. Now that lovely sincerity was gone, and with it Jim felt that the bottom had fallen for ever out of his happiness.

He had been given a full allotment of leave and he spent every moment of it with Christine, not even going home to see his mother. He tried his utmost to win back the old Christine that he greatly loved, and she herself tried hard to be what she knew he wanted her to be. But it was too late. The inherited fever was in her blood, the circumstances of their lives had destroyed all chance of the calm environment which might have stilled it.

Before returning to France Jim Widdington went, by himself, to see his sister at her hospital. He told her that Christine was rather carried away by the excitement of the war but that she was really quite all right and that as soon as it was over and they could start their normal life again, she too would calm down and be normal. Mary knew well enough that this was but a brave pretence, and he must have had little doubt but that she knew it. Still, the pretence was sustained, if for no other reason than that no good could be done by destroying it. They parted affectionately, hiding the misery that numbed their hearts.

This time Jim did not let Christine come to the station to see him off. He could not have borne the contrast with their earlier leave-takings; then, in spite of deep anxiety there had been love and hope in their hearts; now, though love remained, hope of happiness had gone. They clung to each other at parting but they could not speak. Everything of entreaty, of admonition, had been said and Jim knew that it had been in vain; with hope dead there was nothing now left for him to say.

*

The summer drew on towards the great battle that everyone knew
was in preparation. There was some patrol activity and raiding in front
of Ypres, but it was clearly a diversion and when the Fourth Army and
the French launched their offensive on the Somme, the Guards knew
that it was only a matter of time before they would be in it. After bloody
repulses the advance began to gain a little ground and the expected call
came to the Division to move south. Through pleasant back areas they
marched, to settle in the line by Beaumont Hamel, where the attack had
failed, and wait for their turn.

One day Jim Widdington and two friends got a lift in a car and went
into Amiens to enjoy one of the famous Godbert *déjeuners*. The town
was thronged with troops and had almost an air of gaiety. 'Let us eat and
drink for tomorrow we die' was the motto only too bitterly applicable.

Jim enjoyed the good food but he had no mind to follow his friends
in their search of other entertainment, so he wandered off by himself to
look at the Cathedral – not because Cathedrals appealed to him but
because there was nothing else to do. A column of light ambulances was
drawn up in the wide street and he noticed that their drivers were women.
As he walked past a group of them he heard his name called and, looking
back, saw a tall, sturdy figure in a blue uniform detach itself from the
group and stride towards him. It was Helen Wayke.

'Jim! How grand to see you!'

He found himself grasping her outstretched hand. A sudden spasm
of emotion seized him and for a moment he could not speak.

'Helen!' he gasped out at last, and felt a tingle at the back of his eyes.
'Helen! It's . . . it seems like a life-time.'

Helen laughed.

'Well, two years of war are long enough,' she said. 'I heard the Guards
had come down and I wondered whether there would be a chance of
seeing you. They don't let us go any nearer than this, worse luck; we ply
between here and the base.'

'Have you been doing this all the time?'

Helen nodded.

'Yes. It's all right when there's a show on; we're kept pretty busy. But in between times we have to kick our heels a good deal. How are you, Jim?'

There was more in this question than could be answered with a conventional phrase.

'Can we walk about a bit? I'd like to have a talk,' said Jim.

The girl nodded.

'I don't think we shall be moving for a bit. I'll ask.'

In a moment she was back.

'Up and down within sight. I shall be glad to stretch my legs.'

Jim Widdington, looking at his sister-in-law, realised how well the blue uniform suited her fair colouring. She was a handsome woman and the strain and responsibility had added character to her face. In the two years since the cricket match at Chatterleys Jim had thought very little about his boyhood sweetheart but now, with the emotional stress of his unhappiness lying perilously near the surface, he felt a sudden surge of the old tenderness. He longed to open his heart to her in a way that he had not felt that he could talk to Mary.

'I . . . Helen, I've been an ungrateful beast,' he stammered. 'You were always so good to me and I . . . I've let myself drift away from you.'

A wry smile twisted the corner of Helen's mouth.

'It did seem rather like that,' she said quietly, 'but in war people do seem to fly off at tangents. How's Christine?'

That was so like Helen. She was honest to the point of bluntness. No beating about the bush; she came straight to the heart of the matter. And yet there was no touch of malice in her question.

Jim did not answer at once but looked restlessly about him.

'I wish we could go somewhere,' he muttered.

'There's a *café* just ahead. We could sit at a table outside – technically within sight,' said Helen.

A minute later they were seated at the table and had ordered two *cafes crèmes*. Even then Jim seemed unable to begin.

'Trouble?' the girl asked quietly.

Jim nodded.

'I'm afraid . . . frightful trouble. She . . . she . . .'

For a moment Helen laid her hand on his arm.

'I don't think you need tell me, Jim,' she said, seeing what an effort it was to him to speak.

'You've . . . you've heard?'

'I haven't heard much. I don't listen to gossip if I can help it. But I knew about her mother.'

Jim stared at her.

'Her mother? What do you mean?'

'Didn't father tell you?'

'Tell me what? I don't understand.'

'He ought to have,' said Helen Wayke, with the implacable judgment of the young upon their harassed elders. 'He didn't tell me, of course, but I put two and two together from things Mrs. Curling and the servants said when I was young and they thought I didn't understand. She must have been very sweet, Jim; they were all so fond of her though they must have been horrified at first at father marrying an actress. In those days it was even less done than it is now . . . marrying, I mean. But he married her too late, Jim. He thought he could stop her, I expect, but he couldn't. Oh, Jim . . . perhaps I oughtn't to have told you!'

The look of horror in her friend's eyes had suddenly shaken Helen Wayke's calm confidence.

'She . . . she was drinking?'

'Yes, Jim. I'm afraid so. It undermined her strength, I suppose, and she died when Christine was born.'

'My God! How awful! How awful!'

The young Grenadier sat staring at the untouched glass in front of him. The look of utter misery in his eyes touched Helen deeply and she, who had been cruelly hurt by his desertion and had determined to forget about him, she, too, felt the old affection for him revive.

'Jim, try not to mind too much. I've hardly seen Christine since she came back from the convent; she was such a child then that I hardly thought about her. Did she suddenly grow up, Jim? Was she . . . is she very lovely?'

Jim nodded slowly.

'Very lovely, Helen, and so sweet. She was a bit . . . erratic, of course, but it seemed only high spirits and I fell utterly in love with her. I love her now . . . but . . . I'm afraid it's too late, if there ever was a chance.'

Again Helen put her hand on his arm, and this time left it there.

'Poor Jim,' she said. 'I'm so sorry; so terribly sorry.'

CHAPTER VII

THE DREAM IS ENDED

In the month that followed his meeting with Helen Wayke, Jim's thoughts were distracted from his own worries by the intense fighting in which his Division was engaged. On the 15th September the Guards, in spite of heavy losses, thrust deeply into the German lines; on the 25th they broke clean through and from the ridge beyond Lesboeufs and Morval watched the enemy flying in confusion. Now was the time for the cavalry to go through; open country lay before them, with no wire or trenches to impede their pursuit. But the Division on the left had been held up, the gap was too narrow, and the great opportunity was lost.

Once again Jim Widdington came through untouched, though more than half of the officers in his battalion were killed or wounded. He went into these two battles not caring whether he came through alive, and his fearless leadership inspired his men. A year ago the 'immediate award' of a Military Cross would have thrilled him; now the honour found him listless and depressed as the excitement of battle died away, and the withdrawal of the Division to a 'rest area' gave him time once again to think of his tragic marriage.

He had no wish now to go home on leave, though he could have gone whenever he liked. His efforts to save Christine from herself on the last occasion had been too complete a failure to give him the slightest hope of succeeding now. He felt that he could not bear to see her as she was now, that he would rather keep his memory of the lovely, happy girl whom he had married, hoping that a renewal of the fighting would bring him final release.

It was a tragic, and perhaps a wicked state of mind for a young soldier to get into, but the shock he had suffered had been very great; in a few short months he had seen his young wife change from the laughing girl who had swept him off his feet into a nervous, irritable woman, coarsened by drink and taking her pleasure in the company of men and women of a type which he had always regarded with contempt.

Brave as he was in the face of physical danger Jim Widdington had not the moral courage to go back to England and fight that harrowing battle with an intangible foe, the battle which, had he put his whole soul into it, might even yet have saved Christine from the evil which she had inherited.

So, too easily, the young soldier gave up the fight; too rapidly his young wife drifted to inevitable disaster.

There was, as it proved, to be no more heavy fighting for the Guards that autumn. They went back into the line very near where they had left it and settled down to consolidate what they had gained. A hard and bitter winter followed, culminating in a thaw even more detrimental to the health and morale of men. But their discipline carried them through unscathed and in the early spring of 1917 came the German withdrawal to the Hindenburg Line. The change of environment, to a state almost of open warfare during that interlude, heartened the troops and Jim Widdington found himself almost enjoying the problem of thinking in terms of 'advance-guards' and 'outposts' rather than trench reliefs and wiring parties.

Into the middle of this false spring of happiness fell the bomb which finally shattered his married life. It came in the form of a letter from Christine.

JIM (she wrote), I can't go on like this. I have tried to give it up and to be what you wanted but it is too strong for me. If you had been here it might have been different, but it is so lonely by myself that I simply have to go out and be with people and then I lose all control of myself.

I know you don't love me any longer; I could see that when you were home last summer – you looked at me with disgust and I can't blame you. And I know you could have got leave and come home after the fighting ended if you had wanted to.

I am going away and you won't see me again. Forgive me if you can, Jim; I know I have made you very unhappy but I have loved you very much and I always shall. Try to forget me and to start your life over again as if our marriage had never happened. You can divorce me if you want to; I shan't fight it. Good-bye, Jim.

CHRISTINE.

In an agony of remorse and despair Jim rushed off to his Commanding Officer and again got leave at once, although the 'leave season' was now closed. He telegraphed to Christine but his journey to the base was delayed and it was nearly two days before he got to London. He found the flat closed; the porter told him that Mrs. Widdington had left on the previous day; she had not left an address for letters to follow.

Inside the flat he found confusion and dirt. Kathleen, the maid who had accompanied Christine from Chatterleys, had left her months ago, Jim learned from the porter, and very little dusting or tidying had been done. It was a scene of utter desolation, spiritual as well as physical.

Jim rushed off to see Mary. She knew nothing and could give him no help but sympathy. He went home, where his mother knew even less. He went to Chatterleys, where he found Sir Brandon too ill to see him even if he had been willing to do so. He had an interview with the housekeeper, Mrs. Curling, who treated him with anything but favour, regarding him, rather unjustly, as the immediate cause of her young lady's trouble, though she knew well enough the underlying cause. She had not heard of Christine's departure from the flat and knew nothing of her present whereabouts.

Jim went back to London and began to haunt the restaurants and night-clubs which Christine had patronised, hoping – though dreading – to find her with her undesirable friends. She was not there and he could get no recent news of her. He went to his solicitors and instructed them at all costs to find her and to give her a letter in which he assured her of his love and of his wish to live with her again as soon as the war was over. He also made the proper legal arrangements for her support, which he had been too careless to make before. Then he went back to France.

Weeks passed, and months. The solicitors wrote that they could find no trace of Mrs. James Widdington; they had been unable, consequently, either to deliver the letter or to provide her with means of support. Jim's misery deepened, and to it was added remorse, as he realised how much he had left undone that might have helped, if it could not save, his unhappy young wife.

Gradually, as the war drew on towards its dramatic close, his unhappiness was numbed and remorse faded into regretful sadness. He saw Helen more than once and found relief and even forgetfulness in her honest friendliness. The two even arranged to spend a 'Paris leave' together, though in the discreet propriety of separate hotels. It was the happiest week that Jim had known since his first leave revealed to him the dreadful truth.

In March 1918 the great German offensive, striking at the very lifeline of the Allies, thrust all thought of private trouble or private happiness into the background. The bastion held by the Guards Division on the north of the German thrust stood firm and in due course the tide of warfare turned; the Allies, dealing blow after blow on different portions of the yielding enemy line, thrust them back towards their own frontier, to be stopped only by the signing of the Armistice.

That day, the end of bloody, hateful war, so eagerly awaited, brought to Jim Widdington no excited ecstasy of happiness. Like many others, he could hardly realise the change, and before realisation could bring relief there fell, not only on him but on all that army of brave men, the extraordinary reaction of selfishness which, as the problems of demobilisation developed, drove even the disciplined soldiers of the Guards Division to the limit of their self control.

But at last they were brought back from Cologne to England, the extra battalions disbanded, the magnificent units of 'other arms' which had served the Division so well, broken up and scattered. Jim was given a month's leave and found, from the intense weariness of mind and body that overwhelmed him, that he needed every day of it if he was to take up his life as a peace-time soldier again.

When he did go back to duty Jim found the life almost unbearable. Demobilisation had brought every regular soldier tumbling down in rank; men who had commanded Brigades were now commanding Companies and Jim, who had been a Company Commander through nearly three years of warfare, now had to be content with a platoon. Even that might have been all right if there had been any men to command or train, but with the new craze for 'education' every man who was not on a fatigue always seemed to be learning algebra or a 'civil occupation'; the officers spent their time kicking their heels in the ante-room or learning once more to march on markers and halt their men on the proper foot.

After a few months Jim felt that he could endure it no longer. He longed for a wider life and was much tempted by a brother officer to join him on a farming venture in East Africa, whither the attraction of an open-air life and of what was believed to be easy money was drawing many soldiers.

After talking things over with his family he decided to take the plunge, and sent in his papers. There was nothing to hold him in England now. No trace of Christine had been found and, truth to tell, he had not, after his return from France, tried very hard. In the physical and moral reaction which he, in common with many others, had suffered after the war, he had yielded up that battle too easily and, feeling ashamed, tried to forget it. He had no inclination to follow up Christine's suggestion of divorce. In any case, having lost trace of her, it might have been difficult to get evidence and the last thing he wanted was to drag their troubles through the Courts.

One thing kept him in England longer than he might otherwise have stayed. Helen Wayke, who had spent the winter after the war in the south of France and Italy, was coming home for a visit prior to taking up hospital work in the latter country. Jim wanted very much to see her again. During the last two years she was the only person who had taken him out of himself, made him forget his troubles. She was so calm, so quietly cheerful.

She never reproached him, never talked to him about the past unless he wanted to talk, but lived serenely for the present, seeing the best in everyone and drawing from life such quiet happiness as she found it always able to give. The contrast with Christine's restlessness was very soothing to the tired soldier's nerves.

So Jim looked forward to seeing her and, when she came, saw as much of her as he could. Sir Brandon Wayke was dead now and Helen found Chatterleys too sad and gloomy to stay at long. Her brother, Richard, who had been terribly injured in an air crash in March 1918, was still in a hospital at Roehampton, so she came back to London to be near him during the few months she expected to be in England.

Jim found her just the same as ever, ready to walk in Richmond Park or to dine at a smart restaurant and go to a play, whichever the mood suited him to ask her to do. And if she did not want to do either, she said so frankly and Jim, whose nerves would have caused him to flare up with most women, found no cause for irritation in her quiet refusals.

On the night before he was due to sail he took her to dine at the Savoy, intending either to stay on and dance or to go to a show, according as the mood took them. Now that the moment to leave England had arrived, Jim felt curiously reluctant to go, though he could find no explanation of his reluctance. To drive away his depression he drank two quick glasses of champagne before eating anything solid, and the result was entirely satisfactory; he at once felt that the whole thing was great fun, the women beautiful, the men good fellows – even one or two whom a year or two ago he had been calling 'damned embusques' and sworn not to speak to again.

After the fish course he persuaded Helen, who liked to enjoy her dinner, rather unwillingly to dance. The restricted floor space was crowded and they could do little more than shuffle round. Though a graceful and athletic woman, Helen was not a good dancer; she was curiously unresponsive and her partners found that they had more work to do than was enjoyable. For a time Jim, in the elation of his spirits, did not notice this; then, as the dance was apparently ended and they were walking back towards their table, the band leader suddenly broke into one of the old

Viennese waltzes that were so seldom heard in the post-war craze for jazz. Jim put his arm round Helen's waist and swung her back on to the floor. A surge of memory rushed over him; how often he had danced to this entrancing tune with Christine, how she had loved it, how lightly she had floated in his arms. By contrast Helen was as heavy and lifeless as lead.

The wave of depression swept over Jim with renewed and overwhelming force. He stopped dead.

'I . . . I'm sorry, Helen,' he stammered. 'I feel a bit giddy.'

Helen smiled.

'No wonder, my good silly,' she said, 'if you will dance in the middle of your dinner. Come and finish it in comfort and let it settle. The crowd may have cleared a bit by then.'

She slipped her hand through his arm and guided him back to their table, talking cheerfully and at the same time keeping a practised eye open for symptoms of real trouble.

There were none. Jim was well enough but his spirits did not revive. The figure of Christine hovered before him; Christine as she had been when he first married her, laughing, cheerful, the sparkle of happiness and mischief in her eyes.

Jim passed a hand across his own.

'Oh, God,' he muttered. 'What a fool I've been.'

Helen was too wise to question him at once. She went quietly on with her own dinner and did not press him to eat his own.

'It's very hot in here, Jim,' she said after a time. 'Would you like to stay or shall we go? If you don't feel like a show we might drive somewhere.'

Jim did not want to drive anywhere . . . but still less did he want to go to a 'show.'

'Just as you like, Helen,' he said gloomily. 'I daresay some fresh air will buck me up.'

It was a lovely night in late June. Helen had hired a small two-seater coupe for the summer and they had driven to the Savoy in it. With the hood open it was the ideal car for the occasion. But Jim could not get out of his mind that drive of his with Christine to Maidenhead. The memory of her now overwhelmed him with sadness. He sat silently beside Helen and hardly noticed where they were going until the car pulled up in Richmond Park.

Helen took out a cigarette and offered one to her companion.

'Something worrying you, Jim?' she asked.

Jim stirred uneasily in his seat.

'No, of course not; why should there be?' he replied crossly. Then, pulling himself together, he answered her question.

'Sorry, Helen. Yes, I suppose there is. It suddenly came over me what a hideous mess I've made of things – my life, Christine's life . . . and I daresay other people's lives too in a way.'

'Yes. Mine a bit too, Jim. We may as well be frank about it,' said Helen calmly. 'But it's no good going back to that now. You may have been partly to blame but it was much more the War that caused the trouble. Christine was too young and inexperienced and unbalanced to face all that excitement and strain so soon after leaving the convent. And, of course you weren't very old or experienced yourself, Jim, or perhaps you wouldn't have been quite so easily swept off your feet.'

'You mean I ought not to have married her at all?'

'I don't say that, but it would have given Christine a much better chance if she could have grown up quietly at home before being thrown into all that excitement and . . . temptation. With that hereditary weakness she hardly had a chance, poor dear.'

Jim Widdington was conscious of irritation. It is one thing to blame oneself, quite another to hear the blame applied by somebody else. He felt an urge to defend himself hotly, but he beat it off.

'I blame myself more for what happened afterwards,' he said. 'I feel that I ought to have been able to save her, or that I ought to have got her back again somehow.'

Helen Wayke shook her head.

'I don't think so. It was too late then; the damage was done and as long as the war was on you could do nothing effective. After it was over . . . she was gone. Don't go on thinking about the past, Jim. Think about the future.'

Slowly the comfort of her words spread through Jim Widdington's troubled spirit. It dawned upon him that once again, now as at Amiens in the war, Helen was giving him the courage and hope that he in his weakness had almost abandoned.

As he looked at her calm and beautiful face Jim wondered why he had ever allowed her to fade into the background of his life. She had always been his unfailing friend; she had never changed, even when he had treated her with cruel lack of consideration. Whenever he was with her he recovered much that he had lost . . . and now he was on the point of going away and he might never see her again.

An intense longing suddenly overwhelmed him, a longing for affection, for a woman's love, for the comfort and hope that might yet be his.

'Helen,' he said huskily. 'Have we got to leave each other? I have no right to ask you anything. I treated you abominably, selfishly . . . and you've never given me anything but kindness. I have taken it all from you and given you nothing. Is it possible that . . . ?'

He broke off, realising with a shock that there was nothing he could ask her, nothing he could offer. He was a married man and though his wife had offered him freedom he had lost the opportunity to take it.

Helen turned towards him and put her hand on his.

'I know what you are thinking, Jim. We might have got on very well together. I think we could have made each other happy. But it's too late now. We have got to build new lives for ourselves and hope that gradually some kind of happiness may creep back into them. You are going to Africa, I am going to Italy. Perhaps we shall meet again. Perhaps some day we may again mean a great deal to each other, but all that is on the knees of the gods. The one thing we must not do is to look back; there is no hope there. Hope is only in the future.'

She pressed his hand gently and Jim, realising that his sudden dream of happiness was fading as quickly as it had come, turned his head away so that she should not see the tears that had sprung into his eyes.

PART III

WORKING FORWARD

CHAPTER I

THE WAYKES

Inspector Poole did not learn the whole of Christine Wayke's tragic story from Mrs. Curling, but it was wonderful how much the old lady did know. Some she knew from her own observation or the gossip of her staff – butler, ladies' maids and others. Much had been told to her by Christine's half-sister, Helen, during the short period that she was in England after the war. Some even she had learned from Sir Brandon himself; after his second wife's death the lonely baronet had often treated the faithful old family servant as a confidante, and before his death he had unburdened himself of a great deal of his load of grief and anxiety to her and begged her to help, if she could, the daughter whom he had himself treated so harshly.

A good deal of the story he heard later from other members of the two families concerned or from independent witnesses, but for the time being he was content to hear all that Mrs. Curling could tell him. She herself had not seen 'Miss Christine,' as she still called her, since she ran away from home in the first year of the Great War; she believed that no one, no member of the family or friend of her early life, had seen her since the spring of 1917 when she left her husband's flat and disappeared into the unknown. She knew that Captain Widdington had tried very hard to trace her, both then and immediately after the war, but had completely failed.

Poole realised that his next step must be to get in touch with Captain James Widdington. Here Mrs. Curling proved singularly unhelpful; she did not know where the Captain was now; she had heard that he had gone to East Africa and did not know whether he was still there. Colonel Widdington had died not long after the War and Mrs. Widdington had sold Festing Manor and gone away; she too was now dead, Mrs. Curling believed. The people round still talked about Captain Jim, who had been a general favourite, but no one seemed to know anything for certain about him.

'What about his sister?' asked Poole, fully expecting to hear that she, too, was in Kenya – if not Timbuctoo.

'I believe she lives in Devonshire,' said Mrs. Curling. 'That was where Mrs. Widdington went when she left these parts. Miss Mary never married, they tell me, though she was a pretty young lady. She stuck to her nursing after the war, till her mother wanted her.'

Well, Devonshire was better than East Africa, anyway.

'And Miss Helen Wayke?'

Mrs. Curling shook her head and pursed her faded lips.

'I've not set eyes on her for many a year,' she said. 'I did think she'd settle down and look after poor Sir Richard. So steady as she always used to be as a girl and such a help to her father. But, there, the war seemed to upset them all. At one time she took up some kind of hospital work in Italy, I understand, but then she got restless and started travelling about, Poland and Russia and Japan and America and all kinds of out-landish places. The last time I heard from her she was in Australia but that was a year or more ago; she never was a good one to write letters.'

Poole heaved a sigh. Miss Wayke was, or might be, a vital witness. No doubt he could learn her whereabouts from her brother but he doubted if the authorities would run to a trip to the Antipodes for him. Clearly Sir Richard Wayke was the next person to be seen. He probably did not know as much about his half-sister's married life as did Mrs. Curling, because he had been in France almost continuously, the housekeeper told him, until he was shot down in 1918, but at least he would be able to give up-to-date news of his sister Helen and probably, too, of Captain Widdington.

Then there would be family solicitors to see and, after them, a journey to Devonshire. There was plenty of work ahead but at least there was now solid ground to work upon.

Poole decided not to spend any time in getting confirmation of Mrs.

Curling's story at Chatterleys or Festing Manor; that could come later if necessary; at present he wanted to get up to date as quickly as possible. On his journey back to London he went carefully over in his mind all that Mrs. Curling had told him, but realised that it was still too early to frame any sort of conjecture that would link up that sad story of the past with the still more tragic present.

Thinking over the story, one point which struck Poole was the small part played in it by the present head of the family, Sir Richard Wayke. That was natural enough after the war, because the unfortunate man had been partially paralysed by the crashing of his aeroplane when he was shot down in 1918, but even before that he appeared as a dim figure who had apparently had no influence on the lives of his sisters. Mrs. Curling had described him as very quiet and entirely taken up with mechanics; he had had a very thorough technical training and, at the age of twenty-five, was well started on an engineering career when the war broke out. He had at first joined the Royal Engineers but had transferred to the Royal Flying Corps in 1916.

No doubt absence in France accounted for a good deal of his detachment from the family story, but Poole had gathered from Mrs. Curling that both the sisters had been rather frightened of their brother, who was inclined to be morose, though she thought he was really much attached to Helen; of Christine he had seen very little. Sir Brandon had never understood his son, who had none of the interests of a country gentleman of the period, and had allowed him to live his own life, never, she thought, consulting him or trying to train him for the responsibilities he would have to face on his succession.

So Poole had no very clear picture in his mind when he went, on the morning after his return from Birmingham, to the address in St. John's Wood which Mrs. Curling had given him. He naturally expected to add to his knowledge but he had no great hope of making any illuminating discovery.

Sir Richard Wayke's new home, Green Lodge, was a modest house near Primrose Hill, north of Regent's Park. It stood in a small garden of its own but was far from being one of the luxurious modern mansions that border Avenue Road. There was a small wooden garage at the side of the house and the garden showed signs of complete lack of interest on the part of its owner. Poole's ring was answered by a manservant who wore, not the garb of butler or footman, but the plain blue serge of the handyman. He was short, with a cheerful, ugly face, and his voice revealed that he was at home in London.

'Naow, S' Richard's not in,' he replied to the detective's enquiry. 'Any message?'

'I'd rather see him, if possible,' said Poole. 'Can you tell me when he is likely to be back?'

'Back to 'is lunch; not before. If you come at 'alf past two 'e'd be finished by then. What naime shall I say?'

'Poole, but he won't know me. I'll be back at half-past two. Thank you.'

The delay was irritating but could not be helped. Poole had spent the early part of the morning writing up his notes and reporting the new development to the Assistant Commissioner, so that it was now after twelve. There would not be time to start any other line of enquiry before the luncheon hour so, as he was close to Hampstead, he decided to go and have a word with Superintendent Hollis. He did not intend at the moment to tell anyone except the A.C. about the true identity of 'Bella Knox,' but he believed in 'keeping touch.' Something might turn up, some trivial detail, which a police-officer would hesitate to report formally to Scotland Yard but which was easily told in conversation. In any case, Poole thought that the Superintendent had not been very tact-fully handled by Chief-Inspector Beldam and he wanted to re-establish friendly relations.

Superintendent Hollis, though pleasant enough to the C.I.D. man, had no light to throw on his end of the story. As a matter of routine Inspector Hartridge was keeping an eye on Herbert Varden, but the big man had given them no reason for renewed suspicion. He had resumed his normal life of bookmaker's 'escort,' but not to Montie Lewis; the little Jew had evidently become shy of him and Varden had attached himself to one Barney Sprot, an elderly man with, Hollis thought, a dwindling business.

Having had his own modest luncheon, Poole walked down the hill to Green Lodge. In the little drive in front of the door he saw one of the electrically propelled wheeled-chairs which had been such a boon to crippled men since the war; he had often admired the dexterity with which their occupants handled them and the speed at which they were able to travel. When the Cockney man-servant, whom Poole guessed to have been Sir Richard's batman, answered his ring the detective sent in his official card. The man at once returned and led him to a large room at the back of the house, overlooking the garden. There was not the slightest sign of elegance or even comfort in the room, but in the large bay window was what appeared to be some form of carpenter's bench, with a small lathe at one end of it. The occupant of the room was seated in a wheeled-chair in front of this bench, which had an opening to admit his legs; his back was to the door and he appeared to be adjusting the lathe, but when Poole was announced he turned his chair so that he could face him.

Sir Richard Wayke at this time was fifty years old. His body appeared to be sturdy but his clean-shaven face was haggard, with lines of pain about the mouth. The eyes were deep-set, with a hard, penetrating stare, and Poole could well believe that Sir Richard's sisters might have been afraid of him.

'What is it, Inspector? Has my sports car been breaking the law again?'

Poole thought the voice harsh and unattractive but there was a whimsical twist at the corner of Sir Richard's mouth as he spoke.

'Nothing of that kind, sir. I'm afraid I shall have to ask for a little of your time.'

A frown crossed the baronet's face; he glanced involuntarily at the bench, then with a shrug of the shoulders pointed to a chair by the fire.

'Better sit down, then.'

With a quick turn of the wrists he spun his chair across the room. Paralysed as the lower part of his body appeared to be, there was nothing wrong with his arms; his hands, too, had the wiry strength of the mechanic.

'What's it about?'

'About your sister, sir.'

'Helen?' There was a sharp note of enquiry in the voice.

'I should have said your half-sister, sir; Mrs. Widdington.'

Sir Richard Wayke stared at the detective, an expression of astonishment on his face.

'Christine? What on earth do you mean?'

Poole had had some difficulty in deciding how to handle this interview. Considering all the publicity which the case of Bella Knox had received, the photographs in the papers, and the urgent police requests for information, which must have aroused strong local interest, he found it difficult to believe that a man living so close to the scene of the murder should have remained in ignorance of his sister's death; on the other hand he did not want to start by antagonising this important witness.

'You may have read, sir, of the discovery of a woman's body near Highgate Ponds on the ninth of last month; we have just established the fact that the body was that of Mrs. James Widdington.'

Sir Richard Wayke's eyes remained steadily fixed on the detective; they did not waver as he said:

'I don't understand that. Who identified her?'

'She was not identified as Mrs. Widdington at the time, sir, as I said. She was then identified by her landlady as a Miss Bella Knox and it was only yesterday that she was identified through a photograph by Mrs. Curling, your late housekeeper, as Mrs. Widdington.'

'What photograph?' asked the baronet abruptly.

Briefly as he could, Poole explained the steps which had led him to Chatterleys. Finally he produced the photographs themselves. Sir Richard examined them carefully.

'There is certainly a likeness to Christine,' he said, 'but I should not care to swear to an identification. But then I haven't seen her for twenty years or more.'

There was not a trace of emotion in his voice. Poole wondered whether the man was without feeling or whether he had very great self-control.

'You saw these photographs when they appeared in the papers at the time of the murder, I suppose, sir? We were asking for an identification.'

Sir Richard shook his head.

'Not that I know of, but I don't see the daily papers much.'

Poole noticed that the baronet showed no surprise at the word 'murder,' though it was the first time it had been used during their talk. The fact hardened his belief that Sir Richard had in fact read all about the finding of Bella Knox's body and had known that she was his half-sister. It was perhaps comprehensible that the head of an old family should have preferred to keep silent about this skeleton in the cupboard; in any case it would be impossible to prove against him this suppression of identification.

Possibly Wayke guessed something of the detective's thoughts, as he went on to say:

'I'm not prepared to accept this as a fact, you know, Inspector; not on my own identification, which is quite doubtful. And Mrs. Curling must be an old woman now and her eyesight can't be good.'

'Then that will be all the more reason for getting other identifications, sir; your sister, for instance, and Captain Widdington, and the family solicitors.'

A quick frown on Sir Richard's face suggested that he regretted leading that card. But in any case he must know that the detective was bound to follow up the matter now.

'You can try, of course,' he said. 'Our solicitors won't be hard to find but the others may lead you a dance. I haven't set eyes on either of them for years. My sister, Helen, is a wanderer and Jim Widdington was in Africa when I last heard of him.'

'You can give me their addresses, no doubt, sir?'

Sir Richard looked steadily at Poole.

'No, Inspector, I can't,' he said quietly.

Poole felt a quick surge of anger. He was certain that this man was deliberately withholding information . . . but how could he prove it?

'Then the solicitors, please?'

'Gorvin and Bray, 271 Bedford Square.'

No doubt they would be able to supply the addresses, but whether they would know Mrs. James Widdington well enough to identify her from a photograph taken after death was another matter; it was hardly likely that she had had many dealings with them.

'That all, Inspector?'

'No, sir; I must ask you to tell me as much as you can about your sister's married life.'

What Sir Richard knew appeared to be mostly a matter of hearsay. He had seen very little of the Widdingtons after their marriage and had apparently not known much at the time of what was happening. Poole learned only one fact of which Mrs. Curling had said, and presumably knew nothing, and that was the unpleasant little episode connected with Mrs. George Bazeley. Apparently Jim Widdington had told the true story of the flat in Half Moon Street to his wife after their marriage and she, in a moment of indiscretion, had told some one else, and the story had eventually reached Sir Richard. The fact that he now repeated it to the detective and the way in which he told it gave Poole a pretty clear idea that the baronet had no great liking or admiration for his brother-in-law.

Very probably Richard Wayke thought that his unhappy sister had been too lightly abandoned by her husband, a criticism which certainly suggested itself to Poole himself, from what he had so far heard. In any case the baronet had evidently made no attempt to establish friendly relations with Captain Widdington after the war, though it seemed unlikely that he was really ignorant of his brother-in-law's present whereabouts.

Poole decided that for the moment there was no more to be learned from Sir Richard Wayke, so he took his leave and made his way by bus to Bedford Square. He enquired for one of the partners, and after the usual twenty minutes' wait was shown into the room of Mr. Gorvin. The solicitor, an elderly, clean-shaven man, received him with no great show of warmth. Poole came straight to the point.

'I am trying to identify a woman who was found dead near Highgate Ponds on the ninth of October, sir,' he said. 'I won't take up your time with details of the enquiry but I have reason to believe now that she was a Mrs. James Widdington, formerly Miss Christine Wayke, a family for which I am told you act. I came to ask if you could help me with the identification.'

Mr. Gorvin showed no sign of surprise or of any other emotion. He looked steadily at the detective.

'Mrs. Widdington has been . . . missing, shall I say, for many years, Inspector,' he said. 'That is to say, the family lost all touch with her after the war. I only saw her once or twice, when I acted for her at the time of her marriage. I don't know that I could identify her now.'

Poole produced his photographs and handed them to the solicitor. Mr. Gorvin carefully adjusted his spectacles.

'Ah, yes, I think I remember seeing this photograph in the press some time ago. You made an appeal for information, did you not? I certainly did not recognise her at the time, which, under the circumstances, is hardly surprising. But now that you call my attention to the possibility, I can quite see that there is a likeness. Poor woman.'

The last words appeared to be thrown in rather as a matter of form than genuine sentiment.

'Do you definitely identify her as Mrs. Widdington?' asked Poole.

'I should be reluctant to do that, Inspector; not definitely. I am inclined to think that it is she. I would not care to go further than that.'

Unsatisfactory as this was, Poole decided not to press the matter further at the moment. He asked for details of Mrs. Widdington's life and heard yet another and more formal account of the unhappy story; a few details added to what he had already heard from Mrs. Curling and Sir Richard Wayke but nothing very helpful. He turned to the question that most greatly interested him – the present whereabouts of the dead woman's husband.

'Ah, there I am afraid I cannot help you,' said Mr. Gorvin. 'You will realise that Captain Widdington was not my client. I have had no dealings with him since the marriage – or rather, since the arrangements that were subsequently made, or attempted to be made, for Mrs. Widdington through Captain Widdington's solicitors. As you probably know, she was never traced.'

'Then I must go to Captain Widdington's solicitors,' said Poole patiently. 'No doubt you can tell me who they are.'

Mr. Gorvin bent his brow in an effort of recollection.

'I think . . . I must refresh my memory.'

He pressed a button on his house-telephone and in due course announced that, as he had thought, Captain Widdington had been represented by Vastable and Brown.

'But I'm afraid that doesn't help you, Inspector,' he added. 'There was some trouble soon after the war and . . . well, in fact, to put it bluntly, the firm no longer exists . . . as a firm. You may be able to trace the individual partners, but they are hardly likely to be in touch with Captain Widdington now.'

Poole groaned in spirit. No doubt he would in due course find the elusive Captain but for the moment frustration appeared to be his lot. He returned doggedly to the attack. The address of Miss Helen Wayke could no doubt be supplied.

'By the way, she is still single, I take it?' he added.

'So far as I know,' said Mr. Gorvin. 'I have not heard of her being married. Miss Wayke travels a good deal, Inspector, and does not keep me in touch with her movements. Her bank, the Fleet Street branch of the Great Southern, make all arrangements for keeping her supplied with funds and no doubt would know her present address.'

Yes, and no doubt would refuse to part with it without "an order of the Court," thought Poole bitterly; in his experience bankers were even more difficult to get information out of than solicitors. Although Mr. Gorvin had been pleasant enough and by no means obstructive Poole realised, as he walked away from Bedford Square, that he had learned remarkably little from that astute gentleman. He wondered whether a telephone call from Green Lodge had preceded his visit; the thought made him uneasy.

It was too late now to go to the bank and, realising what he might expect from that visit, Poole took a sudden decision to leave the Wayke side of the problem for the moment and go straight down to Devonshire and have a talk with Captain Widdington's sister.

CHAPTER II

THE WIDDINGTONS

Directly Poole saw Mary Widdington he felt that at last he was in the presence of a witness who would be honest with him. Her manner was simple and straightforward; she must, Poole thought, have been good-looking once, though her colouring had faded now, but the frank look in her blue eyes was both attractive and encouraging. She listened quietly to the detective's explanation of his visit and, on being shown the photographs, at once recognised the dead woman as her sister-in-law. Poole did not doubt that her surprise and distress were genuine; she said that she had not read about the case as she 'did not bother much with newspapers.' She declared her willingness to tell Poole everything she knew, though she did not believe that that included anything that might lead to the discovery of poor Christine's murderer.

For more than an hour Poole listened again to the story of which he had already heard three versions. Inevitably it was told this time from the Widdington angle, and Captain Widdington himself appeared in a more favourable light. Up till now Poole had thought of him as a selfish and inconstant man who had married a young girl and, as soon as she showed signs of her terrible inherited failing, had thrown her to the wolves with very little real attempt to rescue her. From Mary Widdington's account it seemed clear that poor Christine had never given him a chance, had made no real effort to fight her own battle and had gone down with hardly a struggle, leaving him heart-broken and forlorn.

However, whichever way sympathy was due, it was the detective's duty to grope his way forward from the past into the present, and try to discover whether there could be any link between that sad story of the Great War and the sordid murder on Hampstead Heath in 1939. Unlikely as that seemed, clearly he could not feel satisfied until he had eliminated the possibility. And the first thing he had to do was to get contact with the dead woman's husband. He must carry the story of James Widdington forward from 1919 to the present day.

In reply to his questions Mary Widdington told him that her brother's farming venture in Kenya had not been very successful. At first, with Government encouragement and an artificial boom in prices, all had gone well, but then had come the inevitable slump and many farmers had gone under. Jim and his friend, being stubborn men, had struggled on, just keeping their heads above water, but in 1925 the partner had been badly mauled by a lion and, losing an arm, had been compelled to give up the hard struggle and come home; Jim, depressed by the loss of his friend, had sold the farm and gone to Australia to try for better luck there. He had in fact done better at sheep-ranching than at seisal growing, and though never prosperous, Mary Widdington thought that he was now comfortably settled.

'And did your brother go on trying to trace his wife?' Poole asked. 'I mean, after the war, as well as directly after she wrote to say that she was going away.'

'Oh, yes, he did,' Mary Widdington assured him. 'He told his solicitors to do everything they could think of – even to advertising in the 'personal' columns of the papers. When he got back from Cologne Jim went himself to all the places she had been fond of going to – restaurants and night clubs and even shops – to try and find out if she had ever been back there. But nobody had seen her and, as far as we know, nobody ever heard of her again.'

'And did he . . . did your brother ever try to regain his freedom . . . get a divorce or anything like that?'

For the first time Mary Widdington hesitated in her answer. There was a hint of anxiety in her voice when she did reply.

'Not for some time,' she said. 'He hated the idea of the story getting into the papers; it was all so terrible. Later on I think he did want to be free but by then it was difficult to get evidence – he didn't know where she was, you see, and there was no question of desertion being enough then. It's different now; that's why . . .'

Again Mary Widdington hesitated. This time she remained silent, biting her lip as she looked out of the window.

Her honesty was so transparent that Poole could not doubt that she was wondering whether she ought to tell something she knew. He felt sure that the only doubt that could deter her was fear that she might injure her brother. He felt a stirring of renewed interest.

'That's why . . . what, Miss Widdington?' he asked.

She turned back to him, decision clearly marked in her expression.

'That's why he's in England now,' she said frankly.

Poole started.

This was significant news, the more so as both Sir Richard Wayke and Mr. Gorvin had led him firmly to the impression that Captain Widdington was still in the wilds. They might, of course, be ignorant of his presence in England, but Poole very much doubted it and their silence made him feel suspicious.

'You mean he has come back to get a divorce under the new Act?'

Mary Widdington nodded but did not amplify her answer. She was looking unhappy.

'I am afraid I must ask some rather personal questions, Miss Widdington,' said Poole. 'Is there any special reason for his wanting a divorce. Does he intend to marry someone else?'

Again Mary nodded and this time, after a moment's pause, she continued:

'I feel sure I ought to tell you about it. In any case you would find out, even if I didn't. He wants to marry Helen Wayke. We always thought he was going to marry her . . . before he married Christine, I mean . . .'

And she went on to tell Poole a great deal more of the story than he had learned from Mrs. Curling.

'. . . After he went out to Kenya he did not see Helen for a long time but I am sure they were always very fond of each other. She travelled a great deal but at last they met again, and when he went to Australia she joined him out there. She still travelled but she went back to him and gradually got to staying longer and longer with him. They couldn't marry, of course, and they are neither of them the sort of people to be happy in an irregular sort of arrangement like that. I don't think many people know about their living together; neither of them has kept touch with old friends and I daresay I am the only person in England who really does know about it . . . or even about their being in England now.'

Poole thought that very doubtful. If Widdington was seeking a divorce he must be in touch with solicitors and probably with other people. There seemed to be a conspiracy of silence that looked rather ugly. It was lucky that he had come so quickly to the one person in the case who seemed to be honest.

Having learned that Captain Widdington was staying at a small hotel, the Hertford, in Bloomsbury, Poole took grateful leave of Miss Widdington and returned to London. Now that the story had been filled out a good deal it seemed to him to contain decided possibilities, but he had no intention of theorising until he had seen Captain Widdington and, if possible, Miss Helen Wayke as well. A good deal would depend upon the frankness with which they answered his questions, and he intended to put up with no hedging from either of them.

His journey to Devonshire and back had taken the greater part of the day but, tired as he was, Poole decided that he could afford to waste not even a few hours in following a trail that was already dangerously cold. Having had a quick meal at the Paddington refreshment room, therefore, he went straight along to the Bloomsbury hotel and enquired for Captain Widdington. Not wanting to arouse curiosity unless it became necessary to do so, he did not use his professional card, nor did he ask to look at the register; there were less clumsy ways of finding out what he wanted to know. He was shown into a gloomy smoking-room which had the one virtue of being empty. Within a minute the door opened and a tall, strongly-built man came into the room.

Although he was now on the wrong side of fifty, Captain James Widdington looked vigorous and healthy. His skin had the colour and texture of a man who spent a great deal of his time in the sun, and his eyes were alert. The one defect of his face, Poole thought, was a suggestion of weakness about the mouth. He looked enquiringly at his visitor.

'I don't think I know you, Mr. Poole,' he said.

The detective shook his head.

'No, sir. I am a police-officer. I have come to see you on a rather private matter; are we likely to be disturbed here?'

Poole thought he saw a flicker of anxiety come into the blue eyes, but Widdington answered him with a smile.

'I've got no sitting-room of my own. This room doesn't tempt many people.'

He pointed to a chair and the detective, after showing his warrant-card, plunged straight into his difficult task.

'I understand, sir, that in the year nineteen hundred and fifteen you married a Miss Christine Wayke and that about two years later you were separated from her. I have to ask you when you last saw your wife.'

There was no doubt about the anxiety in Captain Widdington's eyes now. He sat upright in his chair and stared at the detective.

'Why do you ask me that?'

'I will tell you quite frankly, sir. I am enquiring into the death of a woman on Hampstead Heath on the ninth of October and I have reason to believe now that she was Mrs. James Widdington.'

The blunt statement must be a shock to the man, Poole knew, whether he expected it or not. Widdington swallowed violently, but quickly got himself under control.

'Go on,' he said.

'Did you know that your wife was dead, sir?'

It was a staggeringly awkward question and, after a very short pause, Jim Widdington faced it like a man.

'Yes, I knew,' he said quietly. 'It was quite soon after I arrived in England. I saw the photograph in the papers and although the scar was . . . something new, I recognised her at once.'

'You said nothing about it, sir. We asked for information.'

'I know,' said Widdington. 'I realised that I ought to come forward and identify her but . . . I couldn't do it. How much do you know of the story?'

'A good deal, sir. I know who she was, her family and all that.'

'Then you'll understand . . . at least, I think you will . . . how appalling it would have been to make a public identification. You know how the papers described her; not in so many words but making it perfectly obvious. It meant raking up the whole unhappy story that everyone had forgotten and making it more unhappy still – making it quite frightful. I couldn't do it.'

Widdington paused for a minute and then repeated almost violently:

'I couldn't do it.'

Poole had watched him with great interest. The ex-Guardsman seemed to be speaking almost more to himself, justifying himself, than to his visitor.

'You realise what it means . . . your keeping silent about it, sir?'

Widdington nodded.

'Yes, I do; now that you've found out; damned awkward. Hel . . . I talked it over with a friend, who strongly advised me to go to the police but I stuck my toes in – not only for my own sake, but for her family's. Of course, if this has got to come out, it will be worse than ever now.'

The man was frank, at any rate, thought Poole.

'You realised that she was murdered, sir?' he asked quietly.

'Yes, I realised all that and that I ought to help find the brute – but how could I help? I hadn't seen her for more than twenty years. It could do no good, my telling the world that she was the daughter of poor old Sir Brandon and . . . and my wife. It couldn't bring her back to life or even hang her murderer; it could only throw mud all over her, poor girl, and her family and mine. By God, Inspector, I believe I was right to hold my tongue. It was a gamble but if it had come off everyone would have been the better for it – or rather, it would have saved them from being the worse . . . as they will be now. And me most of all,' he added grimly.

Poole could not help admiring the frankness and courage of this outburst, whatever lay behind it.

'I shall have to ask you a lot of questions now, sir,' he said. 'I won't go into past history at the moment, though I shall have to later, but this is a case of murder and you are a directly interested party; I shall have to ask you straight away what your own movements were that night. You are not obliged to answer or you may prefer to wait till you have taken legal advice, but in that case I shall have to ask you to come to the Yard with me until you have seen your solicitor.'

Jim Widdington's face paled under its tan.

'Yes, I see that,' he said. 'My God, it's coming home to roost with a vengeance now. Well; I've got to go through with it. What exactly do you want to know?'

'In the first place, sir, I must ask you whether you saw your wife after your return to England?'

Widdington's answer was direct enough.

'No, Inspector, I did not. I haven't seen her since 1916.'

'Thank you, sir. Then all I shall ask you tonight is what your movements were on the night in question, the 9th of October. I shall have to ask a good deal more tomorrow.'

Widdington thought for a minute.

'I don't see any point in getting a solicitor to advise me about that,' he said. 'Especially if it involves a night in a cell,' he added with a wry smile. 'I know what I was doing because when I saw the photograph next day and knew that it was Christine I naturally realised that if it came out I should be questioned. I may be a fool but . . . all that sort of thing. Hel . . . damn it, I can't tell you this story without bringing her into it. I'd better tell you straight away, though I'd give my eyes to keep her out of this. I came back to England to get a divorce, Inspector, because I wanted to marry another woman – my wife's half-sister. It was she who advised me to tell the police all about it but . . . I've explained all that. I spent a good deal of my time with her but we had to be careful because of my wanting to get a divorce . . . for desertion under the new Act. She went to a concert or a lecture or something that evening and I was at a loose end. I went to a cinema but the thing bored me and I came out and strolled about a bit and then came back here and dressed for dinner. I stayed in the hotel all the evening. We thought it wisest never to go and see each other after dark. Damned silly rot, of course,' Widdington added with a short laugh, 'but just the sort of thing that a jury fastens on to.'

There was a hint of cunning about that arrangement that Poole did not like; still, it was natural enough.

'What about times, sir; when did you get back to the hotel?'

'I thought about that . . . after I saw the photograph. As far as I could

work it out I must have got back here at about half past seven. I generally
dine about eight.'

And a very crucial time, too, drought Poole. It looked suspiciously
like the deliberate establishing of an alibi.

'Anyone confirm that, sir?'

Widdington shrugged his shoulders.

'Someone may remember, the porter or the woman in the office; but
why should they? The waiter may remember what time I had dinner . . .
but, again, why should he? . . . nearly a month ago.'

At least it was not too pat . . . but then this man clearly was not the
worst kind of fool.

'I'll check that,' Poole said, taking a quick decision. 'You will stay here
for the present, won't you, sir? I shall have to see you again tomorrow.'

'Oh, yes, I shan't bolt. I expect I had better get hold of a solicitor in
the morning.'

'By the way, sir,' said Poole, 'had you begun these divorce proceedings?'

Widdington shook his head.

'No; we only landed about ten days before. We decided to have a bit
of fun first; neither of us had been in London for years. And I had to
look out a solicitor; my own old firm had gone up in smoke years ago.
I'd just got hold of the name of a likely firm when this happened.'

Poole noticed that Widdington made no attempt to conceal the fact
that he and Helen Wayke had travelled home together. It might have
slipped out, of course, but it sounded straightforward.

'Then I must just ask you for Miss Wayke's address, sir, and I won't
bother you any more tonight.'

But that, it appeared, was bother enough for Jim Widdington. His
face flushed and he looked as if he were going to burst out with an angry
refusal, but after a time he calmed down.

'Curse it, I suppose you'll have to worry her. Oh lord, it's making it
worse for her after all, Inspector; I wish to hell I had followed her advice.'

CHAPTER III

APPROACH MARCH

It was too late that night to question the hotel staff, so Poole took the necessary steps to see that no harm was done by waiting till morning. On arriving at Paddington he had telephoned to Scotland Yard to ask for Sergeant Gower and a detective-constable to meet him near the Hertford Hotel; he joined them now and gave them their instructions to keep an eye on the place and not to let Captain Widdington, whom he carefully described, disappear. If the man had killed his wife he might now try to bolt; to do it at once would be his only chance. Poole gave Sergeant Gower further instructions to try and find out whether Captain Widdington possessed a car.

It had been an extremely long day and Poole was thankful to get to bed ... and none too anxious to get out of it again at an early hour. However, he knew that there was a lot of work in front of him now, and he wanted to see Miss Wayke before her lover had had a chance of coaching her. If they really were so discreet about not visiting each other 'after dark' there was quite a good chance of getting there first, so Poole got up at six, had his breakfast, called in at the Yard, and by eight was in Bloomsbury again.

He learned from Sergeant Gower that, so far as was known, Captain Widdington had not left the hotel. So Poole set off for Baxter Street and presently found the quiet and respectable lodging house in which Miss Helen Wayke was apparently awaiting events. Poole judged that this was a superior place, where only one or two visitors were taken and each had a private sitting-room. Certainly the entrance hall was a much pleasanter and less smelly place than he was accustomed to find. He learned that Miss Wayke breakfasted at 8.30 and said that he would wait till she had finished, asking that she should not be disturbed before that. There was, of course, just a risk of a telephone conversation but a private line was unlikely and in any case such a conversation would be very risky.

It was barely nine when the maid came down to tell him that Miss Wayke would see him at once. He followed her up to the first floor with a feeling of keen interest.

Helen Wayke's appearance gave much the same impression as had that of Jim Widdington – an alert, healthy person, accustomed to a hard life and ready to face trouble. Her skin, like his, had been coarsened by exposure, but her eyes had not lost their lustre and there was certainly no hint of weakness about this mouth. Poole liked the look of Miss Wayke and especially the frankness of her expression, though it had not that air of candid simplicity that had been so convincing in Mary Widdington.

Like her lover, Helen Wayke at once admitted that she had recognised the photograph of Christine taken after her death; she said that she had advised Captain Widdington to go to the police and identify his wife but, when he refused, she had decided to keep silence herself, for the same reasons. She was sorry that it had now come out but probably that had always been inevitable.

Poole noticed that Miss Wayke made no attempt to blame Captain Widdington for not following her advice, nor complained at the trouble which his stubbornness would now bring upon them both; she stated the facts and left it at that. An unusual type, from his experience.

'I must just ask you this question, Miss Wayke,' said the detective. 'When did you last see Mrs. Widdington alive?'

Helen Wayke looked him steadily in the eyes.

'Not since before her marriage. I was in France all through the war and she had disappeared before the end of it.'

Poole nodded.

'I shall be grateful if you will tell me about your sister,' he said. 'We assumed at first that this murder was the work of some . . . some recent friend of hers or possibly of some tramp or rough fellow who killed her in the hope of getting money, but we haven't been able to bring it home to anyone of that sort, so I am casting back further. I have heard a good deal but you will probably be able to tell me a lot that other people don't know.'

So Helen Wayke gave her version of Christine's story, revealing many little details of her character as a child, her charm, her waywardness ... even amounting to a wildness which, she thought, accounted for her father's decision to send Christine to the convent in Paris. Helen Wayke spoke very tenderly of her father, but it was clear that she thought his harshness to Christine when she returned from hospital at the beginning of the war was largely to blame for what happened afterwards. If he had been gentle and affectionate she might have settled down to live at Chatterleys and never have been subjected to the temptations which her hectic married life with Jim had thrown in her way. Helen Wayke made it quite clear that she thought it would have been better for everybody if that marriage had never taken place. Poole liked her frankness on that point.

The only new fact that he learned was the story of Jim Widdington's first home-coming from France, when Christine had brought the unfortunate Major Weedon back to the flat. That, Poole realised, must have been the beginning of Jim Widdington's disillusionment and he could well imagine what a terrible shock it must have been to the young soldier and husband. He felt a little more sympathy for him than the stories of Mrs. Curling and Sir Richard Wayke had conjured up.

When the story of the past was over Poole returned to the present.

'You will realise, Miss Wayke,' he said, 'that in view of Captain Widdington's failure to come forward and identify his wife, we have to look very closely into his actions. I have asked him about his movements on the evening of the murder and he has given me a very frank account of them; I must ask you now what you know about them.'

For the first time Helen Wayke showed some signs of surprise.

'You don't mean that you think Jim had anything to do with the murder?' she asked incredulously. 'He hasn't seen Christine for more than twenty years – some time in the middle of the war.'

'He told me that, Miss Wayke, but I have got to look into it all the same,' said the detective stubbornly.

Helen shrugged her shoulders.

'It seems nonsense. Jim wouldn't hurt a fly . . . let alone a woman whom he loved very much.'

It was simply spoken but Poole recognised the conviction in her voice. However, routine duty demanded that he should press his question.

'If you will just tell me what you know about it, please.'

'All right. I remember the night. I went to a lecture that evening. . . or rather it was an address and a discussion about the re-organisation of hospital services in war-time. I'm interested in nursing; I did a good deal of it in Italy after the war. It was at the Cambrian Hall and they had it at half-past six so that people who had been working in shops and offices could get to it – women, mostly. We didn't get out till eight and I didn't see Jim again that night. I believe he went to a cinema but of course I don't know that for a fact. He rang me up after dinner – not about anything special but . . . well, we're rather dependent on each other for company just now.'

That led Poole to a point that he wanted to clear up.

'You must have got a lot of friends in England, Miss Wayke – both of you – as well as relations; it seems curious that nobody appears to know of your being in England. You've been here more than a month, I understand.'

'Perhaps it does, but we neither of us felt like seeing people while this business of a divorce was hanging over us . . . you know about that, I suppose?'

'Yes, Captain Widdington told me.'

'We're rather old-fashioned people and we're neither of us happy about the sort of life we have been living. Of course, when we knew that Christine was dead we could have married . . . if Jim had cared to tell about who she was. He just wouldn't.'

Even though it would have saved them the ordeal of divorce proceedings, which in themselves would rake up the past. Well, no, not publicly, nowadays; the press reported very little of that kind now. Still the whole thing seemed to Poole very odd . . . and rather suspicious.

'Who does know of your being in England, Miss Wayke?'

'So far as I know, only Jim's sister.'

'Not your brother?'

Poole saw Helen Wayke's mouth harden.

'No, we didn't tell Dick. I can understand that you think that strange, but Dick and Jim never got on very well and especially after Jim married Christine. As a matter of fact I've always been rather frightened of Dick myself; he's very hard and cynical. We thought we should be happier if he knew nothing about the divorce, if it was possible to keep it from him. The solicitors would have advised us about that, I expect.'

'You haven't consulted them?'

'No. We didn't at first know who to go to. We heard of a firm but after Christine's death we thought it better to wait a bit.'

'Lying low'; that was what it looked suspiciously like, the detective thought. He did not for the moment press the point about Sir Richard Wayke. He was, in fact, rather at a loss to know what his next step should be; there was much that was suspicious about the story told by these two people, but on the other hand they, personally, both gave him the impression of being honest. Finally he decided to leave things till he had tested Captain Widdington's story of his doings on the night of the murder. He thanked Miss Wayke for her help and took his leave.

When he got back to the Hertford Hotel there was no sign of Sergeant Gower. The latter's relief was on duty at a street corner, and reported that Gower had gone home to bed ten minutes ago, telling him nothing except that Captain Widdington had not yet come out of the hotel. There was nothing for Poole to do but get on with his own enquiries.

He started by talking to the manager, to whom he revealed his identity. He told him that there was, so far as he knew, nothing whatever against Captain Widdington but that he had to make certain routine enquiries into his movements, as well as those of other people, on 9th October. He had to reveal the fact that the enquiries were connected with the murder of the woman on Hampstead Heath because only by doing so would he be able to fix the date in the minds of the people he wanted to question. The manager looked a good deal disturbed but said that he had no particular recollection of the evening himself and certainly none of

Captain Widdington's movements; the most likely people to know were the hall-porter and the waiter who served the Captain's table.

Poole saw both these individuals, as well as one or two others, and got just the sort of results he would have expected from such an enquiry into an event nearly a month old – an event so normal that no one's attention would have been drawn to it. Everybody remembered about the tragedy on Hampstead Heath; some had heard about it on the wireless and some had read about it next day; but no one could say for certain what the movements of one of the hotel visitors had been that night. The head-waiter, looking into his book, could say that Captain Widdington had 'dined in' that night, but he could not say at what time he had dined; he was generally in to dinner, certainly five nights a week. The table-waiter was a dull fellow, who remembered nothing at all. The hall-porter was intelligent enough, and observant too. He had heard the 8.25 p.m. broadcast appeal and remembered the evening well; he was inclined to think that he remembered Captain Widdington coming in that evening at his usual time – in time to dress for dinner, say half-past seven – but, when pressed, he certainly was not prepared to swear to it. A housemaid was voluble but quite unreliable.

Probably the most definite evidence came from a fellow-guest, a Major Daventry, who sat at the next table to Widdington. The Major was a small man with a fierce moustache and was evidently glad of an opportunity to make his weight felt.

'Can't remember the night,' he said to Poole, 'but if the head-waiter says that Widdington dined in that night then he dined at eight, or as near it as no matter. He's regular in his habits; an army man, like myself. Don't know what he was in; he doesn't talk much about himself. I'm a Light Infantryman myself. I dine at eight and Widdington dines at eight; I've never known him more than a course behind or ahead of me and generally we get off the mark together. They keep a very fair table here and I dine in most nights, but Widdington dines out once or twice a week. Never tells me much about himself, but I shouldn't wonder if there was a woman somewhere.'

There was a faintly querulous note about the last sentence, as if Major

Daventry felt it an injustice that he should not know all about his neighbour's nights out – especially if there was a woman in it. But it was an effective piece of evidence and, taken in conjunction with the head-waiter's, it tended to support Widdington's alibi. Still, Poole had sufficient experience to know that if a murder had been carefully planned an alibi of this kind might break down under close examination. He would have to think it out.

As he made his way back to the Yard he refreshed his memory of the 'time-table' of the murder. The latest limit of time was 7.40, the hour at which the body had been found; the earliest appeared to be 7.15, or almost certainly a little later, because the ground under the body had been wet and the rain had started, according to Police-Constable Darby, at 7.15 p.m. Taking everything into account, Chief-Inspector Beldam had put the time at 'nearer 7.30 than 7.15,' and Poole was inclined to agree with him.

The Hertford Hotel was at least four miles from Highgate Ponds and, whatever method of transport might have been used, it was clearly impossible that Widdington could have got back at 7.30 'in time to dress for dinner,' as both he and the hall-porter had put it. On the other hand, assuming that on this occasion Widdington had 'got off the mark a course behind' the Light Infantry Major, that might be put as late as 8.10 p.m., and a quick changer could have done that if he got back to the hotel by 8 – slipping in, perhaps, unnoticed by the hall-porter. Could he have done that if he had left the neighbourhood of Highgate Ponds at, say, 7.35 p.m.? Yes, by car, or taxi, or motor-bicycle, that was possible. Coming down Kentish Town Road and Hampstead Road, at a time when the peak traffic rush was over, that would certainly be possible and it made it all the more necessary to look closely into the alibi.

It also made it all the more necessary to get hold of Gower and learn whether he had made any progress with his 'further instructions.' Gower had been relieved at 9.30 a.m.; he was entitled to go straight home to bed, but Poole, knowing his subordinate, thought it more than likely that the Sergeant might have gone off on a trail; he certainly would have done so if he had received the slightest encouragement in the shape of likely information.

So Poole, on arrival at the Yard, decided to have some luncheon and wait in until his subordinate should report. There was his own report to write up, the problem to be thought out afresh and a plan for future action made.

It was certainly rather a dreary business to go over all that time-table ground again but at least, the detective felt, he did this time know who the victim really was, and there was someone in the offing now who had a very definite motive for wanting her out of the way. Captain Widdington had not given him the impression of being a murderer; he had struck Poole as an honest, if slightly slow-witted man; but the detective knew that murder was the one crime in which character and reputation were not infallible guides.

If Widdington had, in fact, consulted a solicitor and had learned that his grounds for divorce were inadequate or that his chances were seriously imperilled by his having lived with another woman during the period of desertion, then it was possible that he might have decided to take more drastic steps to free himself.

Poole was still thinking along these lines when there was a knock at the door of the Inspectors' room and Sergeant Gower came in. The grizzled little Scotsman never allowed his feelings, his success or lack of success, to appear on his face. He looked now as if he had had a good sleep and had got nothing of interest to report. Poole, unless he was pressed for time, always played up to him.

'Afternoon, Gower,' he said. 'What time are you relieving Platt?'

'9.30 p.m., sir, unless he telephones earlier.'

'Widdington didn't go out last night?'

'No, sir, nor yet this morning, while I was there.'

'Had a good sleep?'

'Not so bad, sir.'

'Hear anything about his having a car?'

'Yes, sir; he's got a car. A Morris saloon, pretty old, dull blue. I've seen it. He keeps it in a garage in Bleak Street, behind the Museum.'

CHAPTER IV

RECONNAISSANCE

The first thing that Poole did after hearing Gower's report was to look up the notes of evidence given by the two witnesses who had seen a car standing in Millfield Lane at about the time of the murder. In the first place, Mrs. Joliffe, whom he had interviewed himself; she had seen a car standing near the point where Merton Lane joins Millfield Lane, facing north. There had been a woman in the front seat on the near side, and she thought there was someone in the driving seat but had not noticed whether it was a man or a woman; she had described the car as 'one of those popular cars and shabby at that.' By a process of counter-checking Poole and Beldam had fixed the time of her seeing the car at about 7.05.p.m.

Then there had been the manservant at Westerham Lodge, Hoskin by name, interviewed in the first place by the Divisional detective, Winterbourne. Hoskin, coming up Millfield Lane from the direction of Highgate Road, had seen the car in approximately the position described by Mrs. Joliffe; it had driven off before he got to it and he had not noticed the driver, but he described the car as a shabby dark saloon; he had put the time of its driving off as between 7.15 and 7.20. This time, if it was correct, seemed too early to fit in with the time of the murder, especially if it had been 'Bella Knox' who was sitting in the car when Mrs. Joliffe passed it at 7.05. Still, the position of the car was a bare five minutes' walk from the place where the body had been found and one or other of those times might be incorrect. It was certainly worth looking more closely into the question of Captain Widdington's Morris saloon – 'dull blue and pretty old.'

On questioning Gower further Poole discovered that his colleague had in fact had only two hours' doze on a sofa, so he sent him off to have a proper sleep before relieving Platt. He himself went straight back to Bloomsbury and soon found the garage in Bleak Street. It was not a large place but appeared to be fairly busy, and the detective soon realised that it was run on business-like lines. The manager, Mr. Hallard, after seeing Poole's warrant-card, at once offered to give any information that was required. Captain Widdington's car was not kept in one of the six lock-up sheds but in the garage itself, where there was room – at a pinch – for twenty cars; as a general rule there were about a dozen being garaged at a time, not counting those which were in for repairs. The car in question was, he believed, in now and he took Poole to see it.

It was a 10 h.p. Morris saloon, once probably a fairly bright blue but now faded almost to a dull grey. It was certainly not a car that would catch the eye but it answered to the description, 'shabby,' given by both Mrs. Joliffe and Hoskin to the car they had seen in Millfield Lane on the night of the murder. A close examination of the vehicle disclosed nothing of any significance, but then it was practically impossible that it would.

Mr. Hallard himself remembered nothing of the evening in question, but there was an efficient system of checking cars in and out that produced evidence of considerable significance. The man who attended to this part of the business produced a book in which were entered the times at which customers took their cars out and brought them back again. No note was taken of the actual driver, but no customer's car would be allowed out unless it was driven either by himself or by someone accredited by him. In this case, Captain Widdington was often accompanied by a lady, who sometimes took the car out or brought it back; as a general rule it was Captain Widdington himself who drove the car and it was taken out most days.

Turning to the 9th October, Poole saw that the car had gone out at 6.35 p.m. and returned at 7.45. It was at once clear to him that these times were highly suggestive. To look at it from a purely negative point of view, there was nothing in them to make it impossible that this was the car seen by Mrs. Joliffe and Hoskin. Bleak Street was within a very easy half-hour's drive of Millfield Lane, so that there was no reason why the car should not have been standing there by 7.05. Ignoring for the moment Hoskin's statement that the car drove off between 7.15 and 7.20, and taking instead 7.20 to 7.25 as the time of the murder, it would have been possible for Widdington, if he indeed were the murderer, to run to the car in little more than a minute and, with the streets fairly clear of traffic, be back at the garage by 7.45. Bleak Street was no great distance from the Hertford Hotel, so that he would have time for a quick change and yet be down in the dining-room very soon after 8.

These time margins, Poole realised, were very fine. To commit a murder by the Highgate Ponds just before 7.30 and yet to be dining in Bloomsbury within a few minutes of 8 was desperately quick work – but it was just within the bounds of possibility. And, of course, either or both Police-Constable Darby and Major Daventry, the two witnesses most directly responsible for fixing these limits of time, might be wrong in their estimates; a mistake of five or ten minutes in either direction would make all the difference.

Poole realised that he would have to get a lot more evidence against Widdington before such a theory would be accepted by a jury. He wished he could learn from the garage people that Widdington had brought the car in in a great hurry and gone off at a run; or from the hotel porter or housemaid that he had arrived back at the hotel just before 8 in a similar state. But neither Mr. Hallard nor his staff remembered any detail about that evening and the hotel evidence had been almost equally negative; the hall-porter was 'inclined to think that he remembered the Captain coming in at his usual time to dress for dinner – say half past seven.' Clearly a lot more spade work would have to be done before a clear outline of that evening was disclosed.

As he walked away from the garage Poole at first felt discouraged, but before long he realised that, quite apart from the question of times, one absolutely vital fact stood out from the evidence he had just obtained; Captain Widdington's car had been out that evening at a time when both he and Miss Wayke declared that they were quite otherwise engaged.

Either one or the other was lying, or else someone else had taken the car out. On that point they would have to be questioned and the sooner it was done the better.

On reaching the Hertford Hotel, however, he found that Captain Widdington was out and there was no sign of the detective who was keeping him under observation. Poole rang up the Yard to ask whether any message had been sent by Platt and discovered that only ten minutes previously the detective had rung through to say that Captain Widdington had collected a lady from 15 Baxter Street and that the two of them were now in a block of buildings in Sussex Street, Strand; the building contained a number of offices, including those of solicitors, insurance agents, commission agents and private detectives.

Of these, Poole thought the first was the most likely objective, with the last as an interesting alternative. Widdington and Miss Wayke had both spoken of having been given the name of a firm of solicitors but of having not yet consulted them; after the detective's visit it was extremely likely that they would want to do so without delay. It was certainly late in the day for such an appointment but the morrow was Saturday and that might have been even more inconvenient to the solicitor.

There seemed no particular point in going down to the Strand; with Platt in tow there was little chance of Widdington slipping his cable. There was a point that Poole wanted to clear up without delay. In thinking over the implications of the Widdington car time-table Poole had fitted the pieces together with one exception; he had set on one side the evidence of the manservant, Hoskin, who had said that the car moved off from Millfield Lane between 7.15 and 7.20. That fact did not fit in well with Poole's theory and he had set it aside, but he knew from experience that it was extremely dangerous to set aside facts that did not fit into one's theory. What he ought to do was to find out whether the inconvenient evidence really did represent fact; if it did it must either be manipulated until it did fit or, if that proved impossible, then the theory itself must be re-examined, altered or abandoned.

Poole thought that Hoskin had only been questioned by the young Divisional detective, Winterbourne. He knew that Chief-Inspector

Beldam had intended to question him but there was in the *dossier* no note of his having done so; Poole could, of course, ask him whether he had done so, but the most satisfactory course would be to go and see Hoskin himself.

As he travelled north again in a bus Poole juggled with the inconvenient 'fact,' and very soon found that it might be interpreted in a way to fit his theory. Hoskin's evidence, as recorded by Winterbourne, was to the effect that the car had moved off before he got to it, but he had not apparently stated in what direction it had moved off. Poole had assumed that it had gone up Merton Lane but it was possible that it had gone down the last bit of Millfield Lane which, as a road, came to a dead end after about two hundred yards at the point where a line of posts blocked its entrance to the Heath . . . and that point was within a few yards of where the body was found!

The detective's pulse quickened as this exciting possibility dawned upon him. Widdington might have driven Christine up to that quiet spot, strangled her in the car, carried her body to the hollow where it was found, and then, returning to the car, have backed it down the Lane until he could turn it and drive away. Backing a car is a noisy process and very thorough enquiries had been made at the houses whose gardens run down to the Lane; nobody had, apparently, heard or seen anything significant . . . but then it was extraordinary how blind and deaf people were to normal sights and sounds. It was a decidedly promising addition to his theory, because it shortened the time that it would take Widdington to get back to the garage and his hotel.

Leaving the tram which had carried him for the last part of his journey, Poole hurried up Millfield Lane. It was getting dark now and the detective could not help noticing what a deserted place the Lane was at this time of the year and day. There was no traffic down it, except an occasional car or delivery van, and no one seemed to be using the many paths which cross the Heath. In the dim light the shimmer of the ponds was eerie, and what lamps there were only served to throw the surrounding shadows into greater darkness.

Westerham Lodge had its entrance about a hundred yards south of the point where Merton Lane and Millfield Lane forked, the one north-east towards Highgate, the other northwest in the direction of Ken Wood. Poole wasted no time in exploration but turned into the drive and went round to the back door of the Lodge; a minute or two later he found himself in a small pantry where Mr. Albert Hoskin was beginning to collect the paraphernalia for his task of laying the table for dinner. He was a thin, dismal-looking man, with bad teeth and none too clean hands, but he had the virtue of telling a straight story in few words.

'I can give you ten minutes,' he said, motioning Poole to a chair. 'Takes me half an hour to lay the table and get the Colonel's clothes out; then I have to lend a hand in the kitchen, which is no part of a man's job . . . but I can give you ten minutes.'

Poole asked for a repetition of the story already told; it was very brief and contained nothing that had not already been reported. Hoskin had been returning from Highgate Road – the route just taken by Poole – and had noticed the shabby saloon standing on the Heath side of Millfield Lane nearly opposite the entrance to Westerham Lodge. It had moved off before he got to it and he had not seen the driver, nor did he notice how many people were in it.

'Which way did it go?' asked Poole quickly.

Hoskin looked surprised.

'Why, away from me, else I'd have seen who was in it. Towards Highgate.'

'Up Merton Lane?'

'Yes; that's the only way out. Millfield Lane don't go on more than a hundred yards or so – comes to a dead end.'

'You're certain the car didn't go down it all the same?'

'Ab-so-lutely. It went up Merton Lane.'

Poole's hopes slumped. That neat manipulation of an awkward fact had broken down; and it appeared to be a fact. But what about the time? Was that equally irreconcilable?

'And what time do you think it was when the car moved off?'

Hoskin nodded.

'Ah, I can see that's an important point. The other young fellow asked me that . . . and lucky he did, because I shouldn't have remembered if you'd been the first – it's a month ago now. I was late out that evening, and that's a fact. You'll see I'm beginning to get things ready now and it's not much after half-past six. But that evening I'd met a friend . . . well, it was at the Blue Ensign, if you want to know . . . and I was late. Soon as I got in here I looked at the clock to see if I could get through in time . . . the Colonel likes his dinner punctual and he's got a temper . . . and I see it was 7.25 – time enough. Allowing for the time it took me to get in here from where I was when the car moved off I put that at between 7.15 and 7.20.'

Damnably precise evidence, thought Poole; it was long odds against his being able to shake it, even if it was not in fact accurate.

'That doesn't fit, eh?'

Hoskin was looking at him curiously. Poole realised that he had allowed his feelings to appear on his face.

'It's very clear evidence and I'm much obliged to you, Mr. Hoskin,' he said.

He walked away from Westerham Lodge feeling thoroughly depressed. If Police-Constable Darby was equally certain about the time of the rain beginning – 7.15 – then it was quite certain that the murderer could not have been in that car. The whole point of the car evidence, in fact, fell to the ground.

No, not necessarily. It was just possible still that Widdington had come up in the car and been deposited at this point to do his dreadful deed, the car driving away and leaving him to get back afterwards . . . how? It seemed utterly unlikely. But if it was the true explanation it meant that there was an accomplice . . . and that accomplice could only have been Helen Wayke!

Ah, but there was another interpretation. What if Widdington *had* driven away in the car, getting back to his hotel in time to establish that eight o'clock alibi . . . and leaving Helen Wayke to ki

It was a horrid thought. Poole's mind flashed over a The two alibis, cunningly separate, were of the type so the one a cinema, a walk, a vaguely fixed return to the lecture at a hall crowded with unknown people, with no one to say who had gone in and out or at what time. Poole pulled out his notebook and turned to Helen Wayke's evidence; she had, she said, gone to the Cambrian Hall at half-past six; even if that was true she might have come out again at once and driven in a taxi to collect the car. Perhaps that was too close to the 6.35, at which hour the car had been checked out, but there was no reason why Widdington should not have collected the car and picked her up at the Cambrian Hall five or ten minutes later; that would still give time for it to get to Millfield Lane and be seen by Mrs. Joliffe at 7.05. Poole had imagined that it was Christine whom she had seen sitting in the car with her murderer, but perhaps it had been Helen Wayke and her lover waiting for the poor woman, come, perhaps, to a meeting already arranged or perhaps because they knew that that was her beat.

Poole shuddered at the horror of that thought. Was it possible that a man and woman of the birth and tradition of these two could plot such a foul crime, to murder a poor woman who was the wife of one, the half-sister of the other? Surely that could not be true to type, let alone the favourable opinion he had formed of both of them. But again Poole reminded himself that murder was not a crime that ran true to type.

CHAPTER V

CONTACT

As his new and terrible theory developed in Poole's mind, he realised how much there had been in James Widdington's story that had not satisfied him. It was not his account of the immediate circumstances of the 9th October that rang false, nor even his failure to go to the police and identify his dead wife; his reasons for not doing so were understandable, however unwise and wrong his decision may have been. What worried Poole was the whole background of this visit to London, the secrecy of it, the fact that two people of good family, who must in the past have had a host of friends in England, should remain in an obscure hotel and lodging-house, seeing no one and not even taking the step which was the ostensible reason for their return to England – a visit to a solicitor for the purpose of discussing a divorce.

Even Helen Wayke's own brother did not know of her presence in England – or, if he did, he had kept it very closely to himself. Surely an innocent woman would have returned to her old home, even though the house was sold; she must have many friends in the neighbourhood – let alone old Mrs. Curling, faithful friend of the family, at Birmingham. The explanation that she was unhappy about her irregular life with James Widdington and wanted to remain in the background until he was free and she was legally married to him, did not accord with her independent mode of life nor with any standard of post-war principle.

Widdington himself, Poole thought, might be reluctant to appear in public until the unhappy story of his marriage had flickered into brief life in the divorce court and died away again. He had, too, told his own sister of his presence inEngland. That was a strong point in his favour, though it was possible that he had done so before ever contemplating murder. Poole wondered again whether there had proved to be a flaw in the divorce plan. It was possible that, in spite of his denial, Widdington had gone to a solicitor directly after his arrival in England and had discovered that the new Act did not meet the circumstances of his case and that other steps must be taken if he were to regain his freedom. If that were so, it surely was a desperately dangerous thing to do, to murder his wife directly after consulting a solicitor about a divorce from her.

But there was a possible answer even to that; he might in the first place have used a false name, have gone to some solicitor of doubtful reputation and stated a case, under that false name, merely to get an opinion as to his chances. If the opinion were favourable, then he could go openly to a reputable firm and start proceedings.

So far had Poole got with his dark imaginings when he found himself back in Bloomsbury. He did not want to question his two suspects until he had thought out his plans more thoroughly. He ought to report to the A.C. before taking any vital step; it might even be necessary for him to consult Chief-Inspector Beldam, though Poole was humanly loath to lose control of the case just as it was coming to life again. But there was one step that he must take at once, in view of his new theory; he must arrange for Helen Wayke, as well as Widdington, to be kept under observation.

Having come to this decision Poole went to Tottenham Court Road Police Station and put a call through to the Yard. All the senior officers had gone home by this time but the Night Duty Inspector agreed to do what Poole asked; a detective would be sent straight up to Tottenham Court Road and Poole could give him his instructions. Knowing that he would have to wait twenty minutes or so before the man could arrive, Poole thought he would go and see whether Widdington was back at his hotel. He found Platt at his usual observation post and learned that the visit to the Sussex Street office had ended at half-past five, Widdington and Miss Wayke had then gone to her lodging, but after remaining there half an hour, the former had returned to his hotel, where he still remained. Platt had not been able to discover which of the offices in the large building his quarry had visited, but that was a point that Poole felt competent to clear up himself.

Returning to the Police Station he found that the detective, Watts by name, had just arrived. He was a man who had worked with Poole before and the Inspector was glad to see him. 'Observation' is one of the most difficult of a detective's duties; unless it is extremely well done it almost inevitably attracts attention and then half its value is gone. Watts would do this difficult job as well as anyone, with the exception of Sergeant Gower, that Poole knew. To increase the man's interest Poole gave him an outline of the case, though he did not say that he actually suspected Miss Wayke of the murder.

Having shown Watts the house Poole thought that he might get himself some dinner, write his report, and go early to bed.

He was still having breakfast the following, Saturday, morning when he was called to the telephone and heard the voice of Detective-Constable Watts.

'They're off, sir.'

'Good God! Where to?'

'Widdington came round in a taxi a little before eight. He went in, leaving the taxi waiting. Five minutes later he came out with the woman, carrying a suitcase. Sergeant Gower had come up in another taxi and I got in with him. We followed them to Paddington and they booked to Denmouth. Sergeant Gower's gone with them; he told me to stay behind and report to you.'

Poole heaved a sigh of relief.

Denmouth was a large port but it was also within easy motoring distance of Mary Widdington's home; it was long odds that they were going there. In any case Gower could be trusted to keep an eye on them and not let them leave the country until he had received instructions from headquarters.

'All right, Watts,' he said. 'I think I know where they're going. You can go and get a sleep now. What time was your relief due?'

'9.30, sir.'

'I'll ring the Yard and tell them not to send him. Very likely Miss

Wayke will be away till Monday but Gower will get local help if he wants it. You'd better be at the Yard by eight, in case you're wanted.'

On the whole this news did not increase Poole's suspicions. It was natural enough for Widdington to go and see his sister and for Helen Wayke to go too. The visit pointed rather to innocence than guilt; probably they were going down to tell the uncomfortable truth and explain why they had not told it before. That, at any rate, would be a natural and proper step for them to take if indeed they were innocent.

But it did not turn Poole from his purpose. He was rather glad to have them out of the way for a time; he had plenty to do without them . . . and would not be at all sorry for a week-end off himself.

In the first place there was the A. C. Sir Leward Marradine sometimes came to the Yard on a Saturday, but more often did not – especially in November, when pheasant-shooting was in full swing. If he was there, Poole would almost certainly have to discuss with him the report which he had written on the previous evening. If not . . . well, he could act on his own for another day or two.

Sir Leward was not there. Chief-Constable Thurston was, and he had a short talk with Poole, but to the latter's relief said nothing about referring the case back to Chief-Inspector Beldam. So the Inspector went off on his own line, which took the present form of a visit to Sussex Street, Strand. The building described by Platt proved to hold only two firms of solicitors, Messrs. Scott and Cavendish on the ground floor and Messrs. Jaunty and Jaunty on the second. Poole took the nearest first, sent in his official card and in an unexpectedly short space of time was ushered into the presence of Mr. Scott.

It did not take the detective long to realise that here was a solicitor who did not welcome a visit from the police but who was still less anxious to do anything to annoy them. Mr. Scott was palpably nervous, though affable in the extreme. He waved Poole into a chair and pushed a box of cigars towards him. The detective took no notice of them.

'I shall be glad if you will tell me whether you received a visit from a Captain James Widdington yesterday afternoon, sir,' he said.

Mr. Scott's face proclaimed surprise – and relief.

'No,' he said. 'No. I have no client of that name.'

'Your partner, sir, perhaps?'

Mr. Scott shook his head.

'There is no Cavendish in the firm now,' he said. 'I am at present the sole partner.'

Poole wondered whether in fact the firm ever had included a bearer of that illustrious name.

'Perhaps Captain Widdington might have given another name,' he said . . . 'on a first visit.'

Again Mr. Scott shook his head.

'The only clients I had yesterday afternoon are well known to me.'

He touched a bell.

'You can ask my head clerk.'

The head clerk was a scrubby little man of obviously non-Aryan extraction. No less nervous than his principal, he declared vigorously that nobody even remotely resembling the gentleman described had visited the firm on the previous day.

Poole was satisfied that he was in the wrong covert and blew his hounds out.

On the second floor he found himself in a more authentic atmosphere. He was kept waiting twenty minutes.

When at last he was shown into Mr. Jaunty's room he was received politely but without enthusiasm. He repeated his enquiry.

Mr. Jaunty did not reply immediately. His steel-grey eyes regarded Poole as if he were summing him up and deciding what would be the best way to deal with him. Poole, as a matter of fact, was not an easy man to sum up by appearance alone. Although just on forty his face had not aged and he had a simple, candid air that had before now deceived people into underrating his ability. Mr. Jaunty, however, was unlikely to make that mistake.

'I'm afraid I can't discuss my clients with you, Inspector, or even tell you who has or has not come to see me. You will understand that that is a confidential matter.'

'I quite understand that your clients' affairs are confidential, sir, but

I am not clear that that applies so far as to the point of whether they *are* your clients. I am enquiring into a case of murder and I am bound to press you for an answer.'

But Mr. Jaunty's thin lips only closed more firmly and he shook his head. Poole, however, was not going to be put off so easily.

'There are generally recognised conventions as to what is professional confidence and what is not, sir. I am quite clear that I am not asking you for a breach of your client's confidence when I ask whether he visited you yesterday.'

'I have not said that this . . . er . . . Captain Widdington is my client,' said Mr. Jaunty.

Poole smiled.

'No, sir, but if he were not I don't think you would be wasting your own time and mine by not saying so at once.'

The hint of a smile flickered across the solicitor's face; his hand rose an inch or two, as if acknowledging a touch. He remained silent for nearly half a minute, then said:

'Very well. I will go so far as to say that Captain Widdington came to see me yesterday.'

'Was that his first visit to you, sir? Had he consulted you before?'

But Mr. Jaunty's expression had hardened again.

'No, Inspector; that is quite clearly beyond the limit of what you are entitled to ask me.'

'I don't think so, sir. You are taking a serious responsibility in not giving me any help. I will formally ask you what Captain Widdington consulted you about.'

'And I shall formally decline to answer, Inspector.'

Mr. Jaunty rose to his feet.

'We shall serve no useful purpose by continuing this discussion. I shall not say anything further about my client's affairs unless I am ordered by the Court to do so.'

Poole had hardly expected to get much direct information out of this enquiry, but it was of indirect value to know that Widdington was now consulting a solicitor and who that solicitor was. The Treasury Solicitor's office would know all about Mr. Jaunty and whether he was likely to handle criminal work; as the question of divorce was now out of the way there seemed no reason why Widdington should rush off to a solicitor unless he was seriously alarmed.

As he walked back along the Embankment Poole wondered what further step he could take to connect Widdington and Helen Wayke with the tragedy on Hampstead Heath. The efforts made immediately after the murder to discover anyone who had been seen near the spot had been so completely barren of result that it seemed impossible that he should succeed now. One line did suggest itself; they had bent all their efforts to an attempt to trace Herbert Varden from the Ponds to the Red Knight at Kilburn; they had questioned bus conductors and appealed to taxi-drivers and others; and they had failed to trace him. But suppose for a moment that his new theory was right and that Widdington had driven Helen Wayke up to Millfield Lane and left her there, driving home himself to create an alibi; in that case Helen Wayke, after killing Christine, would have had to get home somehow, either by taxi, tram, bus, or tube. Would it be possible, after this distance of time, to trace her return?

It seemed a very poor chance, but it must be tried. If he could get a good snapshot of her and have it enlarged, that would probably be the only hope. After all, in his first efforts he had been enquiring exclusively about a man; perhaps even at this late hour a woman of such striking appearance as Helen Wayke might be remembered.

Apart from that, the most fruitful line to follow might be to try and discover whether, in spite of their denials, either Widdington or Helen Wayke had had any contact with Christine since their return to England. It would be as well to go down to Bunt Street and question Mrs. Twist. There again, Poole had enquired exclusively about male visitors to Bella Knox; if her sister had been down there it was just possible that the landlady had not thought it worth mentioning the fact.

Alternatively, it would be as well to enquire whether Bella Knox had visited Helen Wayke or Widdington; that could be done at once and, so far as Miss Wayke was concerned, it would be better done during her absence.

Poole went first, however, to the Hertford Hotel; there should be very little difficulty about finding out whether Captain Widdington had ever been visited, or even enquired for, by poor scarred and painted Bella Knox; such a person would have very little chance of passing a hotel porter without being noticed. The enquiry did not take long. The hall-porter, whom Poole had already discovered to be both observant and intelligent, was shocked at the suggestion; he had certainly seen no such person himself in or even near the hotel, and he very quickly made enquiries of the rest of the staff which resulted in Poole being satisfied that Widdington had not been visited here by his wife.

He then went round to Baxter Street. On his previous visit he had not seen the landlady and he hoped that she would not know who he was, or at any rate, that he was 'hostile' to her guest. He might later on have to question her closely about Miss Wayke's movements on the 9th October, but to do so now would certainly arouse intense curiosity and might put her on the defensive. So he decided for the present to keep the interview on as light a note as possible.

Mrs. Dibbuts proved to be a comfortable body, sufficiently prosperous to be unharassed by the cares that so often beset landladies. Poole explained that he had hardly expected to find Miss Wayke as, on his visit the previous day, she had said something about going away for the week-end.

'I am a police-officer, Mrs. Dibbuts,' he said, 'and I am making enquiries about a relative of Miss Wayke's. I came to see her about it yesterday but I forgot to ask her when it was she last saw the lady. Did you ever hear her speak of anyone called "Christine"?'

Poole felt sure that Miss Wayke would never have spoken of her as 'Mrs. Widdington,' and he was not anxious at the moment to introduce that name. On the other hand it was just conceivable that she might have overheard her lodger and Captain Widdington speaking of 'Christine.'

But Mrs. Dibbuts shook her head.

'No,' she said. 'I can't call to mind that she did. I've heard of a 'Mary' and I've heard of a 'Dick' but 'Christine' . . . I should have remembered that, because it's a pretty name and not common. As a matter of fact she doesn't talk a lot except to Captain Widdington when he comes; that's a friend of hers; great friend, I should say, but nothing wrong or I shouldn't allow it. Not that she isn't getting a bit past anything like . . . well, like a romance. She doesn't seem to have many friends, or they don't come here anyway. Curious, I've often thought, because she's a pleasant lady, always ready to pass a friendly word.'

Poole seized the opportunity to discharge his arrow.

'She hasn't a friend – a woman – with a scar on her right cheek? An acquaintance, perhaps, I should say; a woman in poor circumstances.'

Again Mrs. Dibbuts shook her head.

'Not one that comes here. Of course, I don't know who she sees when she goes out . . . and she's out a good deal. There's not a great deal to keep her in, I suppose. She's not a great reader. Stamp collecting, that's her hobby. Spends quite a bit of time and money too, I daresay; waste of both I always think, little bits of coloured paper. A woman ought to have something more useful to do than that.'

Poole realised that he was getting nowhere and wondered whether he should launch a more direct attack – question her about Miss Wayke's movements on the day of the murder. But if he did that she would almost certainly tell her lodger and a much more definite atmosphere of suspicion would be engendered; at the moment Poole was still on reasonably friendly terms with Miss Wayke and he wanted to remain so, at any rate until he had questioned her again.

He was on the point of leaving when a sudden thought struck him. He drew his bow for a much longer shot.

'I asked you if you'd ever heard Miss Wayke speak of the name 'Christine'; I believe she sometimes used another name – her professional name – 'Bella Knox'; did you ever hear that?'

Mrs. Dibbuts cocked her head on one side; she frowned in an effort of recollection.

'There now,' she said, 'that name . . . it calls to mind . . . I don't think I ever heard Miss Wayke . . . ah, now I recollect; I saw it on a letter. I knew a 'Bella' once and it caught my eye.'

Poole's eyes were alight with eagerness now.

'A letter here?' he asked.

'Yes; it was in Miss Wayke's room. She was doing those stamps of hers and it was lying on her blotter. I think she must have posted it herself because she didn't give it me to take, same as she usually did if she'd been writing a letter and I come up.'

Poole tried hard to keep the eagerness out of his voice.

'When would that have been, Mrs. Dibbuts?'

'Oh, quite soon after she came here; within two or three days, I should say.'

'And she came . . . when?'

'Right at the beginning of October it was. My last guest went out at the end of September and I don't often have a room empty long; my house is well known and I can pick and choose. I should say she came about the 4th October.'

CHAPTER VI

UNPLEASANT DUTY

Here at last was the definite contact for which Poole had been looking. Both Widdington and Helen Wayke had denied having seen Christine for more than twenty years; it was inconceivable that that could now be true. Why should Helen Wayke write to her sister – and under that name – if she did not know all about her and her present life? Why – if she was innocent – should she conceal the fact that she had written? Written, too, within a few days of the murder. There could, surely, be no other explanation than that the letter had lured Christine to her death. Was that letter still in existence? It was not at Bunt Street; Poole himself had searched poor Bella Knox's lodging too thoroughly to admit any chance of that. It was not on her body when she was found. Either she had destroyed it herself or it had been taken from her by her murderer.

The cold-blooded treachery of the crime appalled Poole. Murder of a wife by the husband and his mistress was no new crime, but that people of gentle birth should do such a thing was terrible beyond Poole's experience. Widdington, a soldier who had won the Military Cross; Helen Wayke, a woman who had worked in France throughout the war and since then devoted herself, for a time at any rate, to nursing the sick; what explanation could there be of such ghastly warping of two characters? Passion could account for crime and cruelty but these people did not appear to be of the passionate type; in any case their whole tradition, their creed, their birthright, was to control passion. *Noblesse oblige.*

Much of that old tradition had, of course, perished since the war and this could only be a case where the evil spell of war had disintegrated all that was good in two human beings. The story of Christine Wayke had seemed tragic enough in itself but the destruction of her body seemed to Poole as nothing compared with the destruction of these two souls.

Could he possibly be mistaken? Could there be an innocent explanation of that lie? He wished there was. It was natural for a policeman to want to bring his case to a successful conclusion, but rather than prove this dreadful truth Poole felt that he would gladly find that he was wrong.

Till that was so his duty forced him to go on; he must try every means to reach the truth. For a moment he contemplated asking to be relieved of the case, asking that Chief-Inspector Beldam should resume responsibility. But that was a coward's course. He had faith in himself and he believed that he, better than anyone else, could find the truth, and if it was bitter he must find it none the less. After all, if James Widdington and Helen Wayke had indeed done this horrible thing they were inhuman fiends who should pay the full penalty of their crime.

All thoughts of a pleasant week-end had vanished from Poole's mind. He felt that he must go on until he had proved his horrible theory to be wrong or knew without possibility of doubt that Helen Wayke had lured her sister to that lonely corner of the Heath where either she or her lover had strangled poor Christine Widdington and left her body to a pauper's grave.

There were two things that he could do at once; he could question the Twists again and he could set on foot enquiries among taxi-drivers and transport services in an endeavour to discover whether either Widdington or Helen Wayke had used any of those means of returning from Hampstead Heath to Bloomsbury. Before putting this elaborate machinery in motion, however, it would be advisable to get the approval of one of the senior officers of the C.I.D. – Chief-Constable Thurston, perhaps, or Superintendent Fraser. It was now past one o'clock and, on a Saturday, neither of these big men was likely to be still on duty at the Yard; he could probably find one or other at his home but ... on consideration Poole decided that it would be better in any case to wait until he could get the snapshots which would make these enquiries so much easier. Both the subjects were away in Devonshire, so that nothing could be done for the moment.

That reminded Poole that there might by now be a message from Sergeant Gower; he decided at any rate to return to the Yard, where he could prepare the reports and descriptions which would be required and take any further steps that might suggest themselves.

Both Chief-Constable Thurston and Superintendent Fraser had, he found, gone home, nor had any message arrived from Gower. Poole got some food at the canteen and settled down to his report. An hour later he was on his way to Kentish Town.

Bunt Street looked, if anything, even drearier than when he had last been there. The single plane tree at one end of it had lost most of its leaves, windows were the dirtier for the first November fogs. At No. 53 the ragged lace curtains seemed more tattered than before, the aspidistra drooped more dismally in the cabbage-laden air. As he stood on the unwashed doorstep Poole remembered that even on his first visit he had been saddened by the thought of that poor woman, whose draggled body he had seen lying in the rain in a dark corner of the Heath, returning night after night to this cheerless home; now that he knew who she was and what her early life had been, the picture conjured up a desolate misery that he could hardly bear to contemplate. Poor lonely Magdalen, how bitterly she had paid for the wild folly of her youth.

Mrs. Twist regarded the detective with a sour look quite devoid of welcome.

'What are you after now?' she asked, not moving from the doorway.

'Can I come in, please, Mrs. Twist? I want to ask you one or two more questions.'

Reluctantly Mrs. Twist gave ground and led the way into the back room where their previous talk had taken place. Poole saw that there were seven chairs now round the table.

'I'm glad to see that your house is full again,' he said. 'I hope the room is well let.'

'No thanks to you if it is,' said the landlady aggressively. 'Took me three weeks to find another. What d'you want? I thought you'd given it up as a bad job.'

'No, we haven't done that, Mrs. Twist. We never do that.'

'Well, you 'aven't done much, 'ave you? Not even an arrest and 'er a month or more in 'er grave.'

'That's all the more reason for you to help me now, isn't it? I want to ask you again about her visitors. Did a lady ever come to see her?'

Mrs. Twist eyed him suspiciously.

'What are you gettin' at,' she asked.

'I want to find out whether Miss Knox ever had a visit from a lady – a rather tall, well-built lady of about forty-six or seven. It would have been within a few days, ten at the outside, of her death.'

Curiosity overmastered displeasure. Mrs. Twist's eyes glinted.

'Was it a woman as done 'er in?'

Poole smiled.

'I wish I knew. At the moment I am only trying to trace a possible connection. What about it?'

Reluctantly Mrs. Twist shook her head.

'There weren't no woman come to see 'er . . . not 'ere, anyway; not so much as a district visitor.'

Poole had hardly expected any other answer.

'What about letters? Did Miss Knox get any letters, within a few days of her death, I mean?'

'No, she didn't; she . . . 'alf a minute, though; yes, she did. There was one come . . . it must 'ave been only just before. I remember bein' surprised to see it, 'er not 'avin' 'ad one ever before to the best of my knowledge.'

'This is important, Mrs. Twist. Do you remember what became of it?'

Reluctantly again Mrs. Twist shook her head.

'I never see it again. She didn't say nothing about it and I didn't like to ask though I *was* curious.'

'What was the hand-writing like? Do you remember?'

'It was bold, like. Not the sort of copy-book 'and they teaches 'em in the schools now. I'd say it was a lady's 'and.'

'Would you recognise it again if I showed you some more writing by the person who I think wrote that letter?'

'I might. Yes, I think I might.'

That would be valuable corroborative evidence. It should not be impossible to get a sample of Helen Wayke's handwriting.

'And Miss Knox; did she answer the letter, do you know?'

'Not to my knowledge. I think she 'ad a bottle of ink but I don't remember seein' a letter of 'ers.'

A pity. A letter addressed to Widdington or Miss Wayke would have double-locked that contact. But it was too much to hope for such evidence. There was only one other question.

'Did you ever hear Miss Knox mention the name Wayke or Widdington?'

'Wyke? No, I can't call it to mind. What was the other? Whittington?'

'Widdington.'

Mrs. Twist shook her head.

'Never 'eard of such names, not from 'er nor anyone else.'

Poole took his leave in a more friendly atmosphere. He had advanced one small step but he hardly knew whether to be glad or sorry.

Back he went to the Yard. There was still no message from Gower. He wanted to be absolutely sure that those two people really were at Mary Widdington's. He settled down to wait.

There can be few more exasperating ways of passing a Saturday afternoon than waiting for a telephone call, especially in a large and deserted office. Scotland Yard does not hum with activity for twenty-four hours in the twenty-four and seven days in the week. It has a skeleton staff always on duty, ready for emergency calls, but for the most part it respects the decencies of life, goes home to supper at a reasonable time and takes the normal days off. There was a Duty Inspector to keep Poole company but he happened to be a dreary fellow and Poole was left largely to his own thoughts, which were anything but cheerful. He realised that he had been thinking too much and his thoughts were now going round and round in a circle; he would do better, until action was possible, to find some distraction – a concert, perhaps, or even a cinema – so long as there was no G-men stuff on the programme.

Soon after five the expected call came through and Poole heard Gower's voice over the line.

'They're with the sister, sir, Miss Widdington, as I expect you guessed. She met them at Denmouth. I asked a taxi-driver if he knew who she was and he told me where she lived, so I didn't run to the expense of a car to follow. I thought a motor-bike would be handy in case they went off in a hurry so I went to Denmouth police headquarters and they lent me one. I've managed to get a word with Miss Widdington's housemaid and she tells me they're staying till Monday, but I've got the local police to give me a hand in watching. All seems quite normal so far.'

Poole smiled as he listened to the dry, matter-of-fact account given by his faithful colleague. Gower spoke as if the whole thing was so simple, but Poole knew that it took a good C.I.D. man to do what this elderly sergeant had done; the quick decision not to hire a car to follow a ten-mile trail, the tact which persuaded a County Constabulary to part with a precious motor-bicycle to an unknown detective, the contact so quickly obtained with the household – all these represented years of experience allied with first-class ability. He wondered just how the grizzled sergeant had wormed his way so quickly into the good graces of Miss Widdington's housemaid; going off from London at a moment's notice after an all-night watch, with no time to shave or wash or tidy or change to anything more attractive than his dark suit and bowler hat, how would Gower present himself to the Widdington household? Not as detective, Poole felt sure; probably as a 'traveller,' a business man taking a week-end holiday, a man just looking for a relation... Gower would do it all quietly and efficiently and make no brag about it. But a word of praise never comes amiss.

'That's first-class work, Gower,' he said. 'I don't suppose they're up to anything but let me know any unexpected move. And if you can warn me what time they're coming back I'll have a relief to meet you at Paddington. By the way, if you can borrow a camera I badly want a snapshot of those two, separately or together.'

It was asking a good deal but there was no limit to Gower's ingenuity. If he did it at all he would do it unobserved.

That was all that could be done that night. Poole had a high tea, went to a Deanna Durbin film, and got to bed early.

On the following morning he decided to satisfy himself about the early end of the time-table. He had not been present when Chief-Inspector Beldam questioned the old police-constable, Darby, about the time of the rain starting. He had read Beldam's notes on the subject but he wanted to hear about it himself. There is always the chance of a slip, a misunderstanding or misinterpretation of a piece of evidence, and where a close time-table is concerned a tiny mistake may make a vital difference. So Poole rang up Hampstead Police Station and arranged for P.C. Darby to be there when he arrived.

To his surprise, when he got there he found Superintendent Hollis in his office.

'They told me you were coming up, Inspector,' said the Superintendent, 'so I thought I'd have a word with you, though I generally take Sunday off. I'd like to get this Heath case squared up. Of course, it's in your hands now, but it's still technically my responsibility. I'd like to know how things stand.'

He spoke with a smile but Poole felt rather ashamed to realise how little he had thought about Mr. Hollis's responsibility. He decided to tell the Superintendent a good deal more than he had done on the occasion of his last visit on the day after his return from Chatterleys. He revealed the dead woman's real identity and described the efforts he was making to connect her early, married life with the tragedy on the Heath. He went into no great detail about the different members of the family but said that he was looking into the possibility of a woman being connected with the murder; he described Helen Wayke and promised to let the Superintendent have a copy of any photograph that could be obtained.

Superintendent Hollis listened carefully. He asked a question or two but did not press for details.

'That's all very interesting, Inspector,' he said. 'I take it that you've given up the idea of Herbert Varden being concerned? We've been keeping an eye on him for you; would you like that to go on or not?'

'That is for you to say, sir,' said Poole politely.

Superintendent Hollis smiled.

'I take that to mean that you're not interested in him any longer.'

He paused, rubbing his chin with a thick forefinger.

'Well, I think I'll keep an eye on him for a bit – at any rate till you are quite sure of your case. Now I'll leave you to have a talk to Darby; you can use this room.'

Poole thanked the Superintendent, and a minute later was alone with Police-Constable Darby. The veteran constable clearly enjoyed the opportunity to spread himself before the C.I.D. man. He described in glowing terms the hospitality that he was accustomed to receive from, among others, the friend who was 'cook to a lady in Weedon Grove,' he elaborated his reason for being so sure of the time at which the rain had begun; he had thought that he might be too early and so had looked at his watch; finding that it was 7.10 he had whistled up the cook, who brought him a nice cup of green pea soup; while he was drinking it and having a friendly word the rain had come down sharp and sudden; he had no hesitation in saying that the time of that event was as near as no matter 7.15.

Poole put some questions – about the reliability of the watch, the possibility of the rain having started earlier at the other side of the Heath, and others which he thought might test the intelligence of the constable; when he had finished he felt sure that this was a reliable witness and the time limits already fixed by Chief-Constable Beldam might be taken as pretty well established.

That was all that could be done until Monday, when Widdington and Miss Wayke would presumably be back from Devonshire and would have to answer some rather more awkward questions than had been asked them so far.

CHAPTER VII

DISTRESS SIGNAL

The early part of Monday morning was taken up in discussing the case with Sir Leward Marradine and Chief-Constable Thurston. The Assistant Commissioner had a weakness for cases in which 'the rich and great ones,' as he called them, were concerned. Neither the Waykes nor Widdingtons fell strictly within this category, but they were sufficiently good families to interest Sir Leward. He listened with keen attention to the new developments described by Inspector Poole, who he knew would not bring such a grave charge without good reason. The letter written by Miss Wayke to Bella Knox and, still more, the fact that, having written, she had denied having seen her sister for twenty-five years, did to his mind constitute grounds for suspicion, quite apart from the curious and so far unexplained incident of the car.

'I don't know either of them myself,' said Sir Leward, when Poole had finished. 'but I met old Colonel Widdington once – dining on King's Guard, I think it was. He struck me as very much of the old school and if his son is anything like him this story seems incredible. What do you make of it, Mr. Thurston?'

'Needs looking into, sir,' said the Chief-Constable laconically. 'I think it's time Poole had another talk to these two people; Captain Widdington'll need to explain about the car and Miss Wayke about the letter.'

'I agree. What else do you suggest, Poole?'

'I think we ought to see if we can trace their movements that evening, sir. I hope Gower may have got a snapshot or two and I'd like enquiries made among taxi-drivers and the transport services. It's a long time ago but so far we have only enquired for Varden; nothing was said about a woman.'

So it was agreed, with the addition that enquiries should be also made at the Cambrian Hall, where Helen Wayke had said she had spent the evening, and at the cinema where Widdington claimed to have been.

Before Poole could start on either of these tasks, however, a telephone message arrived from Sergeant Gower, saying that the two people concerned had left Denmouth by a train which was due at Paddington at 2.31 p.m. His borrowed motor-bicycle had developed carburettor trouble, so that he had missed the train and lost touch with them, but the station staff had provided the necessary information. He was following by the next train.

There was still time to make enquires at the cinema and the Cambrian Hall, but neither yielded any positive result; Poole had not for a moment expected that they would. Knowing that he might be very fully occupied for the rest of the day he had a good luncheon and before half-past two was at Paddington, accompanied by Detective-Constable Watts, with a police-car in the background.

The train was only a few minutes late and, in spite of the crowd, there was no difficulty in discerning the stalwart figures of Captain Widdington and Miss Wayke. The former, Poole thought, was looking ill and depressed but Helen Wayke appeared to have lost nothing of her calm confidence.

They got into a taxi and Watts, who was unknown to them, was near enough to hear Widdington tell the driver to go to Baxter Street; a moment later the two detectives were following in the police-car. Poole wanted to question them separately, and as Watts had already had Miss Wayke under observation he decided to leave him in Baxter Street and himself follow Captain Widdington to his hotel if and when he went there.

Praed Street was crowded and progress was very slow; the police car had been cut off from the taxi by a couple of omnibuses and a railway delivery van; if there had been any doubt about the quarry's destination Poole would have felt worried. Entering Chapel Street, however, they quickly caught up, and along the Marylebone Road the way was fairly clear. As they turned out of the Tottenham Court Road, approaching the taxi's destination, Poole told his driver to drop back and stop directly he turned into Baxter Street.

No. 15 was about a hundred yards down the street so that when the taxi stopped in front of it Poole's car was already stationary at the curb and unlikely to attract attention. They saw Helen Wayke get out and Widdington follow, carrying a suit case into the house, while the cab waited. A minute or two later Widdington came out again and, getting into the taxi, drove away. Poole did not want to suggest to him that he was being followed, so, as he knew that Platt was already waiting near the Hertford Hotel he thought it quite safe to let the cab get out of sight. As soon as it had disappeared Watts got out of the police-car, but before shutting the door paused to ask whether he should keep the Inspector informed by telephone of any visits which Miss Wayke might pay.

'Not unless you think there's anything significant,' said Poole. 'If she goes to the Bleak Street garage, for instance, I'd like to know, or that solicitor in Sussex Street. Otherwise . . .'

He stopped short and shrank back into the corner of the car. Over Watts' shoulder he had seen Helen Wayke come out of the lodging-house and walk quickly towards them. Watts, well-trained detective that he was, did not look round but leaned slightly into the car, blocking the interior and keeping his own face hidden. The driver of the car was wearing plain chauffeur's uniform, so that there was nothing to show that it was a police car.

Helen Wayke's swinging stride carried her past and she took no apparent notice of the car. A moment later she had turned to the right down Friar Street.

'Where's she off to in such a hurry?' muttered Poole.

He thought for a moment, then slipped out of the car.

'You stay here,' he said. 'I'm going to see what she's up to. You can get back, James; I shan't want you again.'

He walked to the corner and saw Miss Wayke fifty yards ahead; apart from her the street was empty so that it was not safe to follow closely. Nor was it wise to let her get too far ahead, because Friar Street led into the busy thoroughfare of Southampton Row. As soon as he judged it safe Poole followed on, but when he reached Southampton Row Helen Wayke was no longer to be seen; worse still, he had not been able to see which way she had turned on reaching it, because a little spate of vehicles had turned into Friar Street, hiding her from view. It seemed likely that she would have turned north which was her general direction coming up Baxter Street. There was a bus stop not far away and two buses were just crossing the Euston Road, or rather one was crossing and the other turning right-handed towards King's Cross; she might be on either, she might have got a taxi, she might still be walking along the more crowded street ahead of him.

Poole looked round for a taxi, but none was in sight; he cursed himself for not keeping the car. He hurried towards the bus stop and questioned a man who was dressing a fishmonger's window. The man had noticed no lady getting on a bus, but then he had not been paying attention to bus traffic. Poole hurried on towards the Euston Road and as he reached it a taxi-cab drew up beside him, stopped by the red light. The detective jumped in; he had already decided to follow the bus which had gone straight across; it was a pure guess but it seemed hopeless to hunt down the crowded traffic going towards King's Cross.

The red lights seemed to be on an unconscionable time but at last the amber appeared and his car shot forward. Eversholt Street was clear and before long Poole could see the white top of a bus above the traffic ahead of him. He decided to pass it and await it at the next stop. A moment later the taxi began to bump and the driver pulled into the side and got down.

'Sorry, sir,' he said, opening the door. 'Flat tyre; must have picked up a nail.'

'Hell!' said Poole.

Again no taxi in sight, but behind him another bus – a 68. Poole signalled to it and, as the driver obligingly slowed down, jumped agilely aboard.

'D'you know what the bus ahead is?' he asked the conductor.

'S'far as I know it's a 169,' said the man. 'There's only two routes up here and we're both on a ten-minute service.'

'Where does it go to?'

'Camden Town – Chalk Farm – Swiss Cottage.'

'And you?'

'Camden Town – Chalk Farm. We stop there, but we'll get there before that 169; it goes round by Park Road.'

That might be a real bit of luck; if he could be waiting at Chalk Farm when the 169 came up he might resume contact. But why Chalk Farm?

A sudden thought struck him – Camden Town did have some meaning where his quarry was concerned. At Camden Town she was near Kentish Town, the home of the Twists and 'Bella Knox'; or she could get a tram – or rather a trolley-bus – which would take her up Highgate Road to the Duke of St. Albans on the very edge of the Heath!

Why Helen Wayke should go to either place Poole could not imagine, but these did suggest the only destinations that could have any interest for him and of the two the Heath seemed the least unlikely. Could it be the old story of a murderer returning to the scene of his crime? Surely, with so stable a person as Helen Wayke, that was too far-fetched an idea. Well, it was no good guessing; he would follow the long shot that might yield some surprising result.

A minute later he was at Camden Town and, leaving his bus, changed to another, which took him up to Kentish Town. Here there were trolley-buses running at frequent intervals to Parliament Hill Fields, as the Duke of St. Albans terminus was called, each at five or six-minute intervals, so that Helen Wayke, if she had gone that way, would not have been delayed; still he thought she could not be more than five minutes ahead of him.

At the terminus he saw something that made him think his luck had turned at last – a constable standing on the pavement, ruminantly watching the few passengers as they alighted. He showed the officer his warrant-card and described Helen Wayke.

Slowly the man shook his head.

'No, sir; no one like that. I've been here twenty minutes – waiting for the Inspector, as a matter of fact. No lady's got off here – not what you'd call a lady.'

Poole eyed the man carefully. Yes, he was a reliable type.

'Quite certain?'

294 LONELY MAGDALEN

'Quite certain, sir.'

That ended the long shot. As he got into the return bus Poole wondered why on earth he should have allowed himself to be led on such a wild goose chase. Helen Wayke might equally well have been going in a dozen different directions from the place where he had last seen her – all equally unimportant and unconnected with his case. Well, he had better get back to the Hertford Hotel … and the less he said about this interlude the better for his reputation.

He got off at Camden Town and presently a 169 bus came along – the bus he had been following but in the reverse direction. As the conductor took his penny a thought struck him.

'You come from Chalk Farm via Regent's Park Road, don't you?'

'That's right,' said the conductor.

'Does that go past Primrose Hill?'

'That's right,' repeated the man.

Poole rose to his feet.

'Put me down, will you?' he asked quietly. 'I've made a mistake.'

If he had used his brains a little bit sooner he might have saved some of his lost self-esteem. He had a fair knowledge of London, and 'Chalk Farm' coupled with 'Park Road' – which meant Regent's Park – should have suggested Primrose Hill to him twenty minutes ago. And beside Primrose Hill lived Helen Wayke's brother.

What could be more natural than that Miss Wayke, having had a week-end to talk things over with Mary Widdington, should have decided to go and tell her brother that she was in London, why she was in London, and what a mess she and 'Jim' had got themselves into. That would be the wise and obvious thing to do if she were innocent; it was also the sensible thing to do if she were guilty, because the fact that she had not revealed her presence in London to her brother was one of the facts which looked to Poole so suspicious.

There was no great point in going to Sir Richard Wayke's house now. He could not very well question Miss Wayke there and he certainly could not expect to hear what the brother and sister were saying to each other – if they had not already finished saying it. But Poole's self-esteem demanded that he should satisfy himself that this time his brain had worked correctly. Waste of time though it might be, he was going to make sure that this was where his quarry really had gone.

It did not take many minutes to get from Camden Town to Primrose Hill, but when he reached Green Lodge Poole was uncertain what to do. He could wait outside in the road until Miss Wayke emerged, but as it was an unfrequented road he would run considerable risk of being seen by her, and that he did not want. He could slip into the garden and take cover there; he would have liked to see into Sir Richard's sitting-room, which overlooked the garden, but as it was still daylight there was every chance of his being seen himself. As he strolled past on the far side of the road Poole looked across the garden to its far wall and, from what he could see, judged that beyond it there was another garden belonging to a house in a parallel street. He could just make out the house beyond and realised that the blinds of the upper windows were down; there seemed a fair chance that he might be able to get into that garden and from it look at the back of Green Lodge.

Lengthening his stride Poole walked on until he came to a cross street, turned down it, and presently was in the street parallel to the one he had just left. Counting the houses he soon found the one he was seeking; there was a 'To Let' board in front of it and the garden was unkempt. The detective slipped in through the gate, skirted the house and very soon was standing on a tub and looking over the garden wall directly into the back windows of Green Lodge.

The large window of Sir Richard Wayke's sitting-room was easily recognisable, but Poole realised at once that he could only see a few feet inside the room itself; he could just make out the work-bench but beyond that the room was in shadow; if there were people inside it they were invisible to him. It was a disappointment but not much more. If it had been really urgent to see into the room Poole would have taken the risk of getting closer, but he still did not want Helen Wayke to know that she was being watched.

Poole was on the point of dropping down from his perch when, taking a last look, he saw a head and shoulders suddenly materialise out of the dim interior. Startled for a moment, he quickly realised that the crippled baronet must have wheeled himself across the room to his work-table. He saw an arm stretch out and the next instant table and man were clearly illuminated.

In the bright light Sir Richard Wayke's face looked white and haggard, but Poole was too far away to read its expression. He seemed to be sitting motionless, and a moment later the figure of a woman appeared beside him. Though her face was above the bench-light Poole had no doubt from what was visible that it was Helen Wayke. He saw Sir Richard make a movement with his hands as if in refusal; the woman's figure disappeared into the shadow and a moment later there came the sound of a door shutting.

Still the baronet sat motionless, staring straight in front of him into the gathering dusk.

With that bright light in his eyes Poole knew that Sir Richard could see nothing of the garden. He put his leg over the wall and dropped down on to a flower bed; skirting the wall he was soon in the shelter of the wooden garage, from which he could watch the front door. It opened almost at once and Helen Wayke came out on to the short drive, shutting the door behind her.

As she turned towards the entrance gate Poole could see her face clearly, and realised that for the first time since he had known her the serene composure that was her most marked characteristic had deserted Helen Wayke. She was looking straight in front of her, her eyes rather wide open, but their expression was one of intense disquiet. . . it might even be of fear.

CHAPTER VIII

SURPRISE FOR WIDDINGTON

For a moment Poole hesitated as to whether he should not take this opportunity to question Helen Wayke, while she was clearly outside her normal control. But he put the idea aside at once; there would be a lot to ask her and he could not do it in a public street. By the time he had got her to some more private place – a police-station, perhaps – she would have recovered herself and, knowing that she had been followed, would be doubly on her guard.

So he followed her back to her lodging-house and by that time had decided to revert to his original intention of tackling Widdington first. He regarded the soldier as the less resolute character of the two and thought it good strategy to launch his surprise attack at the weakest spot in the defences.

After a word or two with Watts he went on to the Hertford Hotel and found that Captain Widdington was having tea in the lounge-hall. His face still bore the strained look that Poole had seen on it at Paddington, but he greeted the detective calmly enough and without apparent surprise. A minute later they were once more sitting in the gloomy smoking-room.

Widdington held out a cigarette case.

'I hope your chap enjoyed his week-end,' he said.

Poole started. He had not been expecting a 'first touch' from this opponent. To cover his confusion he took a cigarette, contrary to his custom under such circumstances, and while he was lighting it Widdington saved him the trouble of a reply.

'I happened to see him as he came up to my sister's house on Saturday afternoon,' he said. 'The face was not altogether unfamiliar,' he added with a smile.

'Just a matter of routine, sir,' said Poole, realising the clumsiness of this bromide; 'you went away rather suddenly, taking tickets for a port, and we had to make sure where you were going. I hope he didn't worry you?'

'Not at all. Model of discretion; we were quite sorry not to see him at Denmouth this morning.'

Poole wondered whether this Guardsman, who was clearly not such a fool as he . . . well, as he might have been expected to be . . . had had anything to do with the 'carburettor trouble' developed by Gower's borrowed motor-bicycle. On the whole, he thought not; there seemed no point in such a piece of cheap trickery unless he were going to make a serious attempt to get away from observation, which he had not done.

Still feeling slightly deflated, Poole launched out on his questioning.

'You told me, sir, about your movements on the evening of the 9th October and I have checked them as far as possible; so far as this hotel is concerned what evidence I have been able to get bears out your statement, but I have not been able to get any confirmation of what you told me about your visit to the cinema and your subsequent walk. Have you been able to get any confirmation yourself?'

Captain Widdington lifted his eyebrows.

'I haven't tried,' he said. 'Why should I?'

'It might be advisable, sir . . . under certain circumstances.'

'That's pretty vague. What are you getting at?'

A direct reply was clearly undesirable, so Poole switched to another line.

'Did you have your car out at all that evening, sir?'

This time there was something more than a raising of the eyebrows. Captain Widdington quite clearly saw the implication of that question – much more clearly than Poole had expected, intending as he did to use it as a catch.

'No, I did not have my car out that evening, Inspector; if I had I should have told you. You are poking your nose pretty thoroughly into my affairs and I should like to know what justification there is for it.'

There was a crackle in Captain Widdington's voice that must have come from his soldiering days.

'I have told you that I knew nothing about my wife's death on the 9th October until I saw the photograph in the papers and recognised it. I admit that I was wrong not to come forward and identify her; that was a damn silly thing to have done under the circumstances . . . and I should probably do it again . . . or rather, not do it. But it wasn't criminal and there can't possibly be any grounds for thinking that I had anything to do with her death.'

When he was angry Jim Widdington's face regained some of the handsome vitality of his youth. Poole realised for the first time how attractive he must have been and how natural that these two sisters should have loved him; he remembered, too, the queer and rather unpleasant story of Mrs. George Bazeley and for a moment it flashed across his mind that that old story might hold some key to the present tragedy. But he put the idea away from him as too fantastically improbable. No woman could harbour jealousy and revenge all that long time . . . and if Sir Richard Wayke's description of her was right Mrs. Bazeley must by now be nearer seventy than sixty – if she was alive at all.

The detective brought his mind sharply back to the present.

'I've explained to you, sir, that we are bound to look closely into your movements on the night of the murder; you must see that for yourself. And I must ask you who it was that took your car out that evening if you did not take it out yourself.'

Widdington stared at him.

'Why do you say that? Why should anybody have taken it out?'

'That's what I want to know, sir,' said Poole quietly. 'It *was* out that evening.'

'How do you know?'

'The garage enter withdrawals and returns in a book.'

'Do they? I never knew that. What's the point of it?'

'Probably as a check, sir. They have some responsibility for their customers' cars. I don't say that all garages do it, but most of the big ones do . . . and the most businesslike ones.'

'I see. Probably that's pretty sound.'

If Widdington was fencing, thought Poole, he was doing it well. His

surprise seemed genuinely directed to the methods of garage management
. . . and he had given himself time to recover from what might have been
a pretty severe shock.

'Who can have taken the car out, sir?' reiterated Poole.

'Well, I suppose . . .' The soldier checked himself abruptly. 'I don't
know yet that it was taken out.'

'You can take that from me, sir. I have seen the book. The chance of
their making a mistake is very small.'

Widdington nodded.

'Yes, I suppose it is. But I suppose it is possible that someone else –
some unauthorised person – might have taken it out. That does happen,
doesn't it? Joy-riding, or something like that. They don't enter up *who*
takes a car out, I suppose, do they?'

'No, they don't do that, but the manager tells me that they never
allow a car to be taken out except by the owner or by someone authorised
by him.'

'I see.'

A curious look of discomfort had come into the big man's eyes. He
did not look directly at Poole.

'Did you authorise anyone else to take your car out, sir?'

There was a long pause.

'Do you mean on that night?' Widdington asked at last.

'On that night or any other time, sir.'

The answer came reluctantly.

'Well, yes, I suppose so. Not in so many words. Miss Wayke has often
been with me when I have taken it out and I think she has taken it out
herself once or twice. But not on the night you are talking about.'

'How do you know that, sir?'

'She told me.'

It was Poole's turn to raise his eyebrows.

'You discussed the car with her then, sir?'

Widdington frowned.

'No, I don't mean that. I mean that she told me what she was doing that evening. I can't remember whether she told me at the time but after you had questioned us both we naturally talked about it. She was at a lecture . . . of course, I did know that, because that was why I went to a cinema. She didn't get out till eight o'clock.'

'Yes, she told me that, sir. So we still don't know who took the car out.'

He spoke meditatively but Widdington took it as a question.

'No, we don't. I don't suppose we ever shall. I don't suppose it ever went out at all . . . that night, I mean. Either the fellow who keeps the book made a mistake or, if it did go out, it was taken by someone else. He may have taken it out himself for a joy-ride and entered it up just to cover himself.'

'Pretty risky, wouldn't it be, sir? You might have come in and wanted it yourself.'

'Not so late as that. I've never taken it out so late as that.'

Widdington's composure was shaken now, Poole thought, and the fact interested him. He had seemed assured enough and confident enough when his own movements were being questioned, but now. . . . Could it be that some uneasy doubt had come into his mind? Could it be that he really knew nothing, that he was innocent and she guilty?

Poole thought that he would try one more shaft.

'Would you mind telling me, sir, how it was you first came to know that your wife was using the name "Bella Knox"?'

Widdington looked keenly at him.

'I saw it in the paper,' he said.

'When, sir?'

The soldier frowned.

'I think it was in the account of the inquest. There was no name with the photograph the papers first published; I am sure of that because when we recognised the photograph we naturally looked for the name – and of course you were asking for an identification. I don't think there was any mention of a name before the inquest.'

Poole nodded.

'I think that is so, sir,' he said quietly.

And yet it had been a searching question. Put to him suddenly, if
Widdington had been a guilty man he might well have blundered over
it. When one has something to conceal it is not always easy to remember
how much one is supposed to know. Widdington's answer had not only
been correct, it had sounded convincing.

Yet Helen Wayke had written to 'Bella Knox' at her wretched home
at Kentish Town.

Poole was beginning to form a definite impression in his mind and
he wanted to test it. But he was anxious that Helen Wayke should have
no warning of what she was likely to be asked and he had already prepared
a scheme for preventing this.

'There's just one thing more I would like you to do, sir, if you are
willing to. You told me that you came out of the cinema that evening
because the picture bored you and that you then strolled about before
returning here. I gathered that you didn't know exactly what time you
came out of the cinema?'

'No, I can't say I do know. I had no reason to notice it.'

'Exactly, sir, but do you remember what the film was that bored you?'

'I don't remember what it was called but I remember what it was
about – one of those American back-stage things.'

'Do you remember roughly what was happening. . . in the film story,
I mean . . . when you came out?'

Jim Widdington frowned, in an effort of recollection.

'Ye – es. Yes, I think I do.'

'Then, sir, would you mind going round there with one of my men
and seeing whether you can pin down the time of your leaving. They will
know what time the picture was showing and there will probably be
someone who can identify how long it had been running.'

Widdington stared at him.

'Well, you have got your hooks into me,' he said. 'I don't mind trying
but who the hell do I ask – the Commissionaire?'

'My man will know all about that, sir; he's accustomed to that kind
of enquiry. Platt, his name is; he's out in the hall now.'

'The deuce he is. You don't take any chances, Inspector. All right, I'll do my best. And if you like we will see if I can retrace the stroll I had afterwards. Though there won't be anything to prove that I'm not making it up as I go along,' he added with a grin.

Poole thanked him and they went out into the hall. Platt was sitting in a chair, half hidden by an elderly illustrated paper. When Captain Widdington had collected his hat and coat from the cloak-room he and Poole went out into the street and a moment later Platt put down his paper and followed. A word of introduction and Poole was left alone, watching the two retreating forms.

He had already become aware of a familiar figure strolling down the opposite side of the street. He walked across and joined it.

'Well, Gower,' he said, 'who put water into your carburettor?'

The sergeant grinned.

'Shouldn't wonder if it wasn't that maid-servant,' he said. 'Smart little bit, she was. You got contact all right, sir?'

'Yes, I got, contact all right. And so did Captain Widdington.'

Sergeant Gower stared.

'I don't get you, sir.'

'No; but he got you. He spotted you were trailing him.'

'Did he, sir? Did he? That's one in the eye for me. I thought I was doing the job all right.'

Poole smiled.

'I'm sure you were, Gower, but we all know well enough that one is bound to be spotted sometimes. As a matter of fact I think I have been underestimating Captain Widdington myself.'

Gower was too well-disciplined to enquire further into that handful of consolation.

'I got that snapshot you asked for, sir,' he said. 'Miss Widdington is in it too and the light wasn't too good, but it may do. I took it straight along to the Yard; Cooke is working on it now.'

Poole patted his subordinate on the back.

'Good for you,' he said. 'That puts you right back on the map. Well, I'm going up to Baxter Street to ask Miss Wayke one or two questions. You'd better get off now. Did you get any sleep down in Devonshire?'

'Oh, yes, sir; like a top. The local people were very good about relieving me.'

'Well, anyhow, Platt can keep an eye on him tonight. You can relieve him tomorrow morning.'

When Poole got to Baxter Street he could see no sign of Watts. That probably meant that Miss Wayke had gone out again and the detective felt a little surge of irritation; nothing seemed to go right for him where Helen Wayke was concerned. The irritation may have accounted for a sudden decision to carry the war into the enemy's country; when the maid told him what he had expected to hear he asked for a word with Mrs. Dibbuts.

The landlady seemed quite pleased to see him, so that it was unlikely that her lodger had warned her not to talk.

'I'm going to take you into my confidence, Mrs. Dibbuts' . . . an opening which he often found fruitful. 'I'm afraid I wasn't quite frank with you the last time I came.'

Mrs. Dibbuts' expression disclosed willingness to be confided in.

'The fact is that the enquiry I am engaged on is more serious than I told you. The unfortunate woman I spoke of was murdered.'

Mrs. Dibbuts gasped, her blue eyes goggling with interest.

'Well, I never!' she exclaimed. 'And her a relative of Miss Wayke's.'

Poole nodded.

'Her half-sister. I wonder whether you remember hearing about a woman being found dead near Highgate Ponds – on the 9th October, it was.'

'Ooh! That wasn't never Miss Wayke's sister?'

'I'm afraid it was. That is the woman with a scar I was asking you about.'

'Well! Fancy that! Who would have thought it? Did Miss Wayke know it was her sister?'

'I'm afraid she did . . . and she didn't tell us about it, though perhaps that wasn't unnatural under the circumstances. But it makes it necessary for us to enquire rather closely into Miss Wayke's movements that evening and that is what I have come to ask you about. Do you remember it at all? You might have heard the broadcast.'

'That I did, indeed,' declared Mrs. Dibbuts, 'and it made me feel all queer – just after my supper. I remember saying so to Miss Wayke when I went up to say good-night.'

'She was in to supper herself?' asked Poole quickly.

'Yes, she was. I cook for her myself so I know she was in, but now I come to think she was a bit late that evening; quarter of an hour maybe; I'd done her a bit of fried fish and it's none the better for waiting.'

Poole wondered whether at last he had got on to something tangible.

'What time does she usually have supper?' he asked.

'Quarter to eight. Half-past seven would have suited me best and she wanted eight, so we split the difference. She was good about it as a rule, knowing I like to get done and my own supper eaten before the news, but that night she was late; must have been eight o'clock when she came in, I should say.'

Poole had hoped for something a bit later than that. Eight o'clock meant desperately quick work if the murder had not been committed till 7.25. She would have to get to the car . . . but the car had gone . . . gone by 7.20 at the latest if Hoskin was to be believed. Could it be that the murder had been done earlier . . . ?

It would be best to work that out later. In the meantime . . .

'What was she like when she came in? Did she seem upset at all?'

The landlady shook her head.

'I didn't see her. Milly takes supper up and clears. I didn't see her till I went up to say good-night and ask for orders; that would be about half-past nine.'

'And you spoke to her about the broadcast; had she heard it?'

'She said not. I was surprised; she usually listens in to the news.'

'Did she seem upset?'

Mrs. Dibbuts pondered the question.

'She's not one to show her feelings much. I can't say I noticed any-thing.'

Had Helen Wayke really not known that it was her sister that Mrs. Dibbuts was talking about? If that had been the first news she got, what iron self-control she must have.

He could question the maid but, on consideration, decided not to until he had seen Helen Wayke herself. It was just possible that Mrs. Dibbuts would respect his plea for secrecy, the maid certainly would talk.

An uneasy feeling came over him that Helen Wayke might by now have realised her danger, that she might even now be giving Watts the slip. He felt that he could not wait in Baxter Street but must get back to the Yard, to which Watts would telephone if he were in difficulties.

He hurried to Southampton Row, caught a bus, changed at Aldwych into a No. II and ten minutes later walked into the Yard. The first person he saw there was Watts.

'Good lord!' exclaimed Poole. 'Has she slipped you?'

The detective grinned.

'Not this time, sir; she's here.'

'Here?'

'Come to see you, sir. We wondered where you'd got to.'

CHAPTER IX

A STORY TOLD

Contrary to popular belief, every Detective-Inspector at Scotland Yard is not provided with a well-furnished room, complete with dictaphone, for his own use. Nor, for the matter of that, is every Chief-Inspector so fortunate. However, it was late enough for most of the staff to have gone off duty, and Poole had some hope that he would have the Inspectors' room to himself.

To all outward appearance Helen Wayke had completely recovered the equanimity that had seemed so badly shaken when she left her brother's house. She apologised for coming at so late an hour.

'I thought I had better see you tonight if I could, Mr. Poole,' she said. 'I don't want Jim upset more than can be helped; he is having a pretty bad time, as I expect you can imagine.'

She spoke simply and with a sincerity that seemed genuine enough.

'I had hoped that he need not know what I am going to tell you, but I suppose that is hardly possible now. It was a bit of a shock to him to realise that he was being followed, though I tried to persuade him that it was just a matter of form. I realised how serious things were when I saw that I was being followed too.'

This was a nasty blow to Poole's pride and his expression must have shown as much.

'I saw you in that car in Baxter Street,' went on Miss Wayke with a smile. 'I realised that you would probably follow me, so when I got out of the bus at Camden Town I went into a shop and looked out of the window. I saw you get out of the next bus. You went across to the Kentish Town Road. Did you think I had gone up to Highgate?'

Poole swallowed his mortification as best he could. He did not believe in riding the high horse, so he squeezed up a smile.

'I thought you might have,' he said.

'As a matter of fact I was going to see my brother, who lives near Primrose Hill – as you know, I think.'

It was time to counter-attack and recover the initiative.

'What did your brother say that upset you so much, Miss Wayke?'

'Oh; were you there? Well done, you. My brother was very . . . disagreeable. He told me I had got into my own mess and must get myself out of it. He has never liked Jim and . . . his accident has made him very hard and bitter. It was partly because I felt so completely alone that I decided I must tell you all about it. When I heard that you had been asking Jim about taking the car out I decided that it must be done at once.'

This time Poole did not attempt to hide his astonishment.

'How on earth did you hear that, Miss Wayke?' he asked. Again Helen smiled.

'There is a telephone in the cloak-room at Jim's hotel.'

Poole was very glad that Sergeant Gower was not there. He had been properly fooled and he did not like it. This woman was putting her cards on the table with a vengeance; would she be so frank if she were guilty?

'Perhaps you had better tell me whatever it is you came to say, Miss Wayke.'

He was not in a position to charge her; he did not even know that he intended to do so, so that there was no need for a formal caution nor for a written statement. He knew she would talk better without that. Still, he ought to give her a friendly word of warning.

'You need not tell me, you know,' he added. 'Would you like to ask your solicitor first?'

Helen Wayke shook her head.

'I have made up my mind,' she said. 'I only told you part of the truth when you came to see me on Friday, and I told you a lie when I said that I had not seen Christine since her marriage to Jim. I saw her two or three days after I landed – at the beginning of last month.'

Poole felt his pulse quicken. He felt sure that the truth was coming now and he was intensely eager to hear it.

'It was quite by chance. I had been to see a friend who is nursing in the North Eastern Hospital; that's just off Haverstock Hill, you know. I was waiting for a bus at Camden Town when a woman came up to me and said: "Hullo, Helen." I stared at her and for a moment I didn't know who she was. It was the voice, I think, that made me realise it was Christine. It was pretty awful; she looked . . . terrible. That scar on her cheek and the make-up, and of course she was twenty-five years older than when I last saw her – twenty-five pretty terrible years, poor girl.'

Though she spoke quietly there could be no mistaking the depth of feeling in Helen Wayke's voice . . . or else she was the most consummate actress and the vilest hypocrite imaginable.

'She said at once: "How's Jim?" I didn't ask her how she knew I was living with him. Perhaps she only guessed. I wasn't going to fence with her so I asked her if she wanted to go back to him. She laughed and said that if she had wanted that she would have had him back twenty years ago. All the time that we talked, Mr. Poole, she spoke in a hard, brazen sort of way and yet I felt that, underneath, she was terribly unhappy . . . that she was hiding her real feelings under a kind of veneer of hardness.'

Poole thought that this might well be the truth. He was sure that Christine Wayke had left her husband more for his sake than for her own. He doubted whether either Jim Widdington himself or Helen realised that.

'I couldn't talk to her there, in that public place. I asked her to come back to my lodgings – I wasn't in Baxter Street then – but she wouldn't. I asked her to take me to where she lived and she wouldn't do that either. We went into a little restaurant – it was practically empty at that hour – and we talked there.'

Poole was only listening superficially. He was looking at Helen Wayke's hands. They were clenched upon her handbag and, while her face remained calm, her hands expressed the deep emotion engendered by her story. She wore no gloves, so that the detective could see clearly how large and strong the hands were, as they slowly twisted the bag which lay upon her lap. With sickening clearness Poole remembered the marks upon the dead woman's throat and the words of the police-surgeon as he said that the size of the murderer's hands were the only clue he could give.

With an effort the detective wrenched his thoughts back to the words which were now being spoken by Helen Wayke as she told of the dramatic meeting with her unhappy sister.

'She told me quite frankly the life that she was leading. After she left Jim's flat in 1917 she went on the stage. She loved dancing and thought that she might be able to make a living that way. Of course she had to keep away from West End theatres because she did not want to be recognised. She got on fairly well at first, with touring companies and that sort of thing, but gradually she found it harder to get engagements and she was in great difficulties. Then one night – I think she must have been drinking more than usual, though she didn't say anything about that – she fell with her face on a gas burner and got that terrible scar. It prevented her getting any more work on the stage and there was nothing else that she could do. I asked her why she did not go to Dick, if she would not let Jim or me help her. She laughed – such a bitter laugh – and said that she preferred the men on the streets. She was speaking all the time in that hard voice and putting things as brutally as she could, but somehow I felt that if only I could get under that defensive shell I should find the old Christine, unhappy, lonely, but too proud to ask for help.'

Again Poole found himself impressed by the sincerity with which Helen Wayke spoke. It was difficult to believe that she was vile and that all her spoken sympathy was cruel hypocrisy.

'She told me that she had taken the name Knox from the maid, Kathleen, who had gone with her from Chatterleys when she first married. She hadn't thought about it when she first went to the theatrical agent and when the man asked her name she had to say the first one that came into her head. A placard on the wall gave her the Christian name – "Belle"; it got changed to Bella later on.'

'Did she tell you where she lived, Miss Wayke?' asked Poole.

If she denied that he would know that her whole story would be a lie.

'No, not then. But she wrote to me afterwards. I am coming to that.'

Poole was conscious of a curious feeling of relief. He did not want to disbelieve.

'I asked whether she wanted to go back to Jim now. It meant a good deal to me, that question, because I felt sure that if she did Jim would take her back . . . in spite of everything. He has blamed himself terribly for letting her go too easily. I think he did, but being out in France and . . . all the unnatural strain of the war . . . I think that was some excuse for him. He really has a very high sense of duty, not only as a soldier, and I think he would have taken her back.'

Helen Wayke paused and Poole saw that for the first time her face, as well as her hands, expressed deep emotion. The thought of how near she had been to losing her lover might well account for that.

'I expect I didn't quite hide my feelings,' she went on, 'because Christine said quickly: "Would you mind if I did?" I felt I had better be honest about it, so I said: "Yes, I would mind." She asked me then whether I was living with him and I told her that I was. Then she asked why he hadn't divorced her and I told her that, even if he had wanted to, he could not because he did not know where she was or anything about her; desertion wasn't enough then. "But it is now," she said. She sat thinking for some time and I saw her face harden. I wanted to change the subject so I asked her if she would let us help her now. She laughed – again that horrible, bitter laugh – and said: "I don't want your charity, Helen, but if I can earn my living I will. If you will pay me to keep away, I will!"'

Again that sickening feeling of suspicion swept over Poole. Here was motive, plain and damning – blackmail. Not only the blackmail that meant money, but the more dreadful threat of taking this woman's lover from her just when she could see freedom – freedom to live an open married life – within her grasp.

'It was a horrible shock to me, that,' said Helen Wayke. 'I had not thought that she could hate Jim and me so much. I should have been glad to help her . . . freely, without any threats . . . but she chose to make it so vile. It made me feel very hard; I felt that I could not give Jim up to her now. I determined not to tell him that I had seen her and to go to a solicitor and find out what I had better do. Perhaps we could get the divorce through without her knowing anything about it and then I should feel safe. Jim would not want to take her back then.'

There was an honesty about this confession that Poole found very convincing. He believed that he was being told the truth . . . but what had happened? Was he to hear a confession of even more dreadful truth?

'I told her that it was horrible to talk like that, that I would gladly have helped her but that I was not going to be blackmailed. I got up and walked quickly out of the shop and jumped into a taxi that was going past. She must have followed me in another, poor as she was, because two or three days afterwards I got a letter from her. I had changed my lodgings but I had to leave my new address because I was expecting a letter; Christine's letter followed me to Baxter Street. She said that if I would give her ten pounds a month she would keep away but that if not she would find Jim and stop his getting a divorce. She gave me her address – Bunt Street, in Kentish Town – and told me to write to her there.'

Still the truth but. . . what the end?

'I felt quite hard, then,' went on Helen Wayke, 'and I determined to fight her. I wasn't going to have Jim's life spoilt . . . quite apart from my own. If she had been . . . what she used to be, affectionate, headstrong, even just angry . . . it would have been different. Oh, I know what she had been through; perhaps I was expecting too much . . . but Jim came first for me. We aren't at all well off and without Jim's help I couldn't manage what she asked. But if I could put her off till after the divorce then we could do something for her between us. I wrote and told her that I would do what I could if she would talk it over with me. I asked her to meet me at the same place – at Camden Town. But I wasn't going to talk to her in a shop, where we might be overheard, so I decided to take Jim's car and we could drive to some quiet place and talk in that.'

God! The decoy letter. Exactly as he had guessed. Poole felt a cold sweat break out on the palms of his hands.

'I fixed a day when I knew there was to be a lecture . . . I had had a notice of it. I told Jim I was going to it and should not see him again that evening. I didn't go to it; I went to the garage where he kept his car and took it out; they know me well – I believe they think I am his wife. When I got to Camden Town Christine was waiting, and when I suggested going somewhere quiet she said: "Drive me to Highgate Ponds; I've got a date with a client at seven o'clock."'

Poole felt a quick flutter of excitement.

'I didn't believe her,' said Helen. 'I thought she was just "trying to make my flesh creep," like that horrible-boy in Pickwick. But we drove there and it was very quiet and lonely. I told her I would give her ten pounds then and another ten pounds every month if she would write me a letter saying she had no intention of going back to Jim. She laughed at me. "That would be as good as giving you a divorce," she said; "I shan't do anything of the kind. And if you don't send it me regularly I shall just go back to him. I can find him all right – now that I know where you are. And even if he won't take me back I shall get proof that I tried to go back."'

Motive. Damning motive.

'I still thought that if Jim knew nothing about her we could get on with the divorce without Christine knowing about it – as it was for desertion. I gave her the money – ten pounds – and she said that now she would give herself the treat of telling her friend to go to hell. I still thought she was making all that up. She got out of the car and walked away. I don't know that part well but the Ponds were on our left and she walked straight up the road we were in and then rather to the left where it forked. I sat for a bit watching her and thinking . . . even after she was out of sight. Then it suddenly began to rain and I switched on the engine and drove off, turning to the right at the fork where she had gone to the left. I hardly knew where I was going and I rather lost my way. I found myself down by Finsbury Park and I didn't get home till eight o'clock, which made me late for supper.'

All the times fitted. She had driven away when the rain started – 7.15 – which corresponded to Hoskin's evidence of between 7.15 and 7.20; the garage had clocked her in at 7.45 and Mrs. Dibbuts had said she got home at 8. There was no lying so far.

'When you were in Millfield Lane, Miss Wayke . . . that is the road beside the Ponds . . . did you see anyone?'

Helen Wayke shook her head.

'I didn't really notice. It was very lonely. I think a woman walked past while we were talking in the car.'

That would be Mrs. Joliffe.

'You didn't see any man?'

'No, I'm sure I didn't. I thought of that when I heard about the murder.'

'How did you hear about it?'

She had been so calm when Mrs. Dibbuts spoke of it. It seemed incredible that that could be the first she knew – and even more incredible that she should not have at once recognised the dead woman as her sister.

'I heard it on the wireless. It was a most appalling shock. I don't think I have ever been so near fainting . . . and I am not the sort that faints. Thank goodness, I was alone, and when Mrs. Dibbuts – my landlady – came up and started talking about it I had had time to pull myself together and decide what to do.'

Helen Wayke stopped. She seemed to be thinking how best to go on. Her hands were still now.

'I don't know how I am going to make you understand the next part, Mr. Poole,' she said. 'I know what you are thinking about me and what I tell you must sound pretty thin . . . but it is true. Of course I ought to have gone straight to the police and told them everything. If you can put yourself in my place perhaps you will be able to understand why I didn't. It would have meant raking up all the unhappy story of Christine's marriage with Jim and her leaving him. It would have meant everyone knowing what she had become . . . and that wasn't easy to face, for people brought up as we had been.'

'But you advised your . . . Captain Widdington to tell the police,' Poole broke in.

'Yes, I did. That was different. He ought to have told them and I wanted to put myself right with him. When he decided not to, I was glad, and I did not try very hard to change his mind. But that was different to my telling the police myself. I should have had to tell them about my meeting Christine and about her blackmailing me . . . and I had not told Jim that and I did not mean him to know. I wanted him to keep his old affection for her . . . because it would have made him so terribly unhappy to know what she had become. When I heard the broadcast appeal, though I knew at once who it was, I thought there was no chance of Jim knowing, because he had not seen her for twenty years and knew nothing about her life or the scar. Even when I saw the photograph in the paper next morning I hoped he would not recognise her, but he did, at once. It was only then that I decided to advise him to identify her, because I knew he would expect me to advise him to, but I felt that there was a very good chance that he would not.'

Her frankness was devastating . . . and impressive.

'I don't think I can tell you any more, Mr. Poole,' she said. 'We decided to tell nobody, not even Mary, and to wait till it was forgotten before we went to a solicitor about a divorce. You see, as we did not identify her, we should still have to get a divorce for desertion if we were to marry.'

Poole nodded.

'Yes, I see that,' he said. 'You have been very frank with me, Miss Wayke, and I am glad you have. It still leaves me no nearer knowing what happened to your sister. I should like to think over your story and then I shall probably want to ask you some more questions.'

'Of course; I can quite understand that.'

Helen Wayke rose to her feet.

'Shall I still have to be followed?' she asked with a smile.

'Yes, I'm afraid so; at any rate until I've told your story to my chief. I will try to make it as little troublesome as possible.'

'Oh, I don't really mind . . . now that I've got it all off my chest.'

Poole could well understand the relief that that must be.

'There is just one question that occurs to me,' he said. 'I found in your sister's room in Bunt Street a photograph of Chatterleys; it was through that that I traced her. What puzzles me is that on the back of it was written the name 'Kathleen.' Can you account for that?'

Helen Wayke shook her head.

'Only that her maid's name was Kathleen – Kathleen Knox. I think I know the photograph. She may have meant to give it to Kathleen and then kept it herself. Or she may actually have given it and then Kathleen may have left it behind at the flat when she went away; she left Christine, you know; probably because of . . . of her drinking.'

Poole nodded.

'I knew she was your sister's maid. I did not know about her leaving,' he said.

When Helen Wayke had gone Poole sat on at his desk, thinking over the strange story that he had been listening to. Throughout it had borne the stamp of truth. At every point at which he had a cross-check on it the story, the times, the actions, had proved to be true. The manner of the teller, and especially her frankness, had been convincing. And yet, if it was true, all the theory that he had so carefully built up, that this crime might be in some way connected with Christine Wayke's early life, seemed to fall to the ground, because, though that early life took her right up to Millfield Lane, it seemed to stop at the moment when she got out of the car and walked away from her sister.

If Helen Wayke's story was true up to that point it was difficult to believe that it was not true beyond that. There remained Jim Widdington, who had a fairly convincing alibi – though Platt had not yet reported upon his enquiries at the cinema – and whose whole manner and bearing had impressed Poole just as Helen Wayke's had done.

If neither of them had killed Christine, who had? Within a few minutes of leaving her sister – half an hour at the outside – she had been strangled at a point only a few hundred yards away. Who had done it? Had that dreadful crime after all nothing to do with the circumstances that had brought the unhappy woman to the spot? It seemed unbelievable.

One tiny suggestion did emerge from Helen Wayke's story; Christine had spoken of 'a client' or 'a friend' waiting for her at Highgate Ponds – 'a date' she had called it. Helen had thought that she was making that up, merely to shock and hurt her sister, and there had been no sign of a man there. But if it had been true, here still might be the explanation, though it would surely be impossible now, a month later, to discover who that man had been.

A sudden thought struck Poole; with an exclamation of annoyance he got up and hurried to the 'exhibits' room; taking what he wanted from the tray-drawer that held all the articles connected with the Hampstead Heath crime he hurried down to the Yard and, slipping across Whitehall, was lucky enough to catch a 24 bus just as it was moving off. Ten minutes later he was in Baxter Street.

Miss Wayke had just sat down to her belated supper but she received him at once. As he entered her sitting-room his eye sought the small table in the window where, as he had noticed at his previous visit, a large stamp-album was lying.

'I'm very sorry to disturb you, Miss Wayke,' he said, 'but there is just a chance that you may be able to give me important information. You told me that you gave your sister some money – ten pounds. How did you give it? In a cheque, or notes?'

Helen looked curiously at him. It was the first time that she had seen the detective excited.

'In notes,' she said. 'Treasury notes, I think they are called.'

'They are all called bank-notes now,' said Poole with a smile, 'and a great nuisance it is. Was it in large amounts – two five-pound notes – or ones and tens?'

'Small ones. One pounds, as far as I can remember, though there might have been some ten-shillings.'

There was still a chance. Poole drew from his note-case an envelope and from it took three ten-shilling notes.

'Will you have a look at these, please, Miss Wayke?'

Helen Wayke looked at them vaguely, turned one over, and gave a gasp of astonishment.

'Oh, I remember this,' she exclaimed. 'I tore it badly and mended it with the adhesive paper I use for my stamp collection.'

CHAPTER X

THE UNIFORMED BRANCH

So it was Varden after all!

This torn note, which Helen Wayke declared she had given to Christine Widdington at about seven o'clock on the evening of 9th October, had been paid over the counter of the Red Knight, Kilburn, by Herbert Varden, barely an hour later.

It was inconceivable that the note could have been through any other hands in that short time. Varden had been, by his own admission, on the edge of Parliament Hill, within a mile of the place where Christine was killed at 7 p.m. When questioned about the note he had said that probably he had got it from Montie Lewis, the bookmaker, but he had not claimed that it had come into his possession within that hour. He had got the note from Christine and there could be no doubt now that he had killed her.

But proof? Here was proof, or at least, vital evidence. But his alibi still stood; they had tried their utmost to break it down and they had utterly failed. The murder *must* have been committed after 7.15 – Beldam had put the time at 'nearer 7.30' – and Varden had been in the 'Red Knight,' Kilburn, three and a quarter miles away at 7.55. How had he got there in that time?

Poole himself had tested every possible means by which a man in Varden's circumstances could have made that journey – a car surely was out of the question, taxi drivers had been questioned, buses, trams, trains – all had been tested and discarded. A car or a motor-bicycle seemed the most likely solution, but neither had been traced to Varden, who, in any case, had been seen by an independent witness – Vesper, the London Transport official – walking past the Duke of St. Albans at the edge of Parliament Hill at 7 p.m., exactly as Varden himself had described. He had no motor-bicycle then, nor was he known ever to have had one. And a car seemed even more unlikely.

But he had done it and it was Poole's job to find out how. Late as it was, supperless as he was, he was not going to waste another hour.

The first step was to go up to Hampstead and make sure that Superintendent Hollis had been as good as his word and was still 'keeping an eye on' Varden. The Super would have the laugh of him over that. He would ask the Divisional detectives to renew their efforts to connect Varden with the crime, though it seemed impossible to succeed now where they had failed when the scent was fresh.

Poole snatched a sandwich and a cup of tea at a coffee-stall and soon after nine o'clock was at Hampstead Police Station. Sergeant Jameson was on duty in the charge-room and greeted him with his usual frigid correctness. Superintendent Hollis, he said, had gone home; Detective-Inspector Hartridge was also out but he was expected to look in again about a case that had just come in.

There were two uniformed constables in the charge-room, the veteran Darby and a young constable whom Poole did not know.

The detective wondered whether he should talk to the uniformed men about the case, but in view of Sergeant Jameson's hostility he decided not to.

'I'll wait till Inspector Hartridge comes in,' he said.

'Will you wait in the Superintendent's room, sir?' asked Sergeant Jameson. 'I'm sure he wouldn't mind, but I'm afraid the fire's out and there isn't one in the detectives' room either.'

It was a cold night and Poole had no wish to leave the warm charge-room with its cheerful blaze.

'If I'm not in the way I'd rather stay here,' he said.

The young constable handed him an evening paper and Poole sat down to read it idly.

Ten minutes later the door swung open and Inspector Hartridge strode in.

'Lord, it's cold outside,' he exclaimed; 'you know how to make yourself comfortable, Jameson. Hullo!'

He stopped as Poole rose to his feet.

'What brings you here at this time of night?'

'Work, I'm afraid,' said Poole. 'I've got a line on Varden again. Are you still keeping an eye on him?'

'Christ! I thought you'd done with that mucker. Yes, the Super wanted him taped still. I thought you were after a different sort of hare.'

Poole saw that, in their different ways, the three uniformed officers were keenly interested; this seemed a good opportunity to enlist their help.

'I was, and it was the wrong hare . . . but it led me back to Varden' he said. 'I want your help.'

'Well, that's something from the Yard, isn't it, Jameson?' said the Divisional detective. 'I thought you'd proved Varden couldn't have done it.'

'I thought I had satisfied myself that he couldn't have got to Kilburn by 7.55 . . . but he did. The question is how.'

'Couldn't have walked it,' said Hartridge, 'and the buses go miles round. Must have got a taxi.'

'We tried them. We should have found any driver that picked him up.'

The Divisional detective nodded.

'Car, then.'

'That seems impossible. It seems to me he must have had a motor-bike, though God knows where he got it from.'

'Push-bike's more likely, sir,' said the privileged Darby.

'Cripes!'

The exclamation had come from the young constable, who was staring at Sergeant Jameson with ludicrously gaping jaw.

Poole saw a slow flush spread over the station-sergeant's face.

'What is it, Bliss?' asked Inspector Hartridge sharply.

'Why, that bicycle that disappeared on the Heath; don't you remember, Serg.?'

Hartridge turned quickly to the station-sergeant.

'What's that, Jameson?'

Jameson, his face set, answered quietly:

'There was a bicycle left on the Heath that evening, sir, near Ken Wood. The young fellow put it down somewhere and wandered about with his girl; when he went to look for it he couldn't find it, but it was quite dark then and he didn't know the Heath well so he thought he had lost the place. He had to hurry off to an appointment. It was brought in here by a Park-keeper early next morning.'

Inspector Hartridge's face was red with anger.

'My God, and you kept all that to yourself, knowing that we were trying to find how Varden got away? Why the hell didn't you tell me about it?'

That, thought Poole, was no way to speak to a sergeant in front of his subordinates; still, Hartridge's anger was understandable.

Sergeant Jameson's face was white and his voice shook as he answered.

'If you'll remember, sir, I did begin to tell you about a bicycle, but you shut me up.'

'Well, tell me about it now, then.'

The station-sergeant turned back the pages of his ledger. Poole could see that his hand was shaking.

'At 8.50 a.m. on Tuesday, 10th October, Frank Cadby, 27 Morton Buildings, Webster Street, reported the loss of a pedal-bicycle. He had ridden across the Heath by the cycle-path from East Heath Road to meet a friend, his young lady, by the Bathing Pool, at 7 p.m. They walked towards Ken Wood and after a time he put the bicycle down and they strolled over the Heath up the hill towards Spaniards Road. They sat down on a bench till about 8 p.m., when it was quite dark. Cadby had to get down to Bedford Square to do some work at 9 p.m. When he went to collect his bicycle he couldn't find it in the dark; he said he didn't know that part of the Heath well and thought he must have lost his bearings. He had to hurry off to keep his appointment and didn't get away till 10.15 p.m. He thought he had better go back and look for it in the morning but when he got there there was still no sign of it, so he came in here to report his loss. He said he hadn't done so overnight because it wasn't his bicycle; he had borrowed it without leave. I let him have the bicycle back and sent Bliss to check the facts about who it belonged to.'

When he stopped speaking Sergeant Jameson still looked woodenly at the book in front of him.

Inspector Hartridge had recovered his self-control.

'What time was the bicycle brought in?' he asked.

'6.30 a.m., sir. The Park-keeper found it just after it got light.'

'Where?'

'Near the south-east corner of Ken Wood, sir.'

'Where this fellow, Cadby, said he had left it?'

'Roughly, sir, I should say it was.'

'Roughly!' exclaimed Hartridge bitterly.

Poole thought he had better intervene to side-track trouble.

'If you can get hold of Cadby and the Park-keeper first thing tomorrow morning,' he said, 'I'd like each of them to show me the exact place. If they each show a different one we shall at least know for certain that the bicycle was moved by someone. How far would you say it was from the place where the body was found? Have you got a large-scale map?'

Production of the map and comparison of notes suggested that Cadby had left his bicycle within four hundred yards of the site of the murder.

'He might have started to run across the Heath, stumbled on the bicycle and ridden it right across to East Heath Road and so on by Swiss Cottage to Kilburn. He'd do it in twenty minutes.'

'Wouldn't someone have seen him?' asked Poole.

'Probably not. It was dusk then, not too dark to see the path without a lamp, but dark enough for him not to be seen, except by someone on it or near it, and there are precious few who use that path after sundown except in summer.'

Poole nodded slowly.

'It looks very much as if that is what happened,' he said. 'Now we've got to prove it.'

CHAPTER XI

CLOSING IN

Ten o'clock. Still time for one more job that night. The Red Knight did not close till 10.30.

As Poole rattled down Belsize Road in a 31 bus his mind returned to the curious problem of Sergeant Jameson. Why had he kept that story to himself? The fact that he had started to tell Hartridge about a bicycle and had been snubbed was not in itself sufficient justification for his silence. Although it was probably true that there was not a properly close liaison between the plain clothes and uniformed branches of the Divisional police, Jameson must have heard talk about the case and the particular problem of how Varden might have got from the scene of the murder to Kilburn. Whatever his relations with the Divisional Detective-Inspector, Sergeant Jameson could and should have told Superintendent Hollis about the bicycle.

Had the man some private grudge against the C.I.D. – as Hartridge's description of him a month ago rather suggested? Had he deliberately kept back information that might have helped the detectives in their case? It was an ugly thought . . . but there were other things to think about.

Before he had got far with them, however, he found himself at Kilburn. He walked quietly into the public bar of the Red Knight and looked round; apart from the landlord there was no one there whom he knew. He walked to the end of the counter and ordered half a pint of bitter; as Boscombe handed it to him the detective murmured:

'I'd like a word with you when you've closed.'

'All right, sir. If you'll go through into my parlour. You know the way.'

For a time Poole remained in the bar, then strolled through into the parlour. Soon after half-past ten the landlord joined him.

'That chap Varden been in lately?' Poole asked.

Boscombe eyed him with interest.

'As a matter of fact he was in yesterday,' he said. 'First time he'd been in since you gentlemen started taking an interest in him. Seemed in better spirits.'

The detective did not rise to this bait.

'That night we asked you about – the 9th October. You didn't happen to see a bicycle outside, did you? A Sports Drake, low handle-bars, left grip missing.'

Boscombe shook his head.

'I didn't go outside.'

'Got a yard at the back where a bicycle might have been put – where it would not be likely to be seen?'

'Yes, sir; there is one – pretty quiet as a rule.'

'Then ask your staff or anyone else you think might have been in the yard. Between 7.50 and 10.30. And I don't want it talked about. Understand?'

Ex-Police-Constable Boscombe understood very well, and Poole thought he would get things done more quietly this way. Boscombe had got into Chief-Inspector Beldam's bad books and would be likely to be very careful.

When he was in the bus on his way home Poole suddenly realised how exceedingly tired he was. He had been hard at it all day and had had no proper meal since breakfast. But he had made real progress with the case. There was only one fly in the amber; now that Varden was once more in the picture it was probable that the case would be handed back to Chief-Inspector Beldam. Bad luck on the junior Inspector, but all in the day's work.

The following morning Poole was up early and went straight off to Hampstead, where Frank Cadby, who had lost a bicycle, and the Park-keeper who had found it, were awaiting him. Together with Inspector Hartridge they walked across the Heath towards Ken Wood and Cadby pointed out the spot where he had left the bicycle. He was fairly certain of the position because it was not yet dark when he put it down on the grass. The Park-keeper was even more certain of where he had found it, and that proved to be at least two hundred yards from the spot pointed out by Cadby. Either Varden, when returning it, had been uncertain of the spot where he had found it or, more probably, he had not liked to go back there in case the owner was waiting about; it was, too, unpleasantly close – a quarter of a mile at the outside – to the place where, if their suspicions were correct, he had left the body of his victim lying. It must have required considerable nerve to come back as near as he did, but no doubt he had realised the urgent importance of not letting it be known how he had established his alibi at Kilburn.

There was a fresh point about which evidence was needed – the hour at which Varden had got back to his lodging. At the time when his movements were first enquired into that point had not had any particular significance and it had been overlooked; at any rate there was no note about it in the dossier. Poole would have liked to go straight off to Crouch End but it was time for him to get back to the Yard and make his report.

Sir Leward Marradine and Chief-Constable Thurston listened with interest to Poole's account of the new developments in the case. He described how he had followed Helen Wayke from Paddington to Baxter Street and thence – after a false cast – to Sir Richard Wayke's house at Primrose Hill. His interviews with Captain Widdington and Mrs. Dibbuts followed, and then the story told by Helen Wayke, the story which, with her identification of the torn note, swung the pointer of suspicion back towards Varden.

'I'm damn glad to hear it,' said the Assistant Commissioner when Poole had finished. 'I hated the idea of such a foul job being done by a fellow like Widdington; worse still if she'd had a hand in it too. That was a remarkable day's work of yours, Poole; I congratulate you.'

The Inspector flushed with pleasure.

'I've only brought the case back to where Chief-Inspector Beldam left it, sir.'

Sir Leward laughed.

'What do you say to that, Thurston?' he asked.

A slow smile lifted one corner of the Chief-Constable's mouth.

'That's one way of putting it, sir,' was all he said. But Poole had had his reward.

None the less, it was settled that Beldam should resume charge of the case and Poole was sent off to make his report and discuss it with the Chief-Inspector.

Beldam was generously appreciative of what his subordinate had done.

'I don't know why it shouldn't have been left in your hands, Poole,' he said. 'Nobody could have done better. You've worried out the line on a cold scent and now we're running to view it's hard for you to hand over the horn.'

Beldam had a passion for fox-hunting, though he had never followed hounds himself except on a bicycle.

'Anyway, I'll see that you get any credit that may be going,' he went on. 'What do you suggest as our next step?'

Poole hesitated.

'I thought we had better find out what time he got back to his lodgings, sir. I'm not sure whether he said anything about that but if we could catch him lying it would be a help. But I suppose we're so near charging him that we can hardly question him.'

Beldam laughed.

'You've got a proper respect for the Judge's Rules,' he said. 'I'm not sure that I'm quite so scrupulous where a murderer's concerned. You get along to his lodgings and see what you can find out. We'll get the Divisional men on to seeing if they can't find someone who saw him bicycling across the Heath that night. That would be a useful link.'

It was Gower who had previously been to Varden's lodgings in Crouch End, so Poole thought it would be useful to have the Detective-Sergeant's company. It had been decided that for the time being Captain Widdington and Miss Wayke should be kept under observation but a less experienced man could be used to relieve Gower.

Gower himself was delighted to have a change from the tedious task of' 'observation.' He listened with great interest to Poole's account of how suspicion had swung back to Varden.

'A nasty bit of work, that chap, I thought, sir,' he said. 'Better educated than most and thought himself too good for the company he'd got himself down to.'

'They don't like him up Crouch End way, I think you said.'

'Couldn't find anyone to say a good word for him, sir. Not even his landlady, and they've often got a soft spot for the man they're looking after, no matter how tough he is.'

'You didn't discover what time he got home that night?'

Gower shook his head.

'I did ask, sir, but the woman – Mrs. Gooche her name is – said she always went to bed at ten. He wasn't in by then; that was all she knew.'

'He'd got a key, I suppose?'

'That's right, sir.'

'Well, we must see if we can't find someone else who knows, though it's a thin chance after all this time.'

The journey to Crouch End was tedious, and it was after half-past twelve when the two detectives reached No. 16 Taylor Street. Mrs. Gooche was already dishing up the midday meal for herself and an untidy-looking young giant who slouched on a chair in a corner of the kitchen.

'Very sorry to disturb you just now, Mrs. Gooche,' said Poole. 'I shan't keep you long, I hope. You may remember Sergeant Gower here coming to ask you some questions about a lodger of yours, Herbert Varden.'

Mrs. Gooche, a small woman with beady black eyes, regarded the two detectives with anything but favour.

'I remember 'im, all right,' she said, 'but I didn't 'ope to see 'im again.'

'Is Varden still with you?'

'No, 'e ain't. I packed 'im off. I don't fancy perlice in my 'ouse, pokin' their noses.'

Poole smiled.

'It is rather unpleasant, I'm afraid, Mrs. Gooche. I just want to ask you one question. You remember the night we're enquiring about – the night that poor woman was murdered on the Heath?'

'I remembered it after your precious sergeant come askin' about it. I don't take no interest in murders.'

'You remembered his going out that evening?'

'Yes, I did; and I told this feller all about it.'

'Do you remember what time he came back that night? Varden, I mean?'

Mrs. Gooche slapped a dish of potatoes down on the table.

'No, I do not. I told the sergeant I was in bed by ten. 'E wasn't in by then; that's all I know about it.'

All this time the big man in the corner had remained slouched in his chair, reading a paper and paying no apparent attention to the conversation. Now he suddenly threw the paper on the floor.

'I might be able to 'elp you there,' he said.

Mrs. Gooche sniffed.

'Oh, yes, you can 'elp anybody but your own mother. That's Willie,' she added. 'Out o' work and can't so much as peel the spuds.'

Willie paid no attention to this tirade.

'I wasn't 'ere when the sergeant called before,' he said.

'Mother told me about it when I got 'ome. I remember Varden comin' in that night – the night the pol was done in on the 'Eath. Come in just after me, 'e did, and that'd be close on 'alf-past eleven. I'd been out with some chaps and I was late myself.'

'Ah, an' that's why you're late in the mornin' and gets the sack,' said his mother bitterly. 'You never told me nothin' about 'is comin' in late.'

'You didn't ask me. I don't shoot my gab on a chap unless I'm asked,' said Willie Gooche righteously.

'What was Varden like when he came in?' asked Poole.

'Didn't see 'im. I was in my room and 'eard 'im come up the stairs.'

'You're sure it was him? There's no other man in the house?'

'Not unless mother 'ides 'im under 'er bed,' said Willie with a grin.

'Now, then, none o' that sort of talk,' said Mrs. Gooche sharply. 'And it's about time we 'ad our dinner.'

Poole took the hint. He had got more than he expected, though it was not yet certain how useful Willie's 'close on half-past eleven' might be.

The two detectives walked away from the house in silence. Sergeant Gower was the first to break it.

'I ought to have got that, sir,' he said gloomily.

'You didn't ask Mrs. Gooche if there was anyone else in the house besides Varden?'

'I did, sir, and she told me there was a son, but he was away on a job when I went there. As I'd got all I was sent up for – to find out what time Varden left the house – I didn't bother about the son.'

'Oh, well, it probably doesn't matter. We didn't realise then that the time of return might be significant. Even now there may be nothing in it.'

Whether there was anything in it or not depended largely upon Varden's own account of his movements after leaving the Red Knight, so Chief-Inspector Beldam decided to give his lack of scruples a run and ask the bookmaker's bully some questions.

'Bring him in, Poole,' he said. 'I'll take the blame if anyone objects.'

'Will you have him here, sir, or at Hampstead?'

'Here,' replied his chief with a grin. 'Superintendent Hollis might cramp my style.'

When Poole questioned Mrs. Gooche he already knew that Varden had moved his lodgings; he had got the new address from Inspector Hartridge. He hardly expected to find the man in during the afternoon, so that he was not disappointed to draw blank. There was, he knew, a race-meeting at Hurst Park that afternoon, so that it was quite likely that that was where Varden was. The landlady knew nothing of his movements but expected him back to supper at half-past six.

For a moment Poole wondered whether to go to the railway station and intercept Varden there, but among the returning race-crowds he might well miss the man, and in any case it was better not to have any more publicity than could be helped. So he decided to wait where he could keep an eye on the lodging-house and sent Sergeant Gower off to get a cup of tea and relieve him for a similar purpose later on.

By half-past six, however, there was no sign of Varden and when seven o'clock arrived without him Poole began to feel anxious. Could the man have got wind of what was happening? Young Gooche, for instance, might have given him a word of warning – let him know that the police were asking questions about him again. Although the Divisional Police were 'keeping an eye on' Varden, that did not mean that they had got him constantly under observation, and it would have been perfectly possible for him to receive the warning and slip away unobserved.

Poole cursed himself for not having kept an eye on Willie Gooche, but when he came to think of it it was just as likely that the warning had come from Boscombe, the landlord of the Red Knight, whom Chief-Inspector Beldam already regarded with suspicion.

The thought of Boscombe, however, suggested to Poole that Varden might well be in a public-house, either at the Red Knight itself or in one of the houses in the neighbourhood of his lodgings. He called again and questioned the landlady, who gave him the name of the house which Varden generally frequented, the Three Magpies.

He was not there, so Poole decided that the only thing to do was to try the Kilburn house. It was a long, circuitous journey and it was well after eight when Poole and Gower entered the public bar of the Red Knight. It was fuller than Poole had previously seen it and a noisy group at the bar-counter was clustered round a big man who was evidently standing treat. Glasses and mugs were raised.

'Here's your best, Bert!'

'And one for "Silver Tassel"!'

The big man turned to face the room and with a generous sweep of the arm included all its occupants in his invitation.

Varden's face was flushed with drink and exultation.

'Here's to her!' he cried. 'Are you all in, boys?'

His gaze reached the two men who had just come in. Poole saw the colour drain from his face; for a moment the big body swayed, then pitched forward with a crash to the floor.

CHAPTER XII

FOUR WEEKS AND A DAY

'I hear you made a packet at Hurst Park to-day, Varden,' said Chief-Inspector Beldam blandly.

He sat behind a large desk in the Chief-Inspectors' room at Scotland Yard.

Opposite him sat Herbert Varden, his face still white save for blotches of unhealthy red. At Varden's side was Inspector Poole in another chair.

The big man had taken some time to recover from his faint at the Red Knight but that was not going to stop Beldam questioning him; he knew that Varden was astute and he was not going to give him time to make a plan.

Varden made no answer to the detective's remark. He stared at him with eyes in which resentment was mingled with anxiety.

'No shortage of cash now, I suppose?' went on Beldam. 'No need to worry about a bus fare more or less, eh?'

'What have you brought me here for?' snarled Varden. 'What game are you playing . . . cat and mouse, is that it?'

'Not a game. Just a few questions. We haven't altogether lost interest in you, you know, Varden. For instance, we'd like to know something about your movements after closing time on the 9th October. You remember that night? Ah, yes, I recollect; at first you didn't . . . one night was much the same as another, eh? . . . and then you remembered it after all. Odd that, wasn't it? Well, you told us how you got to the Red Knight – walked across the Heath to save a bus fare. By the way, that ten-bob note you paid for your drink with. Would you care to tell me where you got that?'

'You asked me that before.'

'I know. And now I'm asking you again. It interests me, that note, because I have a feeling that when you started to walk that note wasn't in your pocket.'

'It was, damn you. I never said that I walked because I hadn't got any money. I said buses cost money, and so they do, as you'd know if you had to live on a pound a week.'

'I see. So, on a pound a week you carry notes in your pocket and buy yourself double-whiskies.'

The sweat glistened on Varden's forehead.

'You're twisting my words, blast you. Of course I sometimes have more than a pound a week. If a bookmaker pays me in a lump sum – and they generally do – or if I make a bit myself at a race-meeting, I may have two or three pounds on me at a time.'

'I see. I see. That's quite clear. So that night you had some notes in your pocket, eh? Had a lucky bet or the bookies paid you?'

'Yes,' said Varden sullenly.

Beldam leaned forward.

'Which was it, Varden?' he asked quietly.

'Which was what?'

'Had somebody just paid you? Or had you had a bet?'

'I don't remember.'

'You don't remember? You've got a curious sort of memory, haven't you, Varden. Had Lewis just paid you?'

Varden was silent. Poole saw that his hands were gripped together so hard that the knuckles showed white. Beldam looked at a sheet of paper which lay in front of him.

'Perhaps I ought to remind you of what it was you said last time. Here are your words: "I don't keep a car. I hadn't had a job for some time and buses cost money."'

He looked at Varden and saw the sweat pouring off his forehead.

'How much money had you got on you that evening, Varden?'

His voice was quiet; deadly quiet.

Varden hesitated.

'That was all I had, that note.'

'Given you by a bookmaker?'

'No. I'd had a bet.'

'Where?'

Silence again.

'With Lewis?'

'No.'

'Who with, then?'

'I don't remember.'

Beldam shook his head.

'Very unlucky,' he said, 'this memory of yours. But you do remember that you had it on you when you left your lodging in Crouch End.'

'Yes. I told you so.'

'It wasn't given you by someone on your way across the Heath?'

'No.'

'Nor by someone at the Red Knight?'

'No.'

'Nor by Lewis?'

'No.'

Beldam sat back in his chair.

'Well, that seems to clear up that point,' he said easily. 'Now I'd like to get back to where I started. Will you tell me how you went home that evening?'

A look of relief had shown for a moment on Varden's face when Beldam left the subject of the note. He spoke more truculently now.

'Why should I tell you?'

'Oh, you needn't, of course. Would you like me to tell you?'

Again Beldam leaned forward, looking keenly at Varden. For a moment the big man hesitated. Then:

'I went home by bus.'

'Ah. Money in hand now. You went home by bus. Which way?'

'The usual way, of course.'

'And which was that?'

'By Camden Town.'

Beldam pulled open a drawer and took out a copy of the London Transport bus map. Opening it, he ran his finger along one of the thin red lines.

'Kilburn to Camden Town; that's route 31. Change at Camden Town, eh?'

'Yes, I did.'

'Have to hang about? Wait for another bus?'

'Not long.'

'Quite right, Varden, there are plenty of buses from Camden Town to Highgate, aren't there? And from Highgate to Crouch End; bus again, or walk?'

'I don't remem . . .'

Varden's voice died away.

'Don't you? The end of a tiring day. Mile and a half uphill – Hornsey Rise and all that – and the buses going by. Do you remember walking that, Varden?'

'I probably went by bus,' said Varden sullenly.

Beldam slowly rubbed his hands.

'By bus,' he said. 'And that gets you comfortably home . . . at what time?'

He shot the question at Varden, leaning forward again as if to snatch the answer.

Varden had started.

'How the hell do I know?' he said. 'It's a month or more ago.'

'A month yesterday, Varden. Four weeks and a day since your friend, Bella Knox, was strangled to death on Hampstead Heath . . . while you were walking across it only a very little distance away.'

Varden's face was as white now as when he had fainted. Poole, sitting beside him, felt an instinctive pity for the wretched man, writhing in the tightening coils. He felt more than a little discomfort himself. He did not like what Beldam was doing. He was trapping Varden. Knowing that he was going to charge him, he was questioning him in a way that surely was not within the recognised rules of English procedure. But Beldam had boasted that he had no scruples where a murderer was concerned.

'What time was it, Varden?'

Varden had had time to think.

'Must have been late; half-past eleven, probably.'

'You didn't have to wait for a bus, I think you said?'

'No, but it's a long way.'

Again Beldam turned to the map.

'Kilburn to Camden Town; quarter of an hour, shall we say? Perhaps less at that time of night, but say a quarter of an hour. Camden Town to Highgate; no traffic, say ten minutes counting the change of bus. And by No. 41 to Crouch End another ten minutes. But why guess; we can get the exact times from London Transport. Fifteen and ten and ten; that's thirty-five minutes. And you left the Red Knight at closing time – ten-thirty. Back home by eleven-five, eh? Call it eleven-ten, or even eleven-fifteen. But not eleven-thirty, eh, Varden?'

'You're squeezing the time to suit yourself,' said Varden hoarsely. 'I might have had to wait to get a bus at Kilburn. Or at Highgate. It couldn't be done so quickly as you say.'

'You think you weren't back till half-past eleven?'

'I know I wasn't. I tell you I know I wasn't.'

Beldam sat still in his chair, looking at the white-faced man in front of him. When he spoke his voice was quiet.

'What does it matter, Varden? What does it matter whether you got home at 11.30 or 11.15?'

Varden stared at him, the Adam's apple working in his throat. He was breathing hard and seemed unconscious of the violence of his emotion.

Again Beldam leaned forward.

'Shall I tell you why it matters . . . to you? Because you know that you weren't in till half-past eleven. Because you didn't go home by bus by Camden Town. Because you had a job to do on the Heath that night. Wasn't that it, Varden?'

'No! No, I tell you!'

Varden had half-risen from his chair, his hands gripping its arms. His livid face was working as if some dynamo twitched at his nerves.

Poole half rose too, fearing what he might be going to do. He sank back as Varden dropped heavily into his seat. He was frankly appalled; this was the nearest thing to 'third degree' that he had experienced since he joined the C.I.D. . . . and he hated it. But he could do nothing; he was Beldam's subordinate.

The Chief-Inspector's voice went on inexorably.

'That bicycle, eh, Varden; it had to be found where you had found it . . . just after Bella Knox died. A lucky find for you. Do you want to change your mind about anything you have told me?'

Still that deep, stertorous breathing. Varden stared, wide-eyed, his control nearly gone. But he did not answer.

'Do you want to change anything? About that note? That ten-shilling note that was given you by a bookmaker, for wages or for a win. Was it, Varden?'

'Yes. I told you it was,' gasped the man.

'You are sure that it was in your possession all that evening, till you paid it across the bar of the Red Knight at eight o'clock that night?'

'Yes, I tell you. I swear it was.'

Slowly Beldam drew an envelope from his pocket and from it took a ten-shilling note. Holding it up between the fingers of both hands he turned it slowly over so that the adhesive paper was visible to Varden.

'That is the note, Varden,' he said. 'It has been identified by Boscombe, the landlord of the Red Knight, as the one with which you paid for your drink that night.'

'What of it?'

The words were forced through Varden's dry lips.

'Just this, Varden. We know that at seven o'clock that night this torn note was given to Bella Knox by a woman who had mended it herself with the paper you see. At seven o'clock Bella Knox had this note in her possession. A quarter of an hour later she was murdered and at eight o'clock you gave that note to Boscombe. And you have just sworn that no one else had touched it that evening, no one had given it to you that evening, that it had been in your possession and yours only that evening . . . since you took it from the dead body of the woman you had just murdered!'

'No! No!'

Varden had sprung to his feet and stood swaying, his hands clenched, the sweat pouring from his livid face. Poole stood beside him, ready for anything that might happen.

'I didn't kill her! She was dead! She was dead when I found her! I took the money. I'd got nothing ... not a penny! Not a penny in the world. I took it ... but I didn't kill her. I swear I didn't kill her!'

CHAPTER XIII

CROSS-EXAMINATION

Chief-Inspector Beldam's methods of extracting that admission from Varden nearly got him into trouble; what was much more serious, it nearly wrecked the case. After hearing Varden say that the woman was dead when he found her, Beldam had duly cautioned him and subsequently charged him with the murder. But by that time Varden's nerve had gone; though he still denied the killing he made a formal statement admitting that he had taken the money from Bella Knox's body. He declared that he had had no 'date' with her, but knowing that she was often to be found in that quiet corner of the Heath he had gone there to look for her and had found her lying dead. Beside her was her handbag full of notes; he was in debt and desperately in need; he had taken the money, started to run up the hill towards Spaniards Road, stumbled on the bicycle and used it to get himself quickly to the Red Knight, where he had drawn the landlord's attention to the time, hoping that it would act as an alibi if he were ever suspected of the murder.

When Varden appeared before the magistrate his solicitor at once challenged this statement, declaring that it had been improperly obtained and was therefore inadmissible. His client, he said, had not been cautioned at the beginning of the interview and he had been questioned and bullied in a way entirely contrary to the Judge's Rules of Evidence.

Chief-Inspector Beldam, in the witness-box, blandly met this challenge by declaring that, until Varden's admission that he had taken the ten-shilling note from the body, he had not enough evidence to charge him, had not made up his mind to do so, and therefore was entitled to question him without a caution. He denied having bullied or brow-beaten the accused.

Poole, giving evidence as to the taking of the statement, was closely cross-examined by Varden's solicitor and had to face a terribly awkward dilemma. He could not bring himself to let Beldam and the force down; he declared that there had been no bullying; the questioning, though close, had been fair; when he left the box he was sweating and miserably conscious of having been as near perjury as ever he had been in his life.

After hearing arguments on both sides the magistrate admitted the statement and at the end of the hearing committed Varden for trial at the Central Criminal Court.

As they walked away from the Police Court Beldam gripped Poole's elbow in his strong hand.

'Thank you, my lad,' he said quietly. 'You stood by me nobly and I could see you didn't like doing it. I went too far with Varden; I'll admit it to you. But without that admission I'm not sure that we should have got enough evidence . . . and I mean that – to hang.'

When the case came for trial Varden repeated his defence. He had gone to the Heath, on the chance of finding Bella Knox. He had found her dead body. He had taken the money from her handbag and then, in a panic, started to run across the Heath. Stumbling on the bicycle, he had ridden it in the gathering dusk, without a lamp, along the path which crossed Parliament Hill, and then, after switching on the electric lamp, by Belsize Avenue and Belsize Road to Kilburn. He had ridden very fast and had hoped, by drawing attention to the time, to create an alibi for himself if ever he were suspected of the crime. Realising that a missing bicycle would suggest the creation of an alibi he had, after closing time, ridden the bicycle back and walking it down the hill from Spaniards Road had left it as near as he dared to the spot where he had found it. He had not, on his oath, killed Bella Knox.

In cross-examination, Mr. Whitelock, for the Crown, set about his task of shaking this explanation in the quiet manner which he invariably employed when appearing for the prosecution.

'You say, Varden,' he began, 'that you went to this quiet corner of the

Heath on the chance of finding 'Bella Knox,' as you knew her. Where exactly did you expect to find her?'

Varden's small eyes flickered in his dead-white face as his brain sought for any catch which might lie in this question.

'At the end of Millfield Lane, where it runs into the Heath, through the posts.'

'Near where the body was found?'

'Yes, within fifty to a hundred yards.'

'That is a very quiet place, is it not?'

'Pretty quiet in October.'

'Many people go by there?'

'How should I know?'

'Answer my question, please. Do many people go by there?'

'I don't know. It's a through path.'

'Are there lamps there?'

'I don't know. I shouldn't notice.'

'You heard evidence given by the park-keeper that there are no lamps at that end of the lane. Do you dispute that?'

'I suppose not.'

'But there are lamps further along the lane – where Merton Lane joins it, for instance?'

'If he said so, I suppose there are.'

'He did say so. You accept that?'

'I . . . yes.'

'You had met Bella Knox there before?'

'Once or twice.'

'By chance or by appointment?'

Varden hesitated.

'Generally by appointment.'

'At that unlit spot?'

'Yes.'

'Did you ever meet her there by chance?'

'Yes, I think so. Once or twice.'

'Again at that unlit spot?'

'Yes.'

'Can you suggest why she should wait in the dark rather than in the part of the lane where there are lamps?'

'I should have thought that was obvious,' said Varden with a sneer.

'You would? And yet you heard, did you not, the evidence of Mr. Scott that when she accosted him it was in the lighted portion of the Lane, near the Bathing Pool?'

'I heard him say that.'

'And that it was by the light of a lamp that he saw the scar on her face?'

'Yes. I heard that too,' said Varden doggedly.

'That is in fact the more likely place for her to have picked up a client . . . unless she had an appointment?'

Varden's counsel sprang to his feet.

'My lord . . .'

'Yes, yes, Sir Horace,' said the learned judge. 'You cannot cross-examine the accused on matters of opinion, Mr. Whitelock. Please adhere to questions of fact.'

'As your lordship pleases. But you, Varden, went to look for her in the unlit, quiet corner where her dead body was found. Will you tell the Court how you got there?'

Varden looked surprised.

'I walked.'

'Yes, you walked, but how . . . by what route did you go?'

Again Varden hesitated.

'You haven't forgotten, have you, Varden?' asked Mr. Whitelock softly.

'No, I haven't,' came the surly reply. 'I went by Hornsey Lane and the Highgate Cemetery.'

'Yes, and then?'

'By the Duke of St. Albans.'

'Ah, yes, you were seen there, were you not? By the London Transport official, Mr. Vesper?'

'So he said.'

'So he said. And from the Duke of St. Albans did you go up Millfield Lane – the lighted part?'

'Yes.'

'And did you see Bella Knox there?'

'No.'

'See anyone there?'

'I didn't notice anyone.'

'Not the manservant, Hoskin?'

'Not that I know of.'

'Nor Mrs. Joliffe?'

'No.'

'Did you see Miss Wayke's car?'

'I tell you I didn't notice. I can't remember what I saw.'

'Your memory for that part of the evening is a blank?' Varden was silent.

'I ask you again, Varden; did you see Miss Wayke's car in Millfield Lane?'

'I may have. I don't remember.'

For a moment Mr. Whitelock was silent, looking down at his papers. Then he looked up quickly.

'I put it to you, Varden, that you walked up over the grass in the shadow of the trees and that you saw 'Bella Knox' sitting in Miss Wayke's car?'

'No, I did not.'

'That you saw Miss Wayke give her some money?'

'No, I tell you.'

'That when she walked away from the car you followed her to the place where you had arranged to meet her – that dark, quiet corner of the Heath?'

'No!'

'That you demanded the money and that when she refused to give it you, you killed her and took it? Is that what happened?'

Varden was panting. A froth of bubbles showed on his puffy lips. His eyes sought his counsel, but Sir Horace Toone was looking down at his own brief.

'It's all a lie. I told you what happened.'

Mr. Whitelock's manner relaxed.

'Very well, Varden. Now, about the question of time; what time was it when you found this poor woman's body?'

Varden, too, had relaxed. His face recovered some of its normal sullen appearance.

'I haven't the faintest. I haven't got a watch.'

'No? Then perhaps I can help you. Was it raining when you found her?'

Again that quick look of suspicion, of concentrated thought.

'Yes, it was.'

'Where were you when the rain began? It came on "sharp and sudden," as Police-Constable Darby told us. No doubt you noticed that?'

'Yes, I was coming up Millfield Lane – the lower part of it.'

'Some way away from where you found, as you say, the body?'

'Yes.'

'How far? A matter of five minutes' walk?'

'More than that.'

'Ten minutes?'

'Something like it.'

'So if we say that you found the body at 7.25 we shall not be far out – according to your story?'

'It's the truth.'

'I see. And then, having found the body and the hand bag and having taken out the notes, you suddenly decided that you had better create an alibi for yourself by getting to the Red Knight in Kilburn in the quickest possible time. Is that it?'

'Yes,' said Varden sullenly.

'And in point of fact you were there, if the evidence of Mr. Boscombe is to be believed, at 7.55 p.m.?'

'Yes.'

'Within half an hour. Very quick work. So you calculated that it would be thought impossible for you to have committed the murder only half an hour before your appearance at the Red Knight?'

Varden glared at Mr. Whitelock, his small eyes flickering as his brain searched for danger.

'Was that it, Varden?'

'Yes, it was. That was what I thought.'

'And if you had got there three-quarters of an hour later, instead of half an hour, the alibi would not have been so convincing?'

'No.'

'And as much as an hour . . . no good at all, eh?'

'Not much good.'

Mr. Whitelock looked down at his brief, turned over a page or two, then looked up with a puzzled frown.

'How did you know, Varden, that you reached the Red Knight within half an hour of the murder?'

Varden stared at him.

'I don't understand,' he said, but there was a tremor of anxiety in his voice.

'How did you know that it was not in fact an hour and not half an hour after the murder?'

There was no answer. The big man's breathing was laboured.

'How did you know that the murder took place at 7.25? Was it because you were there yourself?'

'No! No, I wasn't there, I tell you. I found the body. It – it was still warm. I knew she must have only just been killed.'

'*I* see. Remarkable medical knowledge. But Varden, how did you know she had been killed?'

'I . . . I told you . . . I found her body.'

'Yes, you told us that. But why killed? Why "murder"? Why "a crime"? Why should she not just have died naturally? A heart attack for instance?'

'She . . . I could see. She had been strangled.'

'What did you see?'

'Her face was discoloured. There were marks on her throat.'

'What marks? Bruises? Scratches?'

Varden hesitated.

'Bruises.'

'No scratches?'

'I don't know. I didn't notice any.'

'It was quite light?'

'No; it was getting dark.'

'In fact it was very nearly quite dark, wasn't it . . . in that quiet corner of the Heath, away from the lamps?'

'It was pretty dark, yes.'

'But not too dark to see bruises on the throat of the woman whom, you say, you knew had only just been killed?'

'I saw them all right.'

'They were clearly visible?'

'Yes.'

'Dark? Discoloured?'

'Yes.'

'Varden, you claim some medical knowledge; you say that you are able to tell how long ago death has occurred. Can you tell me how soon a bruise becomes visible – dark, discoloured?'

The big man was silent. His tongue passed slowly over his dry lips.

'I put it to you, Varden, that you knew that Bella Knox had died by strangulation, not by estimating the warmth of the body, not by the sight of any bruises, but because you strangled her yourself?'

'No. No. No.'

Mr. Whitelock sat down.

CHAPTER XIV

THE END

In his summing up the learned Judge, going carefully through the evidence, pointed out to the jury that the crucial point which they had to decide was whether they did or did not believe Varden's explanation of how he came to find the body and of how the ten-shilling note came into his possession. They might find it hard to believe that he had not gone to meet 'Bella Knox' by appointment; that, having found her, he should have realised instantly, not only that she had been murdered, and that within a few minutes of his arrival, but that his one chance of escaping suspicion himself was to establish an alibi three miles away within the next half hour. The jury were entitled to take into consideration the general demeanour of the accused when giving evidence and under cross-examination, though they must not be influenced by any opinion they might have formed as to his habits of life. As to why the accused might have gone to the extreme length of murder to obtain money there was no evidence and, though it was not necessary for the prosecution to prove motive, the absence of such proof might suggest a doubt. It was for the prosecution to prove their case against the accused beyond all reasonable doubt, and by reasonable doubt he meant . . .

The jury took two and a quarter hours to consider their problem and at the end of that time returned a verdict of 'Guilty.' As Herbert Varden listened to the dreadful words of the death sentence he made an effort to square his shoulders and to meet his fate like a man.

Inspector Poole remained in Court for some time, talking to the Treasury Solicitor's clerk. When he left the great building the crowds which had been hanging round it throughout the day had melted away, but a little way down the lane which led to Fleet Street he saw two people standing, a man and a woman. As he came up to them he realised that they were Captain Widdington and Miss Wayke.

The faces of both showed signs of the painful ordeal which they had been through in the last weeks, when they had had to lay bare the story that they had tried so hard to conceal. Exposed to the searching light of legal enquiry and public opinion the story had not appeared as a pretty one; selfishness, weakness, immorality, untruthfulness, deception – all these stood revealed and self-confessed, faults common to humanity but, when exposed, none the less bitterly by humanity condemned. And in the last hours they had witnessed the dreadful ordeal of a man who, but for their faults, might never have been brought to this terrible end.

Widdington held out his hand as Poole came up. Rather embarrassed, the detective took it. The soldier opened his mouth as if to speak, but shut it again without saying anything.

'We wanted to ask you to come and have tea with us, Mr. Poole,' said Helen Wayke quietly.

'Yes, do,' said Widdington gruffly.

'That's very kind, sir; I'd like to,' said Poole.

Remembering how keenly he had hunted these two people he did not feel quite happy about accepting their hospitality, but their manner was friendly and he could not very well refuse.

They turned back towards Holborn and, picking up a taxi, were quickly in Baxter Street. Dusk had already fallen and Helen Wayke's sitting-room was curtained, with a cheerful fire burning in the grate.

'After dark, but we don't have to be quite so careful now,' said Jim Widdington with a twinkle in his eye.

Poole laughed.

'I can't help thinking you exaggerated that point, sir,' he said.

'For God's sake don't call me "sir"; we aren't on parade now; thank goodness, that's over.'

Poole nodded.

'Yes, I'm glad too,' he said.

Mrs. Dibbuts appeared with a trayful of tea things. She greeted the detective with a smile.

'All's well that ends well,' she said, without having to dig deep into her collection of clichés.

During tea no mention was made of the subject which was in all their minds, but gradually the attitude of the two men became less restrained, and when they lit their pipes after it they were talking happily about the season's Rugby football Internationals. Helen Wayke sat quietly on one side of the fire, doing some 'useful work' and occasionally putting in a word to show that she was interested.

At last Poole knocked out his pipe.

'I'm afraid I must be getting along now,' he said. 'There'll be some things to clear up.'

At once Jim Widdington stiffened, put a finger inside his collar to ease it, and cleared his throat. Poole saw Helen Wayke smile sympathetically.

'We . . . er . . . we wanted to thank you. I don't mean so much about the result . . . this wretched fellow's death can't bring poor Christine back to life again. But you were very decent about . . . things, when you thought we'd done it . . . or that we might have, at any rate. You might have made things much more unpleasant for us.'

Poole was feeling acutely uncomfortable. Formal thanks were at any time an embarrassment to him and under these circumstances they were an agony.

'That's quite all right, sir,' he said. 'I only did . . . I mean . . .'

Helen slipped quietly into the breach.

'I'd like to say "thank you," too,' she said. 'I didn't at first realise what very good reason you had for suspecting us. You concealed your feelings remarkably well,' she added with a smile.

'I don't know that I did,' said Poole. 'I don't think I really ever felt very convinced about it; it seemed so completely untrue to form that either you or Captain Widdington could have had a hand in such a thing. It was that note to 'Bella Knox' that worried me.'

'Of course it did. I was a fool not to tell you at once. I deserved what I got. Anyhow, we won't say any more about that, though our gratitude is very real. We are going to be married in a day or two and then we shall go back to Australia and try to forget this horrible time.'

'I'm glad,' said Poole. 'I mean, that you are going to be married. I hope you will be very happy indeed. I'm sorry you are going back to Australia, though.'

'Nothing to keep us here, now,' said Widdington quickly. 'You know that Christine is buried at Chatterleys now? There's a private chapel and burial ground where all the family have been buried. We can go now. Dick doesn't want us – he and I never got on together.'

'Poor Dick; he has always been very solitary,' said Helen. 'Mr. Poole, there is one thing I wanted to ask you. Do you believe that what Mr. Whitelock suggested is true . . . that Varden saw me give Christine that money and killed her to get it? It's rather a dreadful thought to me; it makes me more than ever responsible for her death.'

Poole shook his head.

'I'm sure he didn't,' he said. 'From what you told me, she got out of the car some little time before the rain began, say between five and ten past seven. Now Varden was seen at the Duke of St. Albans at seven o'clock and that is at the very least ten minutes' walk from where your car was – more likely a quarter of an hour, because it is a stiff pull uphill. No, I feel sure that he came along just behind Hoskin; he may or may not have seen your car move off, but I don't think he saw your sister there. He would go straight on to the rendezvous and find her there. What does puzzle me is why she went there at all; having got the money from you there was no need . . .'

Poole stopped short, in acute embarrassment.

'You know, I think that was just what Christine would do,' said Helen quietly. 'It was not in her . . . tradition to let someone hang about indefinitely waiting for her. But having kept her appointment she would have taken great pleasure in telling him to . . . well, what I told you she said, only I thought at the time she was making it all up to shock me. Poor Christine, I expect . . . I wonder whether that was why.'

Poole nodded slowly.

'That is the most likely explanation. Varden was expecting . . . sympathy and she gave him the rough edge of her tongue. He is a violent-tempered fellow; if she said really unpleasant things to him he may have flown into a fury and seized her by the throat and shaken her . . . harder than he really meant to. She may have flourished the notes in his face and after she collapsed I daresay he seized them and rushed away. He may not even have known that she was dead until he heard it on the wireless at the Red Knight. That must have been a terrible moment for him. You remember how they noticed him, those other fellows in the bar.'

Helen Wayke sighed.

'Yes, I expect that was it. Poor darling; what a terrible end to her unhappy life. Jim and I have come pretty badly out of all this, Mr. Poole, but I'd like you to believe that we are, that we always have been, terribly unhappy about her.'

Poole rose quickly to his feet.

'Of course I believe that, Miss Wayke. And I ask you to forgive me for even for a moment thinking that either of you . . .'

Helen Wayke slipped her arm through her lover's. They were still a handsome couple as they stood in front of the fireplace.

'I don't believe you ever did think it of my old Jim,' she said with a smile. 'If ever a man had innocence written all over him . . .'

'Oh, dry up, Helen!'

'Me, yes; you might believe it of me. I've often been credited with a poker face. I don't know, though, how you got over the difficulty of my car going off when the rain began.'

'That was the snag,' said Poole. 'I mean, if you were in it, you couldn't . . . quite apart from the general unlikelihood.'

'You never suspected anyone else, I suppose? Varden right at the beginning and then Jim or me . . . or both of us?'

'No,' said Poole, firmly; 'there was nobody else.'

And yet, as he walked away through the drizzling rain, he remembered those hours when a new thought had come to him, a thought almost more terrible than the one already in his mind. The problem of transport – how the murderer had got away – would have been so neatly solved by that swift, silent electric chair, driven by a paralysed man – paralysed below the waist, but with the strong, muscular hands of the mechanic, the steel wrists with which he had seen Sir Richard Wayke whirl his chair across the room with one quick turn. Poole shuddered as he walked on. The end of poor Bella Knox, tragic as it was, had not been so terrible as his thoughts had pictured it.

THE END

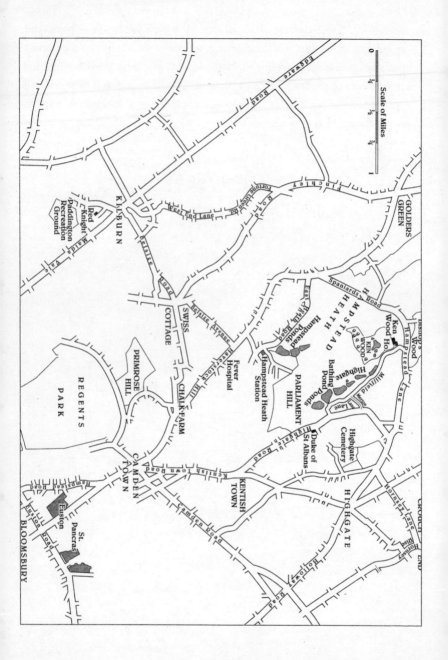

Scale of Miles

0   ¼   ½   ¾   1

GOLDERS GREEN

KILBURN

Red Knight
Paddington Recreation Ground

Maida Vale

West End Lane

Belsize Road

Fortune Green Rd

Finchley Road

Edgware Road

SWISS COTTAGE

Belsize Road

Finchley Road

East Heath Road

HAMPSTEAD HEATH

Hampstead Ponds

Bishop's Wood

Ken Wood Ho.

KEN WOOD

Hampstead Lane

Spaniards Road

REGENTS PARK

PRIMROSE HILL

CHALK FARM

Haverstock Hill

Fever Hospital

Hampstead Heath Station

PARLIAMENT HILL

Bathing Pond

Highgate Ponds

Millfield

Merton Lane

Millfield Lane

CAMDEN TOWN

Duke of St Albans

Highgate Road

Highgate Cemetery

HIGHGATE

Hornsey Lane

CROUCH END

BLOOMSBURY

Hampstead Road

Euston Road

Euston

St. Pancras

Camden Road

Kentish Town Road

KENTISH TOWN

Camden Road

Holloway Road

Hornsey Road